AKITHAR'S GREATEST TRICK

AKITHAR'S GREATEST TRICK

TESHOVAR BOOK I

JASON DOROUGH

For my parents

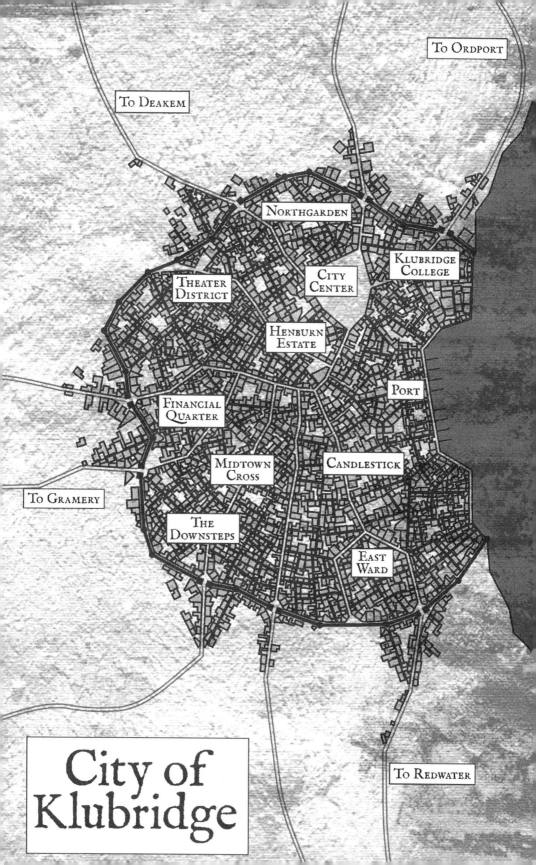

TO ORDPORT

TO DEAKEM

NORTHGARDEN

KLUBRIDGE
COLLEGE

THEATER
DISTRICT

CITY
CENTER

HENBURN
ESTATE

PORT

FINANCIAL
QUARTER

MIDTOWN
CROSS

CANDLESTICK

TO GRAMERY

THE
DOWNSTEPS

EAST
WARD

TO REDWATER

City of
Klubridge

AKITHAR'S GREATEST TRICK

PART I
THE GREAT AKITHAR

CHAPTER 1

Sometimes, when he perched on the edge of a rooftop on a clear night like this one and looked down at the streets, Dorrin felt like a bird. He felt like he could fall forward into the night and leave the rough shingles and glide over the city, his toes brushing chimneys and his fingers cutting through the chill air. He'd ride the wind over the workers, past the stalls, beyond the guards, and above the city walls. He'd leave Klubridge behind and soar into the black sky beyond.

If Dorrin were a bird, though, he wouldn't be the kind that would simply take wing and fly away. He'd be something small, something to match his human form, which already was short and thin for an eleven-year-old. Dorrin would be quick, maybe a hummingbird, darting here and there and slipping through tiny spaces, pausing just long enough to take what nectar he could gather before speeding to the next flower.

But no, the hummingbird wasn't cunning. Dorrin was clever. Dorrin would be a more predatory bird, watching the ground below him and preparing to dive when his eye caught the movement of prey. Even now, Dorrin's own eyes flicked quickly among the crowd, moving from the baker leaving his shop for the night to the old man leaning on a cane to the young woman carrying a bundle of what looked like potatoes. In his mind, lines connected them, visible like a golden thread glowing only for him.

He blinked twice and then let himself slip down from the roof. Instead of leaping into the air, he shimmied off the edge and dropped to the first window ledge below. From there he hopped down and caught himself on a round drainpipe and rode that the rest of the way to the street level. He'd been sitting only three stories above the road, but even that was far enough to muffle the sounds and dim the lights of one of Klubridge's major thoroughfares in the full bustle of early evening.

Up there, it was easy to see the carts and the people. They all were moving and jostling through the road to and from the shops, but with a pattern and direction that made sense. Down here, it was chaotic, and Dorrin came barely to shoulder height on most of the crowd. He was eye level with waistcoats and bundles, cloaks and bodices. He didn't need to see better than that, though. He knew where he was going. He still had that golden thread in his mind, and he sensed it pulling him out into the road.

Dorrin scampered out of the way of a horseman and sidestepped a couple deep in an argument. None of them even noticed the boy in dirty clothes. Even if they had seen him, they likely would have looked right past him, like most of the city did with kids like him. Street kids. That served his purpose well. As he skipped between another pair, he caught sight of the baker, just a flash of white linen in the crowd. Dorrin had guessed his direction correctly, and he picked up a brisk pace to close the distance without running. The people would ignore fast walking, but running always invited trouble.

The baker was less than five steps ahead now and was making a slow pace down the street, caught behind a cart pulled by a tired donkey. Dorrin studied the situation with the speed of experience and spotted the lump low on the baker's back, just under his tunic and above his waist. The tiny sliver of sharp metal was between Dorrin's fingers by the time he was two steps behind the baker, and it sliced a precise slit in his white tunic even as Dorrin pulled alongside the man.

Dorrin stayed alert, his head turning to scan the crowd as he felt the satisfying weight of the purse drop out through the cut in the fabric and into his palm.

Dorrin changed direction and slipped the bag into a deep pocket sewn into his loose trousers less than a second after he made the grab. He didn't check whether the baker had detected the change in weight around his waist. Sometimes they noticed, but by the time they did he always was long gone, either high above them on the roofs or already half a block away, too low in the crowd for them to spot him. This time he was ahead and to the right, just turning the corner as the golden thread in his mind pulled him onward.

The old man was closer than Dorrin had expected. He must have paused at a stall, or something had blocked him. No matter, it was too late to skip him. Dorrin made fast work of his appraisal and saw the leather pouch hanging from the belt around the man's waist. Dorrin matched his pace, just behind and to the left. When the man took a step and leaned to the right on his cane, Dorrin's hand slipped just past his left hip, snipping the belt cord and dropping the pouch directly into another pocket hidden in the folds of Dorrin's pants.

The boy pivoted on his left foot and angled into the flow of traffic before the old man had even completed his step. Dorrin tugged on a hidden lace to tighten the pocket, and the leather pouch bumped against his right leg as he moved. He shifted slightly to compensate so as not to let it slow him down. The gold cord pulled him forward. He knew it led perhaps twenty feet ahead, likely to the left side of the street. He rocked up onto his toes as he walked and spotted the young woman in a glance across the crowd. Her light blue hat bobbed between the people, visible for only a moment, but it was enough. It stood out in the middle of all the gray and black everyone else was wearing at this hour.

Dorrin's path cut through the crowd, and he turned, spun, and hopped right and then left, ever avoiding bumping into or being stepped on by others. She was ten feet ahead now, pausing every few steps to resettle the big sack in her arms. Dorrin's eyes searched her back, and he found her money. She carried it hanging loose in a small bag under her right arm. He was just a few steps behind her when he sensed that she was stopping to juggle the sack again. She turned halfway, as though to look behind her. Dorrin took a brisk step into an alley to his left. That was when hands grabbed his arm, yanking him off balance farther into the alley and shattering his concentration.

He pulled back reflexively and prepared to run, but the hands kept a firm grip. "Skink!" he managed, not sure whether the situation had taken a turn for the better or the worse.

The taller boy snarled at Dorrin and dragged him down the alley. "We've been looking for you. You're late." Dorrin half jogged along, half stumbled. The five purses and pouches banged against his legs with every step.

"I was coming back. I just saw one more-"

"You're coming back now. I'm done having to fetch you every night." Skink shoved Dorrin ahead of him, and Dorrin spotted the girl waiting behind the bins, dressed in rags only slightly cleaner than the ones he and Skink wore.

"Fairy! What are you doing out here?"

She gave him a wry smile and punched his shoulder. "I do get let out on occasion, you know." Her smile dropped, and she fell into stride with the two boys. "Scrounger won't be happy you're late again."

Dorrin knew it was a risk to go after those final three marks, but hopefully the two extra purses he got would prove worth it. Skink grabbed Dorrin's sleeve and yanked him to a rough halt. "How many did you get, anyway?"

Dorrin saw Fairy stare at him pointedly from over Skink's shoulder. She held up two fingers. "Two," Dorrin lied. "I got two." Fairy nodded, relieved.

Skink sneered at him. "So I've outdone his lordship tonight, have I? Look at this." Skink pulled open his dirty coat, and Dorrin saw three small sacks hanging from the inner lining. Dorrin glanced from the sacks to Fairy, but her face was blank now. "What do you have to say for yourself, eh?"

Dorrin looked back to Skink and could smell the bigger boy's sweat. "I... I guess you got me this time," he said.

"Why don't we just count it while we're at it?" Skink shoved Dorrin, and his back slammed against the brick wall of the alley.

Dorrin tried to stammer a response, but Fairy interrupted. "Come on, Skink. We're already late. There'll be time to count when we get back. Let's go."

Skink glared at Dorrin for another instant before giving a curt nod. "Right, let's go."

Fairy pulled aside the dirty blanket that was hanging over the doorway, and Skink pushed past Dorrin to get in first. Fairy gave Dorrin a slight smile and motioned for him to go next. He ducked under the linen and heard Fairy come in behind him. They were the last to arrive, and more than a dozen pairs of eyes watched them from the gloom of the ramshackle room.

The floors were old wood, some nails missing and others poking up at odd and perilous angles. The wood itself was rotting in places with some pieces of planks missing entirely. Dorrin doubted the floor had ever had a proper cleaning. He hadn't seen anyone take a broom to it since Scrounger took charge of the place. The walls were in equally poor condition, the paint having peeled off most of them and something that looked like mildew making a gradual crawl down from two of the corners. It was unclear what this room once had been, or even what the building itself had been. Decades had passed since it served whatever its initial purpose had been. It now slumped low on the side of a street lined with similarly decrepit buildings, most of them full of children and families even more pathetic than the ones in this one.

"Where you been, Skink?" one of the other boys called out. It was one of the younger ones who idolized the older boy.

Skink flashed a gap-toothed grin that looked too nasty to be called anything close to a smile. "Had to collect this one. Dorrin here thinks he's too good for a family meeting, don't he?"

Dorrin gave no response and kept his eyes down. He knew by now when he was being baited into a beating. Fairy touched Dorrin's shoulder as she passed and responded for him. "We all know when the meetings are, Skink. Have a seat, and let's get to it, shall we?"

Skink sniffed in her direction but said nothing. He still squinted in Dorrin's direction even as he dropped to sit on a bare spot on the floor. Dorrin lowered himself more slowly, willing himself to be invisible, and Fairy made her way to the front to stand in her customary spot next to the massive chair, the only thing that was not falling apart.

"Did you know that pirates came as far inland as the East Ward?" The baritone voice came from the next room. All murmuring stopped as the children waited. A stained burlap hanging, probably once a potato sack, pulled back as Scrounger pushed his broad shoulders through the back doorway, beyond the chair. The floorboards groaned in protest under his massive boots.

Scrounger stood in the doorway for a moment, as he always did, sliding his small dark eyes across the assembly. His breathing was heavy through a wiry beard of gray and black, and his enormous stomach heaved with the effort under a shirt stretched too tight.

"They came in at the port, and they went into the tunnels. They couldn't trust one another with their loot, so they went farther and farther into the catacombs to hide their winnings." He stomped a massive foot on the floor, and the boards rattled on their loose nails. "Some of them were right here below us. Just think of it."

The tunnels again. Scrounger was obsessed with the old tunnels that supposedly ran under the city. He thought there was treasure down there, but Dorrin doubted those tunnels even existed. He stayed quiet and let Scrounger go on about them, though. They all did. That's how you got by in the East Ward.

Scrounger trailed off his story, and his lips moved silently as he surveyed the room. Dorrin knew he was counting heads. He wondered once again whether Scrounger actually knew all their names or whether they were just heads for him to count. He certainly knew Dorrin, and he knew Fairy as well. She was a special pick, either because she was good with numbers or because she could keep the others in line. Likely both. Fairy nearly was Dorrin's equal in agility, if not climbing, but Scrounger always kept her back and off the streets. She was too valuable to risk out there, while Scrounger could easily replace most of the rest of them with any street kid with a couple weeks of training.

Satisfied with his count, Scrounger made his way past Fairy and around his chair. He paused there before lowering his bulk into the seat. His long coat crumpled behind him as he sat, and the chair's upholstery sighed. The wood creaked, but it held him on old and sturdy carved legs. It was his throne in this noxious little kingdom between the cracks of normal society.

Scrounger propped an elbow on the thick armrest and scratched at his ear. The room remained otherwise silent, waiting for the usual process to begin. At last he spoke again, his voice coming thick and guttural. "Pray tell, why did we have to wait for you three?" His eyes were on Dorrin, but Skink spoke up.

"Dorrin went off again. He was bobbing about Denry Lane, he was. Me and Fairy had to drag him back or he'd been there all night, most like." Skink finished with a triumphant squint at Dorrin. He knew he had more loot that night, and he could afford some direct shots at the favorite child.

"And what were you doing on Denry, my boy?" Scrounger asked Dorrin, his voice somehow softer but still a rumble.

Dorrin licked his lips and considered his answer, but not for too long. Scrounger suffered being made to wait as little as he suffered lies. "I thought I could pick up a few last marks before coming in. It was a busy night."

"Was that a good decision?" Scrounger asked and watched Dorrin. His eyes glimmered wet, deep beneath his bushy brows.

"I got two purses," Dorrin responded quickly. "I know I should have been back sooner, and I nearly had a third, but I did get two."

"And I got three!" Skink proclaimed. He tore the little pouches out from his coat lining and carried them to the front of the room. He tossed them to the floor, and they landed with the clink of coins in front of Fairy's feet. Skink lingered between her and Scrounger, basking in his moment.

"Well," Scrounger said. He did not even look at Skink's bags. His gaze remained on Dorrin. "It seems you've been outdone this night, does it not?"

Dorrin swallowed hard. Here it came. He had lied to Skink to escape a beating in the alley, but there was no lying to Scrounger. And Scrounger knew what was coming as much as Dorrin did. After a couple of seconds of hesitation that felt infinitely longer, Dorrin managed, "I picked up three more on Second Street before I went to Denry." He slid all five pouches out of his pockets and held them up for Scrounger to see.

A mean light flickered in Scrounger's eyes, and the corners creased with a wicked smile. At last his gaze shifted to Skink, who now stared at Dorrin with a mix of disbelief and hatred. "I suppose you could learn a few things from young Dorrin. Wouldn't you say so, Skink?"

Skink couldn't keep himself from shooting a defiant look at his master. "I would've had more if I'd been out there, too. He only ganked them last two because he was late coming back."

"But you were late, too, weren't you?" Scrounger stood slowly, and Dorrin felt his hands grow cold. He had seen this play out too many times before.

Skink had seen it just as many times. Before he could say anything, Scrounger's cannonball sized fist had closed on his shirt collar. Skink was off the ground, his feet dangling a foot above the floor. At last the boy looked afraid. "I—I'm sorry, Scrounger. I'll do better."

Scrounger pulled him closer until their faces were inches apart. "You haven't yet, have you? How long have I taken care of you, given you a place to live? And you bring me, what? This?" He kicked one of Skink's stolen purses, sending it careening into a far corner of the room. "And Dorrin brings back nearly twice as much as you do. How do you explain that to me? How do I justify the trouble of taking care of you?"

"I—I—"

Skink got only that far before Scrounger hurled him across the room. The boy sailed well over the seated children's heads, but they still flinched away before he slammed against the wall and fell to the floor. Dorrin realized he was holding his breath. He let it out slowly and looked to Fairy. She was looking back at him, her mouth closed tight and her brows drawn together, halfway between pain and fear. Dorrin looked back to Scrounger and saw that the big man was watching him. He gave Dorrin a smirk of satisfaction before settling back into his chair.

~

I t took nearly an hour for Scrounger to make his way through the rest of the children, calling them up one by one and having them drop their ill-gotten gains at his feet. The night had been average, as far as the take went. At five pouches, Dorrin didn't have the most grabs of the evening. That dubious honor went to a smaller, squirrelly boy who picked pockets besides cutting purse strings. Dorrin was solely a string cutter. Getting close enough to slip a hand into a pocket always seemed too dangerous to him, and no one had yet caught him with his current methods.

Even though the other boy had more grabs, once the pouches had all been opened and the money was counted, he didn't have the biggest total for the night. Not surprising anyone in the room other than perhaps the top culprit himself, the five purses Dorrin brought back all bulged with an astonishing amount of seri, and one even held what appeared to be three small diamonds.

"Learn from Dorrin," Scrounger told the group. "He steals smart. He has an eye for who to take from. Pay attention to how he picks his marks, and you might be worth the trouble I put into you one day."

It was the same speech, more or less, that Scrounger gave night after night. Whenever he wasn't droning on about the tunnels under the city, he was telling everybody else to be more like Dorrin. Following his earlier humiliation, Skink had dragged himself back to his spot, and he listened to Scrounger's usual delivery with an unusually sullen face. Dorrin watched the other boy and waited for the jealousy to show. It always did, but it was hiding just then. Dorrin was used to bringing back the biggest take every night, even when he didn't think he'd done it. Twice he'd even made an effort not to be the top earner.

The first time he cut only two purses, but one of those turned out to contain one of the Imperial jewels, making its way through Klubridge by secret courier for an official engagement. Scrounger had seemed suitably impressed, but the stone had been too recognizable to sell. The municipal guard had turned the city inside out, looking for it for nearly two weeks. Dorrin wasn't sure what became of that massive green gem, but he knew what became of the courier when his body went on display, hanged from the Imperial tower at the center of the Henburn Estate three days after the theft.

The second time Dorrin tried to sabotage his own take was a little less than three months ago. He'd had an average night for his own endeavors, but a remarkable one for any of the other thieves in Scrounger's gang. Not wanting to endure another round of praises, Dorrin had dropped half his earnings into charity boxes scattered along his path back through the city. Even having done that, the bags he returned to Scrounger contained more than double the take of any other single thief that night.

No matter what Dorrin did, he always ended up on top and always earned the glares of his fellow thieves. Scrounger had once told the gang that Dorrin had a gift the others should envy. Dorrin thought of it more as a curse.

Scrounger was finishing this night's speech and had stood to leave. Dorrin glanced around the room warily and saw the room looking back at him. Nearly every set of eyes except Skink's, which still stared ahead at the ground. Fairy was looking at him, too, and she knew what was coming.

"Fairy," Scrounger said, snapping her attention away from Dorrin, "Be a good lass and carry these droppings back for me." He gestured to the small piles of money and assorted loot littering the floor.

"Right away," she murmured and sent Dorrin one more look before stooping to gather an armload of coins and pouches. She followed Scrounger out the back of the room, past the burlap flap.

No sooner had the fabric settled into place over the doorway than Dorrin tumbled backwards on the floor. It was Skink, suddenly jerked out of his melancholy and across the length of the room. His hands tangled into Dorrin's shirt at the shoulders, and he leaped astride the smaller boy, shoving until Dorrin's head bounced against the soft and rotting wood. If the floor were in better repair, Skink might have cracked Dorrin's skull.

"You stupid bastard," Skink snarled. His lips pulled back from his crooked and discolored teeth with a fury Dorrin had never seen in him.

"Wait, no!" But there was no stopping it.

Skink slammed a fist into the side of Dorrin's head, and the room dimmed for a second. Dorrin's hands flew up to block the next hit and the flurry that followed. Just enough got through to batter his head against the floor again, and he tried to turn his face away from the direction of the hits. It was no use. They were coming from both sides as Skink flailed wild punches at him. He was cursing as he hit, and the curses soon turned into an animalistic keening that was even more frightening than the coherent profanity had been.

Dorrin tasted blood and thought he had bitten his own tongue. The violence of the beating disoriented him, and he no longer was even sure whether the hits still were coming or whether his head were just reeling and throbbing on its own. Either way, he eventually saw Skink standing over him, a line of spit dangling from his lower lip. The other children had gathered around, looking afraid, but none of them had tried to stop the attack. Dorrin knew they all hated him.

"Learn from Dorrin," Skink snarled in a gross mimic of Scrounger's voice. "Maybe you can learn something for yourself, you little wretch." He punctuated the last word with a swift kick to Dorrin's side. Dorrin could cringe away from the kick just enough to keep any ribs from breaking, but it still knocked the wind out of him. He gasped for air, rolling into a fetal position.

"That's enough, Skink," one of the other boys said and tugged on the taller boy's sleeve. Skink turned on him and drew his fist back as if to add him to the list of his victims for the night but stopped himself in time. He nodded and didn't spare another look at Dorrin as he led the rest of the urchins back out to the streets.

When Dorrin opened his eyes, he knew that time had passed, but not exactly how much. He was still on the floor, and his head throbbed from all sides. It took a few blinks for his vision to return behind eyelids that already were swelling. When he could see again, Dorrin realized somebody was kneeling over him. He flinched back, wondering if Skink had returned to finish the job. Then the light caught Fairy's hair from behind, and he let out a relieved sigh.

"You okay?" Fairy leaned close, not quite whispering.

"I think so," he mumbled and noticed for the first time that his lower lip was puffy and bleeding.

"Let me help you." She slid a hand under his narrow shoulders and pulled until he was sitting up.

The room rocked, and the pain in his head doubled for an instant. It soon subsided to a dull ache. Dorrin tried turning his head to the right and left, up and down, and everything seemed to work as it should. Skink had beaten him, but nothing felt broken. He felt his face with his fingertips and tested the cheeks, the jaw, the nose. Everything was in place but was hot and numb and big all at the same time. Dorrin sighed and looked at Fairy. "How bad is it?"

She raised an eyebrow and grimaced. "It's not great, but you'll live." She glanced over her shoulder and then whispered, "I think there's some ice in the cellar. Should I get it?"

"We have a cellar?"

"Dorrin, listen. Your face will swell. I think I can get something for it without Scrounger knowing."

Dorrin blinked and shook his head. The effort sent a fresh surge of pain into his skull. "No, you'll get in trouble."

Fairy sighed but didn't argue. She was only two or three years older than Dorrin but often seemed much older. Her eyes were weary, and her forehead creased in concern. "Skink was worse this time than ever before. What did you say to him?"

"Me?" Dorrin's voice raised, but he caught himself and lowered it again. Nobody else was in the room just then, but there was no telling who might be snooping around just outside. "Nothing! I didn't say anything at all. He just jumped on me and… well… you can see it."

She looked even more concerned, as if she had been hoping Dorrin had provoked this unprecedented attack. "That's not good. He's getting worse. One of these days—"

"I know," Dorrin interrupted quietly.

She continued, "One of these days he's going to kill you."

"It's the take. Scrounger keeps going on about how great I am."

"Then be less great. Stop bringing back so much money." She didn't know about his disastrous attempts to thwart his own thieving. Fairy thought it was all about pride.

"It doesn't matter," he said. "If it wasn't that, he'd find something else to come after me for."

Fairy knew he was right, and she paused for a moment. Dorrin could tell she was thinking, trying to decide whether to say whatever she wanted to tell him. At last, she leaned even closer. Her tangled hair brushed his face, and she whispered with urgency, "Run, Dorrin."

"What?" He leaned back to look in her eyes to see whether she was joking. There was nothing but seriousness in her gaze. "We can't do that!"

"Not we, you. I'm not in danger here. None of them would hurt me. But you could be killed next time. You probably will be." She took his hand in hers and squeezed. "The next time you're out, just go. It doesn't matter where, just get away from here."

"But what would I do? I need Scrounger—"

"You don't need him, Dorrin. He needs you. You have to understand that." Her words were coming faster now. "You bring him more in your take than anybody else ever has. He won't ever let you go, and he's going to keep setting you up to get beaten. He doesn't want you to know how important you are. He wants you meek. That's why he keeps needling Skink, but it's going too far. Skink's going to kill you."

The thought of leaving was terrifying, but Dorrin didn't think it was scarier than staying and being beaten to death. Either way, he knew one thing to be true. "I can't just go, Fairy. I couldn't leave you."

"I'll be okay, Dorrin. I'll even come find you. I'll get away too one day, and we'll find each other. But you have to go. It has to be as soon as possible."

"What has to be soon, my pet?"

Fairy yelped in surprise and spun around on her knees. Dorrin squinted into the darkness and could make out the lumbering mass that accompanied the gravelly voice. "Scrounger," he said.

Scrounger stepped farther into the room, and Dorrin wondered how much he had heard. The man stood over them now, and Fairy rose to her feet, her hands moving to hug her elbows. She lowered her head and said, "Skink has to stop bullying him."

The casualness with which Scrounger flicked his wrist, back-handing Fairy across the face, stunned Dorrin. The smack was louder than any of Skink's punches, and Fairy's head rocked back. Her legs crumpled, dropping her to the floor. Dorrin gasped and slid back on the floor another three inches. Fairy lay on her side now, her hands on her surely bruised face and tears welling in her eyes. Dorrin looked back at Scrounger and felt the rage rising, but he forced it down.

Scrounger ignored Fairy and squatted in front of Dorrin. Watching him lower himself that way was like watching a mountain bow low. He studied Dorrin's bloodied face for a moment before turning the edges of his mouth upward into something like a smile. "You took that beating well, my boy."

Dorrin didn't know how to respond or whether he should. Scrounger had never hit Fairy before. No one had. There was plenty of violence in the family, but she'd always been the one that was off limits. Things were changing, and Dorrin felt lost and angry and afraid.

Scrounger watched those emotions cycle across the boy's face. He waited them out before continuing. "Fairy means well, but she doesn't know the world the way I do. She needs help sometimes. What would she do without a friend like you here?" Scrounger let the vague threat settle. "You have a gift, Dorrin." This part of the talk was not new. "You can steal like no one else. People don't like it when somebody is better than them. You see how they get. You see how Skink gets."

Dorrin sniffed through the nostril that had not yet swollen shut, and he made himself nod. Anything to appease Scrounger.

Scrounger nodded back. "The way Skink gets, the way they all get? These silly bastards I have to watch over? That's how the world is going to be for you, Dorrin. Nobody likes to be bettered. That's not just here, that's out there, too." He pointed to the door to the streets. "And it's even worse out there. You don't have me watching for you, helping you along." He gave Dorrin a knowing look. "You don't have Fairy out there to clean you up."

The boy looked at Fairy again, and she had not moved from the floor but was staring with open contempt at Scrounger now. The man either didn't notice or didn't care.

"Fairy doesn't see that it's good for you to get knocked around a little. It's what you need to toughen up. You have a gift, but you don't know how to protect what's yours. That's what I'm going to teach you, boy. That's what Skink is teaching you, and he doesn't even know it, the stupid git."

"But I can't do anything to stop him," Dorrin said and immediately wished he had stayed quiet.

Scrounger gave his wicked little smile again and tapped a thick finger against the side of his nose. "Not this time, maybe. But you'll learn it." He stood and towered over the two children again. "You'll learn it, and you'd be wise to learn it soon."

Three months passed, and Dorrin's head no longer felt like it was full of water, and Fairy's bruised cheek had healed. No more attacks had come from Skink during the spring, but there were plenty of glares and threats. Dorrin wondered whether Scrounger might have done or said something to forestall the inevitable beatings, but that didn't seem likely, given his apparent approval of the trouncings Dorrin was getting. Fairy reminded Dorrin occasionally that he needed to leave the gang, but without a recent assault the urgency was fading. The days ticked past, Scrounger kept rambling about his damnable tunnels and the treasures they hid, and the children continued stealing every night.

Some of the kids had tired of pickpocketing and were moving on to more complex schemes. A couple of them ran a shell game down in Candlestick now, and it was becoming so lucrative that they'd had to move their table to a different street every other outing to avoid getting grabbed by their marks from the nights before. Others had started running even more complicated scams that surpassed Dorrin's own comprehension. All these new endeavors were proving worthwhile, but Dorrin stuck to his familiar purse-cutting, and he still brought back the biggest take every evening.

Life went on, such as it was, and Scrounger didn't hit Fairy again. He still called out praise for Dorrin every time he brought back a windfall, but he didn't needle the other children as much. Part of Dorrin wondered whether Scrounger knew he had gone too far the night Skink attacked. Maybe he realized how close he'd come to losing Dorrin and probably Fairy as well. This period of relative calm could be the next part of his game, lulling them back into complacence. If that was what he was doing, it was working. Dorrin felt a bit less afraid each day, and even Fairy seemed to relax a little.

It was a week into the summer when Scrounger called a midday meeting. He usually left the gang to their own devices during the daytime, and most of them used those hours to sleep before going out to prowl in the dark. On that day, word passed quickly through the group that Scrounger wanted a word with all of them.

Dorrin sat in his usual spot on the dirty floor, the same spot where Skink had bashed his head against the planks. Fairy was waiting at the back, near the big chair, and Dorrin raised his eyebrows at her, questioning. She frowned and shrugged. That was when Skink slouched into the room, accompanied by two of the other children who had become his lackeys. He blinked in the darkness until his eyes adjusted and then took a seat against the side wall, away from Dorrin.

The room was full by then, and it wasn't long until Scrounger pulled back the burlap over the back door with his meaty hand and lumbered into the room. He walked slowly, but his eyes were bright with excitement. It was an opportunity, then. Dorrin recognized that expression whenever Scrounger was about to send them after something in particular. His suspicion proved correct when Scrounger dropped into his chair and addressed the children.

"Who knows what is special about tonight?"

The kids shifted and looked at each other, but none of them ventured a guess.

"No one?" Scrounger frowned, affecting a disappointed expression, but Dorrin knew he didn't expect any of them to know what was special about that night or any other, or even what night or month or year it might be. After a long pause, he at last continued. "Tonight is the start of the final week of show season."

Ah, so that was it. Show season had run through the winter and spring, and the theaters always wrapped their current productions in the summer. The last week of show season was the second busiest time of year for the theater district, next only to opening week when all the newest spectacles debuted. Actors, acrobats, musicians, and all kinds of other entertainers put on their best performances to meet the influx of wealthy visitors migrating up to cooler weather from their warmer estates in the south. Everybody wanted to see the final acts of the big shows at the start of their summer holidays. With the show finales came the audiences, and with the audiences came purses worth over ten times the average take. Imperial business and governmental affairs also brought the wealthy, but those were too dangerous. The end of show season was where the easy winnings were to be found every year.

"You'll split into pairs and threes tonight. I want you covering that crowd like never before. Lots of fat wallets needing liberation, lots of drunken 'crats not paying attention to their valuables."

It wasn't unusual for Scrounger to organize them for something like this. Too many kids in one area was a recipe for being caught, but too few spelled missed opportunities. They would go out in groups, with each set assigned to a different part of the main theater street or one of the side streets. Some of the kids would try to run their new scams, but Dorrin knew the end of show season was all about picking pockets and slashing purse strings. By the end of that week, the marks would have wised up and started watching their money more closely. This was the perfect time to hit them, just when they had arrived in the city and were dazzled by the lights and the bustle.

"Rafe and Till, you two are together around the Royale and one block each way." Scrounger was assigning them, and the boy and girl he had just named moved closer to each other to strategize. "You three," he said, sweeping a finger across three skinny urchins sitting together near the back corner. Dorrin wondered once more whether Scrounger even knew all their names. "You'll be at the eastern outflow. Catch them before they head home at the end of the night."

The kids who already had assignments were whispering to each other while the rest of the group got its orders. Scrounger looked at Dorrin and stopped his cadence. That never was good. "Dorrin, my boy. You'll take Fairy with you tonight." Fairy looked as surprised as Dorrin felt. What was going on? Scrounger continued, "You'll be at the Bastion and one block up and down." Dorrin swallowed and nodded, still suspicious. Why was Fairy going out that night?

Scrounger moved on to the next assignment but hesitated again. He looked back at Dorrin with a mean grin, and Dorrin knew what was coming before he said it. "Skink, let's have you at the Bastion as well. We don't want to miss any of the excitement there, do we?"

CHAPTER 2

Samira was in a balcony seat, all alone in the upper level of the Chamberlain. This is where she came when she needed a few moments of peace before a night's performance. She wouldn't be performing herself, of course, but she might as well have had top billing, given how much of the staging and preparation came down to her planning and expertise. She had managed every show in this theater for nearly a decade, ever since she and Caius had scraped together enough money to buy the building outright.

Most of the shows in Klubridge were transient, with performers and companies renting out their stages from stodgy business types who had bought playhouses as investments but knew nothing about the art and craft. Not so with the Chamberlain. It was among a few of what Samira berated herself for calling the real theaters, the ones owned and operated by people who were born to the stage. But she could afford a bit of pride, given what they had done with this place.

They had traveled together and performed in rented spaces, just like those temporary Klubridge acts did today. Unlike most of them, however, Samira had managed their earnings with a keen eye and a stern hold on the coffer. By the time they settled in Klubridge, they had just enough to buy this place from the previous owner, an attempted entrepreneur who had found himself drowning in debt less than a year after acquiring the theater himself.

It had been a rundown hole when they got it, the kind of place nobody would notice even though it was located in prime real estate in the middle of the theater district. There had been a rat problem, and the leaky roof had led to rotten wood across the stage, but those were easy problems to fix. The place had been theirs, and they made it good. Caius had a way of making friends, and he had soon brought a carpenter into their circle. Then an engineer, and eventually a seamstress. The company continued growing, and the theater blossomed with them.

Tonight the Chamberlain was full of workers pushing and pulling crates here and there, hoisting contraptions up to the catwalk, and making sure every detail was perfect. It was thrumming with activity everywhere but here in the balcony, and that's where Samira had retreated to gather herself before wading back into the minutiae of running a show.

This was the final week of theater season, and she both looked forward to and dreaded the coming break. She was a shrewd accountant, and she could stretch a budget with as much creativity as she managed for her stage productions, but the off-season always led to lean wallets. They would give occasional performances to smaller audiences while the other theaters were closed down, and they'd make enough to live on, but just barely. Feeding so many mouths and maintaining a theater the size of the Chamberlain was costlier than she liked to ponder.

Tonight would herald a new flood of curious theatergoers to the city, and that meant the seats would be full again in all the theaters that knew how to draw the crowds. If there was one thing Samira knew how to do, it was how to pack a house, and she fully intended to do so tonight and every night this week. After that, though, the transient shows would move on, and the established theaters would shut down to change up their shows and retool their performances. Those would be the lean times.

"The queen surveys her domain. And does she find it pleasing?"

Samira smiled at the thickly accented query and tilted her head back to see Reykas standing in the door to the balcony. Reykas was tall and dark, with lean muscles hidden under his loose-fitting shirt. He had worked as a courier before he fell into show business, and now he was one of the company's two acrobats. He also was one of Samira's best friends.

"For now," she said. "But something always falls apart, doesn't it?"

He smirked his reply and came to the front of the balcony, resting his big hands on the brass railing.

"Have you talked to Lizzie about that name thing again?" Samira asked.

Reykas gave her a sidelong grin. "Tidal Mirage."

Samira rolled the name around in her head and scowled back at him. "That sounds like a vacation resort."

"She says it represents the way we flow together like water to create illusions for the audience. Shall I tell her you hate it?"

Samira sighed and shook her head. "If that's what she wants, that's what it'll be."

He smiled again. "It truly is dire, isn't it?"

She cut her eyes back at him and laughed. "Are the two of you ready for tonight?"

Reykas feigned shock and pressed his hand to his chest. "You wound me. We are ready as ever. And," he continued, reaching into a pocket in the side of his billowing silk pants, "I wanted to return this to you."

Samira leaned across a seat and took the book from him. "Ah, Pandridge. How did you like this one?"

"It… had its moments."

"You hated it, didn't you?"

His mouth pulled back into a wide grin. "I confess that I probably was not the best reader for such a… bucolic story. But thank you for the loan."

"To be honest, I thought it was trash, too. I just wanted validation."

She laughed and dropped the book into her lap. "I'll get you something better next time."

"Was your librarian to blame for this travesty?"

"The librarian is mine, now?"

"I would say so. For the last two weeks, by my estimation."

"I'm not sure what the librarian would have to say about that," Samira said, but she couldn't stop another smile. He was right. The librarian was hers, and it felt good to have someone again. It had been a long time since things had gone in the right direction for her. She knew she deserved some happiness, but it seemed fleeting. If she acknowledged it, it might disappear just like a tidal mirage or whatever that terrible name was that Lizzie had come up with.

She glanced at Reykas again, seeing the red sash at his waist for the first time. "A new addition?"

"Oh, this?" He looked down and tugged absently at the fabric. "Lizandra thought it was a good idea. I don't know. What do you think?"

"Let's try it and see. It couldn't hurt to shake things up a bit, could it?"

"I suppose not." He gestured to Samira's own outfit, dirty tan pants and a dark shirt with the sleeves rolled up. "It seems you are trying something new tonight as well, eh?"

Samira laughed again and rubbed at a smudge on her right leg that was likely grease. She had pitched in with some manual labor before coming up to the balcony. "I'll be changing soon, don't you worry."

"I didn't think you would miss an opportunity to dress for the final week," Reykas said.

"Speaking of which, I'd better get back down there and make sure the plates don't stop spinning." Samira pushed herself up from the plush chair with reluctance. "How's it looking?"

"No problems that I saw. Apak is cursing over some sort of machinery."

"But what else is new, right?"

"Precisely." He hesitated. "Everything else is prepared, but what about Caius?"

Samira put a hand on Reykas' shoulder. "You let me worry about him. The Great Akithar will be ready."

Tonight it would be the green brocade with silver flowers. Four years ago Samira had received that dress as a gift from a textile merchant who was especially taken by their show. He would take no payment for it and told her he'd had his finest tailor craft the garment in thanks for a remarkable presentation he would not soon forget. She had never seen the merchant again, but the dress was finer than anything else in her wardrobe. She had brought it out the first and last weeks of every season since then, and it had taken on an almost mystical quality for her. Samira was not one to believe in superstitions, but if she were, then this most certainly would be her good luck dress.

She slipped off her shoes and had just begun unlacing her trousers when the door to her office swung open without a knock. She stiffened and then saw the short and stocky man pushing his way in, a familiar frown on his face as his eyes flicked across scribblings on a long sheet of paper.

"I cannot get the blasted thing to fire," he proclaimed.

"I'm in the middle of changing, Apak," Samira said patiently.

He pushed his thick-framed glasses higher on his nose and still did not look up from the notes that stymied him. "Go ahead, I will wait. But then you need to see this."

Samira sighed and stepped behind a wooden room divider to finish undressing. She leaned her head around the edge of the divider. "What seems to be the problem? And can you hand me that dress?"

"Dress? Yes, here." He frowned at the dress draped across the chair, grabbed it up, and thrust it into her hand. "It is the box for tonight. I had completed the preparations, and it was ready to work. But someone..." He looked up from the papers at last, the crease between his eyes deeper than ever. "Someone has sat upon my device, Samira."

She was midway through pulling her arms through the sleeves, and that gave her pause. "Somebody sat on your… what was it again?"

Now it was Apak's turn for exasperation. "The lightning runs through a series of metal poles, yes?"

"Yes…"

"And those poles connect with copper threads to a central box, yes?"

"All right…"

"I am sure that you can appreciate the importance of that box and the significance of someone sitting upon it, then?"

Samira finished pulling the dress down and stepped out from behind the divider. "Can you fix it? And do me up." She turned her back to Apak and waited while he put his paper down on her desk and trundled over to her.

His dark hands were thick and the fingers short, but they were some of the most agile Samira had seen. Apak could assemble machines in a matter of minutes that she could barely even comprehend. Now those adroit hands made quick work of the line of buttons going up the back of the dress. He grumbled the entire time in his own dialect that somehow sounded even more strangely formal than the southern tongues of his birthplace. "Well, of course I can fix it, but the point is that I should not have to. You must speak to the company and stop this carelessness from happening. It is a matter of time until someone damages something that cannot be fixed. And where will we be then, eh?"

Samira nodded gravely to Apak. "I understand. I will say something to everybody else, but for now you should just focus on getting everything ready for tonight." And she truly would speak to the company. While Apak surely was overreacting, they couldn't have pieces of equipment damaged on what was likely to be one of their busiest nights.

Apak looked at her for a long moment before nodding in apparent satisfaction. "Good. That is good." He turned to make his way out of the office but stopped short of the door to go back for the paper he had left on the desk.

"How is Oreth working out?" Samira asked. Apak had taken on an apprentice a few months ago, and the young man seemed to be a quick study.

"Oreth?" Apak blinked absently. "Ah, Oreth, yes. The boy does good work, but he would be well advised to withhold his mirth."

Samira kept a smile off her face as she hummed in agreement. "Too many jokes can't be good for the engineering."

"Precisely!" Apak stopped and squinted at her over his glasses. His mouth turned downward in the midst of his close-cropped black beard. "You mock, but technology requires a seriousness that the boy lacks. Perhaps my instruction can set him right."

"Perhaps," Samira said but hoped not. Oreth had been a welcome addition to the company when Apak found him in a tinker's shop, not unlike the one Apak himself had owned when she and Caius first met him. Just past his eighteenth birthday, the young man had been well on his way to blowing himself up with some project gone wrong. Oreth had enthusiasm for engineering, but not much in the way of knowledge or discipline.

He had been building spring loaded joke boxes to sell to children, but they all were roughly constructed, and half of them didn't work. Apak had bristled at the shoddy craftsmanship and ordered Oreth out of the tinker shop and into the theater company, where he would learn the proper ways of engineering. There had been no resistance from Oreth, and Caius had welcomed the addition. Since then, Apak had been hammering the essentials of metalworking, rudimentary chemistry, and basic physics into the young man's head. He seemed to be learning the material but drove Apak up the walls by turning the older man's lessons against him. Just yesterday Samira had heard the dressing down Apak gave Oreth when the young man had rigged a loud buzzer to trigger when Apak sat at his workbench.

Samira turned to look at herself in the tall mirror she kept in the corner of her office. She was hardly vain, but appearances mattered in the theater business. She pushed a strand of dark hair behind her ear and smoothed her hands down over the front of her dress. "What do you think, Apak?"

He'd gone back to the scribblings on the paper but looked up at her reflection. "Perfectly adequate," he huffed before wandering back out the door.

Samira tilted her head toward his departure with a grin. That was the best compliment she had heard him give in ages.

As showtime neared, Samira felt the little flutter in her stomach that was a mix of nerves and excitement. It didn't matter how many performances they had—and she had lost count long ago—that flutter always was there, just before the house lights dimmed and the spectacle began. How would the audience react? Would the acts land properly? Would they be entertained? Of course they would, but the questions came back every night. The doubt and the flutter always came strongest when they had a full house, and that's what she was feeling just now.

Samira had been off the side of the stage, watching the theater fill. Stagehands and assistants were bustling about behind her, but she left them to their business. They knew what they were doing, and her interference would only slow them down. Her attention was on the audience that had been pouring into the theater in a steady stream for the last few minutes.

She always tried to profile the audience, to guess what they were there to see. Over the years she had honed the craft of predicting how they would react to the various parts of the performances before they even took their seats. That man in the blue coat, for instance, would be astounded by the trickery Apak's lightning machine was sure to provide. And that older woman in the bonnet would be aghast at the very notion of anything unnatural. She might be in the wrong place. And the young man in the third row? Lizzie would be what he would remember from that night.

Every guest had a tell, and it required some educated guesswork, but Samira was good at it. It looked like they would have a full house that night, so there would be plenty of opportunities to put her talent to the test.

Samira moved down the steps at the side of the stage and made her way up the aisle on the right, past the attendees who were finding their seats. There still were plenty of seats to fill, but they soon would be taken, at the rate the people were coming in. Samira reached the back of the room, cast one more glance across the audience's heads, and pushed through the door to the lobby.

It was an ornate entryway with a polished marble floor and curved staircases winding up on either side, leading to the balconies. Potted plants decorated the edges of the room, and gilded mirrors on the walls gave the illusion that the space was twice or three times as large as it actually was. Samira caught her own image in one of the mirrors as she passed, and she smiled at the green dress again. It had yet to let her down, and she was sure tonight would be another success, no matter what that flutter might want her to think.

She stepped outside the front doors and checked the ticket window. There was a line waiting to buy tickets, always a good sign. The new barker Caius had hired was out there as well, still roping the populace into the theater. "Good people of Klubridge! Come in and see unexplainable wonders of science and mystery! You there in the hat, yes you! Once you've seen the Great Akithar, you'll leave here a changed man!"

Samira kept her eyes from rolling at that last bit. It seemed to work, because the man in the hat had stopped to look up at the theater and the giant stylized painting of Caius in full regalia. Samira looked past the man and saw the boy weaving through the crowd. She knew what was about to happen long before it happened, but she kept watching anyway.

The boy was skinny and short, with messy black hair and tanned skin, and he wore old clothes that were ragged and dirty enough to keep the upper crust disinterested in him but presentable enough for him to blend with the theater crowd. It was a deliberate look, and Samira recognized it both because she knew a costume when she saw one and because she had pulled similar stunts in her time. The boy walked with the flow of the crowd, only deviating for an instant, but it was long enough. Samira's brows rose in appreciation. He was good. The man in the hat wouldn't know the boy had robbed him until he tried to pay for his ticket at the window. It was a shame to lose a paying customer, but Samira thought this one was worth it.

She came fully out into the street and dropped into traffic behind the boy. He hadn't seen her and continued his path upstream. He moved with and around the other pedestrians in a pattern that looked almost random, but Samira soon spotted the woman just ahead and to the left. She was the next target. She watched the boy glance around the crowd, and she saw him move swiftly beside the woman and dart away just as easily and quickly. Samira blinked, a new appreciation forming. He had been good when he grabbed the man's wallet, but this one? His ability was astounding.

The boy was moving along, surely with someone else in his sights, when Samira spotted the officer half a block ahead. He wore the dark blue uniform of the city constabulary, and his head was turning constantly, monitoring the crowd for just this sort of trouble. The boy, too intent on his next target, didn't see the guard. Samira took a deep breath and plunged forward through the crowd.

She was moving with something just shy of the boy's speed now. As he rounded a couple walking hand in hand, she dipped past two businessmen on their way to a show. He hopped out of the way of a heavyset man, likely a banker, and that gave Samira a chance to gain on him. It wasn't long before she was a half step behind him, and the guard loomed ever closer, just off the right side of the road. The boy slipped to the right, ever closer to his target but also closer to the patrol. Samira saw the target now, a young man with a satchel. Probably an actor heading for his show. She frowned at that. Rob the public, rob the wealthy, but you always leave the performers alone.

The boy was nearly within striking distance of the actor and clearly in view of the guard when Samira grabbed his wrist in a tight hold. He barely had time to realize what was happening as she spun him in the opposite direction and pulled him back up the street, back toward the Chamberlain. "What—"

"Quiet," she said and gave him a meaningful look. Samira had little experience with children, but somehow that worked, and he stumbled along in her wake, pulled by the arm. They probably looked like a stern mother dragging her child off for a good scolding, and the crowd parted before them, not wanting to impede impending discipline.

Samira didn't stop until they were just short of the theater and well away from the guard. She moved back to the right and pulled the boy into the alley next to the Chamberlain. Out of the flow of traffic at last, she took a moment to look at him, keeping a hold on his wrist. "What's your name?"

The look he gave her was somewhere between terror and shame, but he managed, "Dorrin. Dorrin Vester." His fear was enough that he had not even bothered with an alias. Samira knew he was telling her the truth.

Her face softened, and she squatted to meet his eyes. "You're not in trouble, Dorrin. I pulled you away because a guard was about to see you."

At that, his eyes widened, and he protested, "They couldn't! I'm—"

"Quite good, yes. I saw you. But everybody slips up now and then." She smiled. "My name is Samira Tandogan. Do you live around here?"

He shook his head slowly, likely trying to comprehend what was happening. "No, we—I live with Scrounger. I mean, in the East Ward."

"You work for this Scrounger?" Samira asked. She knew the answer already, and that told her too much about this boy and the hard life he surely lived.

"He takes care of us," Dorrin said, and it came out as a protest.

"Does he treat you right?" Her grip on his hand loosened, and Dorrin looked down, surprised. He didn't answer immediately, and Samira smoothed a tangle of hair off his forehead.

He finally dropped his head. "I need to go. Skink's going to be looking for me."

Samira watched his face, full of far too much fear and worry for a child his age. "Do you know what this building is, Dorrin?"

He looked past her, up at the brickwork, and asked, "A theater?"

"This is not just any theater. This is the Chamberlain. Do you know what happens in there?"

He said nothing but looked at her for the answer. Everyone in Klubridge knew about Akithar and that the Chamberlain was his domain. Of course this boy knew what happened inside the theater, but he was reluctant to admit it.

She leaned closer and whispered, "Magic."

CHAPTER 3

Dorrin felt the hairs on the back of his neck stand up. Of course he'd heard what went on inside that theater, but he hadn't believed a word of it. Who would be stupid enough to do magic in the middle of Klubridge? And then to advertise it? No way it was true.

But now, there he stood in a strange alley with a strange woman who was telling him it was true, that there was magic inside. The lady, Samira, took his hand. "Come with me. You'll want to see this."

Growing up on the streets and surrounded by scoundrels all his life, Dorrin had learned to be wary. He should have bolted as soon as this lady released his wrist after pulling him into the alley, but he stayed. Why did he trust her any more than he would trust any other person in the crowd? She wore a fancy dress, which usually meant money, but that wasn't it. He couldn't see her as a mark, and that stymied him as well. You struck where you could, when you could. You got what you needed to survive, and he didn't even know this woman. And yet he felt compelled to like her.

Samira stood to walk deeper into the alley, and Dorrin followed along, his hand still in hers. This could be a dangerous situation. He knew all the cautionary tales about children getting themselves snatched up and never seen again. It was a daily occurrence in some parts of Klubridge. Not generally in the theater district, granted, but he could be the first. But something told him to follow her, and so he did.

They reached a green door tucked into an alcove that recessed about two feet into the red bricks that covered the side of the tall building. Dorrin had been so startled by the turn of events that he hadn't really thought about this building he was about to enter. The Chamberlain was one of the biggest theaters in the center of the district, and people said there was a wizard inside. Ridiculous, Dorrin reminded himself. But what if it wasn't?

He glanced back toward the street and watched the busy crowd continuing to move past, oblivious to his own little drama that was unfolding just a short distance away. That's the way he always liked it as he floated unseen through the currents. Something about being unseen and unknown now seemed exciting to him, because he also would be unmissed. Well, unmissed by all but Skink and Fairy. He had already ducked away from them long before the lady found him. Skink had had a look in his eye, and Fairy had seen it, too. It was a dangerous look that made Dorrin feel like he might not make it back to Scrounger's slum that night.

Samira was unlocking the door now with a short key tied to a band around her wrist. He saw a few other keys dangling beside it, and they all disappeared back up the sleeve of her dress after the door swung inward. She put a hand on his back and gently encouraged him into the building.

Dorrin took a step inside and saw they were in a dark hallway that ran to the back of the building before making a turn to the left. It was warmer inside than out, and Dorrin could hear music coming from somewhere deeper in the building. He looked up at Samira, and she smiled at him again and went down the hallway toward the turn. Dorrin followed her, still unsure what he was about to see, but he was becoming eager to find out.

A man in dark clothes and with graying hair rounded the corner and nodded to Samira before quickly passing them and disappearing into a discrete door Dorrin hadn't noticed. He and Samira continued toward the back, soon taking that very corner, and the hallway opened into a larger room. It was brighter there, but the gas lanterns around the room remained dimmed from their full luminescence. The floor was pale wood, which brightened the area, and Dorrin noticed crates and equipment arranged around the room. Black metal ladders hung down on either end of the room, extending up into the darkness above. The music was louder here, and he realized they must be behind the stage. People were busy carrying satchels here and there or stopping to have quick conversations, and nobody took notice of the two of them.

Samira asked Dorrin in a hushed tone, "Have you ever been in a theater?"

"No," he said but then caught himself. "Yes, once. It was a prize fight."

She laughed. "I'll bet you left with quite a prize yourself, didn't you?"

He gave a slight smile and nodded, both proud of his take that night and concerned by how this lady might react.

"I'd appreciate your not lifting any purses while you're here tonight. You are our guest." She took his hand again. "Come now, the show's already started."

He followed her to the front of the room and through a small doorway that led to a much darker room. Dorrin blinked in the blackness, wondering for an instant whether she had tricked him into a trap. Was he about to be one of those unfortunate disappeared urchins after all? But no, his eyes adjusted, and he realized there was another exit from the room, an open doorway leading directly onto what must be the stage. The music was louder still, moaning strings punctuated by occasional percussive hits of a tambourine. Dorrin could not see the musicians, but he did see something else on the stage. He took a step forward and tried to decide what sort of animal he was watching.

In the center of the stage, bathed in a light that presently was shifting from purple to green, some sort of creature stretched. With a start, Dorrin saw that it was a snake, bigger than any he had ever seen before. It was pale, with a dark streak slashing diagonally down it, and its head reared up in the dim lighting, undulating in pace with the music. How was this possible?

But as soon as he blinked, the thing no longer was a snake. It had become a butterfly, extending its wings wide, arcing up as if about to take flight in the now orange glow of the stage lighting. Even as the creature flexed its wings back in, Dorrin heard a collective gasp from the audience, out of sight before the stage.

He looked up to Samira, barely visible in the reflected light from the stage. "What is it?" he whispered, careful not to let his voice disrupt whatever mystical event he was witnessing.

She was watching it, too, and tugged at his hand. "This way. You can see better."

Dorrin followed her through the darkness at the side of the stage, not able to see where they were going but trusting her navigation. They paused, and Samira pulled back a curtain. Dorrin ducked under it, and now he was in the main room of the theater. The house? Is that what they called it? He saw the audience now, facing him, but all eyes affixed to the transformations occurring on the stage. Dorrin followed their gaze and gave a gasp of his own to see that the enormous butterfly now was a horse.

The steed raised onto its hind legs, and Dorrin leaned forward with incredulity. He now could see that this thing was neither a snake nor a butterfly nor a horse, but it was in fact two people. A woman with pale, glowing skin and hair so blonde that it was nearly white was the front of the horse. She wore a thin and flowing white gown that draped behind her as her arms moved and her back arched in uncanny ways to create the illusion. Lifting her from the ground were two strong, dark hands clasped at her waist. The man was big, with lean muscles tensing deliberately in the lights which now were yellow. He wore no shirt, his torso making the black body of the creature. His legs were covered with dark and baggy pants that made Dorrin think of his own, replete with hidden pockets. But these were no thief's pants. These looked like silk and flowed with the movements, giving the appearance of the horse's back legs. A red sash tied at his waist punctuated the image, giving it a shock of color that both betrayed and enhanced the illusion.

The man lowered the woman, and she collapsed in a boneless way that startled Dorrin. He heard another intake of breath from the audience and knew he was not alone. The man stood over her for an instant before tucking his head and rolling his body into an impossible shape, arcing down over her prone form. She slipped upward from the floor, moving like Dorrin had never seen anyone move before. The music turned and changed with the pair's movements, and even though Dorrin knew he was watching two people, he also was seeing a giant bird before him, its head cocked to the side and the suggestion of an eye blinking at the audience.

As soon as the bird had formed, it dissolved again. The woman shot straight up into the air, a thin arrow that disappeared into the dark upper regions of the stage. From where Dorrin stood, he could see that she had grabbed a bar dangling from ropes suspended from a catwalk above the stage, but to the audience the bird had launched into flight. Dorrin thought he had never seen anything as wonderful in his life.

There was a brief intermission after the first act. Some of the audience had gotten up to mill about the lobby or to talk with each other, and Dorrin had turned to see what Samira had thought about the performance. She had disappeared sometime towards the end, though, and he stood alone at the side of the stage. He thought about going backstage again to find her, but another part of him focused on the audience. It was a reflex, really. A golden thread, visible only to Dorrin, angled out toward a gentleman in a top hat, facing away from the stage while he talked with a couple sitting behind him. From there, the thread wove its way up the center aisle to a younger man who had somehow fallen asleep in his seat. His head nodded back, and Dorrin could see his mouth moving with each breath. Continuing toward the lobby, the thread found a woman engrossed in reading a pamphlet and oblivious to the rest of the people sitting and wandering around her.

No, not in here. The thread shivered and then dissolved into sparkling, silent dust. Samira had been good to him, and he would not repay her by stealing from her patrons. That reserve felt like a betrayal of something, not striking at the opportunity when he could. Of course, it was a betrayal of Scrounger. The stern man expected all his charges to take every chance to fill their pockets and bring the contents back to his lair. But the looming threat of not having enough for Scrounger felt more distant here. Even Skink and his flailing fists and snarling face were far away. Dorrin had been in the theater for only a few minutes, but it already felt safe to him.

No sooner had Dorrin made up his mind not to rob the theater crowd than the house lights dimmed once, then twice. He blinked up at the glowing lanterns and wondered how they could change in intensity like that. The light fixtures hung above the audience, emitting their constant glow, and there was no one near them to tend to them manually. They didn't look like any gaslamps he'd seen, and they weren't wax candles. Thin wires that looked metallic wound up the ropes from which each fixture hung and disappeared into the ceiling. Maybe that had something to do with it.

He had little time to ponder the rigging, as a man brushed past Dorrin and made his way to the center of the stage. He wore a black coat and white shirt with gray trousers that didn't quite match the upper part of the ensemble. His prodigious belly hung over his trousers, fully obscuring the belt that likely held them up. He was balding and sported a day's growth of stubble on his face. It was when he spoke that Dorrin remembered seeing the man outside the front of the theater earlier that evening. He had been calling to the passersby and trying to hook them into the show.

Now the man spoke with that same booming voice, and this time it echoed from the front to the back of the theater and caught the attention of every ear. "Visitors, friends, and guests, we welcome you once again to the Chamberlain!" He allowed the murmurs of conversation to fall silent. Satisfied, he continued, "You came here tonight to be astounded, and you already have witnessed the transformations and contortions of the greatest acrobatic illusionists of our time, the incomparable..." He hesitated an instant and looked offstage before shrugging and saying, "Tidal Mirage!" The audience applauded, and Dorrin eagerly joined them in clapping. That act truly had been marvelous.

The barker nodded in agreement and let the applause continue for a moment. He then raised his hands, and the room fell silent again. "You no doubt were thrilled by what you just saw, but that was only the beginning. Yes, we have something even more amazing in store for you."

Dorrin knew the next act had to be the wizard himself, but he didn't know what to expect. He saw a good portion of the audience shift forward in their seats. Whatever came next was what they came to see. What possibly could have been better than the acrobats?

"My friends, prepare yourselves for miracles, if such preparations are possible. You are about to see the uncanny brought before your eyes. We request that you remain seated and that you attempt to keep your composure. In just a moment you will cross into a realm from which you may never return. Your understanding of the natural world will be challenged. I bring before you a man who shall perform feats you never have seen before and never will see again." He paused again and took a dramatic breath. The audience hung on his words, and Dorrin didn't know whether to watch the eager faces in the crowd or the stage itself. At last, the barker finished. "I introduce to you the mysterious, the impossible, the Great Akithar!"

The lights in the theater extinguished all at once, and Dorrin's eyes opened wide in the blackness. In the absence of the barker's voice there was silence, and then he heard the audience shifting uncomfortably in their seats. The darkness persisted, and a few people began whispering to each other. Someone cleared a throat, and someone else giggled. The audience's noise grew to a low murmur during what seemed to be an hour but really was only fifteen seconds. Dorrin counted it off, just like he'd learned to count as the distance closed between himself and a mark.

As he hit the fifteenth second and the murmuring was on the verge of ascending into jeering shouts, the room erupted in light, accompanied by an enormous bang. Dorrin jolted, and the audience jumped. The seats creaked on the floor, and feet stomped in surprise. Someone yelped, and a couple of others laughed nervously in response.

The light came from a huge lantern at the back of the stage, nearly five feet across, Dorrin reckoned. He saw no flame inside it. How was it so bright? Silhouetted in front of the light was the form of a man, tall, maybe six feet. He was thin and wore a tall hat, but Dorrin could make out no other details as the man stood backlit by the strange glowing circle. The audience was silent again, stunned and likely anxious to see what would happen next.

The man on the stage raised his arms slowly, and Dorrin saw that he was wearing a short cape of some sort. It draped down from his arms, creating a growing shadow across the audience. The silence broke when the man spoke. His voice projected through the theater with an astounding resonance that grabbed every person in attendance.

"I am Akithar." His arms fell, and the great lamp behind him disappeared as spotlights flooded the center of the stage. He was tall, just as Dorrin had thought, with dark hair and pale skin. His eyes stared confidently into the crowd, and he frowned with pronounced intensity. A thin black mustache covered part of his upper lip, but he had no other facial hair. He was wearing a tuxedo, the white shirt and black suit finished with a straight black necktie and a cloak with a bright red lining, the only thing with actual color on the stage.

"You have come to see magic, have you not?"

Dorrin's eyes widened at that word, and in Akithar's pause the audience shifted again. Dorrin heard someone whisper something to a neighbor, and they sounded nervous. As well they should, being in a place where someone would even mention this sort of thing. But Akithar was smiling a devilish grin.

"No doubt you have heard that I am a sorcerer." He raised his right hand, and fiery sparks shot from his gloved fingertips. Dorrin swallowed hard and looked from the stage back toward the entrance to the theater. How could someone dare to do this, and in a theater in front of an audience? "No doubt you have heard that," Akithar continued, "but who would be foolish enough to proclaim himself a sorcerer on a stage in this city? Let us instead say that I am a man of science. Does that make you more comfortable?"

At this cue, gears rumbled to life, and something began to rise from a hatch in the stage's floor. It was a metal structure, some sort of machine. The lower part was a nondescript gray box. A thin pole raised from the top of the box, upon which sat a fat metal orb. Akithar rounded the device as it came up onto the stage, taking deliberate steps to bring himself behind it. It finished raising, and the gears clanked into place. Akithar now stood behind the device, and the orb came up midway on level with his stomach. He snapped his right hand into view again and dragged the white glove off it. He did the same with his left hand and carefully folded the two linen gloves into an inner pocket in his jacket.

"I was born in a small village far away from here. That is where I learned my singular craft." He rested his hands on the orb as he spoke. "It was there, far up in the mountains and distant from modern society, that I was taught the esoteric activities that you come tonight to see. And so, I share with you, my... science."

Akithar's hands pulled away from the orb, and with sharp crackles tiny flashes of lightning jumped between his palms and the ball. The stage lighting had dimmed, and these jolts of electricity now lit the strange man in flickering blue light. His fingers curled, and his hands moved in swaying patterns over and around the metal ball. He seemed to sculpt the lightning, and he never flinched away, never was shocked. Dorrin's fear and confusion gave way to utter fascination, and he leaned forward toward the spectacle.

Akithar slid his palms together on the upper curve of the ball, and then he scooped them up like drawing a cupped handful of water from a basin. But instead of water, his hands came away full of jagged little lightning bolts. A tiny storm raged in his hands, still sparking and cracking with growing intensity.

"This is electricity," Akithar said, and he continued to shift his handfuls of lightning so that the bolts danced wildly among his fingers. "This is humanity controlling the elements."

"Blasphemy!" Someone in the audience shouted.

Akithar raised an eyebrow and smirked. "And against whom would you say that I blaspheme? As I said, I am but a man of science. What could be less unnatural than that?"

Machinery from somewhere made a clanking noise, and a spotlight illuminated the audience and turned to find the man who had interrupted the performance. The man was middle-aged, dressed in a shabby dark suit, and he had risen from his seat to confront Akithar. Dorrin felt like he knew the man from somewhere. "Your sorcery will be felled by our glorious ruler. Even you can't escape his gaze!"

"Mm, perhaps you are right," Akithar said with a tilt of his head. "Perhaps you would like to carry a sample back to him?"

With that, he drew his hand back and flung it toward the audience. An explosion of sparks flew from his palm when it opened, and the man in the audience shuddered and fell back into his seat. His eyes were saucers, and he convulsed from the unseen force but remained otherwise unharmed. Others around him pulled away, trying to avoid whatever energy the sorcerer had thrown at his naysayer.

Dorrin watched all of this unfold with his mouth agape. This was real magic, happening right here in Klubridge. Surely the guards would be upon them any moment now.

He watched the stricken man in the audience recover quickly from the attack, stand, and make his shaky way to the aisle and then toward the exit. It was then that Dorrin realized where he had seen the man. It was the same person who had brushed past when he and Samira were in the back hallway. It was one of the theater company... The man was in league with Akithar! Crestfallen, Dorrin looked back to the performer and saw everything differently. Akithar's right sleeve bulged slightly from some sort of rod that barely poked out the edge of his cuff. Dorrin watched sparks fly from the end of the rod as Akithar made another sweeping motion.

It was all fakery. This was no magic. Just a moment ago, Dorrin had been terrified that the law was about to take the whole theater apart, searching for illegal magic. But now he realized excitement had accompanied that terror. He had been in the presence of wonder and greatness, but now he knew it was just another lie. Another man preying on the gullibility of others.

Dorrin scowled and glanced at the exit from the stage door. He could slip away and get back to Fairy before anyone even knew he was gone. He looked back to the stage and watched Akithar preparing for his next trick. Even as Dorrin watched, the man was discarding his previous hidden contraption, surely getting ready to replace it with some equally disappointing prop. Akithar's right hand went behind his back, out of the view of the audience, and the spark-throwing rod slid down and out from his sleeve.

Dorrin waited for it to slip out and drop to the floor, but that didn't happen. As soon as the tool cleared Akithar's sleeve, the man's hand gestured subtly, and the rod no longer was there. It was not that it simply disappeared or fell too quickly for him to see it. No, it ceased existing. Starting at the bottom and moving to the top, the rod, nearly a foot in length, shimmered before evaporating into a light wisp of purple smoke.

No one else had seen it happen, but Dorrin knew what he saw. As soon as the rod was gone, Akithar turned his head to the left and looked straight into the dark wing of the stage, directly at Dorrin. He smiled and winked. Dorrin felt a chill run up his arms, and he froze in place, all thoughts of escaping out the stage door now forgotten.

CHAPTER 4

"Where do we put the calipers when we are finished with them, Oreth?"

The young man looked up from the toolbox, a mix of shame and confusion on his face. "In here?"

"Precisely," Apak said, handing the tool over.

"Sorry, Apak." Oreth took the calipers and rummaged in the box to make room. "I was just thinking about how maybe we could get some more spark out of the rods if we—"

"This is not the time for that. What have I told you?" Apak's tone was patient, although he was sure that he had asked the same question in the same circumstance a hundred times.

Oreth nodded. "Focus on the task at hand. But if we—"

"And what, would you say, is the task at hand?"

"Packing up after the show?"

"You are correct. Complete that, and then we can talk about new designs."

Oreth had a good head on his shoulders, and he had a knack for coming up with ingenious designs and unexpected ways to implement them. What he lacked was focus, and he could use a bit more serious-ness as well. Apak reminded himself once again that his apprentice was young, still only eighteen, and he told himself the boy would grow out of the mischief. Sometimes he wondered, though.

The calipers at least were put away now, and—Apak paused. He glanced over his shoulder, and his eyes narrowed as they scanned the row of crates along the side wall. Something. But what?

He rubbed at his chin, and the graying whiskers scratched against his fingers. Apak took one step toward the crates, and then another. Everything had a place, and something most certainly was not in its place. Reaching the first of the wooden boxes, he rested his hand on the top. No, this one was shut tight. He knew without checking that it was full of fabrics. The next one, then? He walked down the row and trailed his hand lightly over each crate. No, that one was extra wiring. And the next? No, not that one either.

His slow pace halted at the fourth crate. It was a sturdy one, about three feet tall, and covered in flaking yellow paint. The front was stenciled with "HARDWARE" in bold black letters, and Apak knew it was only one quarter full of smaller boxes of screws, attachments, and other technical accoutrement. It was his job to know these things, and he took his job seriously. He studied the box in silence for a moment before sighing and grasping one edge of the lid. It came up more easily than it should have, and Apak slid it off and gently rested it on the floor, one edge propped against the crate.

"I suppose you should introduce yourself," Apak said as he peered over the edge and into the box.

Looking back up at him was a pair of wide and frightened eyes, staring out of the dark crate. The boy said nothing, and Apak huffed in disapproval.

"If you are going to crouch atop my supplies, you at least could have the courtesy to speak, boy." When there still was no response, Apak reached a hand down. "Come out of there."

The boy shrank impossibly farther into the box. Apak sighed again. "Oreth, could you please assist me? We appear to have a stowaway."

Oreth closed the box he had been filling and made his way over to the open crate. He stood beside Apak and blinked down into it. He looked at Apak and back at the crate, a smile forming. "What is this?" Oreth asked, looking like he expected a punchline.

"It appears to be a boy, and I would appreciate his removal from this box before he damages something."

Oreth's eyebrows raised, and he stepped closer to the box. "Okay, pal. Time to be up and out." He reached inside, grabbed the boy under the arms, and hauled him over the edge.

When the boy's feet touched the floor, he looked ready to bolt, but Apak put a firm hand on his shoulder. The lad was dirty with a thin dusting of grime, and his tousled hair looked unwashed. He obviously had come from the streets, but how had he gotten into the theater, much less backstage, and why was he hiding?

"What is your name?" Apak demanded, and the boy shrank even more, refusing to speak.

"His name is Dorrin, and you're scaring the life out of him." Samira rounded the corner to the prop room, and Apak saw the boy's gaze shift hopefully to her.

Apak had to look up to meet the taller woman's eyes. "This boy, Dorrin, he is your guest, then?"

"He is, and I was wondering where he got off to." Samira smiled at Dorrin and eased Apak's hand away from his shoulder. She squatted next to him. "Now, then. What did you think of the show?"

Dorrin looked from Samira to Apak to Oreth and back again. Uncertainty clouded his face, and he finally managed, "I've never seen anything like that."

"The sparks?" Apak asked. "It is admittedly a spectacle but quite simple to accomplish."

Dorrin shook his head. "No. I mean, yes. That was great, too, and the people becoming animals. All of it. But..." He hesitated, and Apak shot a hard look at Samira. Now he knew what had so captivated the boy and also what had driven him into hiding.

"What happened to the spark rod," Apak said. "That is what you saw."

Dorrin's eyes widened, and he licked his lips before responding. At last he gave a short nod but looked as if he regretted it as soon as it was done.

Samira returned Apak's look, but hers was softer. She smiled gently and told Dorrin, "It's okay. What you saw isn't going to get you into trouble."

"But... how? I mean—Isn't it illegal to..." He could not bring himself to say more.

"Illegal? Yes," Samira said. "But we won't tell if you don't. And I don't think you're going to tell anyone, are you?"

Dorrin shook his head, his expression of fear giving way to confusion.

"See?" Samira said, "We're all friends here, and everything is okay." Then, to Apak, "Dorrin has had a hard night. And I suspect more than that. He is my guest, and he's welcome for as long as he needs to stay."

Apak pinched his lips together into a disapproving scowl before releasing it and exhaling in resignation. He extended the hand that previously had clamped onto the boy's shoulder. "My name is Apak, Dorrin. This is my apprentice, Oreth. Welcome to the Chamberlain Theater."

Dorrin stared at Apak's sturdy hand before cautiously accepting it and shaking it.

Apak looked back to Samira. "Did you tell Caius about this?"

"I did, and he's interested in meeting our young friend. Would you be so kind as to show him the way?"

The pinched scowl returned for an instant, but Apak pushed it away. "All right, boy. Let us go. You have people to meet."

Dorrin tried to trail behind Apak, but the engineer was having none of it. He kept the boy at his side as they wound through the hallways backstage, eventually coming to a small waiting area. It was scarcely more than a walk-through closet, and there was barely room for the two crates that flanked a closed door in the wall opposite the doorway where they had entered. Apak squinted through the dark window in the door. "He is not quite ready for us." He gestured to one of the crates. "Have a seat."

The boy sat wordlessly, his legs dangling off the edge of the box and his feet brushing at the polished wooden floor. He still was watching Apak with a mix of emotions that Apak thought might be fear and suspicion. That would not do. If Samira said this boy was to be their guest, Apak could not have him sulking about.

Apak grabbed the lid of the other crate and gave it a hard tug. It popped up and slid aside with a high-pitched groaning of wood. He reached inside and rummaged. "You saw the entire performance, eh? Not just the part that frightened you, I trust?"

Dorrin did not reply, but he nodded when Apak cast a look back at him. Satisfied, Apak went back to the box. "Akithar is a master of the sleight of hand. He can make anything seemingly vanish or appear with a wave, solids and liquids alike, as incredible as the latter might seem. Much of that comes from practiced tricks. Illusions he has perfected over many hundreds of hours of practice and that you, too, could learn. Some of what you saw surely cannot be explained in the time we have here, though." Aha, there it was. He grasped a thin metal tube and pulled it out of the box, presenting it triumphantly. "But some of it can."

Dorrin's eyebrows raised, confirming for Apak that the boy had spotted the rod slipping out of Caius' sleeve. That was perceptive. Perhaps Samira had seen promise in the boy after all. "Do you know what this is?" Apak asked. Dorrin shook his head, and Apak scowled. "I am trying to show you something interesting. At least say something."

Dorrin blinked. "Okay."

"Answer the question. Do you know what this is?"

"No... sir."

The "sir" was a surprise, and Apak humphed before turning the rod over in his hands. "I built this. That is what I do here. I build things that make wonder. Not everything you saw on that stage was... magic." Apak leaned in to say that last word and watched Dorrin bristle at the word. That was good. Having a fear and respect for it should keep him safe. "In fact," Apak said, raising a finger, "almost everything you saw Cai—the Great Akithar do tonight was thanks to devices like this one." He tapped the rod and gave his head a meaningful bob.

Dorrin studied the metal cylinder carefully and finally asked, "What does it do?"

"I am glad that you asked. This, my young friend, is what Oreth likes to call a spark slinger. Please do let me know if you can invent a better name than that, and I will be happy to rebrand this thing. As for what it does? We shall start by secreting it away, like so." He slid the rod up his sleeve so it extended midway up his forearm with the downward end resting in his cupped palm. His sleeve was tight, and it held the device securely in place.

"And now that it is in place, it is hardly perceptible, yes?" He raised his arm, and the rod was small enough that it did not create a bump or crease on his sleeve. "But now we come to its true purpose." Apak stared gravely into Dorrin's eyes. "Are you prepared, young man?"

Dorrin nodded, leaning forward on the edge of his crate.

Apak splayed his fingers and flexed his hand upward, his palm thrust forward. The rod caught tighter between his shirt cuff and his arm. He felt the small click an instant before the rod flared to life. A burst of bright sparks shot out the end, showering the space between Apak and Dorrin. He released the switch just as quickly, shutting the device down before it could burn the whole blasted theater down.

The sparks lingered in the air a bit longer than one might expect. That had been a bugger to figure out, and Apak had gone through three scorched shirts before he got it right. But he did get it right in the end, as he always did.

Dorrin's eyes were wide, and he now regarded Apak with a grin. "That's what he used in the show!"

"Indeed, it is." Apak closed his hand and tugged the rod out. He held it toward Dorrin, and the boy reached to take it. Apak pulled it back, but gently. "Not just yet. We simply look and learn for now."

Dorrin nodded in understanding and lowered his hand. He said,

"So it wasn't… magic, then?" Even now, he looked afraid to utter the word, and his voice dropped to a whisper when he said it.

"It was science. Science and engineering." Apak turned the rod and pointed to a slight protrusion partway down one side. "This is the activator switch. When you depress it… Well… Here, go ahead. Give it a press."

Dorrin studied the cylinder and carefully slid an index finger along the side until he found the bump. He pressed for an instant and jumped back, both startled and delighted as sparks flung out the end once again. He beamed at Apak. "It's wonderful! How did you do it?"

Apak gave the boy a small smile. "This is what I do. I engineer the contraptions that go on the stage. Tell me, have you ever built anything?"

The boy frowned in thought. "Nothing like that. I—wait! I have made something!"

Dorrin bounded off the crate to stand before Apak. He spread his feet wide and reached down to pull up one of his filthy, baggy pants legs. Apak blinked in confusion at what appeared to be a second pair of trousers beneath the first. The inner pants leg was secured to the boy's own leg with a series of brown straps that wound around and around, disappearing up into the outer pants.

"I do not understand," Apak said as he knelt to examine what he was being shown.

"See, here," Dorrin said, and now he was pulling open the pocket on the side of that same leg. He thrust his hand down into the pocket and continued pushing until his arm had disappeared past the elbow. "The pockets go all the way down, see. So when I put something in, it falls down my leg, and I can keep more and more in there. That's all it was when I first made it. Well, Fairy made it, but I told her how I wanted it." He was excited now, and Apak remained quiet, letting the boy tell his story.

"But when it was like that, everything just went straight down, and it jangled around and was too heavy at the bottom. I couldn't run, and anyway you'd hear everything clinking and clanking around. So then I had her put these straps in." He pulled at one of them. "They go all the way up and around here." He raised the bottom of his shirt to reveal that the straps came up the pants and wrapped around his waist. "And if I pull on different ones, they make it tighter in different places. Like this!" He yanked at two of the laces, and Apak saw the inner pants leg tighten toward the bottom of the leg.

It all came together then. Dorrin was a thief, and this was how he carried his ill-gotten gains surreptitiously and in a way that allowed him to remain agile when a hasty escape was necessary. Apak rocked back from his crouch to lean against the opposite crate. He favored Dorrin with a brief inclination of his head. "That is quite clever." Now he was looking at the boy with a different appreciation. Perhaps Samira had known what she was doing after all. "Would you like to learn to make more things? Things like this?" Apak asked, indicating the rod still in his hand.

Dorrin was dumbstruck. "I wouldn't even know how to start making something like that."

"Of course you would not know how to make this," Apak grumbled. "I asked if you would like to learn."

Dorrin hesitated. He clearly wanted to answer in the affirmative, but he was unsure. "I don't know if I could learn. I'm… I'm nobody."

Apak rested a hand on Dorrin's shoulder, the same hand that had clamped that same shoulder in a tight grip just a few moments ago. "Everyone starts somewhere, Dorrin. You met my apprentice, Oreth."

"He was rough when he picked me up."

"Well, you should not have been hiding in our hardware," Apak scolded and then continued. "I found Oreth working in a joke shop, of all places. I brought him into the company at the theater, and he has been learning my craft ever since then. You, too, could learn, if you would like."

Dorrin was halfway to an answer when the window in the door illuminated. He and Apak looked at each other for a brief second, and Apak pushed himself to his feet. "That conversation can wait. For now, you have a magician to meet."

∾

The Great Akithar was an institution in the city of Klubridge. Anyone who walked through the theater district would see the immense lettering above the entrance to the Chamberlain, and the name Akithar even was on tongues in the distant financial quarter and all the way through to the less glamorous Downsteps. This strange man who made his life's work the flaunting of a magical stage show fascinated the people of Klubridge, while the Empire snuffed out every whisper of magic that it could find. The public's awe at Akithar's brazenness was matched only by its curiosity about his identity. They knew him only as Akithar, always clad in the same black suit or a series of black suits, all identical, always completed by a gaudy black cape with a red lining.

If questioned about the man's private life, the average citizen likely would conjure their own fantasies about the strange hours he kept, the otherworldly guests he surely entertained, and the ancient manor he must inhabit. Despite his public claims that his shows were merely science and not magic, everyone knew the truth. The man had to spend his hours away from the stage bent over wicked cauldrons and laying out grotesque runes. He probably even now was summoning up some unearthly demon to do his bidding from within his elaborately appointed laboratory, garish silks and tapestries hanging from the walls and ceiling, and chilling mementos adorning the shelves that lined the room.

Those thoughts always brought a droll smile to Apak's face when he passed through the door into the magician's office. It was a cozy enough room, and it did have shelves along the walls. The public would be disappointed to see not a grimoire in sight. Instead, they would find texts about mundane chemicals, volumes on practical physics, and a few books concerning biology. Electrical currents were of particular interest at the moment, and the few manuals that were available on the subject already lay open and stacked on top of each other across the surface of a small desk.

The sorcerer himself did not sit at the desk or stoop over a mystical altar but instead reclined in a burgundy upholstered chair, the fabric run through with intricate golden stitching. He wore that same black suit, but the collar was undone, and the cape was nowhere to be seen. He had his left leg crossed over the right, and he propped his left elbow on the arm of the chair. A cup of what surely was tea sat on the small round table to his right. The steam still curling upward from the cup was the only thing in the room that seemed truly magical. Off the stage, he looked younger, perhaps even more human. He smiled as Apak and Dorrin came in.

"Have a seat, Dorrin. Can I call you Dorrin?"

Dorrin was watching him warily and nodded as he went to the armchair that sat angled toward the other one. "Okay."

"Sorry there's not a chair, Apak."

Apak clasped his hands behind his back. "Not to worry. I am fine standing." This meeting was not about him, anyway. He took a step back towards the wall, just outside the glow of the lanterns hanging about the room. Dorrin was sitting in the chair now, and Apak knew he was trying his best not to fidget.

"My name is Caius Harrim," the magician said.

Dorrin blinked. "Not Akithar?"

"I'm Akithar when I'm on the stage. I'm Akithar to people who don't need to know who I really am. To my friends, I'm Caius. And I think we will be friends, Dorrin. What do you think?"

"I don't know. I don't know what to think. I was just outside in the street, and the lady brought me inside."

Caius smiled. "I understand you're quite skilled out there, in the street."

Dorrin took a moment to answer. He was studying the man's face, his encouraging smile, his gray eyes. Apak realized that Dorrin was a shrewd judge of character, especially for his age. "I guess so," the boy finally said. "You know what I was doing?"

"Samira told me a little, but why don't you tell me yourself?" Caius clasped his hands in his lap and uncrossed his legs. He leaned forward, ready for a story.

Dorrin took the encouragement. "I take things. Money, usually, but sometimes other things."

"Where do you live?"

"Not near here. I live with Scrounger. And the others. There are several of us." Dorrin paused and then added with a touch of defiance, "Scrounger looks out for us."

Caius nodded. "I imagine so. Do you give Scrounger the things you take? The money?"

Dorrin nodded back.

"How long have you been doing that?"

Dorrin glanced back toward Apak in the shadows. He looked concerned now. Caius read his worry and said, "It's okay. You're not in trouble, Dorrin. Quite the contrary, if we're being honest. Samira was impressed with the way you moved through the crowd and how you took things without being caught. She thought you must have been doing it for a long time. You have a talent."

Dorrin was looking at Caius again and pulled the corner of his mouth tight. "That's what Scrounger says."

Caius sat back in his chair and drew a thumb down his jawline. Apak had seen him do that enough times to know that he was weighing his next words. After the brief pause, he asked, "Are you happy working for Scrounger?"

Dorrin's shoulders raised just enough for Apak to notice the tension. The boy waited half a beat before blurting, "Are you a real magician?"

Caius' eyebrows went up a tic, and he huffed a quick laugh. "Straight to the point, aren't you?"

"Well, are you?" Dorrin's tone was challenging now.

"Why do you ask? You saw tonight's show, didn't you?"

"I saw you making sparks with the spark slinger thing. And I saw you doing tricks with machines and wires. But then, afterwards, I saw what you did with the rod." Dorrin stopped talking abruptly. He looked as if he had said too much.

Apak could tell that Caius liked the boy. He always appreciated directness. Nevertheless, Caius' response was less than direct. "We all have our skills, Dorrin. You are good at moving through crowds but making yourself unseen. And you're skilled at, ah, obtaining things that previously weren't yours. I'm good at making an audience see what I want them to see. I've been doing this for a long time, and I suspect you've been doing what you do for a long time as well."

Dorrin did not look satisfied with the answer, but he seemed to know better than to press. "I guess."

"Did you have parents before Scrounger?"

"Batten took care of me for a while."

"Who is Batten?"

"I don't remember much about him. I know he took care of me, but then..." Dorrin trailed off. Something had happened to this Batten, and then Dorrin had landed alongside the creature he called Scrounger.

Caius lowered his head in understanding. He leaned forward again, his elbows on his knees, so he could look into Dorrin's eyes on a level with the boy. "Before coming here to Klubridge, I didn't have a family, either. Samira and I both were on our own for a long time. Then we found this city, and we found friends. Good people. People like Apak and the rest of my company here. They became my family, and we take care of each other. Things are better when you have someone to take care of and know someone will take care of you. Don't you think so?"

Dorrin looked back at Caius but then dropped his gaze. "Maybe."

Caius watched him for another moment in silence. Then his eyes flicked past the boy, toward Apak. His forehead was creased in wordless query. Apak knew his own response would matter more than the small boy in that chair could ever imagine. It mattered for the company at large as well, though, and it was not something they should take lightly on either account. Apak sighed, and at last he closed his eyes and nodded to Caius. Caius gave a small smile and nodded back.

"Dorrin, you can stay here with us if you want to. You don't have to go back to Scrounger."

Dorrin's eyes widened, and his breath caught. He looked up at Caius and turned to look at Apak again. His expression was one of hope, but just as quickly as it had come, it fled beneath suspicion. "You just want me to steal for you. Just like him. That's what this is about."

"No," Caius said gently and held his hands up, palms open. "If you stay here, you never have to steal again if you don't want to. You deserve a chance to grow up and not have to fight for your living."

Dorrin said nothing at first, but his chin wobbled. "He'll come for me." The boy's eyes shined in the lamplight as tears formed.

"That's not something for you to worry about," Caius said. "If you want to stay with us, we'll take care of you. You won't be harmed. I promise you that."

Dorrin tried to blink back the tears, but that only set them free. Once the first tears rolled down his cheeks, he bent forward, and his small back shook. He buried his face in his lap as the shaking became more violent. Apak took a step forward, concerned, but Caius motioned him back. "It's okay," he said. He placed a hand softly on the boy's back. Dorrin now was crying in earnest but still without a sound other than ragged gasps between sobs. "You're safe here. Do you want to stay?"

Apak felt compelled to help the boy, but he did not know how. He clasped his hands tighter behind his back and stayed away, as Caius had motioned for him to do. After what seemed to be an eternity of tears, Dorrin's quaking slowed. He had exhausted himself. Caius still had his hand on the boy's back, which now was rising and falling with more regular breaths. Between loud sniffs, Dorrin raised his head slowly and wiped his hands across his face. "Yes," he said, "I want to stay."

CHAPTER 5

F airy had given up trying to scam coins off unsuspecting victims nearly half an hour ago when she realized how long it had been since she'd seen Dorrin. She, Dorrin, and Skink had made their way from Scrounger's place up to the Bastion in time to hit the prime theatergoing crowd. It didn't take Skink long to split off from them without a word. Dorrin had been so focused on the crowd that he barely noticed, but Fairy noticed. She wasn't about to let the bigger boy sneak around an alley and catch Dorrin unawares, so she stuck close. She'd been with him all the way down the street past the Bastion, and that's where the crowd got thicker. It was then that Dorrin had said they needed to split up to get this done faster. She'd reluctantly agreed, and she now was cursing herself for that lapse in judgment.

Had Skink come back around and grabbed him somewhere? Was Dorrin lying beaten or worse in some trash bin somewhere? It had been too long since she'd seen him, and that was a fact.

Calling out for Dorrin would have been useless. There were too many people, all being loud, and all much taller than Fairy was. If she'd yelled for him, the mob would have eaten her voice. She likely would draw too much attention, too. Before leaving Scrounger's, she had put on her nice blue dress, but even she knew that what passed for nice there was barely passable here. It wouldn't take long for somebody to see the dirty ragamuffin screaming her head off, and they'd call the guards, and then where would she be? Nowhere good, and that's a fact too.

She had made a pair of laced-leg pants for herself after Dorrin came up with the idea and had her make a pair for him. She wore them under her dress now, and she could feel the weight of her paltry winnings of the night bound close to her ankles. It wasn't nearly as much as Dorrin always brought back, but it would be enough to land her in some trouble she couldn't talk her way out of.

So she held her tongue and jostled her way through the bodies, all packed too close together and all dressed in scratchy clothes and all towering over her. Fairy tried going up on her toes a few times, but she still couldn't see over their heads. Where was he?

She was halfway down the street when the worry started giving way to dread. Her memories turned back to that night three months ago when Skink had very nearly beaten the life out of Dorrin. The same night Scrounger gave her a bloody lip of her own. She touched her now-healed mouth and slipped around a pack of old women. She'd warned Dorrin that night. She'd told him Skink was going to kill him, but it was hard to tell how much of that got through to him. She still fully believed Skink would murder him if given half a chance.

There had been no fighting since that night. No more attacks, no more bullying, even. That made it worse, somehow, like there was something evil lurking just below the surface, waiting for the right time to strike. Fairy had let Dorrin out of her sight, knowing that Skink was in the vicinity and unsupervised. This very well could be that perfect time.

Dread was turning into despair, and Fairy stepped out of the street and into a narrow alley to catch her breath. The people kept streaming past, and she watched them with waning hope. What would she do if she'd let Dorrin get himself killed? How could she live with that? He should be out and away from Scrounger and Skink and, yes, even her. Some kids were hard and suited for a life like this, but

Dorrin wasn't one of them. Fairy sank to the ground and tucked her knees up to her face.

No sooner had she folded herself onto the pavement than a foot gave her a sharp kick in the leg. "Ow, hey!" She slid away from it and jumped to her feet. "Skink!"

He was standing over her, grinning an ugly grin. She knew that expression. It was malice laced with glee, just the way he looked whenever he'd done something particularly horrible to someone.

"What did you do?" Fairy shouted. She shoved his chest, and his grin disappeared as he nearly staggered backwards into the street. "Where is he?" She couldn't help the outburst, no matter who might see and call a guard on them.

"Hey, hey, wait!" Skink was backing up and had his hands up now. "I don't know what you're on about, but your little boyfriend got hisself nicked."

She was about to scream at him again, but she froze. "He's not— What do you mean?"

"What I said." Now that the assault had abated, some of his cockiness was pushing the grin back onto his face. "I seen it with my own eyes. Dorrin was doing what he does, and somebody nicked him. He's done for now." He laughed a mean chuckle. "What you think about that, eh?"

Fairy's mind spun. He wasn't dead, then. That was good, but if he'd gotten caught, that introduced a whole new problem. How could anyone have caught Dorrin, anyway? He was the best of them on the street, and she couldn't imagine how he could have messed up. "Where is he?" Fairy asked.

"Doesn't matter, does it? He's done for now!" Skink was laughing down at Fairy, but she cut his mirth off with another sharp shove.

"It does matter, you idiot. If he's been caught, we have to get him back."

"Now hey, I'm not about to go sticking my neck out for—"

Fairy exhaled deeply and grabbed both of Skink's arms. "Listen to me. He knows where we live. He knows all about us. If they make him talk, he's not the only one getting nicked. Compre?" It was the only way Fairy could think of to get him on board for a rescue. She couldn't care less if Scrounger and all the rest of them got rounded up, but it was an angle she knew would work on Skink.

Skink stared at her for a long minute while his slow brain slotted the pieces into place. "Compre," he said, sounding disappointed.

"Where is he?" Fairy asked again, this time calmer.

Skink looked up the street, back in the direction Fairy had come. "That way, the big one with the magic man in it."

"The Chamberlain? The one where Akithar performs?"

He nodded, "Yeah, I guess?"

"Was it a city guard? Where did they take him?"

"I don't know. Some lady. She was dressed all fancy-like, and she pulled him in beside the building and gave him a talking to. You shoulda seen it, Fairy, he was like to fall over he's so scared." Skink laughed again, and Fairy yanked at his arm.

"Come on," she said, "show me where."

The Chamberlain was one of the largest theaters on the street. Fairy had seen the facade every time she'd been in this district, the name spelled out in giant golden letters above the entryway. Of course Skink couldn't read, but even he knew that this was where the Great Akithar performed. She'd be surprised if anybody in Klubridge didn't know that. There were tales about the kinds of sorcery that went on inside that building, but Fairy knew enough of the world to know that no one would be stupid enough to flaunt real magic in this day and age and especially in this city, and that was a fact. There was some sort of trickery on the stage, not that different from the scams she and her fellow gutter rats ran for Scrounger. The only difference was that the public willingly handed over their money for this one.

The crowd on the street was not as thick by the time Skink and Fairy got back to the Chamberlain. It was well past showtime, and most people with legitimate business there already were inside the theaters, tucked away in their seats and watching whatever the wealthy liked to watch. Those still on the street at this hour rocked a tenuous balance between the keepers of the law and the breakers of it. Fairy recognized several cutpurses and nodded to them as they gave each other the professional courtesy of a wide berth. The thieves were waiting for the audiences to pour back out into their snares, and the police were waiting to catch them in the act. No more of that tonight for Fairy.

"We're here. Where did the woman take Dorrin?" She had Skink by the shirtsleeve and practically dragged him along behind her.

"Hold up, will you? They went down that way." He was pointing down an alley to the side of the theater, and Fairy pulled him into it with her.

"Then where?" she asked. It went all the way through to the next street, and all she saw along both sides of the alley were refuse bins.

"There's a cubby she shoved him into, right along there."

Fairy followed his gesture and spotted an alcove she had missed at first glance. It was tucked into the side of the Chamberlain, just past the light from the street. She released Skink's shirt and headed toward the opening with purpose.

"Whoa whoa, hey," Skink called, hopping after her. "You don't want to go in there."

"If Dorrin is in there, I most certainly do," she said without looking at him. There was a green wooden door inside the alcove. She stepped to it and pressed her ear against it. The street was still too loud, even this far into the alley, for her to hear anything happening inside. The door seemed thick, too, so she might have heard nothing even if it had been a quiet night.

"Fairy, you know about this bloke, yeah? They say he has demons in there."

Fairy looked away from the door long enough to give Skink a dramatic eye roll. "They say a lot of things, Skink. You don't have to go in here, but I am, and I'm not coming out without Dorrin." Before he could say anything else, she tried the doorknob. Locked. Of course it would be locked.

She took a step back and surveyed the door and its frame. All sturdy, nothing giving way. She might have been able to pop the latch, but she'd left her kit back in the East Ward. It was supposed to have been a routine night of picking pockets, not locks. She left the alcove with a sigh and went deeper into the alley.

"Wait! Where are you going?" Skink sounded afraid, but he was still trailing after her.

"I'm getting in here, one way or another." She was behind the building now and peeked around the corner. Another alley extended in that direction, running between the back of the Chamberlain and the rear of whatever building backed up to it. It was just as deserted as the first alley, save for a gray cat that scampered when it spotted her.

"Let's go back, Fairy, come on. We can tell Scrounger what happened. Everything'll be dice, you'll see."

"You go if you want. I'm staying." She moved around the back of the building and craned her neck to find a way in.

"Come on," Skink pleaded again. "This ain't fair. You know I can't leave you here. Scrounger'll have me dead."

There! A ways up the wall, higher than the top of the green door had been, there was a rectangular window, propped open with what looked like a metal bar. It was a few feet long but looked fairly narrow from top to bottom. Still, it should be enough space for her to squeeze through. Skink saw what she was looking at and shook his head, "No, come on, Fairy. Please come on. Just leave it, can't you?"

She ignored him and grabbed a downspout at the corner of the building. She yanked on it with both hands, and it didn't budge. It was dark metal and looked bolted into the bricks. Fairy knew she was light enough to make it work, and she hoisted herself up and then began pulling herself hand over hand, holding onto the pipe below her with her legs. Dorrin was better at this than she was, but she could make it work.

The downspout ran right beside the window, well within reach of the sill. Fairy let go of the pipe to swing herself over to the opening. It was only after she was hanging by both hands above a perilous drop to the alley that she considered that someone might be just inside that window. Too late to worry about that now, she supposed, and pulled herself up to where she could throw a leg onto the ledge. She heard stitches pop in her dress, but she could worry about that later. For now, she had a boy to rescue.

~

Skink's fear of Scrounger apparently outweighed his fear of potential demons, and that's how Fairy ended up in the rafters with him. The window had led into a dark storage room, which gave way to a darker upstairs hallway. There were doorways lining one side of the hallway with heavy curtains covering them. Fairy had poked her head through one curtain but yanked herself back as soon as she realized it opened into the theater's crowded balcony. She had nearly bumped headfirst into a matronly woman who was watching the show through ivory theater glasses on what probably was a golden handle. If not for those glasses, Fairy would have been spotted, and she simultaneously thanked the gods for the distraction and wished she had time to purloin the glasses for herself. No time for that, though, and too risky besides.

That close call had prompted Fairy's quick and silent scamper down the hall and up a narrow flight of black metal steps in the opposite wall. She didn't wait to make sure Skink was with her. If he got caught, he could figure his own way out, but she knew he'd be right behind her. Those stairs went up and up, and Fairy had to be careful not to clang a foot down too hard on the bolted steps. All they needed was to draw the attention of every eye in that theater.

Eventually the stairs ushered her onto a catwalk suspended above the audience. It was little more than a skinny metal platform with long bars along each side. Fairy saw similar catwalks suspended from the ceiling at intervals across the theater, but thankfully all of them were empty except the one right above the stage. She could see two or three crew members moving in the darkness over there, working to keep the performance going, and no doubt providing the secret wonder behind Akithar's supposed magical feats.

Fairy held onto the bars as she made her way midway across the catwalk, and only then did she look down. The theater was packed, and all the people looked tiny beneath her. Whatever was going on at the front of the room had them enraptured, and Fairy turned her attention to the stage. And there he was, the Great Akithar.

"It's him," Skink said, squatting beside her on the catwalk.

Fairy gave him a sharp look and shushed him.

"It's him," he said again, this time in a coarse whisper. "Just look at him."

She already was looking and wasn't too impressed with what she saw. It was just a man in a suit, strutting about and waving his arms. The crowd hung on his every word, and some of them were whispering among themselves. More interesting to Fairy than Akithar was the rig that was lighting him. There were big cannisters mounted on the catwalks above the stage, and they poured light out, brighter than any lantern she'd seen. She'd heard that some wealthier buildings in Klubridge had switched from lanterns with flame to lanterns with odd wires inside, but none of them were this bright. It wasn't sorcery, and that intrigued her even more.

She pulled her attention away from the lights and scanned the audience below, looking for any sign of Dorrin. She saw plenty of puffed-up aristocrats and rich weekenders who breezed through the city on a whim, but there was no sign of Dorrin or anyone even close to his description. Maybe he'd already escaped on his own. They couldn't risk that, though. She had to find him, even if it meant going down into the midst of all those people.

Fairy started to move back to the stairs, but Skink caught her arm. "Fairy, wait."

"What?" she asked, irritated that he was slowing her down, much less even up here with her.

"Look, there."

She followed his finger down above the audience, just to the side of the stage. Fairy squinted into the darkness. Someone was standing on the edge, just out of sight of the audience. One of the giant cannister lights swept across the stage and illuminated the figure for an instant. Fairy caught her breath. "Dorrin!"

"What you reckon he's doing?" Skink asked, and for once Fairy didn't have an answer. He was by himself, just standing there watching the performance. It made no sense at all.

"We have to get to him," Fairy whispered, and she didn't wait for a response before she took off down the catwalk, headed for the right-angle junction with another walkway. Skink was whispering something after her, but she didn't wait. She was already on the second catwalk, making a quick and stealthy pace toward the front of the theater, far above the audience. If anyone looked up, they might catch sight of someone running above their heads, but Fairy hoped they would think it was someone in the crew. They all were too caught up in the show to be looking up at her, anyway.

Something lit up the stage, and Fairy saw sparks shooting from somewhere. The extended catwalk blocked her view of Akithar, so she wasn't sure what he was doing, but the gasps from the crowd made it seem impressive. She glanced back at Skink and saw that he had stopped to lean over the edge of the walkway. His eyes were enormous, and he looked as thrilled as the rest of these people. Let him moon over the spectacle if he wanted to. Fairy had a job to do.

She was at the intersection with the next catwalk that spanned the width of the theater. She took the right side and looked down as she moved. This one was much closer to the stage, just one beam away from the catwalk with the crew and the big lights. She couldn't risk going farther that way, so she had to hope this was close enough.

Fairy was most of the way toward the end of the walkway when she stopped and knelt on the beam. She held onto the rail with both hands above her head and leaned out into the open space of the theater. There he was. Dorrin was just below and ahead of her, still a long way down, but much closer than he'd been.

"Dorrin!" she hissed in a loud whisper she hoped would reach her friend without alerting anyone else. It still came out louder than she intended. She held her breath and waited for someone to spot her, but nothing happened, and the show on the stage continued.

Skink dropped into a crouch next to her again. "You're mad, is what you are," he said.

She was too busy watching Dorrin to respond. He was just standing there by himself, watching the show and occasionally looking out across the audience. No one was holding him there. What was going on? Now he was staring at Akithar, just a few feet away from him. This was one of the most famous shows in Klubridge. How had Dorrin ended up on the side of the stage, let alone in the building at all? And where was this woman Skink had seen dragging him inside? None of this made sense.

Fairy frowned and looked from Dorrin across to Akithar. He had just finished some trick and was talking to the audience. He finished his speech, and Fairy swore he turned and looked directly at Dorrin. She was sure of it. And then he smiled and winked at the boy.

Fairy's hands grew icy, and her heart thudded in her chest. Everything fell into place as she remembered what she had told Dorrin months ago. What she always told him. He wasn't safe with Scrounger, and certainly not around Skink. She had told him to get out and go far away. Somehow he had done it. He had escaped into this theater, and he was here because he wanted to be, not because he was being held. This was his way out, she was sure of it.

She looked at Skink, and her heart sank. He had seen the wink, too, and he knew she had seen it. Just like that, he had put the pieces together in his stupid brain as well. A furious gleam was in his eye. Fairy leaned back into the catwalk. "Let's go, Skink. You were right. Just leave him to his foolishness. It's his own fault for getting caught, right?"

Skink's gaze shifted from Fairy back to Dorrin, and a sinister grin wrinkled his ugly face. "We're here now. Ain't this what you wanted?"

"It was, but I changed my mind. We need to get out before the show ends. We can tell Scrounger that Dorrin got pinched. That's how you wanted it, isn't it?" Her words were tumbling out, and she knew her desperation was betraying her thoughts, but she couldn't help it.

Skink was still grinning. He knew Dorrin was out, and he knew Fairy wanted to protect him. One more glance down at Dorrin in the darkness, and he said, "All right. Yeah, let's go back to Scrounger," and Fairy knew things were about to get much worse.

Skink and Fairy were among the last to arrive back in the East Ward. Most of the others already were sitting on the floor, whispering among themselves. Some of them were holding their night's takings, bundled in various rags or cloths, and more than a couple seemed nervous, unsure whether the amounts they were bringing back would be sufficient. Skink dropped down to sit with his usual cohorts. He hadn't stopped smiling the entire way back, and everyone recognized that he had regained some spark that had been missing for the past few months. His friends packed tighter around him, eager to find out what had happened. The others shrank back, not wanting to be on the receiving end of whatever that new spark might bring with it. Fairy moved to the side of the big empty chair, taking her usual post, and tried not to look at him.

Fairy had gotten more of an education than the others, though that wasn't saying much. Scrounger had needed someone to keep the balances for him, and she had been the one he picked. He'd taught her math and basic accounting, and she'd had lessons in reading and grammar that he'd denied the others. He'd even taught her some basic cartography so she could help him chart up maps of his dumb tunnels that were supposed to be running under the city. Scrounger told her at least one of his brood needed to seem respectable. That was a fair answer, but Fairy suspected her gaining basic competence in the world helped balance out Scrounger's conscience after denying and abusing the rest of the rabble.

As if summoned by Fairy's thoughts, Scrounger pushed back the heavy drape that covered the door in the back wall. All talk hushed, and he had the room's full attention as he lumbered around the chair and sank into it with a heavy grunt. "Welcome back, my mice. I trust your evening at the theater was a profitable one."

He turned his head toward Fairy, his tangled beard catching on his barrel chest. "And you, how was your night out on the city?"

It was rare for Fairy to go out on a run with the rest of the gang, and she still wasn't positive why he had sent her. Possibly to make sure Skink didn't kill Dorrin, but then why even group the three of them together in the first place? Some wicked amusement, most likely. She held up a sack with the coins she had collected from her leg pouches. She knew it would be lighter than he wanted, but it was all she could offer without betraying her fear.

Scrounger took the small bag in his massive hand and gave it a perfunctory jangle. His lips pursed, but he did not comment. That would come later, she was sure. For now, he turned his attention to the rest of the room. His gaze moved from one dirty face to the next in a lazy appraisal, and he grunted again when he had taken them all in. "Where is Dorrin, Fairy?"

She had been trying to work out an answer for that question all the way back from the theater, and she had prayed that she would be the one asked and not Skink. Relieved, she began, "He—"

"He's flown the coop," Skink interrupted.

Scrounger had been looking at Fairy but slowly turned to Skink. Fairy closed her eyes and took a deep breath.

"What's this, now?" Scrounger asked Skink.

"What I said. Me and Fairy and him was out at the Bastion, just like you said. I figured it best to split up, so I took the up street. Hadn't been twenty minutes but I spotted him off with some lady."

"Some lady?" Scrounger looked to Fairy for this.

"I didn't see her," she offered weakly. "Skink came and found me and told me Dorrin had gotten caught by a lady and taken away."

"Only he didn't get caught after all, you see," Skink was quick to add. "He went off with her, and he thinks he can live the high life now."

Scrounger wiped a hand down his face and turned to Fairy again. "Can you explain this nonsense to me, girl?"

So there it was, her chance to help Dorrin, and Skink had already spoiled it. She drew another deep breath before beginning. "It started like Skink said. We were near the Bastion and decided to split up. Skink went off on his own, and Dorrin and I stayed together for a little while, but then we split up as well. A little while later, Skink found me and told me he'd seen a lady hauling Dorrin off. I made him show me where they had been, but they were gone. He'd been taken away, maybe caught lifting a purse."

Scrounger's bushy eyebrows raised almost imperceptibly. "Skink seems to think otherwise."

Skink had no hesitation in jumping in. "Fairy's got it right up to that part. But then, see, she had the idea to go looking for him. So we got into the place—"

"What place is this?" Scrounger stopped him.

"The big theater with the magic man."

"The Chamberlain," Fairy mumbled. He was going to hear it, regardless.

"Right," Skink said. "So we got in there, and the show was going, and there Dorrin was up on the stage. He's joined in with them. I reckon he ain't coming back."

No one spoke for a moment, and then Scrounger asked Fairy, "Is this right?"

She nodded slowly. "I think he's gone from us now."

Scrounger grunted and stroked at his puffy lower lip. "You did well in spotting this, Skink."

Skink grinned back and cast a nasty look at Fairy. "Fairy should get the thanks, too. It was all her idea to go in after him. We wouldn't even know he'd left on his own if not for her." Fairy's stomach felt heavy as the weight of that truth became real. Skink continued, "Just give me the word, and my boys'll get him back," Skink offered, and his friends nodded their agreement. "We can rough him up for you too, you believe it."

"No."

The word hung in the air, and Fairy had no idea what could be coming next.

Skink frowned. This wasn't what he'd expected, either. "Now wait, we can—"

"No, Skink." Scrounger's eyes had narrowed and brooked no argument. "If Dorrin is at the Chamberlain, then that is where he will stay for now."

But Skink pressed on, undeterred. "If it's because of the magic man, you don't need to worry. There ain't demons or none of that. It's just some fancy man in a suit, we seen him."

Scrounger slammed a fist down on the arm of his chair, and the thud shook every child in the room. "I know about Akithar, and I know about the Chamberlain. We do not need the kind of exposure a conflict there would bring us. There may be chances for Dorrin to return to us in the future, but this is not how it will be done. I am not fond of explaining myself to you, Skink. Do I make myself clear?"

Skink's mouth hung open, and his face colored with disappointment, but even he knew better than to push any farther. He clamped his jaw shut and nodded.

Scrounger nodded back. "We will skip our usual proceedings." He pushed himself up out of the chair, and the floor groaned under his weight. "Fairy will collect your take. We are finished for tonight." He moved to leave but turned back to Fairy one more time. His eyes burned into hers, and the anger was palpable. She prepared herself to be struck again, but he lowered his voice and whispered, "Whatever happens to Dorrin now is your fault."

PART II
THE SCARLET KITES

CHAPTER 6

Salkire Hold stood less than five miles from the outer city walls of Salkire itself. Constructed on a rise in the midst of a vast field, it was one of the first castles the High Lord Peregrine seized when he first rose to power, countless centuries ago. At least, that's what the legends said.

Nera had been inside the hold only three times in all her years in service to the Empire, and never by specific invitation. She had that invitation now, though. It had arrived by courier three days earlier, when she was reviewing her newest recruits far to the south in Bria. The letter, inscribed in calligraphy on thin parchment and sealed with the blue wax insignia of the High Lord's Aerie, read that the High Lord demanded her service. She had left the inspection immediately to summon a small caravan and was provisioned and on the road less than an hour later.

Three days of hard riding with brief stops had brought Nera and her company of three guards through Salkire, and they now were riding out of the last close of trees and into the wide-open space that housed the castle. As they left the modern city behind and approached the hold, Nera could feel the centuries disintegrating before her. Time marched forward throughout the Empire of Teshovar, but it seemed to stand still wherever the High Lord had staked his claim. To visit any part of his domain that he personally oversaw was to visit a world of the past, where the progression of technology and architecture froze in place. Their horses' hooves pounded the road that connected the castle to its city, and Nera realized it had transitioned from a paved surface to packed dirt. She could feel the fine dust of the road working its way into her skin and her uniform.

Night had already fallen, but the light of the moon silhouetted the ancient structure upon the hill on the horizon. Torches burned along the top of the walls and flickered between the crenellations. Beyond the outer walls, lifted even higher on the rise, candles illuminated windows throughout the inner towers. The lights, still distant, glimmered hazily in the dark, as if burning behind a film. The hold was busy, and that kind of activity likely came only when the keep was inhabited. Nera's pulse quickened now that her destination was in sight. She had never met the High Lord before and didn't even know anyone else who had been in his presence. Eagerness and a twinge of fear commingled to make her urge her horse to cover the last span more quickly.

Nera's breath caught, and she forced herself to inhale through her nose, out through her mouth. She shut her eyes against the panic that threatened to engulf her, and she fell back on old tricks that still served her well. One road, two guards flanking it ahead, three soldiers accompanying her, four horses in her party. Before she got to five, Nera was in control again, and she allowed her eyes to open.

Just ahead, the pair of armored men stood to either side of the roadway, a torch flaming in a mounting beside each of them. Nera remembered the small shack to the right side of the road from the last time she was here, and she shuddered in her saddle. The guards extended their arms as the caravan approached, their pikes crossing at the middle of the path. "State your business," the one on the left called. The men wore dark blue and yellow, the colors of the Aerie, and their armor was new but styled like warriors of old, functional but bulkier than the plates Nera wore.

Nera reined her horse to a slow walk and stopped in front of the crossed weapons. "I am Nera Mollor, Commander of the Scarlet Kites and servant to the High Lord. I am summoned, and I demand passage."

It was a ceremonial exchange, but one that Nera had dreaded. The guard on the right called, "Passage is permitted for a company of four."

Nera tried not to look at the shack, but her eyes betrayed her and strayed to its single window. Someone moved inside, and the window lit with a quick flash of violet light. Nera forced her gaze away in time to see the film peeling back from the horizon before her. It was an invisible barrier, held in place by some incantation, and it had pulled open to exactly the width of the dirt road.

The guards uncrossed their pikes, and Nera walked her horse between them, leading her group now in single file to pass through the barely perceptible doorway. The hairs on her arms and the back of her neck tingled with dancing energy as she moved inside, and her horse gave a nervous whinny. She gave the horse a sympathetic pat on the neck but didn't know whether it would help. Getting her own neck rubbed would do little to reassure Nera every time magic disarmed her like this.

After she and all three of her companions were inside, Nera turned back in her saddle to watch the barrier reseal. They now rode within an impenetrable bubble that enclosed all of Salkire Hold and most of the field surrounding it. They still were outside with the night sky overhead, but everything external to the shield seemed muted and distorted. Stars hung elongated, and the moon was hazier than it should have been. Nera made herself focus on the road ahead, but the magic was oppressive. This appointment was worth any measure of discomfort, but she would be glad to have Salkire Hold behind her as soon as possible.

The distance from the checkpoint to the gates of the castle itself was blessedly short, but the ride felt to Nera longer than any of the three previous days' worth of riding. As they approached, a draw-bridge lowered, spanning a small moat that had been dug around the perimeter of the walls. Nera went first and looked over the edge as her horse's hooves clopped across the sturdy timbers. The water beneath was inky black under the night sky with an oily reflection of the moon staring back. Something shifted in the water, splitting the moon into sudden ripples. There was no telling what might live down there, breeding and changing through dozens of human generations.

Once they were inside the walls of the hold, Nera dismounted and motioned for her soldiers to do the same. Attendants hurried forth to take their reins. "I am Nera Mollor—" she began, but the attendants had already left, leading the horses to a small stable to the right of the gates. Nera looked to her company, and they stared back, clearly uncomfortable and waiting for her command. "Wait out here for me. I'll send word when I know why we are here."

With that, she turned and began a slow climb up the hill to the doors of the keep and whatever awaited her within.

The outside of the keep, constructed from large, pale stones fitted together with an ancient and primitive mortar, was formidable and stark. Nera had nearly forgotten the contrast to the inside until she stepped over the threshold. The servant holding open the massive oaken door wore a dark blue waistcoat and tie, with the Aerie insignia embroidered on the left side of the chest. The man was indeterminably old, his sparse white hair having given way to spotted skin. He had combed back what hair he still had, and his white mustache was thick and shaped in the severe style of the northerners. His eyelids drooped over watery eyes, but he still stood at attention to usher Nera into the entryway.

A thick cobalt carpet ran the length of the room, centered on the stone floor. Tapestries hung to the right and left, showcasing the emblems of the baronies and duchies in favor at the moment. Nera counted twelve domains represented and noted that her home, Trowood, was not among them. That was hardly surprising, given the ineptitude of her local lord. In another life, perhaps she would have been in that seat of power, but politics had never interested her. Her focus had been decidedly martial, and she held no fondness for petty bureaucrats and their plots. Even now she suppressed a sneer at the people moving through the hallway, all on some diplomatic errand that ultimately would prove pointless and would require Nera's skills to resolve.

From the ground floor, sweeping stairs curved up on both sides, meeting at the top on a landing with a balcony that overlooked the entry. That same cobalt carpeting ran up the stairs and disappeared over the last step. A house guard stood sentry at the top of the stairs, looking down. Nera nodded to her, and she gave a sharp nod back. Nera had never been upstairs, but she guessed there must be at least eight stories in the keep, once it branched out into its towers, maybe more. All her previous encounters had been in meeting rooms on this ground floor, and that's what she expected on this visit as well. But, then again, she had never received a summons to meet the High Lord himself. No one had.

"This way, Commander," the servant said in a quiet voice that she almost had to strain to hear. He led her to a door on the right, between the hanging tapestries of Esterburgh and Tresa. Nera's riding boots were loud on the stones when she stepped off the rug. Too late, she noted that they also likely were leaving muddy tracks after the long journey. The servant was polite enough not to comment, and he motioned her into the room. "If the commander could wait here. Refreshments are available, and I am sure the summons will come soon."

It was a parlor, finely decorated in the same blues and yellows that adorned the rest of the castle. A table at the middle of the room held silver platters of pastries, fruits, and meats, a more ostentatious spread than Nera was used to seeing. Another servant stood nearby holding a matching silver pitcher, ready to pour into any of the crystal goblets collected on a side table. Murmured conversation halted as Nera entered and was surveyed, but they quickly resumed. A pair of men, most likely representatives from some far-flung hamlet, sat across the room in armless chairs, leaning forward into whatever talk had them engaged. In the opposite corner, a tall and thin woman wearing the customary orange and white uniform of Tresa's lawmakers stood alone, nursing whatever drink she was holding. Nera caught her eyes, and the woman looked away.

Nera saw her own reflection in a mirrored panel and was neither surprised by nor ashamed of the disheveled mess that she had become. Riding north with barely a stop showed in the dirty smudges on her otherwise pale cheeks and in the tangled nest that her auburn hair had become. She pulled off her riding gloves and tucked them into her belt before raking a hand through her hair. That was all the capitulation she would give the finery of this place. The High Lord would understand her road weary appearance, and what the rest of these people thought was of no concern. She had, however, worn her light dress armor for this occasion and left the heavier tarnished and dented full suit she actually used for battle at home. She adjusted a pauldron and thought a little shine in the presentation never hurt.

Under the armor she wore the tabard of the Scarlet Kites, flaming red and trimmed in white that presently was dulled with dust. The front of the jerkin hung just past her knees, where it ended in a point where the two halves angled into each other. On her chest she wore the emblem of the Kites, a black bird in silhouette, taking wing over the red field of fabric. The tabard had no sleeves, of course, but the laced-in quilted sleeves of a matching red gambeson covered her arms. Her dark riding breeches completed the standard uniform.

Nera prided herself on being as one with her soldiers, but she had worn her mantle of rank to this meeting. It was cleaner than her riding clothes, having made the journey packed in a saddle bag until just a few moments ago. The mantle of her command was the same red as the tabard and draped over her shoulders, covering the armor there. In back, a cloak hung nearly to the floor, red with intricate gold stitching around the edges. She wore the attached hood thrown back, as was custom when indoors at Salkire. Less customary was the leather belt she wore with her regulation sword still at her side. No one had asked her to surrender the weapon, but then she doubted that something as mundane as steel could harm the Lord Peregrine.

She looked over the food on the table but was not hungry. She was too eager to get the meeting underway. Something to drink would help, though. Nera picked up a goblet and turned to the servant but froze after her eyes met the girl's dazed expression.

"A drink, my lady?" the servant asked in a vacantly breathy tone, but Nera did not respond. The girl looked to be in her early twenties, perhaps ten years younger than Nera. Rather than the livery of the Aerie, the girl wore a long, plain, light gray cloak, bound at the waist with a simple corded belt. Her hair was dark and thick, but Nera could see the telltale bald scar line that ran up the sides of her head. She knew the scars would curve inward to meet at the back, making a horseshoe shape if viewed from behind. The girl had been a mage, like the dangerous and wicked ones Nera herself regularly captured and delivered into the care of the Empire. Surely she was harmless now, but magic never can be trusted.

"A drink?" the girl asked again, her voice still flat and distant.

Nera swallowed hard and placed the goblet back on its table. "I seem to have lost my thirst," she said through tight lips and took a step away from the creature. She kept her hand from straying to the comfortable hilt of her sword, but barely.

Just then, the old doorman appeared again and beckoned to Nera. "He will see the commander now."

She cast one last suspicious glance at the mage before following the servant back out of the parlor.

Nera was still thinking about the mage in the parlor as the servant led her through the keep to her meeting. Had the girl's power been silenced? Or had she been turned and controlled? If the choice were Nera's, she would obliterate all magic, and no trace of it would remain. Even the High Lord's immense power, though wielded with precision, the right intent, and the experience of centuries, made her uneasy. Magic was an invitation for doom, and the world would be better with none of it. That's how Nera would have it, but she knew that most of the renegades she and her forces and the other squads like hers collected received reeducation and found a new purpose working toward the interests of the Empire and its people. They used their magics only when and how directed by authorities, all answerable eventually to the Lord Peregrine. Even so, she still didn't like it.

Thinking about the High Lord snapped Nera's attention back to the present as the gravity of what she was about to experience descended upon her. She was being led through halls and antechambers, deeper into the keep than she had ever been. They still were on the first floor, but by now they had to be nearing the far extent of the building. Would he be waiting when she arrived? What was the proper greeting, anyway? She knew the protocols for dealing with her subordinates, her equals, and her superiors, but she had never imagined that she would converse with the highest superior of them all. The most powerful person in the world, truth be told.

Butterflies fluttered in her stomach, and she forced them away by pure will. This was an opportunity, not a punishment, and she would react accordingly. But what would he even look like? Her mind spun with the possibilities, and her aversion to magic seeded more worry into her nerves. There was no doubt that magic was what sustained the High Lord Peregrine, the longest-lived person in any history that could be recalled or recorded. His existence transcended written history as the world knew it. Calendars numbered this year 3212, and many speculated that the numbering began with his birth. The general understanding was that he had been born human, but Nera wondered how much humanity remained after this long. There were rumors that he no longer truly lived as a man but had become some sort of undying shade, lingering in between death and life. Nera didn't believe that, but it was undeniable that he had changed himself in profound ways through spellcraft.

The servant had paused before a closed door that gleamed a brilliant white, and Nera stopped quickly behind him. The entire door looked as if it might be ivory, inlaid with delicate filigree. There was a thick rod of gold affixed horizontally across the door, and the servant was pulling at a lever attached to it. Was the Lord already inside and waiting for her? She breathed in deeply through her nose, held the breath, and blew it out softly between her lips. The panic she expected remained at bay.

A mechanism in the door clanked loudly, and Nera became aware of the otherwise silent corner of the keep. No one else was within earshot, and she had seen none of those groveling politicians in the last several rooms through which they had passed. She was alone here with the doorman, and perhaps with the High Lord. The door pushed inward and swung heavily, the bottom brushing a thick, black rug. The servant bowed and stepped back, motioning for Nera to enter. She took one more breath before stepping into the room.

It was empty.

She exhaled sharply, both relieved and disappointed that the Lord had not yet arrived. By now, her apprehension at meeting him was matched only by her eagerness to have it done and over with.

The door swung shut behind her, and she approached the big, low desk at the center of the room. This was some sort of office, but it lacked any of the personal decorations she was accustomed to seeing. No weavings, no documents or proclamations of accomplishments on the walls. It all was austere, except for that thick rug. Two wooden chairs angled toward each other in front of the desk, and a larger chair, this one upholstered, sat behind it. There were two bookcases against the wall behind the desk, but they were empty. This was a disused office, she realized, running a finger along the back of one of the wooden chairs and feeling the thinnest layer of dust.

Her hand jerked back from the chair as the door made the same clanking noise, and she spun to face it. Her back straightened to attention, and she clasped her hands in front of her. No, behind. She held them behind her back, squeezing her fingers to stop a tremble, and raised her chin, hoping that it did not shake as well.

The door was swinging inward, pushed by the same servant, and he stepped back and out of the way once it was open. A form moved into view, filled the doorway, and then was in the office. It was a man, not a wraith or a shade. He had black hair parted precisely down the middle, and a familiar thin mustache lined his upper lip. Nera blinked and frowned. "General Bekam?"

He strode quickly into the room, pushing the door shut behind him. He was in his traveling uniform, the Aerie blue a contrast to Nera's red tabard. He paused at her query and stared at her with his icy blue gaze. "You sound surprised."

"Is the High Lord with you?" she asked and immediately regretted the question.

Bekam smirked and raised an eyebrow at her. "How long have you been in service to the Empire, Commander Mollor?"

"Since I was eighteen, sir. Just over thirteen years ago. But you know my devotion has been a lifelong privilege."

"Indeed. And in that time, how many people do you know who have had a private meeting with his excellency?" Bekam's smirk was turning into a sneer as he rounded the desk and stood in front of the chair behind it.

"None, sir."

"And you thought, what? That you were special?" He let the question hang just long enough for Nera to feel it as a physical manifestation dangling in the air between them. Nera swallowed, and Bekam nodded. He had chipped a piece off her confidence and now was satisfied. That was what he did. "Have a seat, Commander." He was cordial now, the tense moment all but forgotten.

Nera took one of the hard chairs facing him and made herself push past the embarrassment. "I came as quickly as the message arrived."

"You made good time," he allowed, and Nera accepted it as a compliment. That was his way. Break you down before building you up. "I'm about to depart myself. I was just waiting for your arrival. Do you know what this is about?"

She looked into his eyes again and wondered if this might be a test or a trap. Her thumb worked slowly at the edges of the tabard in her lap. "I do not, but I noticed that we aren't in an ordinary office. I presume you have something sensitive to tell me."

Bekam's lips parted in a thin smile, showing a sliver of teeth. "Your perception did not fail you, even if your pride might." She didn't rise to that barb, but she felt it just the same. He waited for a response and seemed mildly irritated that she showed none. "You're right, of course. You have a new assignment, and it's an important one. The High Lord is here in spirit, if not in person, and this mission comes directly from him."

Nera's eyes widened. She had not been a complete fool, then. Peregrine had a hand in this. "I am an instrument of the Empire. What would the High Lord have me do?"

The meeting took less than half an hour, and Nera already was back out the front doors of the keep and headed to a much smaller building positioned against the outer walls. During the past two hundred years or so, the Empire had built lodging for guests separate from the primary towers. What had begun as a very basic two-story building full of small dormitories had evolved into something of an inn with its own tavern. It still looked like an old-fashioned tavern and lacked any modern comforts, but it seemed to serve its purpose. Nera could hear the music inside as she approached, and she finally felt some of the tension in her shoulders and neck abate. A representative of the castellan had offered her a room for the night within the keep, of course on the first floor, but she had declined in favor of rejoining her Kites.

A soldier was coming out the front door as Nera approached, and he stepped aside to let her in, giving a nod of respect. She nodded back and went inside. The door opened into the tavern area, and it was lively but nothing like the inns they had encountered along their journey. This one still was within Salkire Hold, after all, and some modicum of propriety was necessary. Still, drinks were aplenty, and a couple sat on stools at the back of the room, the man plucking some ancient stringed instrument Nera didn't recognize while the woman sang. They were concluding a jaunty song, something about a girl looking for her cat, and the listeners cheered loudly, some banging their steins on the wooden tables.

Nera scanned the room and spotted one of her Kites sitting alone on the far side. He'd been leaning back against the wall and watching the performance but caught sight of Nera as she approached. He stood with a slight bow. His dark hair cropped close over his smooth face made him look even younger than he was. "Commander."

"No need for formalities in here, Tomos. Mind if I join you?"

"Please do." He sat again but didn't quite lean back on the wall. He would be at ease when she was there only to a degree, Nera noted, and she approved. Order was crucial, and respect for rank was a part of that. "Are we staying the night?" Tomos asked.

"We are. You will have your own room."

Tomos' shoulders relaxed. Nera knew he didn't enjoy changing with the others. Armor was constraining enough, but she couldn't imagine how he dealt with the binding as well.

"Where are the others?" she asked.

He gestured to the door. "Morcan and Wil went to check the horses. They should be back in a moment."

The musicians were preparing to play again, and Nera watched them for a moment before leaning forward to cross her arms on the table. Her bracers clanked uncomfortably, and she shifted to let them rest. She'd be happy to get this blasted armor off and have a night's rest before starting off again tomorrow. A brief respite before things really got interesting. "Tomos, is there a messenger stationed here?"

"I think I saw a coop on the wall when we were riding in. Do you have something you'd like for me to take?"

"I do." She hated standing again so soon but pushed herself up from her seat. Her feet ached in the riding boots, and she longed again for the bed she knew would come soon. She motioned for Tomos and headed back toward the door. She heard his stool slide back as he rose to follow.

Outside, the air felt unnaturally still, and Nera swore she could feel that buzzing again that she had felt lift the hairs on her neck when they passed through the shield. She was looking forward to sleep, but the sooner morning came, the sooner they could be out from under this terrible bubble. She looked up at the sky and scowled at the muted light from the stars and the streaky face of the moon.

Tomos was with her now, and she beckoned him around the side of the inn. He followed her into the shadows, and she looked back towards the door before speaking in a low voice, nearly a whisper. "We have our new assignment, and I need a message sent to Lieutenant Gieck. He should be in Gramery now. Tell him to gather the rest of the Kites and set out east immediately to meet us."

Tomos listened carefully as she spoke, and she knew he was recording every word. He would transcribe it onto a tiny scroll that Salkire's message keeper would attach to one of their pigeons. "Should I encode it?" he asked.

Nera concurred. Why had she not thought to mention that first? The tiredness really was upon her. "Use the thirty-second key. Lucian knows that one by heart." He should have known all the keys, but she knew that he didn't, so she made concessions and tried to use only the ones she knew he had learned during his brief time in the Academy.

"I'll send it straight away. Where should they meet us?"

"We leave in the morning for Klubridge," she said. "We have a traitor to catch."

CHAPTER 7

The city reeked of filth and desperation. Lucian Gieck crinkled his nose and scowled at a ragged beggar who made the mistake of holding her grimy bowl out to him with a trembling hand. He spat into the bowl and backhanded the woman out of his way. The bowl spun out of her palsied grasp, and the few coins she'd collected bounced off across the cobblestones. Two other peasants scrambled out of the shadows to grab at the woman's lost earnings. They probably would take the bowl, too.

This is what happened when a city wasn't properly governed. Gieck never would openly criticize the High Lord, but he had always thought giving Klubridge this much leeway would lead to nothing but trouble. And so it had, from the dingy dregs of the Downsteps to the rich pissants in Northgarden. None of them knew their proper places, and all of them got above their stations. The criminals had organized themselves here, and those who could stop it did nothing. The city's lawkeepers would round up a cutpurse or stop a crime in progress if they bumbled across it, but they did nothing to break up the guilds that had formed among the thieves and murderers. Even worse, they allowed the wealthy to overstep their stations and run the upper city as if they were landed aristocracy rather than puffed-up pansies. Their time would come.

Gieck had arrived in the city the night before, leading the seven Kites who had been with him in Gramery. Command had sent them to investigate rumors of a rogue mage at work in the town. As it turned out, there was no mage, but Gieck still had his fun there. Perhaps more importantly, he'd made sure that his mates had had their fun, too. Reports might get back to command, but with eight Scarlet Kites in the stew together, they all would vouch for one another, and it would blow over, just like it always did. It helped that Nera never believed a word against Gieck. They all were soldiers, and soldiers needed some relaxation. He'd found ways to get it and to slide between the cracks of oversight.

He was walking through the Downsteps now, not quite the worst part of Klubridge, but far from anything remotely respectable. Most of the quarter was ramshackle or abandoned, and it was a haven for the homeless. Nasty old wastrels swaddled in rags huddled on broken-down stoops, many of them without five teeth among a pair. They would look hopeful when they first spotted him, a well-dressed man who looked like he had money to spare. But word traveled fast, and it had taken scarcely a night for most of them to know he was not one to bother. And yet he still hoped they would.

The Scarlet Kites were lodging in the Henburn Estate at the city center, where the municipal government carried out its business. The primary structure on the estate was a castle rising from the midst of smaller buildings surrounding it and flanked with towers, the only remnant in the city to show that the High Lord's old ways still persevered even here in Klubridge. Gieck had no business down here in the slums, but he had time to kill before Nera arrived. Every man had his hobbies, and Gieck's were particular. He wasn't wearing his uniform down here. He had no desire to dirty it with these peons' muck.

That was secondary to his own sense of self preservation, though. As he was, witnesses could describe him as a big man, well over six feet in height and broad at the shoulders. They might even describe his hair as light brown or dusky blonde, hanging to jaw length on the sides and front but cut short in the back. If they got close enough, they even could say he had green eyes of a reptilian shade. All of that would be accurate, but he still would be just some big, anonymous bloke dressed in nondescript brown trousers and a loose-fitting green shirt with bishop sleeves. That could be anyone in this city of thousands. It would be much easier to identify and locate a giant man stupid enough to wear his flaming red uniform out for a jaunt. The anonymity protected him, but it also made him seem ordinary, and that made people misjudge him.

Gieck was counting on that when he pushed through the door to one of the seedy pubs that called the Downsteps its home. Poor and pathetic as these people might be, they wouldn't go without their swill. The poorer they were, the more they liked to drink, and the more they liked to drink, the stupider they got. That's a large part of why Gieck found himself drawn to these hovels in every city he encountered.

This one was The Lying Bees. A wooden sign hanging above the door had probably shown the name at one point, but time and weather had worn away everything but the grungy painted partial outline of a bumblebee. He didn't need to read the sign to know this place. A bum had described it last night after some convincing. There were no windows to the outside, and Gieck had to stand in the doorway for a moment before his eyes adjusted to the dimness, even in the middle of an otherwise bright day. He was glad for the darkness here, as glad as he was for the wastrels leaning against the sorry excuse of a bar far earlier than it was proper to be that drunk.

There were three of them, all paying more attention to each other and their drinks than they were to the man who just came in. The bartender saw him, though, and knew what he was there for. He was a clean-shaven man, looked to be in his fifties. His hair was white and long, standing out from his head in unruly tangles. He was wearing a stained white shirt under a brown vest, probably something he thought made him look upscale, better than those he served. Gieck had to grant that the barkeep at least was savvier than his clientele. The man put away the mug he had been wiping and threw the brown speckled hand towel over his shoulder. He came around the bar to look Gieck in the eyes.

"Do what you came for, and then leave. Don't wreck me bar, and mind the glasses." Without waiting for an acknowledgment, the barkeep was out the door and closed it behind him.

Gieck snorted at that. Perhaps there were some worthwhile wretches down here after all. That would be something to think about later. For now, he had business. Gieck rolled his head around his neck and pressed his right fist into his left palm. The loud cracking of his knuckles finally pulled the drunks' attention away from whatever they had been discussing, and they turned their sloppy gazes on him as one.

"Hello, boys," Gieck said with a wicked smile. "Which one of you is first, or shall we all go at once?"

Nera and her three lapdogs arrived in the city about three hours later. That gave Gieck time to finish his business, get back to the city center, and present himself cleaned up and uniformed. Nobody would ever find two of the drunks, and the third couldn't identify his attacker if he didn't have a tongue, could he? Gieck had been less worried about the barkeep, but the older man still nagged at the back of his mind. Perhaps he'd go back and tie up loose ends later. For now, he had other errands to address.

Jona came to get him when Nera's caravan reached the castle. She knew he'd been up to something, but she didn't ask about it, and he knew she wouldn't voice her suspicions to the commander. Jona was one of the good ones. Besides that, she knew that Gieck knew what she got up to as well, and that held her in check.

"Commander Mollor is downstairs," Jona said. She was in her uniform, minus the red tabard. Nera would expect them all to be in full regulation dress from this point forward, and Gieck understood Jona's wanting to steal a few more minutes without that coarse thing hanging on her. A little light insubordination directed at their leader was of no concern to Gieck.

Jona hadn't bothered knocking, and that did concern him. Maybe he was allowing his soldiers to get too comfortable, too familiar. He let it go for now. "Did she say anything? Any indication of why she summoned us to this dung pile of a city?"

"Nothing. Just to fetch you."

Gieck rankled. "Fetch me, eh?"

Jona quirked a half smile at him and pushed her hair behind her ear. She had black bangs in the front that tapered down to a shoulder length cut on the right. The left side tilted the opposite direction and was trimmed short, over that ear. "Fetch, call, retrieve, you know, the usual." She had crossed the room now to the desk where he was sitting and leaned over him. "What are you working on?" Her hand was light on his shoulder.

Gieck looked at the hand and hesitated. "Never mind that," he said and swept the parts he'd been piecing together into a small box. "I've been fetched, and I must be called to heel."

"Such a good dog," Jona whispered and trailed a finger along the back of his neck.

He pushed his chair back and turned on Jona, her hand suddenly wrapped in his much larger one. She gasped and looked up to meet his eyes. "Not now," he growled.

"Later, then." She grinned, her tongue stuck between her teeth.

Gieck shoved past her and headed to the door. He looked back at her. "Are you coming?"

"You're no fun," she pouted and pushed off the desk to follow him.

When Jona reached Gieck, he grabbed her face and pulled it close. "Do not mistake this for fun. We're here and have a job to do. Is that clear?"

Her forehead crinkled, and she pulled back from him. "Yes, gods, I understand."

He narrowed his eyes at her response but once again decided not to rise to the conflict. Let her call on her supposed gods, if that's what she wanted. He pushed her back roughly and let go of her face, and he was out the door and headed down the stone stairs before she could retort.

Nera had assembled the other ten Kites in a meeting room off the main hallway. The castle was well appointed, especially considering its age and the state of the rest of this deplorable city. A red carpet covered the floor, and varnished benches filled the mid-sized room. The soldiers had lined up on the benches like back alley parishioners, and Gieck sneered again at Jona's invocation of the gods. Several of his troops looked to the door as he entered, and he saw they all were in their formal gear already.

He suspected the city committee used this room for meetings when it was not being appropriated by the military. The walls were bare rock, except for the Klubridge banner hanging at the front. Nera stood in front of that banner now, her hands resting on a teak lectern. She had been talking to someone on the front bench, but her eyes caught Gieck's as he came in. A quick smile gave her away, and she turned her eyes down to the podium, no doubt silently flagellating herself for that slip.

Nera was pretty enough, no doubt. Pale skin, red hair, slim but with enough curves underneath that dowdy tabard and mantle. It wasn't hard for Gieck to play the part he needed to play. He rounded the benches to approach the front of the room and greeted her. "Commander Mollor."

When she looked back at him, it was all business, but he could see the lingering fondness around her eyes. The eyes were where it was the hardest to hide. "Lieutenant Gieck." She extended a hand, and he clasped it. He held it a fraction longer than he normally would have and let his thumb gently stroke the back of her hand just before he let go.

"I trust your journey here was an easy one?" he asked and watched with satisfaction as she touched the back of the hand he had held.

"It was." Her eyes lingered on his face, and she finally pulled them away to look at the gathered troops again. "Is everyone here now?"

"Sorry I'm late." Jona was the last in and was still pulling her tabard straight. So she had been smart enough to grab it on the way after all.

"No matter," Nera said, "We're all here now." She waited for Jona to take her seat toward the back, and Gieck took a step to the side to stand at his customary station to Nera's right.

"I'll get straight to the point. We've been assigned a retrieval mission that was handed down directly from the High Lord Peregrine himself."

It wasn't often that she could take Gieck by surprise. He usually knew every twist and turn before they happened, mostly because he was the one planning them. This one caught him off his footing, though. The High Lord himself! And for a retrieval mission. But that made no sense. "Why did he send this to us?" He couldn't stop himself from asking. "Klubridge is Tereth's purview, isn't it?"

Nera nodded. "It is, but Commander Tereth is detained with an uprising in Karsk. It's unlikely that he'll be able to get away within the week, and our task is too urgent to delay." She waited for the implied gravity to sink into each of the soldiers before she continued. "The Empire has learned that a traitorous spy is on the way to Klubridge as we speak. They are in possession of classified documents of critical importance to the High Lord's efforts in the borderlands. I don't think I need to explain why having these documents in the wrong hands is a very bad thing."

She let her words settle before continuing. "Our intelligence suggests that the spy is a rogue mage. That makes this a Kites issue. Further, we believe this spy has scheduled a rendezvous with a rebel contact within Klubridge. The contact may or may not also be a magic user. Now, here is the critical part. The purpose of this rendezvous is to arrange safe passage for the spy out of the city. The rebels are so keen to get these documents that they are bringing the spy directly to Stormbreak."

Gieck's mouth opened and closed, and he saw a similar response from the rest of the room. The rebels never brought someone directly to their headquarters. They always had waystations and drop points they would use to obfuscate any trackers. Their methods had proven effective, and no one had gotten any closer to finding a pattern or base for their operations, or even any sort of leadership structure. If transport directly to this much rumored Stormbreak Sanctuary were being arranged, that meant that either the spy or the contact in Klubridge already knew exactly where that base was located.

This was big. Big enough to make a career, Gieck thought. Big enough to ensure that he no longer needed to tease and grovel at the feet of this lesser commander. The person to learn the whereabouts of the rebels' operations effectively would deliver a victory against the entire rebellion to the High Lord. That was not the kind of thing that went unnoticed. That was not the kind of thing Nera Mollor was competent enough to manage on her own.

"What is your order?" he asked Nera.

"Disperse through the city. Cover every district, and consult every contact we have. We need to find out who the Klubridge agent is before the spy arrives. Detain the agent, and bring them back to us alive. If they are indeed magically inclined, we will silence their magic and then interrogate them to learn what they know."

Gieck turned to the congregated soldiers. "Scarlet Kites, you have your orders. Begin your search immediately, and report back with anything you find."

Nera was watching him with approval and gave him a nod. "You are dismissed," she told the Kites. "Go find our traitors."

"You look pensive," Nera said. She was sitting next to Gieck on a bench in the dining hall, but of course not too close. They were the only two people in the big, echoing chamber, and she still couldn't risk a thigh brushing his.

"Do I?" He had already finished his dinner and pushed the metal plate a few inches away, resting his hands on the table in front of him. Truth be told, he was pensive. Ever since Nera had delivered the orders, his mind had been turning, building plot after plot and trying to find the one that could spin this situation in his favor. It would result in his ultimate betrayal of Nera as he pushed her down under his boot heel and climbed out of the morass of his posting in the

Scarlet Kites. Bringing in the location of the traitors' base would be the talk of every town in the Empire. His superiors would celebrate him as a hero, and Nera would remain behind, little more than a convenient and needy stepping stone.

He turned his head to face her and gave a gentle smile. "I suppose I was just enjoying having a few moments alone with you. They are rare."

"They are," she said and returned the smile. She really was quite pretty, but maybe a shade older than he'd have liked. He enjoyed the way a strand of that auburn hair had fallen loose and hung with a slight twist beside her eyes. He thought that color was called hazel, but maybe these were browner than that. The crease in her skin beginning to show at the corner of that eye was unfortunate. The blossom began to wilt after they reached thirty or so. Gieck was a year her senior, but he knew it was different for men.

On an impulse, he reached to her face and stroked a thumb across that small wrinkle. Her eyes widened, and he felt her stiffen, but she didn't pull away. She might like to play the chaste and frigid soldier, but he knew what she really wanted. What they all really wanted. She'd never get it, of course, but that was the whole point of the game, wasn't it?

He waited until he felt her angle her head ever so slightly into his palm before he withdrew his hand. "Who issued the order?"

She looked confused. Good. "What? What do you mean?"

"You said the order came from the High Lord himself, but how was it delivered to you?"

"Oh," she said. Gieck practically could see the gears shifting in her brain as she pulled herself back on track. No doubt she would be chastising herself for being distracted once again. She always did, and that threw her off balance. Made her easier to interrogate without her even realizing it. "It was General Bekam. He called me to Salkire and delivered the briefing."

"In the keep itself?"

"Yes, but in a back office. He stressed the importance of secrecy for this one."

Gieck gave her a knowing grin. "Either that, or he just wanted to get you alone. Can't say I blame him."

The color rose in Nera's cheeks. "I don't think that's—I mean, he would never, and you know I would never." The perfect amount of protest.

"Well, I should hope not," he said. "Certain fraternizations among officers are hardly professional."

She didn't respond but was looking at him with that little line between her eyebrows, like she did when she couldn't quite figure him out. She had never truly figured him out. That would be a bad day for at least one of them. But he let her feel like she broke through the surface every once in a while, only to confound her again. That was the nature of the game, too. Draw her in and then push her out again. It kept her off balance, and that usually was enough to get Gieck more than he otherwise could have gotten.

This time it was a name. Tenez Bekam had delivered the order and would be the one waiting for a report of success. That explained Mollor's involvement. Bekam knew Gieck's parents and had visited their estate many times when Lucian was young. He'd shepherded the boy into the service and was the one who pulled the right strings to get him into the Academy to train for the Kites. Bekam had always liked him, and Gieck respected Bekam's methods. He'd picked up a trick or two of his own from the general over the years. Bekam would be more than happy to see Gieck overstep Nera and might even facilitate his advancement himself. The general knew Nera was unsuited to her station, between her anxiety and her unhinged zealotry for destroying any trace of magic, and setting her up for this mission was a gift for Gieck. Bekam had lined everything up perfectly. Gieck just had to deliver that location.

As if on cue, Gieck heard the outer door open and close, and sharp footsteps approached on the stone floor. Nera snapped her attention away from him and rose from the bench. Back to business, Gieck supposed. He stood and stepped over the bench to stand a few feet away from her as the soldier came in. It was Eyral, one of his own. The young Kite at first looked to Gieck. Before he could approach,

Gieck jerked his head toward Nera. Eyral got the message and approached her instead.

"Commander, we have someone who claims to know about a rebel sympathizer who also is a mage."

"A mage? Known here in Klubridge?"

"Yes, Commander. It could be the agent in the city who will be meeting with the spy."

"Who is this mage?" Gieck asked, eager to rush this conversation along.

"He didn't say, sir. He told us he'll take us to his own master, who has all the details. I'm not convinced that the boy even knows the agent's name, but I thought it right to bring it to you immediately."

"You did well, Eyral," Nera said.

"What do you know about this boy?" Gieck asked. "Or about this master?"

Eyral shrugged. "Not much. He's a street kid, probably a thief. Goes by the name of Skink."

"Time is wasting," Gieck said. "Take us to him."

CHAPTER 8

Fairy grabbed the back of Skink's collar and yanked him toward her. He wasn't expecting it and tumbled backwards into the open doorway of the empty shop where they'd been hiding. Skink fell hard on his backside with a grunt and glared at Fairy. "What the bloody—"

"It's bait, you idiot," she hissed, pointing at the woman he'd been just about to rob.

Skink glared at her one more time and then looked at the woman. She was about five feet away from them, just standing there and facing out toward the street. She wore fashionable green breeches and a white blouse with mid-length sleeves. Around her waist she wore a dark leather belt with an old fabric pouch strapped onto the back, and that was the target Skink had been eyeing.

"You're mad," Skink said, but Fairy noted that it was under his breath. He at least was being wary, even if he still didn't see it.

"I'm not, and you were about to get nicked. Look." She pointed again. "That pouch doesn't match anything else on her. She's dressed like a fine lady. Why would she have that ugly thing just hanging off her? And see how she's just standing about. What's that for? She's not waiting to meet anybody here. All these shops are closed up. She's bait, you nutter."

She could tell Skink wanted to be skeptical, to prove her wrong, but he saw the truth. The city watch had been stepping up its game lately, and Fairy had had to pull Skink out of three traps already, this one making four. He'd been careless the last two weeks, ever since Dorrin left. When Scrounger wouldn't let them get him back from the theater people, Skink sank into an even more miserable state. He snapped at everybody now, even his own mates, and he'd gotten sloppier with his work than ever before. His mind wasn't in it, and that was showing with the rapidly decreasing returns he was showing on their nights out.

That wasn't the only change among Scrounger's crew. After Dorrin left, they'd been one man down. To make matters worse, the one they were missing was the top earner, and Scrounger wasn't happy about that, even if he never mentioned Dorrin after that first night. He didn't mention Dorrin, but he made sure Fairy knew it was her fault he'd left. Skink had learned not to bring the boy up to Scrounger after the second time he had to pick himself up from the floor. Since then he'd been nursing a grudge against the big man, with no way to address it. He'd gone from being a rallying point for the bullies to being a sulking loner. Fairy's part in the group had changed, too. Scrounger still expected her to handle the accounting, but now he was sending her out on the street every night. Ostensibly it was to make up for their lagging income with an extra set of thieving hands, but Fairy knew it was to punish her for letting Dorrin get away.

Even though she was bearing the brunt of it, Fairy was glad he'd escaped, and she hoped he was living safely among better people than he'd found down in the East Ward. She didn't know whether she'd see him again, but she hoped she would, once she worked up a plan and got her own self out of this place.

Tonight they were in a broken-down neighborhood near the city center. Scrounger had gotten word that some military types were in the city, and that always brought the street vendors to congregate. Wherever there was government money, there would be hands to put it into. And with the money came the cutpurses, and Fairy had watched an exodus of thieves from the theater district down into the middle of Klubridge, dozens of eager rogues hungry for Imperial coin. Naturally, anytime there was a rise in crime, the city watch was quick to respond. That's how Skink very nearly fell into his fourth trap and was instead brooding inside that shop with his knees tucked up under his chin.

Fairy told herself the next time he went off stupid like that, he could get himself arrested, and that was a fact. But, even in the telling, she knew she wouldn't let that happen. She didn't have a way out, and if Skink got nicked, he would turn over on the whole gang. She couldn't have that, so she'd keep rescuing his sorry carcass even if he deserved more a swift kick to the head.

She was watching Skink in the dark and thinking about how much she'd like to deliver that kick and at exactly what angle it would be most effective when she saw his eyes widen. He sat up straighter, and she peeked around the doorjamb to see what had gotten his attention.

It was a strange man dressed all in red. He had shaggy black hair, but his dark face was clean shaven. Fairy could tell he was one of the military types from the uniform and from the insignia on his chest. It looked like some kind of bird, but she couldn't see what type, and she didn't recognize the tabard. He had a sword sheathed on his left hip, and he moved with a hand hanging near it, looking like he was used to walking with the weight of it. He'd come around the far corner, and his eyes were busy taking in all the storefronts. Fairy pulled back into the darkness when he looked toward their shop. He probably couldn't have seen them lurking in their hiding place anyway, but she'd rather not risk it.

Fairy shifted around the small room in silence to get a better look at the man. Skink had slid closer to the door, still in shadow and out of sight of the street. Fairy swallowed hard when she realized the stranger was walking directly toward them. Had he seen her after all?

No, he had stopped now and was talking to the woman Skink had tried to rob. "Anything yet?" he asked her.

"Nothing," she said, "and I'd thank you not to linger. It's hard enough netting the little bastards in without them seeing me consort with the enemy."

"See?" Fairy hissed at Skink, but he was too caught up in the conversation outside to pay her any attention.

"This is more important than catching a few pickpockets," the man said, his voice low and serious. "I have—"

"Yes, yes, orders from the High Lord himself, and I'm a priestess of Shathre."

"I'm serious," and he certainly seemed to be. "If we don't find this mage—"

The woman interrupted him again, but more gently this time. "I know, Eyral. You've made it abundantly clear. I haven't heard anything, but you'll be the first to know if I do hear about any magicians lurking about my city."

Fairy was tiring of the eavesdropping and had started to sidle back towards the rear exit from the shop. She was about to motion for Skink to follow her when she realized Skink wasn't there.

"I know where you can find a mage!"

The man and woman both spun at the voice, and the man—Eyral —had his right hand across his body, the sword half pulled from its sheath. Skink had burst out of the doorway and either didn't notice or didn't care that he'd nearly gotten skewered. Fairy knew immediately what he was doing, and she shrank farther into the dark until her back pressed against the cool planks of the rear wall. Don't do this, Skink. Just stop talking. But, of course, he didn't stop.

F airy tore through the streets faster than she'd ever taken them. She wished she had Dorrin's speed, but this would have to do. Behind her, somewhere back there in the city center, Skink was selling out the entire gang. She knew he'd be satisfying his simmering rage and exacting his revenge on Scrounger, and in the process he'd be taking the rest of them down and likely dooming Dorrin as well. Skink was too thick to realize he'd be condemning himself as well, but it was too late to worry about him. She just had to reach the East Ward before Skink brought the police or the red soldiers or worse.

Fairy hit a crossroads, the uptown toward the theater district to her left and down to the ward on her right. There was a chance Skink would lead them straight to the Chamberlain. It sounded like he was about to tell them all about Akithar. Skink still swore the man was a magician, even after he'd seen all the rigging and special effects. He'd want them going after Akithar, just to deprive Dorrin of whatever new life he'd found.

But no, he'd send them to Scrounger first. Scrounger, who had been so adamant about not wanting to involve the gang with the authorities. Scrounger, who had beaten on Skink just a few too many times. He'd want to get them all in one swoop, and that would start with Scrounger and eventually lead uptown to the theater. The East Ward would be their first destination. Fairy took off down the street to the right, her resolve set.

Leaving Scrounger to his well-deserved fate never was a consideration. Yes, he should get whatever misery Skink was trying to pile on top of him, but the rest of the kids didn't need that kind of trouble. There were stories about what happened to thieves after they got taken in, and none of them were pleasant. And besides, if Scrounger went down, they assuredly would take down Akithar and his troupe as well for whatever they thought he'd done. That would put Dorrin in danger, and she couldn't have that. Given no other choice, she had to save Scrounger, of all the unlikely people.

Fairy's two weeks of night runs had reacquainted her with Klubridge. She had always known the city's twists and turns, but being set loose on the populace brought everything back fresh, and the new familiarity quickened her pace. She didn't know how long it would take Skink to finish telling his story, but she was sure the watch woman and the soldier man would take interest and follow up on his tip. The usual governmental processes might slow them down before they left for the East Ward, but they'd be coming, and that was a fact.

When Fairy burst through the front door into the hovel she shared with the other kids, she ran straight into that moth-eaten blanket that hung over the doorway. She stumbled into the front room and yanked at the thing to get it off her. It ripped free from the nails above the door, and she let it drop to the floor. Scrounger wasn't there. Of course he wasn't. It was midday, and he'd be wherever he went when he left them there. Maybe he had some other job elsewhere in the city, or maybe he was a demon that vanished into the morning light. Whatever the case, the other kids were there, all sprawled across the dirty floor asleep. A couple of drowsy heads popped up when Fairy came in, and bleary eyes stared at her in the dim light, no doubt wondering why she was panting and covered in sweat.

"Get up," she called and banged on the wall. The other kids shifted, and some were sitting up now. "We have to go. Come on, get up!"

"What's this?" The deep voice caught her by surprise, and the familiar wide hand pushed away the fabric that covered the back door of the room.

"Scrounger!" She wasn't sure whether she was pleased or terrified. "Skink's sold us out. He's talking to guards now, and they'll be here soon." It spilled out in a torrent of words, and Scrounger held up a hand to stop her.

"Slow down, Fairy. Tell me who Skink is talking to."

She couldn't tell whether Scrounger was worried, but she had to make him understand. "There was a red soldier looking for a mage in Klubridge. One of the military types who came in. He was talking to the city watch, a woman, I don't know her."

"Did the soldier have a black bird on his chest?" Scrounger asked.

She nodded. "Yes, I remember that. He did."

"Scarlet Kites," he said. "They're magic hunters. What would they want with us?"

"They're not after us. I don't know who they're after, but Skink wants them to go after Akithar."

"Because of Dorrin." Scrounger sighed and rested a forearm on the back of his big chair. The other children were listening by now, no doubt trying to make sense of what had happened.

"Right. Only, I think he's bringing them here first. I think he wants to get back at you."

Scrounger digested this more calmly than Fairy would have liked. He stroked at his lower lip and frowned in thought.

"We have to go! If we don't leave now—"

"We're not going anywhere," he said and made his way around the chair, finally dropping heavily onto the seat. He had planted himself, and Fairy knew there would be no budging him.

"What? Why? They're coming to get you! All of us!"

"If they come, they will come. But I suspect this is a situation that could be turned to our advantage."

She was dumbfounded. How could she make him understand the danger they all were in? Even as she stared at Scrounger in disbelief, she heard the hooves approaching outside. They were here.

The first person through the door was the soldier Fairy had seen in the street outside the shop, the one who had nearly gutted Skink with his sword. Eyral, the woman had called him. He didn't knock or wait for an invitation. He just pushed the door open and stepped inside like he owned the place. Fairy noticed that he kept his right hand across his body, ready to draw that sword at a moment's notice.

Scrounger was still sitting in his chair, right there in the front room, but said nothing. Eyral didn't speak, either. He looked around the room, now empty except for the big man in the chair, and stepped to the side of the door, kicking the fallen tarp out of the way. When she heard the horses approaching, Fairy had rushed all the kids into the back room, and she now was watching through a small gap the heavy fabric left in the doorway. Scrounger hadn't protested when she started shoving everyone back there. He was being obstinate, but he wasn't stupid. If the government came across a full-blown den of thieves, there wasn't likely to be a happy outcome.

After Eyral came another man, bigger and broader but dressed in that same red uniform and armor. Scarlet Kites, Scrounger had called them. Fairy wondered whether Scrounger had run across them before. She knew very little about this man who controlled all of their lives. The bigger soldier was lighter skinned, with his hair long in front and short in back. He looked meaner than Eyral, and Fairy was glad to be out of sight. With luck, these Kites would keep their attention on Scrounger and wouldn't be interested in the back room. If they decided to search the place, she'd have to come up with another plan and fast.

She thought that second man would be the last one, but soon Skink himself staggered into the room. He looked as surprised to be there as Fairy was to see him return. He saw Scrounger at the middle of the room and visibly deflated. He hung his head, not wanting to meet Scrounger's undoubtedly fierce gaze.

Behind Skink came one more soldier, a woman. She had the same uniform as the others, but she also was wearing a cloak of some sort. From the way the other two looked to her and moved aside, Fairy could tell she was in charge. The woman stepped farther into the shack and dropped the hood away from her head. Her hair was pulled back into a braid, and it looked dark in this light, but Fairy could see hints of red in the gloom.

"Moeply Raseul," she said. "Or do you prefer Scrounger?"

Scrounger barked a laugh. "My reputation proceeds me... Commander?"

"Mollor," she said. "It's our business to know you and every other two-penny thug haunting the underside of this city." The look she gave Scrounger was like she'd bitten into an apple that had gone bad. And Moeply Raseul. Was that truly Scrounger's name? Fairy had never heard it before, and somehow it had never struck her as odd that he didn't have a name other than Scrounger. Of course he'd have another name. After all, she had, and Skink had. Dorrin had been one of the few that didn't get a second name when Scrounger took him on.

"You've been holding out on us, Scrounger," the commander said. Her tone was more familiar than it would be if she had just looked him up. How did she know him?

"And you are here to balance that, are you?" Scrounger asked. He didn't sound afraid. At least, not as afraid as Fairy felt.

Mollor didn't respond, but the bigger man stepped closer. "We are." Fairy swallowed hard. He had looked mean when he came in, but the malice in his voice was even more palpable. "Your boy here tells us you know about a mage in the city."

"There could be many mages in Klubridge. I don't keep those accounts. As I recall, that's your business. Or has the mandate of the Kites changed since the last time I spoke with your generals?"

The big soldier looked at his commander, but she didn't move. He seemed satisfied and turned back to Scrounger. "Who is the mage?"

Scrounger chuckled under the hateful eyes of the soldier. "My memory is lapsing a bit in my age. I'm certain it would improve if some enhancements could be made to the existing arrangement I have with the Empire?"

Fairy frowned. What was he talking about? What kind of arrangement could Scrounger have with the Empire that would permit him to run a ring of child thieves like he'd been doing for as long as anyone could remember?

The soldier pulled his lips back into a tight grin. "Money. It always comes to money with you types, doesn't it?"

"I do have a fondness for the coin," Scrounger admitted, and he sounded almost mirthful. Fairy was confounded.

"Eyral," the soldier said, "Do you have a purse on you?"

"I do, Lieutenant." He pulled a cloth bag from a waist pouch and handed it over. The lieutenant gave it a little toss, and it jangled in his hand. Satisfied, he let it slip through his fingers so he held it by the drawn top part of the bag.

"I'll make you a deal," the lieutenant said. He held the bag out, and Scrounger reached for it. An instant before the money changed hands, the lieutenant whipped his arm back and slammed the coins across Scrounger's face. His head rocked to the side, and Fairy heard blood spatter across the floor. It was dark, but she still could see a few shiny wet drops on the rotting wood.

Fairy's eyes were wide, and she clamped her teeth together to keep from crying out. Skink had given an audible gasp when it happened, and he now was looking between Scrounger and the lieutenant. Maybe he finally was realizing what he'd stepped into. For her part, the commander was looking away from the scene with a pointed interest in a blank spot on the wall. She didn't like what was happening, but she wasn't going to stop it.

Scrounger gave another laugh, this one thick and wet. "I must refuse your generous offer, lieutenant. And I seem to have forgotten a few more details. That happens when I'm beaten about the head."

The lieutenant held the money bag at his side now, the drawstrings in his fist. Fairy could see dark spots staining it that weren't there before. He paced in front of Scrounger, and a wicked smirk turned up the corners of his mouth. "You're hard, is that it? A hard man running children in this heap of a city. Something to be proud of. To be paid for, even."

"I like to think so," Scrounger said, and the sack of money slammed across his face again. More blood hit the floor, and this time Fairy heard something firmer tap tap tapping across the ground. A broken tooth clattered to a halt just past the doorway where she was hiding. It was covered in blood.

Scrounger's head lolled to the side, and he spat on the floor. He rocked his head back up to look at the soldier, but it seemed to take more effort this time. When he spoke again, it was even thicker, and there was a wounded lisp. "You think you can beat what you want out of me. Me!" He paused and spat again. "You can shove that sack of coins up your ass. You're getting nothing from me."

The lieutenant drew his arm back again, and the commander finally spoke. "Lucian, wait." The lieutenant—Lucian, apparently—halted in his backswing. He looked at Mollor. She approached Scrounger and gestured for the other two men to back away from them. Now she stood over the wounded man, and her face was stern. Fairy had seen her disapproval of the beating, but she was masking it now.

"Moeply, you provide a great service to the Empire, but you have delivered nothing to us in quite some time."

"It's been less than a year—"

"That's too long for us to wait. The Empire has its needs, as you well know. You're tardy, but your service still is valued. For that reason, your existing arrangement will continue. Unaltered," she added with a pointed stare. "I will ask you once more whether you know of a mage in Klubridge that you have not reported. When you answer, please remember that withholding the identity of a magic user is a capital crime in the Empire." She remained silent long enough for Scrounger to digest her meaning, and then she asked softly, "Where is the mage?"

"The theater!"

Mollor half turned as Skink broke his silence. "What's that?"

Skink looked like he was about to cry. He was more miserable than Fairy had ever seen him. "There's a wizard, works up in the theater row. He's the one you want."

The commander wasn't pleased. "Why did you have us come all the way to the East Ward? You could have told us about this before."

Fairy knew why. Skink had wanted his revenge on Scrounger, but he hadn't thought about what that would look like until just now. The boy shrugged and looked away.

Scrounger shifted in his chair. "I don't know about any mage. This boy is always creating trouble."

Mollor ignored him and continued questioning Skink. "Tell me more about this mage, boy. What's his name?"

Skink shrugged again, "I don't know. He does magic on the stage. He acts all like it ain't real, but you know it is. He's a wizard, everybody knows it."

"Where can we find this wizard?"

"He's got his own show. It's a big theater house uptown. I don't know the name."

The fool couldn't even remember Akithar or the name of the Chamberlain. Thank the gods for his stupidity, for once. Mollor turned back to Scrounger. "Do you have anything to add to this? It's your last chance."

Scrounger wiped a big hand across his injured face before answering. "I don't know what the boy is talking about."

Mollor nodded slowly and almost looked regretful. To her soldiers, "Arrest him for aiding a suspected magic user."

"Now wait—" Scrounger started up from his chair, but the lieutenant forced him back down with a firm hand on his chest.

"I can execute him here," Lucian said, and Fairy could tell he was hoping for an affirmative.

"Not without due process. Bring him back in our custody, and he'll be tried," she said.

"What about the boy?"

"Leave him. With the thanks of the Empire." Without another word, she was gone. Fairy heard one of the horses clopping back up the street.

"Get up," the lieutenant ordered Scrounger. He grabbed the front of his shirt and yanked him to his feet. It amazed Fairy to see that Scrounger wasn't as tall as the soldier, not by far. He had always seemed so huge before. Now he stood, defeated, before these two men. The lieutenant kept an eye on Scrounger as he told Eyral, "You will now witness that he attempted to escape arrest."

"Sir?" Eyral asked, confused.

In the blink of an eye, Lucian was behind Scrounger, and there was a quick zipping noise. Fairy couldn't tell what was happening at first, but then she saw Scrounger buck backwards with a wheezing grunt. The soldier had some kind of cord around his throat and was pulling tight. Scrounger flailed an arm back, trying to knock the soldier off him, but he was too thick, and his hands couldn't reach far enough. He took two steps forward before he fell to his knees. Lucian still was at his back, and Fairy saw that he had a knee in Scrounger's back now, pushing the big man forward while he pulled back with the cord.

Scrounger's hands flopped at his neck and then at the floor, reaching, grabbing at nothing. A couple of guttural gurgles escaped his lips, and as soon as it had begun, it was over. Lucian bore Scrounger down onto the floor, hard. His head thudded against the wood, and his face was turned toward Fairy. She never would forget the sightless eyes staring at her above a ruined and bloody nose, broken from the beating. Worst of all was Scrounger's fat tongue sticking out of his mouth and the line of drool connecting it to the floorboards.

Lucian was still kneeling on the dead man's back, and he released the cord with his left hand. It made that zipping noise again as it retracted into a strap he wore on his right wrist. As he stood up, pushing his weight off Scrounger's body, he asked Eyral, "What did you see?"

The other man's eyes were wide now, like Fairy's, but he knew what to say. "You tried to arrest him, and he attacked you. You had no choice."

"That's right. You'll need to have him picked up and processed to the potter's field. Do that straight away. What did you see, boy?"

In the horror, Fairy had forgotten all about Skink. She looked past Scrounger, back to the dark wall, and saw Skink pressed against it. He was terrified now, looking back and forth between the soldiers and trying not to look at Scrounger. "I... I..."

The lieutenant looked back at Eyral. "Loose end. Take care of the boy." Fairy's entire body turned cold.

"The... boy?" Eyral asked carefully. He clearly understood but didn't want to do it. But Fairy knew he would. He was as afraid of this Lucian as she was.

"He doesn't need to be seen again. Do it quickly." He watched Eyral and waited.

Skink's mouth trembled in fear, and all at once he looked directly at the fabric covered doorway, right at Fairy. She thought he might have seen her and worried for an instant that he was going to say something. But that moment passed, and he made a break for the front door. Skink was fast, but his foot caught the edge of the fabric Fairy had torn off the door. Eyral was faster. The sword was out in a flash, and Eyral didn't even have time to strike. Skink tumbled straight into the blade, and it passed all the way through him. Skink and Eyral were face to face, neither of them looking like they could believe what was happening. And then Skink was dead, dead just like Scrounger and just like Dorrin was going to be.

CHAPTER 9

Nera's horse trotted through the city at a brisk clip. She was careful to weave around the few pedestrians that failed to move out of her way, and they slowed her only minimally. She knew it would take Lucian and Eyral time to bring their prisoner back to the castle, but she wanted to get ahead of that delivery and start sending the scouts out immediately. They had a lead, tenuous though it might be, and it needed pursuing as soon as possible.

She did not approve of Lucian's rough methods, but she had to admit that, in the end, they got the job done. She'd known he was a rough man from the moment she met him, when he showed up under her command years ago. His willingness to skirt the line of appropriate and even legal behavior for a Kite should have repulsed Nera. She should have sent him back to the Academy and demanded a new lieutenant. But she knew he was a special placement, pushed up through the ranks by important parents and ushered into her care by General Bekam. She had to keep him, and it wasn't long before she realized she liked him.

He was a brute, and maybe that was part of his appeal. Lucian was dangerous, but he always knew how to limit himself. He had never strayed fully outside the boundaries of how he should perform his duties, and the Kites under his charge never had a cross word to report about their superior. His edge, and even more his ability to control that edge, made Nera pay attention to him. It made her think about him far more than she should.

That same control she admired in him had helped her to stay within the professional parameters of her own position. She was reluctant to admit to herself that she felt an attraction to him, one of her subordinates, but there it was. And she knew he felt something, too. But he had never acted on it, and that only heightened Nera's own attraction. Lucian managed himself well, and she was loath to think about what might have happened between them if he didn't keep such a tight rein on himself. For that she was both appreciative and, in truth, mournful. Perhaps something real could be there in the future, but not while he was under her command.

Lucian Gieck was a good man. Everything Moeply Raseul was not. Nera had heard of Raseul by reputation, but this was her first encounter with him, and she hoped it would be the last. The Empire relied on independent citizens at all corners of the realm to provide for the future, as Raseul had done. Most of the finders Nera had encountered were people of honor, and they took pride in the service they provided. Not Raseul. He had adopted this Scrounger identity and ran street thieves in Klubridge, of all things. Worse yet, he forced the children to live in squalor and dressed himself to match the part when she knew he lived outside the East Ward in a mansion paid for by Imperial taxes. She doubted his urchins knew anything about that side of his life.

Nera had not planned to arrest him, and having him imprisoned would put the Empire down one finder, but she felt justified in giving the order. He was actively obstructing her Kites' search for a mage, and nothing would impede that without consequence. Magic had no place unchecked in Teshovar, and Nera admitted that pulling Raseul off the streets might even do the Empire some good. There always would be someone else willing to step up and fill the void he left in the program, and she felt certain anyone else would be better than this wretch.

When Nera reached the city center, she found Jona in the common room, picking through her lunch. Jona was one of Lucian's proteges, and Nera felt sure the young soldier would follow him to her doom if she had to. That kind of loyalty held the Scarlet Kites together, and Nera was proud to lead such a tight squad.

Jona looked up from her food as Nera entered and pushed herself up to stand at attention. "Commander," she said with a crisp nod.

"Lieutenant Gieck and Eyral will be coming back soon with a prisoner. Send word to prepare a cell for him. And do you know where Tomos is?"

"He was somewhere uptown, but I think he just got back. He should be in his quarters upstairs."

"Thank you, Jona. That will be all."

Jona nodded again and scooped her plate off the table. She carried it out of the room, quick to follow Nera's command. Nera watched her leave before turning and heading out through the opposite door. If what the boy had said about a mage operating openly in the theater district proved to be true, the man shouldn't be hard to find. Surely someone would not be so foolish as to think he could hide in plain sight like that, but Nera had encountered much stranger things in her time at the head of the Scarlet Kites. One way or another, she would have her answer soon, and she headed up the stairs to assemble her vanguard.

Ordinarily, Nera would have taken the boy's claim of a wizard doing magic openly in a theater with more skepticism. Raseul's silence and then his insistence that she not listen to the boy only made the wild claim seem more likely. That, combined with the other Kites' failure to turn up any substantial information in other directions, had Nera and five Scarlet Kites canvassing the theater district on foot.

Klubridge was one of the largest cities on the Empire's eastern seaboard. It had no real material exports other than its money, and that flowed out in a steady torrent. The wealth disparity between the citizens was greater than Nera had seen anywhere else in Teshovar, with the poor living in rotting and even burned-out slums like the East Ward, while the rich sat literally above all that on rising hills. Cutting through those uptown boroughs was Klubridge's famous theater district, unquestionably the modern world's center of stage and performance. At last count in the Imperial arts registry, there were over ninety theaters, some of them small playhouses and others massive and ornate institutions.

The boy hadn't known the name of the supposed mage or the theater where he performed, but it didn't take long for Nera to answer both questions. She ducked into the very first shop on the street, little more than a souvenir stand hawking overpriced booklets and trinkets to wealthy tourists in town to see a show. With the theaters in their off-season, there was less foot traffic than she imagined the shop usually saw. There were a few racks of gaudy merchandise along the two side walls, and the owner stood behind a short counter at the back of the room, which really was only a few steps away from the front. She was broad shouldered, with strong arms that Nera imagined knew a life of farming before ending up selling to passersby in Klubridge. The woman wore a plain brown dress that was good enough for working in the theater district but not good enough for partaking in it.

"You're two weeks late if you're here to see a show. What do you want?"

The woman's directness broke Nera's stride. She was used to people scattering out of her way or bowing respectfully or doing any number of other, more appropriate things when they spotted the red tabard of the Scarlet Kites. This was something new.

"You talk like you've known Kites before," she said.

"I've known everything is to know in this town. Sooner or later, you see it all. And it's getting to be later, don't you know?" The shop-keeper looked to be in her sixties, with deep lines in her forehead between her stark white hair and her cool blue eyes. The expression she gave Nera was a tired one. "So what is it you want?"

Surprising though it was, the directness was also refreshing. "I'm looking for a performer who does stage magic. I'm told there is a theater here in—"

"The Great Akithar," the woman interrupted, her voice mocking. "You'd think he did real magic, the way he's talked about."

"You know who he is?"

"Everybody round here knows of him. Not many seen him outside his theater. He keeps most to himself, you see. Part of his show, I say, but you should hear the lookies." The mocking voice again. "Oh, he made a woman fly up in the air! Oh, he made fire out his fingertips!" She made a spitting noise, and Nera was thankful that she didn't follow through with substance. "It's just a bunch of talk. What you want with him, anyway?"

Nera didn't answer but asked, "What makes you think he's not doing real magic?"

The woman leaned back and gave Nera a snort. "You lot, is what. Who'd be stupid enough to go waving it about with you prowling after them?"

"Who, indeed," Nera said. "Where does this Akithar perform?"

"Chamberlain. Big theater down near the Bastion. Can't miss it."

Well, then. That was almost too easy. "Thank you for your help."

"You can help me back with not scaring off my paying customers."

"I'll be going," Nera said and gave the woman a smile. Brusque as the shopkeeper was, Nera liked her.

Tomos was waiting for her outside the store. "We have a name," he said.

"The Great Akithar?" Nera asked with a raised eyebrow.

He raised his own at that. "I suppose that's a confirmation, then."

"What did you learn about him?"

Tomos walked with her back into the street. "He's been in town for years and owns his own theater. He's famous throughout Klubridge for his illusions. Local legend is that he's an almighty wizard."

"The woman I talked to seems skeptical of that," Nera said, leading them around a horse that had stopped in the middle of traffic.

"It was the same from the man I found. It sounds to me like this

Akithar puts on a show and makes his living by pretending to be a mage, but the locals see through it. He probably dupes outsiders."

"The boy Skink said something about this Akithar claiming to use science instead of magic. His master seemed eager for us not to find out about him. Why would he say that if he's trying to run a con? There was something between this scoundrel Raseul and Akithar."

Tomos considered for a moment before saying, "That works two ways. One, he's covering himself by openly saying he's not doing real magic. And two, what's the surest way to get somebody to believe you're doing magic?"

"Tell them you're not doing magic," Nera said.

"Right."

"You think this Akithar is not our man?"

Tomos shook his head. "I'd be surprised. I don't know what Raseul was hiding, but I doubt it was real magic. Maybe Akithar has him duped, too. Maybe Akithar owes him money. Who knows? But no agent of the insurgency is going to want to draw this much attention to himself, mage or not. This is just some carnival trickster who's found a way to earn a wage off gullibility."

"There's no crime in that," Nera said.

Tomos angled his head. "Maybe not, but couldn't we do something to discourage it? It can't be good for him to be making people think he's getting away with doing real magic without consequence."

"If he's not a mage, then he's doing nothing illegal." Nera hated to admit that, but it was the truth. She abhorred magic, but the Empire had defined the laws and put them into place for Nera and those like her to uphold. The High Lord Peregrine had seen fit to allow his people a measure of freedom that the populace frankly did not appreciate and often took for granted. His strictest mandate was against the use of magic, but there were no laws against faking it. She'd seen stage magicians before, and there always were aristocrats eager to whip out card tricks or practiced sleights of hand at dinner functions after they'd gotten too much liquor into them. There was nothing illegal about it, but it was unquestionably immoral. And, by the High Lord's wisdom, morality was not an enforceable virtue.

"There it is," Tomos said, pointing.

The Chamberlain was big, standing taller than the theaters on either side. Huge, gilded letters mounted on the front of the building proclaimed its name, and they arced over a window that undoubtedly was a ticket box. The ticket window was dark, the last tickets having sold weeks ago. The street was slow just now, but Nera knew the crowd would thicken even without new performances, come nighttime. She planned to be well out of that throng by then.

"Want me to go in?" Tomos asked.

She shook her head. "Keep watch out here. I suspect this won't take long." She left him beside the empty ticket window and tried one of the front doors. It was unlocked and swung open. Nera gave Tomos a nod before going inside and letting the door swing shut behind her.

This wasn't the first time Nera had been inside one of Klubridge's many theaters. She'd been to a play once, when she was nine, almost ten. She remembered little about that trip into the city or what theater had put on the performance, but she always would remember the play. It was a musical comedy and had been the most wonderful thing she'd ever seen. In retrospect, she knew they wrote it for children, but that didn't lessen her love for the show. She had seen it only once but still believed she could remember every ornate costume and every line of dialogue, and she still caught herself humming a few of the featured songs from time to time.

More than anything else, though, she treasured those memories because it had been the last trip she had taken with her parents. Nera's mother was a clerical worker, and her father was a respected lawman. It was rare that their schedules aligned, but on that occasion they both were in Klubridge on business, and they had brought Nera along. It was wonderful, and she smiled sadly as she recalled the way the colors and lights from the stage illuminated their laughing faces on either side of her. That had been less than a year before they were gone, before she had moved to Rifast to live with her father's successor,

Nezar. There had been no blood relations left after her parents died, but Nezar was the next best thing, and he had loved and raised her as his own daughter.

Nera blinked, surprised to feel that her eyes were moist. She gave them a quick wipe with the back of her hand and forced herself to ignore the phantom burning pain in her shoulders and upper arms. That was a long time ago, and what was done was done. She pulled her attention away from nostalgia and into her current duty. The boy had claimed that this supposed magician was the real deal, and his master had been eager to cover something up about the situation. That piqued Nera's suspicion, but Tomos likely had the right of it—that this was just a charlatan making money off the superstitions of his audience. Part of Nera hoped that would be the case. The thought of an actual mage flaunting his magic openly like this gave her a disgusted shudder. But, of course, if this Akithar ended up being her man, then her job here would be all but done.

It was still early in the day and was in the off-season, but Nera was surprised to see two technicians at work in the front hallway as if they were preparing for the next performance. There was a busy hum inside the theater that seemed odd two weeks after the season's closing shows. Nera walked through the back doors into the grand room and stared at its size. The theater had looked big from the outside, but nothing had prepared her for the vast vault it held. Rows of seats stretched across the wide room and extended far to the back of the building, where the elevated stage presented an unobstructed view for any seat in the house. There were balconies suspended above her, and she saw narrow catwalks spanning the ceiling far above that. She couldn't remember the theater where she had seen her musical, but she was certain it couldn't have been this enormous.

Nera took a slow stroll down the center aisle and stopped beside the front row of seats to watch a young boy busily digging through a crate next to the stage. He was well dressed, with crisp suspenders holding up his pants, and he looked to be perhaps eight or nine years old. He must have sensed her watching him, and he stopped searching for whatever it was to look over his shoulder. He met her gaze and froze in place, his dark eyes wide beneath his tousled black hair. He was small, but Nera thought she might have underestimated his age by a couple of years. He was young but had earned experience in those eyes.

"Hello," she said.

"Hi." He was uncertain, and Nera thought she might be the first Kite, Scarlet or otherwise, that he had seen.

"What's your name?" she asked.

He stood from the box and waited a moment before answering. "Dorrin."

"It's nice to meet you, Dorrin. My name is Commander Mollor." She immediately wondered whether she should have dispensed with titles and just given him her first name. She wasn't good with children.

"Can I help you, Commander?"

Nera had been so intent on talking to the boy that she hadn't noticed the woman approaching from the other side. She looked to be about Nera's age, perhaps a year or two older, and the woman had about an inch of height over Nera. Her long, dark hair was pulled back from her face, and she wore a green blouse over brown work pants. She undoubtedly was part of the theater crew, and her demeanor placed her high on that rank. Perhaps a manager?

"You have a marvelous theater. I was surprised to find it open in the off-season," Nera said.

A gleam of pride slipped through as the woman gave a small smile of appreciation. "We still perform at least once a week while the other theaters are closed." She looked to the boy. "Dorrin, run along back-stage. You can help Lizzie."

He bolted away without a response, and Nera added another name to the roster of children she had unintentionally terrified.

"Now," the woman said and asked again, "How can I help you?"

"You heard my introduction, but I'm afraid I am at a loss. You are...?"

The woman hesitated, almost a mirror of the boy, Dorrin, but sighed and said, "Samira Tandogan."

"Marvelous," Nera said. "I'm sure you can guess why I'm here."

"You're a Scarlet Kite. There's only one reason for you to be anywhere, as far as I know." There was disdain in the woman's wariness. That intrigued Nera but also gave her an instant dislike for this Samira. Scarlet Kites went wherever magic was to be found, and they snuffed it out, as was the natural order. Anyone opposed to their presence was not fully opposed to the extinction of magic and was no friend of Nera's.

Straight to business, then. "I am here to see the man who calls himself the Great Akithar."

Samira's shoulders visibly tensed, and she began, "He's not—" But she stopped short, and Nera followed her gaze to the same stage door through which Dorrin had escaped. There was a tall man, thin and paler than Samira, but he had the same dark hair, the same general look. Perhaps they were related?

"The Great Akithar, I presume?"

"You presume correctly. It's a pleasure to make your acquaintance, Commander." He was wearing a black suit, far more formal than anything else she had seen in the city until now. His voice rang clear and deep, perfect for the stage.

Samira started, "Akithar, I can—"

He smiled at her, and Nera did not miss the intensity of the look he gave her. "It's okay, Samira. You can go back to what you were doing. The Commander and I are going to have a chat."

Samira didn't respond but backed away slowly. Just as Nera had seen the look Akithar gave Samira, she also caught the brief glance of distrust and hatred Samira shot her way before she pushed aside a dark curtain and disappeared into the depths of the theater.

Akithar was smiling again when Nera looked back to him. The edges of his thin mustache curled up, and Nera marveled at how precisely the man had fashioned himself to look like what any audience would expect a magician to look like. "Samira is a bit protective of me," Akithar said. He motioned for Nera to follow him. "Shall we?"

"What would she be protecting you from, exactly?" Nera asked.

They went through the stage door and were in a hallway now. He was leading her back, presumably to his office.

"My performances here are popular with the audience, but they tend not to go over quite as well with those who have real experience with magic. A nasty business, that."

"Your performance is not real magic, then?"

Akithar gave her a surprised look and a laugh before continuing down the hall. "It wouldn't be very smart for me to admit using magic to a Scarlet Kite, now, would it?"

"It would make my job easier," Nera said. They had stopped in a small alcove, between two crates, and Akithar was unlocking a door.

"When something is taboo," he said, "it becomes the thing that people most and least want to see and experience. My audience fears magic, loathes it, even. But they can't resist coming to see whether the real thing might be happening here, behind the doors of the old Chamberlain theater."

He pushed the door open, and Nera followed him into his office. The decor was sparse, a proliferation of books being the room's dominant feature. She wasn't sure what she had expected, but it was unlikely that he'd bring her into an office replete with all the trappings of his nefarious wizardry if he were a true mage.

"So you put on a show? You sell them the fantasy of magic, then? A lie?"

"Well, I prefer not to call it a lie. It's no more a lie than what any other performer gives their audience," he said. He motioned to a chair, but Nera ignored the offer. "I give them a spectacle, and then I tell them how I did it."

"How do you do it, then?"

He picked up a book with a blue cover from a small table and tossed it to her. She caught it on reflex and looked down to read the title aloud. "Modern Chemical Investigations. What is this?"

"It's how I do it." He tapped the covers of three more books spread across the table. "I am a man of science. I've studied chemistry, engineering, physics. Electrical phenomena is my newest interest. I've been educating myself in the latest advances practically all my life."

"You're saying the show, this spectacle you give your audience, is all a product of the science you've learned?"

Akithar took a breath and clasped his hands behind his back. "I know you have a job to do, Commander. I don't begrudge you that. You have a duty to find out whether I'm using unlawful magic. I understand and respect that, but you will not find what you're seeking here. It's true that I perform miraculous feats on that stage, but hidden inside each of those feats are marvelous contraptions. Wires, gears, steam, magnets, electrical currents, those are my magics. I employ a chief engineer to design and build my illusions, and he has a staff of workers under him. This is a production company, not a coven."

Nera watched his face, searching for the telltale signs of a liar. Any sort of giveaway that would let her know the truth. She saw none. This man was an experienced performer who may or may not lie to audiences every night, so he naturally would be adept at deception. But something in his tone rang true for her. Still, something wasn't right. All the evidence was right here. There were blueprints and sketches of machinery, books about every scientific topic she could imagine and some she'd never even dreamed existed. She couldn't find the lie, but she felt it deep inside. Something was off.

"Is there anything else I can do to help you, Commander?"

She gave him a tight smile. "No, not for now. Thank you for your time and your candor."

He returned her smile with a warmer one of his own. "I trust you won't go telling my audience about our discussion. It wouldn't do for them to know how the soup is made, as they say."

"Of course." Her eyes focused past him, and there it was. She forced her expression not to change. "I can see myself out."

Nera thought she might have left the office a little too quickly, but Akithar made no move to stop her. She retraced the path back through that long hallway and into the auditorium, which now was completely empty. She didn't stop there to wonder where the workers had gone but instead made a quick trip up the aisle, through the lobby, and out the front door.

Tomos was waiting for her, just beside the doors where she had left him. He fell into stride next to her as they moved out into the street. "Did you meet the Great Akithar?"

"I did," she said and glanced back at the theater as they moved away from it.

"Well? Is he our mage?"

She didn't hesitate. "He is, and we are going to bring him down."

CHAPTER 10

Samira's office window overlooked the street in front of the theater. It was mirrored from the outside, so she knew she could lean against the wall beside it and peer down without being seen by anyone looking up from the roadway. The Scarlet Kite, Mollor, was leaving the theater now, and one of her soldiers met her next to the door. They walked into the street as they talked, and Samira kept them in her sight until they disappeared to the right, down the street.

Once she was sure they had gone, she cursed under her breath, pushed away from the wall, and made a quick trip down the stairs and to the back of the theater, toward Caius' office. She passed through a work area where Apak was scolding Oreth about something or other, and he looked up in surprise as she stormed through. No time to explain.

The window above the door to Caius' office showed light inside, and she pushed in without knocking. Caius had his back to her and was looking down at something in his hand.

"What's that?" Samira asked.

He looked over his shoulder, and she saw that he had already peeled the false mustache off his upper lip. "It's Apak being careless again." He closed his hand and dropped whatever it was into his pocket. His tuxedo coat hung over the back of his chair, and he started working at the tie as he turned to face her.

"How much does she know?" Samira asked.

"She doesn't know anything, but she has her suspicions. Will you help me with this damned thing?"

Samira made quick work of the knot and pulled the tie off from around his neck. "Are you going to change your hair?"

He frowned and touched at it gingerly. "I'd better. But we need to hurry." He opened the door at the back of the office and stepped through into his private washroom. Samira waited in the office and listened as he rinsed the dark powder out. "Where are we going?" she called to him.

"I suppose there's no use in asking you to stay here." His voice was muffled under a towel.

"You know better than that. So what's our plan?"

"We need to find out how serious they are this time."

There had been other inquisitors in the past. Running a magic show in this town was a magnet for unwanted attention, but it had always been manageable. They usually had visits from Commander Tereth or one of his lackeys. Those Kites knew Akithar well, and they were reasonable, for magic hating governmental sorts. This Commander Mollor was an unknown quantity. What had happened to Tereth, and why was she here? Samira asked that last bit aloud.

"That's something I dearly would like to know as well. How do I look?"

When Caius came back into the office, his hair was a much lighter shade of brown, his natural color. He also had changed out of his trademark suit into a much more nondescript outfit befitting a middle class laborer. No one would look twice at him, and they wouldn't pick him out as Akithar, infamous sorcerer of dark repute.

"You missed a spot," Samira said and wiped at his temple with her thumb. The smudge of wet powder came away easily. "You're good now. Do I need to change?"

"You'll be fine, as long as we don't run across the Commander again. Let's go."

Caius and Samira left down that same hallway. As they passed through the workroom, Caius said, "Apak, we'll be gone for a bit. You're in charge."

"I will want to know what this is about," Apak said with a concerned frown.

"And so you will, as soon as we know."

In the lobby, Samira said, "They went to the right when they left."

"Probably headed back to Henburn," Caius said. "We're going left, anyway."

Samira followed him out the door and into the street, where they immediately became just two more faces in the city. Still, she remained vigilant for the city watch and especially for any red tabards. "Have we ever had Scarlet Kites here?" she asked.

"Not at the Chamberlain, at least," Caius said. "It's always been Tereth and his blue Kites in the past."

"This isn't even the Scarlets' domain, is it?"

"Not as far as I know, but they're always changing things. Maybe Tereth is assigned elsewhere now."

"Or maybe this Mollor was sent on a special mission," Samira said.

"Maybe."

They turned left at the end of the third block, and Samira knew they were heading toward the city's outer walls. For all its decadence, Klubridge still was a city under the control of the High Lord Peregrine. As such, it was encircled with a tall, stone wall with enormous gates providing the only means of exit. There were three gates to the south, two to the west, and another three to the north. They now headed for the westernmost gate on the south wall.

Even before they got there, Samira knew what they would find. The street was becoming more crowded, block by block, and traffic eventually slowed to a crawl. Voices grew louder and more discontent, the closer they got to the gate. She looked at Caius, and he raised his eyebrows. He was thinking the same thing she was. The guards had closed the gates and either were monitoring all entrances and departures or had stopped them entirely. The gates had been closed only a handful of times in the years since Samira and Caius had arrived in Klubridge. The city watch had closed them once when a rebel assassin had killed a visiting noble. A few years later, Tereth's Kites had ordered the gates closed when there was suspicion of a plot to take the city center by force. And yet another time, a high decree had closed the gates when a band of insurgents gathered outside in a meager attempt at a siege.

Samira touched Caius' elbow and guided him off the main street and onto a side way lined with grocers. "This is not an ordinary inquiry," she said. The city was noisy, but she still kept her voice low.

"You're right. We should check the other gates, just to make sure."

And so they did. Their walk took them near the other two southern gates, but they couldn't get closer than a block to either of them before the traffic bottlenecked again. If the southern gates were closed, it was likely that all the others were shut as well. Magic hunters had come to Klubridge, and the entire populace was locked in with them.

Samira sat slumped so that her chin rested on her hands, which she had crossed in front of her on the table. Caius was across from her, staring down into a now half-empty mug. He looked that way when he was trying to work out a problem or come up with a way to pull off a new trick. She'd seen it hundreds of times, and she knew to wait it out. There always would be an idea.

While she waited for Caius' idea, Samira's mind was turning as well. She was about to interrupt his contemplations to ask a question when his attention snapped away from the mug. "Brius!"

A stocky little man in a half-tucked shirt had just come in the door and now was squinting into the gloom of the tavern. He had two days' growth of beard on his face and a crinkled brown beret shoved down over a mop of curly graying hair. He dressed similarly to Caius, in what looked like work clothes, and Samira wondered if it might be a costume just as Caius' was. The man caught sight of them, gave an uncertain wave, and made his way over.

"Averet," he said, greeting Caius. Averet?

Caius clasped his hand and motioned to the empty seat next to him. "Brius, this is my sister, Tilla." Tilla?

Brius gave Samira a thick lipped grin, and she saw that he was missing most of his upper teeth. The tip of his tongue poked through the gap in the front, and it gave him a wet lisp when he talked. "Well! Hello then. You never said you had a sister."

Samira had been in these kinds of situations with Caius enough to know how to play along. "I'm visiting," she said. "From the west."

"You picked quite a time to visit, lady." Brius laughed deep in his throat and leaned over to look into Caius' mug. "Half gone, blast you. Where's a server?"

"Brius is the new friend I told you about, Tilla." Caius smiled winningly across the top of his mug. "Remember, the one who helps dispose of excess property?"

He was a fence, then. "Ah, right. You did mention him to me. The best in Klubridge, as I recall."

Brius was looking for a server, but that brought him back into the conversation. "It's good to be known. By the right people, you see. Some people, you don't need to be known at all." He grinned again, and Samira returned the smile. Where was this going?

"I told you about Brius' ability to handle goods, but I think I neglected to mention that he also can acquire nearly anything you need as well."

"Nearly, pah," Brius said. "You need it, Brius can get it." He took the beret off and slapped it onto the table before scratching at his hair. "Usually."

Caius leaned in, sympathetic. "Troubles, my friend?"

Brius gestured toward the door, toward the street. "You've seen what they're doing? The whole bleeding city's been shut."

"We did comment on the traffic, didn't we, sister?"

"Mhm," Samira said, watching this play out.

"It's the Kites that shut it down. Looking for some mage or other."

Caius said, "It must be somebody serious that they're looking for."

Brius shrugged. "Must be, but I wouldn't know. Brius just hears

127

what he hears, and that was just that they're keeping everybody from coming in and out those gates."

"That must make it hard for you to do business," Caius said with a sympathetic pat on the man's shoulder.

"Had a wagon supposed to come in today, but of course they had to turn back. Wouldn't do to have the watch digging through my affairs, now."

"Not a bit. So you don't know anything else about why they've shut the gates down?"

Brius shrugged. "Just as I said it. They think there's some mage they want on the loose here. Dumb as a lump of kittens, all of them. Whoever it is, they're probably long gone from here, and now Brius has to get the punishment."

Caius looked into his mug again, and Samira picked up the thread. "Surely a man as resourceful as Brius would have some way around them. Yes?"

Brius looked at her, then at Caius, and then back at her. She was giving him her most earnest smile, complete with raised brows and wide eyes. At last he gave that gapped grin again. "You know old Brius. Always a way through, and if not, a way over or under." He leaned into the table on his elbows and lowered his voice to a whisper. Samira doubted anyone else was listening to their conversation, but she leaned in and humored him. He tapped at his temple. "Always a plan working up here. They've shut the gates, but they don't have enough bodies to cover the harbor."

The simplicity of it stunned Samira. "The Kites are stopping traffic in and out through the gates, but they aren't checking the boats?"

"I told you, stupid as a pile of pups. You need anything, Brius can still get it for you, and don't you forget it."

"We won't," Caius said. He looked at Samira as he clapped a friendly hand on Brius' back. "I'm afraid we have to make our exit now, though."

"Not even going to join me in a drink?" Brius looked wounded.

"Tell you what, my friend." Caius flipped a coin onto the table. "Your first one's on me."

"Well then," Brius said, and Samira saw he'd already palmed the coin.

"It was nice to meet you, Brius," she said as she rose to follow Caius.

Back out in the street, they took a right and headed uptown. The foot traffic thinned in that direction and gave them an opportunity to talk without bodies and ears packed around them.

"Now I'm your sister?" Samira asked with a smile.

"The closest thing to it, anyway. You played that well."

"And Brius? How do you know him?"

"That disappearing box I had imported a few years ago? That was from a shipper who moved away a few months ago. Brius took over his business."

"Ahh." It was a massive, coffin-like box with a false back. Caius had incorporated it into the Akithar show for a few months and used it to disappear himself mid-show, only to seemingly materialize in the middle of a crowded balcony box, much to the gasping amazement of the audience. Naturally, everyone in that balcony box was a plant. Caius had bored of the disappearing box's banality after a while, and he had it stowed away in one of the many storage rooms in the theater ever since. "I suppose Brius confirmed it. The city is shut down for a mage hunt."

Caius nodded. "They've never done that in the time we've been here. Not just to find a mage."

"Not unless it was someone extraordinary," Samira agreed. "What do you think?"

Caius slowed his pace and stepped to the side of the road to stand by a pillar holding up a store that was closed during the daytime hours. "I think this is something we need to take seriously."

"You think they're after you."

"I don't know. If they were after me, Mollor could have taken me today. But they're still stopping everyone at the gates and searching."

"So," Samira said, "they at least aren't sure you're the one they're after."

"No, but the gates could be just due diligence. You didn't see the commander in my office today. She thinks I'm the one they want."

"Then why didn't she take you?"

He chewed at his lower lip, and his eyes flicked to watch the people passing by. "She knows she's here for a mage, and she thinks I'm her target, but she has to make sure. They're going to be watching the Chamberlain. They'll wait for me to slip up, for some chance to pin me with evidence."

"That doesn't sound like the Empire," Samira said. She was used to seeing whole buildings emptied by squads hunting for magic users. Soldiers would take them all in and process all of them for various trumped-up crimes, just to make sure they got something for their efforts. "This is too pointed, too precise."

"I agree. There's something special about this one."

"What does that tell you?" she asked.

"That Commander Mollor is someone we should fear." Caius pressed his lips together in a resigned frown. He exhaled and looked at Samira.

She knew the expression and had dreaded it for the decade they'd been in Klubridge. She wanted to disagree, to tell him there was another way, but she already knew they were in agreement. "It's been a good run, but it's time to go," she said.

Caius nodded sadly. "We've been here long enough for people to know us. They talk."

"They know Akithar, but they don't know you. Who you really are."

"All the more reason for us to end this before they find out."

Samira scowled at the street and cursed under her breath at the Kites, off rambling through her city somewhere. "What do we do about the Chamberlain? It's everything we have. And so many people rely on it. Apak, Reykas—"

"We've known this was coming. It's happened before, and we've moved on before. We just got to stay here a little longer than we've had anywhere else."

"But the others," she protested.

"They can come with us. We aren't just a pair now. We're a family, and everyone who relies on us will be welcome to come with us. In fact, I think anyone who stays behind will be in as much danger as we're in right now."

Samira drew her eyebrows low, and her forehead crinkled in consternation. She didn't like it, but she knew Caius was right. They had settled in Klubridge years ago and purchased the theater, but a part of her always knew they eventually would have to leave it. It had become home, and they had built relationships there, not to mention a reputation that had served Caius well. But all of it could come tumbling down in tragedy if they stayed and the Kites ran them down. The time of the Great Akithar was ending.

"Okay," she said at last.

"Okay?" Caius asked.

"Okay. How do we do this?"

～

B rius had been right. There were police at the port, but they hadn't shut it down like the gates. Surely it wasn't an oversight. The Empire was calculating, cruel, and seemingly omnipresent, but it was not foolish. If the harbor was open, Samira was sure there was a reason and a plan behind it. Nevertheless, it was the only way out, and that was where they went.

The shore of the Madigus Sea bordered Klubridge on the east, and the city operated one of the largest harbors for imports on the eastern coast. There weren't many notable exports, and larger ports to the north had a greater hand in trade, but there never was an end to the crates shipping into Klubridge. With its heavily urbanized center and the city's sprawl blocked by its walls, Klubridge lacked any trace of agrarian culture. There were a few small farms dotting the west and south, just outside the city, but the bulk of the food and provisions came in by boat, most from the Broganwell-Westfall holdings.

The shipyard was where the many shopkeepers got their goods as well, and while there was a booming fashion industry in the city, nearly all the threads and materials that supported it were imports. Beyond the necessities, though, were the countless crates that arrived daily full of luxuries to be trollied uptown and dispersed among the wealthy.

One such delivery was being unloaded when Caius and Samira reached the docks. A small retinue from some important citizen waited dutifully beside a small ship as the crew hoisted box after box onto the pier. The lead representative had pried the lid off the first crate and was digging through the hay packed inside to examine the contents. Samira spotted a statue of Khealdir buried in the box as they passed by. It looked to have been marble, no doubt an expensive addition to some collection of religious relics hidden in the upper floors of a mansion somewhere on the north end of town. As wealthy as the purchaser likely was, Samira doubted any amount of money would stop Commander Mollor if she got wind of religion in the city. Worship and idolatry were second only in punishable infractions to the practice of magic, and the two frequently traded places in that ranking, depending on who you asked.

Caius had brought them up some stairs that led away from the ships, and they now were standing on a stone balcony overlooking the proceedings. Caius held his hand up to shade his eyes as he surveyed the boats that were currently docked. Samira scanned them as well, but she knew Caius knew them better than she did. She'd been running the theater for most of the waking hours she'd spent in Klubridge, while Caius had seen to their everyday needs. Those needs often involved supplementing the theater's income, especially in the early days, and that's how he came to know characters such as Brius and how he could recognize exactly which ships would bend the rules a bit and which ones would turn them over directly to the Kites.

Still, Samira knew a few of the captains with whom they had dealt, and she spotted the familiar green and black checked flag flying from the mast of an unusual, multi-decked galleon at the same time Caius did.

"There," he said, pointing.

"Not on your life," she said. "Ergo Drass is not the solution to this."

"Then what is, Samira? If you have a better idea, I'm ready for it."

"Don't you know any other ships? Anyone else we can trust to get us out of here?"

Caius shook his head. "Not that are docked in the harbor at this exact moment. Drass is a scoundrel, but we can trust him with this. Unless we didn't leave at all. There are so many people in the city. We could close the theater and disappear into the crowd. We have places to stay, and we could keep watch."

Samira knew that wouldn't work. "You're talking about hiding the entire company. We might get away with that for a few days, maybe a week, but what do you think would happen when the Kites saw that we'd left the theater? There'd be a bounty on our heads."

The Great Akithar was a celebrity in Klubridge, and while Caius could change his appearance, too many people knew the woman who managed the theater. And affections in the city ran only as far as the next coin would reach. She'd be sold out at the first chance. Maybe even by someone in the company, reluctant as she was to admit it. Neither of them wanted to leave, but they both knew she was right. If they stayed, they eventually would be found, and likely sooner rather than later.

"But does it have to be Drass?" she asked.

"I don't know any of these other ships," Caius said again. He gave them another look but shook his head. "Drass is the only one we know here who wouldn't hand us over. He hates the Empire as much as we do. Maybe more."

"The last time you trusted him—"

"I know. We lost money on that deal, but that was because he prioritized smuggling supplies to the rebels over doing illicit business with a bunch of wealthy theater people. Things are different now, and he'd be striking a blow to the Kites by helping us."

"But he still is a mercenary. He's going to want money."

"No doubt. Let's just hope we can afford him."

They made their way back down the stairs and turned left on the boardwalk. The planks were old and knotted and stained with grease, fish innards, and who knew what else. Samira stepped over ropes sailors had tossed aside and walked around a few wet spots. The last thing they'd need was for her to slip and tumble into the sea. The walk was thankfully short, and before long she saw the bow of Drass' ship peeking around a smaller one. She saw the name burned into the hull: *Sephare*. Samira didn't know who Sephare was or had been or even if she existed, but she appreciated wordplay on a seafaring vessel.

"Caius Harrim!" a voice bellowed from above. Samira looked up and saw the old pirate peering down from the deck. He exaggerated a double take and yelled down, "And Samira Tandogan as well! It must be an auspicious day indeed!"

Caius went first up the ramp to the ship, and Drass met him with a firm handshake. He offered his hand to Samira as well, and she congratulated herself for hesitating only a second before taking it. The upper deck was empty except for Ergo Drass and two crew. The sailors were cleaning the railings and watched Samira and Caius with curious gazes they didn't even try to hide. Drass glanced at the two men and then jerked his head aft. "Let's retire to my office. Too many birds with ears in this harbor."

They followed him back to the quarterdeck, and Samira watched his loping stride. Drass was a man more accustomed to being on the sea than on land, and he looked and dressed the part. His outfit was a variation on the classic Imperial naval uniform, with a long, braided coat in dark blue, set with golden epaulets on the shoulders. A lifetime at sea and a tendency not to alter his wardrobe had left Drass' uniform sun bleached and salt stained in spots that would have driven a proper naval captain to shame. Drass was no proper captain, though, and had not been for many years. He made his living skimming just below the notice of the Empire and mixed legitimate imports and contraband in his cargo holds below decks.

He ushered them into his office, and Samira had to admit that it was impressive. The room was larger than her and Caius' offices combined, and a red velvety material covered its curved walls. Windows at the front looked out the back of the ship, and Samira swallowed heavily as the horizon bobbed, reminding her they no longer were on dry land. There was a wide and deep black desk at the center of the room, with bird skulls ornamenting the corners. They looked like ivory, and Samira commented, "This is Imperial work."

"The lady knows her furniture," Drass said with a wry smile. He offered no further explanation before dropping himself into a padded chair bolted to the floor behind the big desk. "Now," he said with a twinkle in his eye, "what strikes your fancy today?"

Straight to business, then. Caius took one of the chairs facing the desk, and Samira took the other. Caius leaned in. "We're not buying or selling today, Ergo. We're seeking passage out of the city."

Drass' bushy gray eyebrows raised, and he scratched at his wiry and equally gray beard. "Well, then. That's something else, isn't it? Where are we going?"

"Where are you headed?"

Drass didn't respond at first. He leaned back in his chair and studied the two of them for a long moment, and Samira was sure he was going to turn them away. But he didn't. "Just the two of you?"

"No," Caius said. "The whole company."

The pirate chuckled. "Caius Harrim, I'd say you've stepped into something this time. This will be one way passage?"

"It will. And the sooner the better."

"Well, there's the task," Drass said. "I'm already secured for transport. I don't have a problem with letting a few more passengers aboard, but we're in port until my shipment arrives."

"Time really is of the essence," Samira said.

Drass frowned at her. "For you, for me, and for those who entrust me with their goods. I will not be shoving off from this city without my cargo." He looked back to Caius. "I can take you, and gladly, but you'll have to wait until then. It's expected within the week but could be delayed due to the excitement in this city, which I now am thinking makes a bit more sense."

Caius looked to Samira. She knew he wanted to take the deal, but he was deferring the final decision to her. She chewed at her lip and tried to think of something, anything else that they could do. But this was it. Any other captain would anticipate that bounty on their heads and would be just as likely to turn them in preemptively. The city ran on money, and commerce was the language of the ships. "All right," she finally said. "Let's do it."

Caius nodded, and Drass nodded back. "Now," Drass said, "there is the matter of your transport fare."

"What will we owe you?" Caius asked.

Drass leaned back again and looked to the ceiling as he counted. "Fare for your entire company, and leaving, I expect, without the notice of some particular red birds. You'll need provisions for the journey, and I wager you'll end up being more trouble than I'm bargaining for." He rocked forward and rested his forearms on the desk. "Twenty thousand seri."

Samira balked. "Twenty thousand! That's robbery!"

"What business did you think I was in?" Drass asked her with a slow smile. "Twenty thousand, and you all get passage on my ship, no questions asked, no Imperial involvement."

"We don't have that," Samira said. She did the bookkeeping and knew exactly what the Chamberlain's coffers looked like, and they were nowhere close.

"We can get it," Caius said, and Samira stared at him incredulously.

"Where are we going to get twenty thousand seri?" she asked.

"We'll get it," he said again with a finality that made her realize he already had a plan. She hadn't liked the situation to begin with, and now it was getting worse, but she held her tongue.

"You'd better be quick in getting it," Drass said. "I'm leaving after my cargo arrives, whether you're on board or not."

"We'll have it in time," Caius said.

"All right, then." That was good enough for the old pirate. The twenty thousand clearly didn't matter to him, and his client would pay him well for the cargo he planned to smuggle, regardless of whether they made it onto his ship.

"Where will we be going?" Caius asked.

"Wherever I'm going," Drass responded with a wink.

CHAPTER 11

Lizandra pressed the back of her hand to Reykas' forehead. "You're freezing and soaked with sweat. You're not going out there."

Reykas looked like he wanted to protest, but Lizandra gently pushed him back on the chaise. He started to sit up again but couldn't manage it, so he flopped back and stayed for once. It was always like this. He did too much and tried too hard, and when the chills came, he still thought he could fight through them.

They were in the smaller of the dressing rooms, tucked into a back corner of the Chamberlain, away from the bustle of the crew making preparations for tonight's weekly show. Small though it was, Lizandra loved the room. Its walls were a pale yellow, and silks of various colors draped down from the ceiling, giving it a light and happy feeling that so much of the rest of Klubridge lacked. The furniture in here was sparse but plush, comprising the chaise on which she currently was trying to keep Reykas, an accompanying chair, and a dressing table with a large, round vanity mirror. It reminded her of her people, of the carnival that had raised her, and she always felt secure back here.

Lizandra's straight, white-blonde hair normally hung to her waist, but she had it wound into a bun while she tended to Reykas. She had not yet changed into her stage costume, a gauzy and silky gown that would flow with her as she spun and moved under the lights on the stage. Reykas already was wearing his costume, a billowing white shirt and black pants, but Lizandra knew she'd have to change him out of them soon enough. His sweat had already bled through the material, and it clung to him like a second, wrinkled skin.

"I have to get up," Reykas said, never truly relenting in his protests. "We have to perform."

"You're not fit to sit up, much less perform, my love." She rested her warm, pale hand on the side of his cold, dark face. "You know you have to rest, and this will pass. You can perform again later, but leave that to me for tonight."

He stuttered and coughed before speaking again. "You cannot do it alone. The animals—"

"I won't do the animals tonight. I'll use one of our older routines. This is an off-season show, and these people will be nearly as awed by some contortions and tumbling as they would be by our animals." She smiled at Reykas and wiped a bead of sweat away from his right eye. "They're not hard to please."

Reykas sighed, and Lizandra knew she had won at last. This same script played out every time his illness surfaced, and she knew the lines by now as well as she knew the twists, the bends, and the leaps in every performance they had done together. Reykas was resting now, but he asked, "Have you told Samira yet?"

"She's out with Caius on some errand. I told Apak."

"He agreed to have you performing alone?"

"Well, he grunted, but I took that as agreement. You know Apak." She sat on the edge of the chaise beside Reykas and took his hand. "I need to talk to you about something else. Something is happening in the city."

"What is it?"

"I don't know yet, but a Scarlet Kite came to the theater today."

Reykas was fully alert again, and he shifted as if to sit up, but

Lizandra squeezed his hand and laid her other hand on his arm. Weak as he was at the moment, he still felt as strong and sturdy as ever. His lean muscles tensed with the strain of the illness, and she could feel his damp forearm shaking with the effort, almost imperceptibly.

"Peace," Lizandra whispered. "She came and asked questions, but she didn't stay long. Dorrin saw her and told me."

"Scarlet, and not Azure? What did she want?"

"I don't know." She stopped talking and weighed whether she should continue. Reykas was sick and shouldn't be excited, but his illness was precisely why she had to keep going. "I think she may be looking for you."

Reykas frowned but didn't argue. "She could be hunting a mage. She could be here after Caius."

"She could, but it seems bigger than that. Apak said they've shut the gates. They never do that, not even when they're looking for a mage, unless it's something big."

Reykas sighed again, and Lizandra knew she didn't have to finish explaining her fears. He understood, because he lived with the same fears. The Kites usually showed up to hunt magic, but that wasn't their only assignment. They were enforcers of the High Lord's will regarding the welfare of all peoples of the Empire, and that extended to culling the mortally sick from the population. A sneeze was something to be hidden when Kites were near. Coughs were to be suppressed. Sniffles could be a symptom of something worse—something incurable that could spread and infect all of Teshovar. Lizandra had protected Reykas and helped him hide his condition since she first met him, when she was fourteen and he was sixteen. It seemed like ages ago. Had it really only been five years?

"But no one knows," Reykas said. "How could they?"

"You've never said anything to anyone outside the company," Lizandra said.

"Of course not. No one knows," he said again.

"Then it could be someone within the company."

"No, Lizandra." The look he gave her was part reproach and part disappointment. "No one here would do that to us. We are family."

"Can you stake your life on that, though? Mine?"

"Absolutely." He was loyal, and she loved him so much for that. But she feared that his loyalty was fierce enough to be his undoing.

She held his hand and bore his stare in silence as she constructed the next thing she needed to tell him. She finally said, "We need to leave, Reykas. It doesn't matter how they found out, but they might know, all the same. You know the city doesn't close its gates unless the Empire compels it, and a quarantine would fit that better than hunting out a mage would. We have to leave, and soon."

"We cannot do that," he said. "We have a duty to Samira. To Caius, Apak, everyone else."

"That's precisely why we must go, my love. If the Kites are after us, we'd bring them straight to the theater. We may already have done so." Her eyes pleaded for him to understand, but she already could tell it was a lost cause.

Reykas shook his head slowly. "I love you more than all the world, but we cannot simply flee. If the Kites already have come here, then they already have met Caius and likely suspect that there is more to him than he would have them believe. I will not abandon him or anyone else under this roof."

That had been what Lizandra expected, but she had hoped to sway him. She bent to press her forehead against his clammy hand before kissing his forehead. She knew her lips felt fiery hot against his skin when he was in this state. "Okay," she whispered, her face next to his. "We'll stay. And I'll kill anyone who tries to take you from me."

Reykas' chills subsided after two hours, and he could walk with assistance after three. He still was in no condition to even consider stepping on the stage tonight, but he at least had accepted his lot to watch from the wings. He had also refused to consider leaving the theater company, and Lizandra eventually gave up on talking about it. Reykas was sitting up on the edge of the chaise, and Lizandra had just finished changing into her costume when a knock came at the door.

"Enter," Reykas called. His voice was back, deep and rich, and it made Lizandra smile into the mirror as she fastened a clip into her hair, now hanging in shimmering sheets. That voice just might be her favorite sound in all the world.

The door opened slowly, and Lizandra knew it was Oreth before he even poked his head into the room. He always was tentative and nervous around her, especially when Reykas was present. Oreth idolized Reykas, but he very obviously adored Lizandra. He was coy about it and thought he kept it hidden, but Reykas and Lizandra had shared many amused glances in Oreth's presence. One such glance passed between them just then, Lizandra catching Reykas' eyes in the mirror. He smirked and turned his head to watch the young man enter. Oreth was only a year younger than Lizandra, but his eternal wide-eyed enthusiasm blended with staring bafflement made him seem much younger than that.

"Reykas, hey, hello." Oreth was smiling at Reykas, and he very deliberately had not yet looked at Lizandra.

"Hello, Oreth," she said, and he practically flinched. He finally met her smile in the mirror. He was a sweet boy, and by all accounts he was learning well from Apak, and neither Lizandra nor Reykas begrudged him his crush or his hero worship.

"Hi, Lizzie." He slumped his head forward and scratched at his short red hair. "They sent me, er, Apak did, that is. The company is meeting. Or, well, some of us are."

Meetings before performances were not unusual, but Lizandra suspected there would be more to this one than simply planning out the show and making sure there would be enough spark slingers for Caius. Reykas looked to be thinking the same thing. "Did they tell you what this is about?" he asked.

"No, you know, they just had me come tell you, so I did. So, I guess I'll see you there?"

"You'll see us there in a moment. Thank you, Oreth." Lizandra gave him a smile, and he beamed back before practically bounding out the door. When it slammed shut, she looked back to Reykas in the mirror. "What do you make of that?"

His face had lost its lightness, and he was staring at the closed door. "I suppose we should find out."

Lizandra helped him up and out into the hallway, and they made it to the common room in back of the stage with only a few stumbles. The door was shut, unusual for that room, but Lizandra pushed it open and brought Reykas in with her.

Samira stood from her seat at the table next to Caius and went to take Reykas' other arm. "Is it bad today?"

"Not so bad," he said, but Lizandra and Samira shared a look that filled in the untold anguish.

"Let's sit you here," Samira said, and Lizandra helped maneuver him into the closest chair to the door.

Once she had him settled, Lizandra took the chair next to him and looked around the room for the first time. Ordinarily meetings were an open affair, with all the stagehands, crew, and performers included. Not so, this time. Samira and Caius were across the table, and on the other side of Samira sat Apak. He was ignoring the rest of them as he squinted at a tablet in front of him and scratched numbers onto it with a nubby pencil. Caius was handing something across the table to Apak. The engineer took it with some surprise, nodded to Caius, and tucked it into his vest pocket before resuming his calculations. Oreth was next to Apak, trying to pretend that he wasn't looking at Lizandra and instead was studying Apak's bizarre numerology. And beside Oreth sat the newest and smallest of their family, Dorrin.

"We're all here now," Caius said and stood. Apak put his pencil down and gave Caius his attention. "You've probably noticed that this is a closed meeting. We almost never have those, but this is important. As far as I know, you are the only ones who saw or know about the visitor we had today."

"The Kite," Lizandra said.

"Her name is Nera Mollor. She's a commander in charge of the Scarlet Kites. We don't know where the Azure Kites are or why Tereth hasn't made an appearance, but Samira and I were able to find out a little about this new one from some of my contacts at the docks and in the city center."

"Why is she here?" Reykas asked.

"She's hunting a mage," Samira said, "but there's something special about this situation. The Kites have closed down the city, and they don't do that for just every rogue magic user."

"And unfortunately, we don't know what makes this one special," Caius said. "Based on the commander's visit here today, we have to assume that she's after me. She didn't take me when she had the chance, though, so she may not be sure that I'm the one she's looking for. A watch captain I know near the Henburn Estate told us that Mollor has a reputation for being especially strict and operates by specific mandates. She wouldn't take me unless she's positive, so that could buy us some time."

"To do what?" Lizandra asked.

Caius breathed heavily before dropping his decision on the room. "We have to leave Klubridge. All of us."

It lay in the air, spoken, but still incredible. How could they just abandon this city? This theater? It was what they had built over the past decade, and it was all they had. Lizandra had been ready to flee with Reykas, but she had never considered Caius proposing that all of them leave.

"Preposterous," Apak said. He was looking down at the writing on his tablet again.

"Apak?" Caius asked.

"Where do you propose that we go? How do you propose that we get there? As you said, the city is closed."

"The gates are closed," Samira said. "The harbor isn't. For the time being, ships still are able to come and go."

"Why would they close the gates but not the port?" Lizandra asked. It didn't make sense.

Caius said, "That's something else we don't know. But we do have a captain willing to take all of us away from here. We can bring some of our belongings, but we'll need to travel light. We can relocate somewhere else and start again. There are other theaters, other cities."

"There's no other Klubridge," Lizandra said, and they all knew it was true. They might settle elsewhere and rebuild their company, but it never would be like it had been as a darling of theater row in the greatest city for the performing arts in the entire Empire.

"We can make it work," Caius said. "We have to. There's no alternative. If we stay here, the Kites will move on us."

Apak grunted and pulled his eyeglasses down off his nose. "When will we be leaving with this captain?"

"Soon. As soon as possible. We can't afford his fare just yet, but we will be able to."

"His fare?" Apak put the glasses back on his nose and looked at Caius with incredulity. "You say that we are in imminent danger, and now we must haggle with some ship's captain? Is he even someone to be trusted?"

"It's Ergo Drass," Samira said, and Apak scowled.

"He is a mercenary and a pirate," he said.

"He's our mercenary," Caius said, "if we can pay him. He's the only captain I would trust with this. Drass hates the Empire, and I don't worry about his deciding to cash in on turning us in to the Kites. He works with the rebellion and has just as much to lose as we do."

"It sounds more like he has much to gain. How much is he asking?"

"Twenty thousand seri," Samira said quietly.

The room was silent, and Lizandra almost laughed. That was more than they'd earned in the past three months combined, and she was certain the theater didn't have that much money readily on hand. Apak knew the numbers, too, and he did laugh, but it was an ugly thing that he spit out. "As I said, Drass is a pirate. We cannot afford twenty thousand seri. What did you tell him?"

"I told him we'd have it for him." Caius stared at Apak, and his confidence pushed Lizandra back in her seat. She glanced over at Reykas, and he was watching this drama unfold in silence. She took his hand, and he squeezed hers.

"This is preposterous," Apak said again. "We do not make that much seri, and you know it. If we must leave, then I am in favor of taking the ship by mutiny and forcing Drass to take us away."

"We're not on the crew," Oreth muttered.

"What?" Apak snapped.

"Don't you have to be on the crew to do a mutiny?"

Caius rapped his knuckles on the table, and Oreth and Apak looked back to him again. "We're not taking Drass' ship by force. He's an enemy of the Empire, the same as we are. We do not hurt our allies, even if they're just the enemy of our enemy."

"Your honor will end you up in a dungeon," Apak warned.

"Maybe so, but I'll at least have come by it honestly," Caius said. "We're not going to hurt anyone on our side. We never have, and we never will. Does anyone take issue with that?"

"You know I do, but carry on," Apak grumbled.

Caius ignored him. "We are in between seasons, but we're still running occasional shows like we always do in the off-season. We're the only theater on our block in a position to put on regular performances during the gap. The summer brings larger crowds into Klubridge than any other time of the year, and they're always eager to jump on any show they can find, this time of year. We always see increased ticket sales from new visitors, and we get another bump whenever we revamp our show. If we increase our ticket prices and present an entirely new performance, something they've never seen before, we should be able to make enough. We do have a small savings that we can combine with the tickets to make the twenty thousand. But we have to fill every seat consistently."

"How are we going to plan and build a completely new show that quickly?" Lizandra asked. "Reykas can hardly stand."

He pulled his hand out of hers, and she immediately regretted saying it. "I will be able to stand anywhere I need to stand," he said sharply. "We will do our part," he told Caius.

Apak spoke again, and he sounded somewhere between amusement and resignation this time. "You are saying that we must assemble a performance unique and outstanding enough to draw larger audiences than we ever have seen here, and you want to do it while charging every one of them more than they ever have paid to see a show in Klubridge?"

Lizandra could tell Apak finally was on board. The man was grouchy and less than cordial, but he couldn't turn down a challenge. She saw that Caius knew it, too. He gave a half smile. "That's about the size of it."

Apak slapped the table and began gathering his tablet, pencil, and other papers. "Then we had best put on a damned good show."

PART III
HARANIUM

CHAPTER 12

"How long have you known Caius and Samira?" Dorrin asked. He had his chin propped on both hands and was watching Apak sketch out ideas on a long scroll of paper. They were back in the biggest of the props rooms, where Apak had a long table of unfinished wood, across which were strewn various bits and bobbles on which he had been tinkering for the last hour.

Apak looked up over his small glasses but kept his head down, and his hand continued working on the drawing. "I have known them for a long time. For as long as they have been in Klubridge."

"You were in Klubridge before them?"

"I was." He drew a perfect circle with the practiced deftness of decades of experience, then turned it into a cylinder.

Dorrin followed the pencil with his eyes but soon grew bored again and asked, "What did you do before you knew them? Did you make props?"

Apak connected two lines with a third and pressed the back end of the pencil against his lower lip as he considered the new lines. He waited to draw again before responding. "I did not make props, but I already was an engineer. I owned a shop in the city."

"What did you sell?"

A brief and rare hint of a smile danced across Apak's mouth, and then it was gone again. "Do you know what automata are?"

Dorrin shook his head, and Apak laid the pencil down. He pushed himself up from the table where he had been working and rolled his shoulders once before walking to a plain-looking cabinet that he had placed into one corner. He pulled one of its two doors open and looked over the shelves. So many relics from the past, so many creations. These were the special ones. The ones he had not dared show to his customers and the ones he had not dared discard when his life moved forward from that tinker shop. He selected one off the second shelf from the bottom and carried it back to the table.

What he placed before Dorrin was an assembly of metal and wood, hundreds of pieces interconnected and intertwined. On the whole, the contraption had the basic rectangular shape of a metal box with holes in the sides to show the tiny machinery and inner workings. A spring was visible through a gap in the housing, as were multiple gears and rods, all small and connected in an intricate design. The top of the box was a wavy piece of metal into which Apak had carved many swirling lines. "The ocean," Dorrin said, reaching out a hand to trace a finger over the still waves.

"Ah, ah," Apak said, pulling the box away an inch. "You must look before you touch."

Apak reached his right thumb and index finger into a hidden nook near the bottom corner of the box, grasped a grooved stem, and began turning it. He watched Dorrin as the small machine clicked with each wind. The boy was watching what Apak was doing, but Apak could tell that he also was watching the pieces move within. That was good. He needed to understand these things if he were to learn the craft.

The winding stem gave a final click, and Apak released it. All the parts, those hidden and those exposed, lurched to life, and Dorrin's eyes widened. The metal sea atop the box shifted and rocked, and the carved lines cleverly conveyed the believable rise and fall of waves. A tiny ship of carved wood sprang up from the side of the box, suddenly afloat on the artificial ocean. The details on the boat, from the individually laid timbers to the little flag flying at the top of the mast, were incredible on that small scale.

Gears propelled the ship across the sea along a slotted track that was all but imperceptible in the cunning way the waves disguised it. When the ship had reached the midpoint, it slowed and halted, and a group of miniature people appeared on deck. Dorrin was leaning in closer now, his mouth open and his attention fixed on the display. The people on board the ship moved to the front of the deck and raised their arms. With a soft clank, a metal bouquet of flowers flew off the ship and disappeared into the sea. There was a brief pause, and the ship began to rock as the sea surged higher.

A head, as big as the ship itself, broke the surface of the water, and soon the figure of a giant woman came up from the ocean to loom above the boat. Seaweed cut from light, porous wood wrapped around her, and her hair was intricately beaded metal. She stared down at the ship with serenity, and the people on board, worshipers, raised their arms to her again and again. After a few seconds, the woman fell back into the sea, the people disappeared into the ship, and the ship snapped back around the side of the box. The ocean finished its rocking and came to rest as a still, solid lid.

Dorrin looked from the contraption to Apak and back again. "That was dice!"

Apak allowed another small smile and tapped the top of the box. "That is automata. That is what I made and sold before I knew Caius and Samira."

"Who were the people on the ship? Who was the lady? What were they doing?" Dorrin's questions came at a fast clip, and Apak waited him out before responding.

"Have you heard of Ikarna, Dorrin?"

"From the old grampa stories."

"Grampa stories?" Apak asked with a frown.

"You know, the ones everybody tells but knows they aren't true."

Apak shook his head. Of course the boy would not have known the truth of Ikarna, raised as he had been.

"Ikarna created the oceans. She is as old as time itself, and before there was water, there was Ikarna."

"She made all the water?" Dorrin looked skeptical.

"She did," Apak said.

"I've seen a lot of water, but I've never seen her."

"Ikarna created the wellspring of life, from which the oceans flowed. From which all water arose. The water you have seen, that you have drunk, came originally from that same wellspring."

"She's not around now?" Dorrin asked.

"Creating the wellspring of life was a hard task. She set the seas into motion and built a system that would replenish water and the life in it for all eternity. Only after ensuring that life could continue without her direct intervention did she allow herself to rest."

"Where is she now?"

"She sleeps wherever the waters flow. She is within every ocean, river, stream, even the puddles you see on the ground after the rain. And she is in the rain itself. She rests, but she always is with us, ready to return and help us if we need it."

"Is that what she was doing there?" Dorrin gestured to the automata. "She was coming back to help?"

"Precisely. She heard the pleas from those who know her and love her, and she awoke to bless them."

Dorrin was chewing at his cheek, his eyebrows drawn down. "I don't know about this. Scrounger always said there wasn't anything bigger than the High Lord."

"It sounds as if Scrounger is a fool," Apak said. He thought for a moment and reached into his vest pocket. From it he withdrew an oval trinket, the same one Caius had found and returned to him earlier. It was similar to a locket, hanging on a light chain, but it did not open. It was pale pink and had been shaped and formed from what Apak believed to be compacted sand and shell. The unmistakably serene face of Ikarna looked out from the carving, surrounded by swirls of engraved water. Apak looked at the small relief once more before handing it across the table. "Here, take it. I misplace this thing more often than not. At least I will know where it is if you have it."

Dorrin took it and looked into the goddess's face. Despite the boy's skepticism, Apak felt Dorrin could grasp some of the truth and the weight behind what he had been told. The boy looked up from the idol, seriousness across his face. "I'll take care of her for you, Apak."

Something inside Apak ached, and he wanted to say something meaningful, something appropriate to Dorrin. Instead, as always, he could summon nothing substantial that could convey his feelings into words. "Yes, well. We all have an obligation to do good where we can. I must be going."

Apak gathered the scroll and a few other documents and tucked them under his arm. With a last look around the workspace, he made quick strides to the door and left Dorrin alone in the room with Ikarna.

~

A pak felt agitated, and he made the walk to Caius' office a brisk one. His designs and sketches were in his hands, but his mind was on the conversation he had just had with Dorrin. Apak felt the absence of his totem acutely, and he wondered whether he had made a mistake by giving it to the boy. Perhaps Dorrin would discard it without a second thought. But no, surely he understood its importance and the magnitude of Apak's having given it to him. But perhaps he did not understand. Boys were wont to foolishness.

He pushed the office door open and entered to find Caius sitting at the side table, the theater's financial log opened before him. Samira stood to the side and was pointing at something in the ledger. They both started when Apak entered, and Caius said, "No need to knock. Just come right in anytime, I guess."

Apak closed the door behind him. "I did, thank you." Caius and Samira exchanged a smile as Apak came over to the table and dropped his documents and drawings before them.

"We were in the middle of something…" Caius began.

What could be more important than this? They had not just risked their very souls on the chance that a boy could learn about universal truths, as he had. Apak waved at the air. "I am certain you can resume this shortly. We must discuss the mechanics of our upcoming performances." He pushed the newest drawing in front of Caius, and Samira frowned down at it. Could they not see?

"What is this, Apak?" Samira asked. She smoothed the curled edge of the paper and traced one line with her finger. "Is this… Is that a kettle?"

"No, of course it is not a kettle," Apak snapped and turned the paper ninety degrees.

Samira studied the new orientation. "Nope, no idea what that is, then."

Caius gave a quick chuckle, and Apak slapped the tabletop with his palm. Caius blinked, and Samira drew back. He had their attention now, and they at least were taking him seriously. Had he stepped too far again? He thought he had. He took a breath. "I apologize for intruding on your conversation, but what we must discuss is a serious matter, and I ask that you save your mirth." Apak looked from one to the other, and they both gave him nods, so he continued.

"Caius, you have set before us the nearly insurmountable task of raising twenty thousand seri."

"Ten thousand," Samira said in a halting voice.

Apak frowned. "Ten? Not twenty?"

She slid his drawing aside and indicated the ledger she had been showing Caius when Apak entered. "That's what we were looking at," she said. "We can't sell the theater without drawing the Kites' attention, but we do have assets within it that we could liquidate quickly."

"We also have a small savings set aside," Caius added. "Samira estimates that we could raise enough from selling some of our equipment and fixtures from the theater to combine with the savings and leave us about halfway to our goal."

Apak leaned over the desk and made a show of studying the ledger. He was brilliant with numbers and math, but he had no head for finances. Not anymore, at least. Not since he ran his own shop, and perhaps not even then. His focus always was on the intricacies of machines and the grandness of their purpose, not on the resources necessary to bring them into existence. He had no interest in nor time for such annoyances. Still, he gave the logbook a long look and nodded his approval. Although he did not have a head for finances, he knew Samira did, and he trusted her estimation, even if he could not bring himself to tell her so.

"So we need ten thousand," she said. "Still a lot, but not quite as bad."

"Hm," Apak said and brought a thumb to his lip. "That still is a hurdle, but you are correct. It may be possible now." His attention snapped back to the drawings he had brought. "That makes this even more important."

Caius studied the papers again. "What are we looking at, Apak?"

"If we are to raise the ten thousand seri that we need, we absolutely must sell every seat for as many nights as we can, even after raising our price of entry. The audience will be available to us, with the dearth of other performances in the district, but we will be competing with our own previous acts. With our own reputation for marvels."

"It's always been a competitive job," Caius said.

Apak nodded. "And now, more than ever. If we are to draw the audiences at the rates we will charge, we must give them something miraculous on the very first night. We want for every member of the audience to tell two more people about what they saw, and then those two must buy tickets and tell others. And so on."

Samira spoke slowly. "We're in agreement, but we already knew that. Do you have a way for us to get the audiences excited? Something to spur the word of mouth?"

"I believe that I do," Apak said, and he could not help but feel a swell of pride and a hint of excitement. He rapped the central drawing with his knuckles. "This is the device that will bring us the attention we need."

There was a box at the middle of the drawing, and attached to it were cylindrical tubes extending out and downward. There were straps on one side, and Apak had rendered part of the drawing as a cutaway to show additional, smaller tubes, wires, and small coils hidden within.

"Tell me what this is," Caius said.

"I believe that it is an accepted truth that our audiences generally are easy to impress with sparks and pops. I designed the rods—"

"The spark slingers?" Samira asked.

Apak squinted at the name. "Yes, those. They serve us well, but they are expected now. A few sparks will not be enough to inspire the type of awe we need. That is why I have designed this. It is a harness that you will wear beneath a customized jacket," he told Caius. "The box will rest on your back. I still have adjustments to make in the design to flatten it sufficiently to prevent the audience from seeing its bulk. These tubes will run down your sleeves, and you can activate them with your hands without being noticed. The activators are powered by coils in the pack that must provide a substantial amount of energy. We will need a source of haranium for this to work properly."

Caius was nodding along with Apak, and when the engineer paused, he asked, "But what does it do?"

Apak could not help himself. His face split into a grin, and he said, "Simply put, it will ignite a blazing inferno that will consume your entire body."

CHAPTER 13

The next morning, Samira left home early and headed across town to the educational center of the city. Wealthy business-people had funded the Klubridge College of Finance nearly three hundred years ago. The founders had no genuine interest in higher learning or in edifying the city's next generation. Rather, they had tired of financing other buildings and projects and decided as one to pour their money into a school. Always trying to outdo the others, every Klubridge aristocrat always was throwing money at the targets most likely to get them public recognition, and the recipient of choice had been a small trade school that had been training up blacksmiths and builders for a few years. The new influx of money had chased off all hints of manual labor as the donors' names were carved into the fronts of new buildings that were sure to bring up a so-called better class of society.

Knowing nothing as well as they knew their own money, the founders insisted on the college having a focus on finance, and the name stuck. Over the centuries, the school diversified into more disciplines, but it still carried the same name, just as the buildings still bore the names of long forgotten gentry. Samira smirked as she neared the Treemore Library and wondered what old Treemore would have thought about the library becoming public and admitting the likes of her. Klubridge's upper class had always been toadies under the Empire, of course, and Samira enjoyed the blasphemy she was visiting upon the establishment with her presence, tainted by association with magic as Klubridge had branded her. The large wooden doors were propped open, and Samira went up the steps and through the entry.

The library was larger than it had any right to be, originally overbuilt with repeated payments from Treemore, whoever that had been. It had eventually filled up with books and documents, though, becoming the most extensive literary repository within hundreds of miles. Samira stopped in the entry hall and admired the enormous brass sculpture in the center of the room. It was, predictably, of a giant book, opened at the middle and trailing the brass tassel from a huge bookmark over the edge of the base where it stood. Treemore would not be accused of being overly creative.

Samira knew her way around the fiction shelves, but today she headed past them, farther back into the research stacks. She made her way through Philosophy, through Biographies, through Languages, past Military History. All the sections had their categories engraved on large metal placards that were affixed to square columns at the heads of the aisles. Agriculture, Geography, Mathematics.

She had reached the back of the library and craned her neck to look up at the open balconies of the floors above her. She could see others roaming through the upper stacks, mostly students by the looks of them. She headed for the curved wooden staircase at the back corner and climbed it to the second floor. Music. Medicine. There seemed to be no order to these categories. Why was Folklore next to Biology?

Shaking her head, Samira put her hands on the rail and leaned to look over the first floor. The library was mostly silent, but from here she could hear the shuffling of feet on the stone floor as students trundled their piles of lore from tables to shelves and back again. She looked up to the third floor, where the library offices were located. Samira pushed away from the rail and began climbing another flight of stairs. These were narrower, leading to the top floor. There were no books up there, just the staff, and the grandeur of the common areas tapered off as she reached the landing. This floor was more utilitarian, likely to save some of that precious Treemore seri.

She passed the first three offices and was halfway around the upper level before she found the door she wanted. The nameplate on the closed door said this was the office of Aquin Mirada. Samira tapped softly on the door, but in the silence of the library she thought her rap sounded like stones knocking together. Nevertheless, there was no answer. She tried again and waited. Still nothing. She cast a glance around at the other office doors across the open gallery but saw no one.

Samira looked back at the door and ran a hand through her hair. One more knock? She reached to tap at the door again, but midway there she changed her mind and tried the doorknob. It turned, and the door swung open on silent hinges, perfect for this audible crypt of a building. But, once the door was open, Samira could hear a voice coming from within. She leaned in cautiously and peeked around the door. The office was empty, just a small desk and a chair with two bookcases against the far wall, all lit by the morning sun through a large window in the side wall. The voice was coming from another doorway across the room.

"Hello?" she called into the office and flinched when her voice echoed back around the upper floor. Instead of calling again, she stepped inside and pushed the door shut behind her. The low sound of a voice was unmistakable now, but she couldn't make out what it was saying.

Samira sniffed at the air. Something sweet but unrecognizable, just present enough for her to detect. Intrigued, she moved farther into the office and stepped carefully past the desk, toward the far door. The other room was dark, but an occasional flicker of light from within hinted at a candle.

She hesitated at the doorway and placed her hand to the side of the opening, leaning just far enough in to hear the voice more clearly but not far enough to cross the threshold. It was talking low, repeating something over and over again. Samira still couldn't make it out, and the hushed tone made it impossible to discern anything about the speaker, but something about it sounded familiar. She squinted and leaned closer, and then she realized it was the old tongue, Aevash, a language that had been dead for hundreds of years. Banned, even, but Samira knew the sound of it because she heard Apak making similar quiet chants late at night, when he thought everyone else was gone. It was a prayer to the sea goddess, Ikarna.

Samira caught her breath, and the voice halted. She backed away, but it was too late.

"Hello?" The voice in the room was soft and tentative. It sounded scared.

Samira considered heading straight for the door, but she stopped herself. "I'm sorry. It's me." She leaned back into the door and this time peeked around the corner. "I didn't mean to intrude."

The room was completely dark, except for the single candle burning on a wooden table pushed against the near wall. Its meager flame hinted that this likely was a closet, small and compact with shelves along the two side walls and the back wall. Someone was kneeling before the table, and in the dim light Samira could see the woman's features only in vague silhouettes. The dark of the closet turned her into a spectral figure with a thick head of dark hair that draped out and down past her shoulders in tight corkscrews. Samira's eyes moved to the table, and she saw the remains of some sort of herb, partially burned in a bowl, alongside a small carved icon similar to the one Apak had.

The woman stood slowly from the floor. "Samira. This is not what is looks like."

"It's okay," Samira said. "I won't tell anyone. I just didn't know."

The other woman was silent for a moment. Samira felt her eyes on her from the dark room but could not see them. She took a hesitant step back, and some of the daylight from the office fell into the closet. If Samira's breath had caught when she realized the woman was worshipping Ikarna, it stuttered again when she saw the woman illuminated. Aquin stood slightly taller than Samira, and she was a few years younger. Her brown skin contrasted with the white scoop necked blouse she wore and with the blue scarf that draped loosely around her neck and reached down her back. She wore a green patterned skirt that hung nearly to the floor, the design a unique one but the style familiar to Samira from her time with Caius in the south, around Plier Gleau.

All of that was arresting, but it was her pale blue eyes that stole Samira's breath now and every time she'd looked into them for the past two weeks. Now that she could see them again in the light, Samira couldn't imagine how she hadn't seen them even in the dark. They seemed to glow of their own accord, staring back at Samira, still with doubt and some fear. The woman pushed back a strand of the thick hair that Samira knew was even darker than it had appeared in the closet's gloom, so black it looked nearly blue. This was the most beautiful person Samira had ever seen, and she still was not used to the vision.

"You didn't tell me," Samira started. "About Ikarna."

The woman spoke again, and her accent was slight. She was from the southern coast but had been in Klubridge for enough years to shift her speech. "It's just... research."

"Really. It's all right." Even so, Samira checked over her shoulder to make sure she had closed the office door before she continued. Her voice lowered. "I know about Ikarna. I told you about my friend, Apak. He worships her. You have nothing to fear from me." She took a cautious step forward and took Aquin's hand. "You never do."

Aquin stepped closer to Samira and pulled the door to the closet shut behind her. Her eyes flicked toward the outside corridor and then back to Samira. "What do you know about Ikarna?"

"Apak has told me about the wellspring and how she's worshipped. And I lived in Inport for a little while. A long time ago." She started to say more but forced herself to stop. "This isn't a problem, Aquin."

After another quick hesitation, the other woman sighed. "I am sorry. Truly. I never meant to deceive you."

Samira squeezed Aquin's hand and touched the side of her face with her other hand. "It's okay. Really. I understand why you didn't tell me. We've only known each other for a couple of weeks. And with the Scarlet Kites in the city…" She didn't have to finish. They both knew what would happen if the Kites found a worshipper of Ikarna.

Aquin managed a smile and tilted her face into Samira's hand. "Still, I should have known better. I do trust you, Samira."

They stood in silence for a long moment before Samira said, "The Kites are why I'm here, actually."

Aquin pulled back, stiff again. "What has happened?"

"You know they've shut down the city?"

"I heard as much from the students. No one can enter or leave?"

"That's right. They're searching for a mage. They came to the theater."

Aquin's eyebrows raised at that. "What do they want with you?"

"Nothing with me. We think they're after Caius."

"How serious is this, Samira?"

She hesitated again before answering. "We may have to leave the city. We have a way out, but we have to pay a smuggler for safe passage."

"You are leaving?" Aquin dropped Samira's hand.

"That's why I came here. I want you to come with us if we do leave."

"I cannot leave Klubridge," Aquin said. "My entire life is here."

"We can build a new life wherever we end up. You can be there with us. With me."

"You don't even know where you are going."

"Not yet. It's complicated, but we have to be prepared to leave."

"Why can't you stay? Why do you have to go? Why not just Caius?"

"You know I can't do that. He's my family. They all are. And we can't stay in the city. With the gates closed, it's only a matter of time before the Kites come back, and next time it will be worse."

Aquin walked around her desk and dropped into the chair, her face sullen. "So you came here to tell me we are finished if I do not leave my entire life to go off with you and some smuggler."

"No, that's not it."

"That sounds like it is indeed it."

Samira wiped her hand over her face. This was not going at all like she wanted or hoped it would go. "The plans haven't been settled yet. I just wanted to tell you what's happening before anything happens. We don't even have the money to pay the smuggler yet."

"Will you be selling the theater?"

Samira shook her head. "We can't. The Chamberlain is too well established. If we tried to sell it, we'd surely draw attention from the nobles uptown."

"And then from the Kites," Aquin finished.

"Right. We're going to try to earn the seri with additional performances. Apak—he's our engineer—is developing new ideas. We're... what?"

The corners of Aquin's mouth had quirked upwards. "Do you have any idea how ridiculous this is? You are putting on a magic show to earn money to pay a smuggler to take you away from magic hunters. Was the goal to make the plan as convoluted as possible?"

"No," Samira muttered.

"A pity, because you already would have succeeded." Aquin sat forward and propped her chin on her hand. "You see how foolhardy this is, yes? You are smart. That is one of the many reasons that I care about you."

Samira groaned. "Caius refuses to steal the money. And we have to pay this pirate to get us out of the city. There's no other way that we've been able to find."

"His principles will be your undoing."

There was no other chair in the office, so Samira put her back against the wall and sank to the floor beside Aquin.

"What is the plan?" Aquin asked. "How are you going to earn this seri from a few shows?"

"We need a spectacle big enough to draw crowds consistently. Enough to fill the theater night after night, and we're raising the ticket prices."

"You'll draw the Kites as well."

"They won't know the rest of the plan. As far as they are concerned, we're doing business as usual."

"But you're not. What are these ideas your friend is developing? Tell me about the spectacle."

Samira shook her head. "This is the part where it goes wrong. Apak wants to make a machine to turn Caius into some sort of flaming demon. He says the fire won't actually touch him, and he says he'll be able to control the size and intensity and possibly even the color of the flames."

"How does he plan to do that?"

"He has these hidden rods he wants Caius to hold under his sleeves. It's similar to some of the other tricks they've already done. But he's never wanted to set anyone on fire before."

"This does not sound safe," Aquin mused.

Samira threw her hands up. "And yet." She brought her hands down and ran them through her hair again. "Apak says he needs haranium. Do you know what that is?"

"Some sort of explosive, isn't it?"

"It's a metal that's been banned by the Empire. He wants to get some and use it to make coils or springs or something to power the fire machine."

Aquin accepted this in silence and waited a moment before angling her head down toward Samira on the floor. "This is the worst idea I've heard all week, and I work with university students." She dropped her hand down to take Samira's again. "I can't go with you when you leave, but I am here with you until then."

"We can't use haranium. It's too dangerous."

Apak looked at Samira over his glasses and then back down at the assorted parts in front of him. "Of course we can, and where have you been? And why are you smiling?"

"I'm not smiling."

"You are, and it is disconcerting. Particularly when you arrive ranting about explosive compounds."

"This is serious!" Samira closed the stage door behind her. "And that's exactly my point. I've been reading about haranium, and we're not putting Caius anywhere near it."

"You went away for a few hours, and you have become an expert on haranium? Is that what you mean to tell me?" Apak slotted a thin rod into a matching cylinder and pressed it home. It remained together for the briefest of seconds before the opposite end of the cylinder popped open, and a spring shot out across the room. It ricocheted off the nearest wall, and Samira heard it whiz past her, lost somewhere among Apak's other experiments, all strewn across shelves and piled into crates on the floor.

"What is that, anyway?" Samira asked and took a few steps closer to the workbench. Not close enough for flying debris to hit her, but close enough to see what looked like the dismantled innards of a large clock, only more dangerous.

"This will be one of the triggers for the device Caius will be wearing. It will fit through his sleeve, and he will activate it with his palm."

"Was that spring supposed to do that?"

Apak looked over his glasses again and frowned. "It is a work in progress."

The door behind Samira opened, and she turned as Caius came in. "Samira, you're back! Good. Apak wanted to show us what he's been working on."

"He's already been showing me. It flies into multiple pieces spectacularly," she said.

Caius gave her a wry smile that Apak wouldn't notice. They both had borne witness to Apak's creative process. It always began with a brilliant spark of an idea before crashing into repeated failures, eventually emerging with something more clever than they ever anticipated. At present, he was in the failure part of the sequence.

"Where did you go?" Caius asked. "I wanted to go over the numbers from last night but couldn't find you."

"She was undermining my plans. That is where she went," Apak said. He picked up a pair of magnifying goggles from the workbench and sat his glasses to the side. He wiped at the goggles' lenses before slipping them onto his head.

"I was at the library," Samira said.

"Seeing your librarian," Caius said with a sly grin.

"You've been talking to Reykas too much. I also did some reading while I was there. How much do you really know about this haranium, Caius?"

He shrugged. "I know it's dangerous, if that's what you're getting at. But I trust Apak to make sure I'm not roasted alive."

"Did you know the Empire uses it to scourge entire towns?"

"That can't be true. Can it, Apak?"

Apak was peering through the goggles at some tiny metal parts but nodded. "Oh, yes. It is an extremely efficient and effective tool for rapid extermination. It has not been used in that manner for several hundred years. Peregrine had it banned after his own soldiers mutinied and used a supply of haranium to level one of his own castles."

"Even the High Lord has some sense every now and then," Samira said.

Caius frowned. "If it's not used anymore, where would we even find it?"

"It still can be found, even here in Klubridge. The High Lord may have outlawed it from military applications, but he most certainly has no qualms in using it elsewhere." Apak gave Samira what she assumed was a withering look, but the goggles made it hard to know for sure. "Haranium has been distilled into metalworking. It has proven to be quite useful when forged properly."

That hadn't been in any of the books Aquin had helped her find. "Then it turns inert? It's not explosive anymore?"

Apak chuckled. "No, no. It still is rather explosive. It now tends to be used primarily for disintegration canisters produced for Imperial use. An item is placed within, the haranium is activated with an agent, and the container implodes in a small and controlled blast."

"That's no more reassuring than anything else you've told me," Samira said. And then to Caius, "There has to be something else we can do. We can't sell the theater, but we can get the money somewhere else. We can borrow it."

"Who would loan us that much money? Especially while the city is closed down? This is the only plan we have, and it's going to be okay." Caius looked like he truly believed it. "Like I said, I trust Apak. If it were not safe, he wouldn't have me doing it."

"I would not call it safe, exactly," Apak said. His attention was back on the small parts spread before him. "However, I can assure you that I will minimize the risk. In the end, you will see that the risk is worth the benefit." He flipped the goggles up and gave Samira and Caius a genuine smile. "Sparks and bangs, my friends. Sparks and bangs."

The argument went on for another hour, and Samira eventually had to accept that it was not one she would win. Apak was dead set on putting together this device that would make Caius burst into flames, and Caius was showing even less sense than usual by agreeing wholeheartedly. Samira suspected he even was looking forward to seeing how it worked and what it would be like for fire to envelop him on the stage. That's how he had always approached these kinds of things. Commit to the outlandish, and deal with the practical later. It was bad enough that he'd have to do it once, but the plan was for him to pull off this trick night after night, until they had earned enough money to pay Ergo Drass.

Samira had racked her brain to invent an entirely different plan, but she could come up with no better illusion. Apak was right when he repeatedly asserted that bangs and flashes were what the audiences wanted to see. Caius had tried dozens, perhaps hundreds of tricks over the years. The cerebral ones were the most interesting and confounding, but they had nowhere near the impact on the crowd that fire and sparks had. It had to be something showy and dangerous.

But perhaps they didn't even need to earn the money that way. Caius wouldn't hear of forcing Drass to waive his fee, and he also would not approve of robbery. He was adamant that they not commit any crimes that would hurt the innocent people of Klubridge or those who might side with them against the Empire. If they stole seri from one of the city's banks, the bank would shuffle funds out of the accounts of its poorer clientele to ensure that the theft impacted no Imperial accounts. Bank robbery was out of the question, then.

What if there might be a different way out of the city? The gates were closed, but the guards wouldn't have descriptions of all of them. And even if they did, surely it would be easier and less expensive to pay off a couple of guards to let them pass than it would be to pay Drass' exorbitant fee. She had already mentioned that possibility to Caius, and he had disliked the element of risk. There would be guards willing to take a bribe and look the other way, but many of them were devoted to the cause of the Empire, not just to its coin. If they approached the wrong guard, they could hasten whatever the Scarlet Kites had planned for them.

So, haranium it would have to be. Samira sat at the meeting table with the rest of the company again and scowled at her having believed she could research the problem away. It was foolish and a waste of the day. Her mind turned to Aquin, and she thought perhaps it had not been an entire waste. She might have occasion to go see her librarian again sometime soon.

"I'm sorry, but did you say you are going to set Caius on fire?" Lizzie's question snapped Samira's attention back to the meeting.

"He will appear to burn, but the flames will not touch him," Apak said, less testy than he'd been when Samira had confronted him earlier. She guessed he'd chalked that argument up as a win, and he didn't need to argue as strenuously now that he had Caius on his side.

Lizzie laughed and opened her hands. "This is insane. You're not setting Caius on fire. Does no one else have a problem with this idea?"

Samira considered voicing her objections again, but she knew there was no use. The plan was decided, and going against Caius and Apak would not be good for the unity the company needed, going into this opening series of elaborate performances. Both Apak and Caius glanced at Samira, and Caius favored her with a subtle nod of thanks when he realized she would not protest.

"Apak is working out all the details, and this will be perfectly safe,"

Caius said. "I have no doubts about it, and you shouldn't, either. Let's focus on the rest of our plan."

Lizzie looked to Samira, and Samira felt like a traitor when she returned a tight smile to the girl. Lizzie sighed and sat back in her chair, her arms crossed over her chest. She wasn't happy with the plan, but she wouldn't try to block it.

Caius continued, "What we do need from you and Reykas is a new routine. Something so creative and amazing that it'll have everyone on the street talking about it."

Lizzie looked at Reykas, sitting beside her, and said, "We've been talking about some ideas. We don't have anything ready to show you yet, but we'll get it done."

"Fire would enhance those ideas," Apak said.

Samira scowled at him. "Ignore Apak, Lizzie. You and Reykas will come up with something good."

"Well," Caius said, "since the fire is the topic of the moment, let's talk about the haranium. It's very illegal and, presumably, very hard to get hold of. How much do you need, Apak?"

"Only enough to make two small coils. Less than a quarter pound of the material should suffice."

"That doesn't sound too bad," Caius said. "Where will we get it?"

"I have no idea," Apak responded.

That dropped into the room with an almost audible thud, and nobody said anything for a moment. Samira broke the silence. "You've been making all these plans that rely on our having haranium, and you don't even know where we'll get it?"

"I knew that we would find it somehow. We always find what we need."

"Apak, this is a highly explosive compound that you can't just pick up at the market."

Caius forestalled further argument with a raised hand. "Apak is right. We always figure something out, and we'll do it again this time. Apak, you said earlier that haranium isn't used by the military now, but the Empire still keeps it on hand."

"Yes, it still is used in a few applications."

"Like those boxes you mentioned."

Apak nodded. "Sensitive documents often are stored in containers built from a haranium alloy. It is a convenient way of disposing of them, should the need arise."

"That's a start, then," Caius said. "If we could get one of those containers, would you be able to use it for what you need?"

Apak rubbed at his eyebrows, and his forehead creased in thought. He was moving his mouth silently, and Samira knew he was doing calculations. After running through the numbers, he tilted his head. "Perhaps. Yes. I could extract the haranium, but we likely would need several of the containers, depending on their size." He motioned with his hands, describing something about a foot long and cylindrical. "I believe they usually are tubes, like this. If so, I would need… Five? Yes, five should provide enough of the compound."

"Where are we going to find five of these things?" Lizzie asked. "It sounds like finding one would be hard enough."

An idea struck Samira, and she blurted it out before she even considered restraining herself. "The bank!" Everyone was looking at her now, so she pushed ahead. "I was thinking we probably could find several at the bank. The banks run on an Imperial charter, and they handle money and property for all the nobility. Surely someone must have stored documents there in these haranium tubes."

Apak raised an eyebrow. "That is not a bad idea. The nobility likely have some of these containers in their residences, but it would surprise me to find more than one or two possessed by a single family. It is far more likely that we would find several together in a bank vault."

"But we don't rob banks," Samira added, dragging down her own suggestion.

Caius shook his head. "We don't, but this wouldn't be a bank robbery. We won't take any money. We're just after these cannisters, and it sounds like all of those belong to people we wouldn't mind hurting a little, anyway."

Reykas spoke for the first time. "We are thieves now? I am unsure about this, Caius."

"I can help!" Samira had forgotten that Dorrin was in the room, but there he was, sitting behind her and to the right. "I've stolen plenty of stuff, and I'm good at it."

Caius smiled at the boy. "Thank you, Dorrin. I don't think we need to send you off to do our thieving for us, but I do appreciate the offer. What we do need is more information. There are several banks in the city. We need to find out if any of them actually have these things and, if so, how we're going to get them out."

"Where do we do our banking?" Lizzie asked, looking to Samira.

"We don't keep Imperial accounts. It's too unstable for anyone who isn't nobility."

Lizzie scowled. "So you keep all the theater's savings stuffed in bags under your floorboards?"

"Not exactly," Samira said. The bags were in her walls. "But we do not use the banks."

Lizzie chewed at her lip and said, "The bank in the city center would be the most likely. It's the biggest one and is nearest the High Road. That's the bank the most nobles would be using."

"That makes sense," Caius said. "We need to verify that these tubes are in fact being kept there, and we need a plan for getting them out."

Lizzie gave another long sigh and spread her hands on the table in front of her. "As much as I can't believe I'm volunteering for this, I think I have an idea."

CHAPTER 14

Lizandra peered into the full-length oval mirror and squinted. "Is this truly how the rich people dress?" During her performances, she was sparing with makeup, using only as much as she needed to prevent her skin shining in the harsh lights. What she wore now was comical, her cheeks seeming to glow bright pink and her eyes rimmed with thick black borders that narrowed out to dark triangular points at the outside corners of both eyes. Her lips had become fuller, and Samira had colored them a bright, wet red that shimmered in the candlelight. She had also dabbed a conspicuous black mole just below and to the right of her mouth, punctuating the whole ordeal. It reminded her more of her uncle's clown routine than it did of any nobility she'd seen.

Samira removed a clip from her mouth to laugh and clamped it deftly into place behind Lizandra's head. "I'm afraid so. At least, this is what they look like when they're out on business and trying to look important."

Lizandra tilted her head toward Reykas, reclining in a nearby chair and watching the deceit unfold. "What do you think?"

"Hold your head steady," Samira said and pulled her face back toward the mirror.

From the corner of her eye, Lizandra could see Reykas' smile. "You look ridiculous."

"At least I know you'll never lie to me, my love."

"Never," he said. "And I would be lying by omission if I did not tell you how little I enjoy this plan."

"I'm not too keen on it, either, but it must be done," she said. "This Kite woman, Mollor. She's already seen Caius and Samira and who knows who else. She hasn't seen me, though. If she's put out notices on them, I'll duck right under."

"There, I think that does it," Samira said and released the tight grip she'd taken on the back of Lizandra's neck.

"Am I at last permitted to move?" Lizandra asked with a smirk.

"You can move yourself over to the vanity."

They were in a dressing room near the one Lizandra and Reykas customarily used, but this one was bigger, with walls painted blue and bare floorboards that someone had varnished to a shine. The white furniture around the room also looked as if it had gone unused for several years. This was where Samira had chosen to dress her up, though, and so that is where they had gone.

Before following Samira to the vanity, Lizandra angled her head to see what the other woman had done to her hair. She was used to leaving it long and straight, hanging past her slim shoulders. She knew it looked like white gossamer in the lights of the stage and flowed with entrancing fluidity as she and Reykas moved through their acrobatics. It wasn't often that she had done anything with her hair other than keep it straight and clean or pull it up into a bun for convenience, but now it was pulled up into an invisible array of clips and pins. Waves of hair curled up at the sides into thick rolls that barely shifted when she moved her head. Twin braids twined down at the front, draping back over her ears and getting lost in the rolls. She couldn't quite see what the back of her head looked like, but she imagined it was equally ornate and laughable. This was what she had asked for, though, so she hardly could complain.

Samira was waiting at the table, next to which she had hung a dress that she had scavenged from some costume closet in the deep recesses of the theater. The top was an embroidered bodice, gold at the center with eight red stones set into it in two vertical rows of four. Lizandra guessed they were cheap and painted paste, but at a glance they truly looked like gemstones. The sides of the bodice were a deep green and looked like velvet, with puffed shoulders and long sleeves to match. The dress draped to floor length with similar green fabric, opening in the front center to reveal a white panel of some silkier material. She knew it would be something cheaper than actual silk, but, again, it looked the part.

"You'll need help getting into this," Samira said, "but I think it'll fit you."

Lizandra shrugged off the dressing gown she'd been wearing, and it puddled to the floor. Reykas reached across to pull it out of her way as she approached the dress. He folded the gown onto the floor beside his chair and said, "Surely there is some other way to do this."

Lizandra smiled at him. "I appreciate your concern, and I understand it. I wouldn't want you going off on something like this. But it needs to be done, and I'll be fine. This is simply reconnaissance."

"If anyone suspects that you are not…"

"Lady Rethi Terake."

"They will not hesitate to jail you, or worse."

"Then I'd better make sure they don't suspect." She was smiling, but truth be told, she felt every bit as unsure as Reykas seemed. She really was the one best positioned to carry out this task, and it had to be done, but she was no actress. Lizandra had grown up a performer, but all of that had been true. She had built her stage persona around her own abilities and talents and physicality. She could flip, bend, and soar better than anyone. Better, even, than Reykas, but she never would say that aloud. She was no Caius, though. Lizandra had little experience with direct subterfuge, and most of the actual secrets others had shared with her over the years had been all but impossible to keep when she'd been pressed. If she did mess this up, it wouldn't be just the end for her, but likely for the whole plan and therefore the whole company. It would be the end for Reykas. She couldn't let that happen. Wouldn't. She would make this work, somehow.

"If there is trouble, you will run, Lizandra." Reykas was sitting forward now, his elbows on his knees, serious.

"I'll run," she agreed. She was midway into the dress, with Samira lowering it gingerly past the elaborate creation she'd spent the past hour making on Lizandra's face and head.

At last, the dress was on, and Samira tugged at hidden straps along the sides to tighten the bodice. "How does that feel?"

"Like you've found an overly complicated way to suffocate me," Lizandra said.

"All right, then." Samira stepped back to survey her handiwork. "Spin around."

Lizandra twirled in place, and the dress billowed out just a bit. The fabric was too heavy to flow like the gowns she was used to wearing, and the whole thing felt too constraining, but she would make the most of it. "Do I look the part?"

Samira nodded. "If I didn't know you, I'd try to rob you myself."

Lizandra was used to loose-fitting clothes, and she became more aware of how constricting this dress was with every step she took. It was tight around her chest and stomach, and she felt as though her ribs were being crushed every time she tried to inhale. Below the waist, the dress had more space, but there was so much material, most of it heavy, that she felt just as constrained. How and why would anyone choose to dress this way? Half a mile into her walk, she had discovered that the bottom half of the dress, the part with the heaviest fabric, was merely a skirt pinned onto the bottom of the bodice. It was a cost saving concession made for the costume, and Lizandra hoped it would stay pinned and wouldn't give away her outfit as a fraud.

She had left the theater through the side exit into the alley and had followed the alley around behind the Chamberlain and past the neighboring building behind it. That led her into the next street over, which she had taken south toward the center of the city. Caius and Samira had concerns that the Kites might be watching the theater and would see her leave out the front. She'd been watching out the front windows herself for more than an hour before Samira dressed her and didn't see anyone suspicious. Still, she supposed a bit of caution wouldn't hurt.

Lizandra had to stop to rest just after the bank came into view. She'd made it all the way through the city in this horrible costume, and her breathing came ragged. Samira had made her wear shoes with tall heels, and she could feel her feet bruising from the weird distortions. It was only because of her acrobatic training that she'd managed not to fall the entire way there. She put a hand on the corner of a brick building to steady herself. Breathe in, breathe out.

Truth be told, it wasn't only the journey that had her out of breath. She'd spent the entire time going over the plan in her head, hoping against hope that she didn't do or say anything to betray this ridiculous character she was playing. Lady Rethi Terake, indeed. She slowed her breathing and worked to center herself, just like she did before a performance. This time she would not be flipping through the air or balancing herself on Reykas' outstretched hand, but her current circumstance was far more precarious.

One more breath in, one more out, and she was ready. She pushed away from the building and picked up an aloof stride as she crossed the last street toward the bank. It was a tall building, as was everything here in the middle of Klubridge. The facade was built up from some sort of white stones, and there were four grand columns of the same material, spaced at the top of the steps leading up to the entrance. At this time of day, the bank was busy. Lizandra decided she liked that. Less opportunity for her to stand out, and less time any single person would spend paying attention to her.

To her relief, she saw that she was far from the only person dressed like a fancy mummer. On the corner near the bank stood a man in a garish purple suit. He was smoking a long pipe and took it out of his mouth to duck his head to her in a polite greeting. She gave a quick curtsy and hoped after the fact that that was a suitable response. She didn't wait to find out and instead took the steps up to the bank two at a time. She nearly tripped once on a wobbling heel and cursed these demonic shoes Samira had forced her to wear. She added Caius to her list of curses and wished they could just barge into the bank and take the seri they needed instead of going through this farce with haranium.

Up next to the bank's main door was a strange woman in a straight, gray dress. She didn't have the gaudy makeup Samira had smeared onto Lizandra, but her hair was a spectacle, with the entire back shaved off and the front hanging long. Her skin was pale white and unsettled Lizandra almost as much as the woman's dead eyed stare did. Both probably resulted from a long-term frost addiction. The city watch always upended the poor districts when they made their frequent sweeps for narcotics. They'd have much more success looking in the noses, throats, and arms of the nobility, and they likely knew it.

A man coming out of the bank held the door open for Lizandra, and she dipped another brief and awkward curtsy to him. Then she was inside, and it was time to convince people that she belonged. She smoothed her hands down the front of the bodice and felt the invisible bump where it met and attached to the costume skirt. It looked as much like a dress as she was going to look like a noble.

She took as deep a breath as the tight lacing would allow and glided across the shiny marble floor to a bank attendant. It was a balding man in a plain, dark suit, and he wore tiny silver glasses that reminded her of Apak's gold ones. He was clean shaven with a face that hung low, the jowls drooping in concert with his eyelids. "Yes," he said as she approached.

Lizandra had gone over the script a hundred times at the theater. She'd made Reykas pretend to be a bank manager and run lines with her. "I am newly arrived in your city, and I require a place to secure my valuables." She hadn't been able to deliver that line to Reykas without laughing, but she pulled it off this time. Had she used the right posh accent, though?

The bank attendant did not look impressed but also didn't seem suspicious. That seemed like the best she could hope for. "Name?" he asked, opening a thick ledger on the podium in front of him.

"Lady Rethi Terake," she said. The words tasted false on her tongue, but she thought she delivered them well.

He scribbled on a line in the book before looking up at her above the glasses. "For how long will you need to secure your belongings?" His voice had a droning buzz that was almost lulling.

"Oh, this will be a permanent arrangement," she said.

He pulled a sheet of paper from a stack next to the ledger and pushed it in her direction. "I trust you can write?"

"Of course I can." She didn't have to act the contempt, at least.

"Complete this, and take it to the window."

She had anticipated this move, and the whole plan hinged on it. "Not quite yet. If I am to entrust you with the safety of my valuables —" She'd already said "valuables." Was that too many times? Was she being obvious? Too late, push ahead. "—I must see the measures you take to secure your clients'… valuables." No, no, stop it, Lizandra.

The attendant stared at her for a long moment, but the look on his face was more one of annoyance than suspicion. He finally breathed out a deep sigh. "Very well. I suppose you would like a tour of our facilities."

"Well… yes, that would be… splendid." Was this actually working?

He turned to another attendant standing at a podium to his right. "I am taking Lady Terake to vault three." The other attendant nodded, and they were off. Lizandra followed him through the bank lobby, past an assortment of workers and clients. Most of the clients wore high town finery not unlike her own, and that helped quell her nerves. She still had to stay sharp, but perhaps this whole thing wasn't about to fall apart.

The attendant selected a large iron key from a ring at his waist and used it to unlock a metal door on the back wall. It swung inward, and he pushed it open, stepping aside to let Lizandra through. Once she had cleared the threshold, she heard the door slam shut again, and the attendant locked it. They were in a sealed room at the top of a set of stairs that led downward into a hallway lit on both sides by rows of burning sconces.

"This way," the attendant said, and Lizandra followed him down the steps and into the hallway. There were large, numbered doors on both sides, between the gaslamps. They passed the first two and stopped in front of the one with a giant "3" engraved on the front. The attendant selected a different key, this one silver, and used it in the cavernous lock on the front of the door.

Lizandra was making mental notes the whole time, and her doubt was rising. How would they hope to get through that first door and down the stairs, much less into one of these vaults? It seemed that all the vaults might have different keys. And how would they even know which one held haranium tubes, if there even were any haranium in the whole place? This plan was looking more impossible by the moment, but she continued absorbing everything she saw and heard so that she could report it back to Samira and Caius.

The door to vault three hissed open on enormous metal hinges. The attendant stepped back and extended a hand. "After you, Lady Terake."

She tilted her chin up like she imagined these nobles would do and stepped past him and into the chamber. This was nothing like she had imagined a vault to be. The room was square, maybe five paces in either direction, with a steel table bolted to the stone floor. Wooden chairs sat facing the table on both sides, and that was it. There were no shelves, no safes, no boxes of jewels or money or haranium cylinders. Just a table and chairs, and a narrow window slotted high into the back wall, letting daylight into the empty chamber. It was less a vault and more a cell.

Lizandra's eyes widened as she realized what was happening, but when she spun around, she knew she was too late. The door already was swinging closed with the attendant on the outside. It slid shut with a soft clang, and she heard the giant bolt slide home.

"Well, hells."

~

H ow had he known?

Lizandra had been locked in the room for what must have been an hour by then, and she was sitting in the chair that faced the door with her chin propped on her left hand, her right hand resting closed on the table. There was no mechanism on the inside that she could use to unlock the door, and it hadn't taken her long to accept that she was locked in until someone decided to let her out. How long would it take before Reykas went looking for her? She hoped he would have the sense to stay away, but she knew he wouldn't. She wouldn't, if he were the one in trouble.

Of course, there was the chance that the attendant just didn't like her, and her present entrapment had nothing to do with Caius, the haranium, or any of the rest of the complications that continued to pile atop them. But no, he knew. Somehow she'd given herself away.

Was it something about the dress or the makeup? Maybe she'd said something wrong. It was the "valuables" thing, wasn't it? As likely as it might be that the attendant had seen through her transparent ruse, none of that seemed right. He'd locked her in a vault and just left her there. That's not something you do unless you need to keep someone in place for a specific reason.

That reason arrived a few seconds later when the bolt clanged open again, and the door hissed inward. Lizandra sat back in the chair and pressed her shoulder blades against it to keep her nerves from visibly shaking her. Keeping calm and admitting nothing. That was the way out of this, if there could be a way out.

She inhaled through her nose when the red nightmare walked through the door. Lizandra had never seen the woman, but she recognized her all the same. It was Nera Mollor, the Scarlet Kites' commander who had been at the theater. There was no mistaking the red-haired woman in the red tabard with the command rank and the bird on her chest. This was getting worse by the moment.

Two guards, dressed in similar crimson uniforms, followed Mollor into the vault and moved to either side of the door. One was older than the commander, with silver at his temples and in his tight beard.

The other was much younger, probably recently added to the retinue after he graduated from whatever training these soldiers went through. The young one was looking at Lizandra, studying her with interest, but the old one's eyes were straight ahead. He appeared to have no interest in their prisoner, but Lizandra suspected he'd be the one to cut her down if she made a run for the door.

The bank attendant, that odious little man, came in after the guards and faded himself into the far corner. He didn't look at Lizandra, either, and kept his head bowed. He looked ashamed or regretful for what he'd done to her. She thought he should be, and she wished she'd have a chance to express that to him.

All thoughts of exacting revenge on the wormy banker flew to the back of Lizandra's mind when the final person stepped through the thick doorway.

"You little sneak," Lizandra said and then realized it was out loud. So much for keeping quiet and denying everything. It didn't matter now, anyway. She knew how they'd caught her.

The strange woman in the gray dress, the eerily pale one with the dead stare, now turned those bleak eyes on Lizandra. It all made sense, and she wanted to kick herself for not recognizing the telltale shaved head. "She's a mage," Lizandra said. "One of your pets." Mollor stood on the other side of the table and held herself erect, looking down at Lizandra. At the accusation, the commander's face twitched once but otherwise gave away nothing. Lizandra already had her brain running mathematic calculations, reciting poetry, remembering carnival acts, and doing anything else she could do to obscure her present thoughts. "She read my mind, didn't she?"

Mollor grasped the back of the chair before her and pulled it away from the table. It scraped across the floor, and the sound of the wood on stone echoed in the otherwise empty room. She took her time in stepping around the chair and sitting, now level with Lizandra and still staring at her with cool disdain. "You seem familiar with magic users," Mollor said. "Why might that be?"

Lizandra met the other woman's eyes and managed not to blink. Her heart was thudding, but she thought she was doing an admirable job of hiding it. "Why do you have me in here?" How much had the mage woman gotten out of her head? Did she know everything? Did she know about Caius, the plan to escape, the theft, everything?

"You are not Lady Rethi Terake. Why did you lie?"

There was no use in denying what they already knew. She had to be careful not to tip her hand on anything they didn't know, though. "I lied because I didn't feel like using my real name." Lizandra wanted the face she presented to Mollor to be defiant, but it was hard for her to know how effective it was. She wasn't used to posturing under this coating of makeup.

Mollor tightened her lower lip and clasped her hands in front of her on the table. "You came here to prepare for a robbery. You plan to take twenty thousand seri. Why do you need that much money?"

Confusion passed through Lizandra's mind before she realized what the woman was talking about. On the way into the bank, Lizandra had mused that it would be simpler just to steal the money than it would be to take the haranium and go through the ordeal of earning the funds. The mage had missed everything but her desire to take the money. Sloppy. Sloppy and useful. Lizandra forced fright onto her face, just enough to be convincing. She said nothing and hoped that made her look even more guilty. As long as they focused on money, they wouldn't be thinking about haranium.

The mage blinked once before stepping away from her place against the wall. She leaned and whispered into Mollor's ear. Mollor recoiled a fraction of an inch away from the mage but got the message. With new determination in her eyes, she asked, "Who is Harah Nym?" The mage stared triumphantly at Lizandra and moved back to the wall.

It was Lizandra's turn to blink, and she had to swallow hard to keep from laughing. She'd let haranium slip through, but the daft mage woman hadn't understood what she had meant. She kept her composure and made herself stammer, "Please… please don't hurt him. He's the one who needs the money."

Mollor watched her and narrowed her eyes. Was she buying it? "Is he the spy or the contact in the city?"

"I don't—"

"We can find out. It would be easier if you would tell us yourself, though. Easier on us and easier on you as well. Which one is Nym? Is he the spy?"

It was hard to process this while masking her thoughts, so she didn't try to figure it all out just then. Instead, she let her mind spin a yarn. "He's new to the city. He doesn't—"

Mollor's hand slammed against the tabletop, and Lizandra flinched back. The sound of her fist pounding the metal surface was enough to startle the bank attendant and the younger guard, too. The mage and the older guard were unmoved. "This is your opportunity to do the right thing. We know that you are in league with a magic user. We know that a rebel operative is in the city and is meeting with a contact. It will do you no good to protect your friend. What does he plan to use the money to do? Is he building a resistance in Klubridge?"

Lizandra pulled her hands into her lap. Mollor was giving away far more information than she should have. They had to have picked up some details in her mind that made them think she was part of some grand conspiracy involving the rebellion. If that's what they were after, maybe they didn't want Caius after all. Maybe this whole thing was a case of mistaken identity.

"Is Harah Nym the real name of the magician who calls himself Akithar?"

Lizandra's pulse quickened again, and she knew her thoughts would betray her to the mage's probing if she stayed in that room for one more minute. Her chair slid back two inches, and the legs made a crunching sound against the floor. The older guard was the only one who noticed, but he moved quickly. "Commander, there's glass!"

Lizandra kicked down and leapt to stand on the chair in a crouch. She'd broken the window above her while waiting alone in the cell, and now was her moment. Lizandra's feet crushed the broken shards of glass that she'd pushed out of sight beneath the table, and she abandoned her impractical shoes in the leap onto the chair. Someone cried out, probably the bank attendant.

The older soldier was halfway to her, and Mollor was rising from her chair when Lizandra spun and flung the fistful of sewing pins she had hidden in her right hand. Without waiting to see how effective her attack had been, she made another spin to pull the costume skirt loose from the bottom of the sash where it was attached. She threw the heavy material at the approaching guard and, in the same movement, she pistoned her legs down. The same motion she'd made dozens of times, hundreds even, when leaping high above the stage. The chair gave a loud crack, and she was up, impossibly high above the others' heads.

Her right hand caught the edge of the windowsill, and she swung her body up, her legs now free to move. Her feet slapped together, and her toes pointed in unison as she flung herself through the space where the window had been. The opening was small, but there was just enough room for her to fly through.

The sunlight blinded her for an instant as she landed on her back on the hard cobblestones. The vault she had escaped was below the ground, and the window was just above street level. She made a fast kick up to her bare feet and took the briefest of seconds to look around. She didn't have her bearings, but she knew she was on a roadway, and that was all that mattered. Lizandra shoved away from the side of the bank and darted into the opposite alley. She was free.

CHAPTER 15

Nera Mollor was interviewing the owner of the Bastion when the messenger came for her. She heard the horse approaching at a fast clip and excused herself from the conversation. She was stepping out to the street by the time the rider dismounted.

"Commander Mollor, a message for you." The young woman handed her a folded paper.

Nera read the note, just a single line: "Conspirator held at central bank." There was no signature, but she knew it came from Wil. He'd been in her service for long enough for her to recognize his block letters and clipped writing.

She folded the paper again and slipped it into her pocket before turning to Tomos, just then emerging from the theater behind her. "Bring the horses around. We have business at the bank."

Moments later, Tomos was riding on his horse behind hers as she navigated the winding streets of Klubridge. They were making the trip at as quick a pace as she dared, but a full gallop was out of the question. With the city gates closed, the streets were becoming more and more full of displaced or trapped citizens. Nera wanted to get to this conspirator as soon as possible, but not at the sake of running down some poor pedestrian along the way. She knew other Kites under other commanders might not have that courtesy, but she felt proud that her own regiment followed her example.

It wasn't long before they turned the corner to the city's central district, and Nera saw the bank ahead, gleaming white in the midday sun. Wil was waiting outside, his red uniform visible even from this distance. Citizens still were going about their business in and out of the bank, but Nera noted the berth they gave her tall friend as they departed. It was good that the Scarlet Kites still ordered the respect of the populace here. Think what she might about the state of the city's underworld and the sharp divide between the rich and the poor, Nera had to admit that Tereth had done an admirable job of keeping the Kites relevant and recognized. She would remember to compliment him after this task was complete.

Nera pulled her horse to a slow walk and then a stop beside Wil. Tomos fell into line beside her mount, and one of the city watch took their reins.

"What do you have?" Nera asked as she approached Wil.

"One of the mages picked something up."

Nera wrinkled her nose, and Wil said, "I know. They can be useful, though."

"We'll see. Where is the halflock?"

Wil pointed up the steps to the woman standing beside the bank door. Nera recognized her as the one called Magra, one of several mages General Bekam had sent for her to use after her latest report reached him. Magra was an odd looking one, short and with a bulbous head that seemed too large for her body. Her hair hung long and black and stringy in the front but had been shaved in the back, where Nera knew she would have the telltale surgical scarring. She was in a gray dress, similar to the gray robe the Imperial mage had worn when pouring drinks at Salkire. Her skin was the color of death, and her eyes, ringed with dark sleeplessness, stared wide at the people coming in and out of the bank. Nera knew she was reading minds, what the Empire had sent her to do, but it still unsettled her. Magra's gaze passed over Nera, and they locked eyes for an instant. Nera felt a chill run the full length of her spine, and she broke the connection by looking back at Wil.

"What did she get?"

"A woman trying to pass herself off as nobility. Magra says she's connected to magic somehow. That's what caught her attention."

"Connected how? Is she a mage?"

"Unknown. Magra can't sense magic. She just reads minds." Wil glanced back at the bank and gave a quick look around before adding, "There's more. Magra says the woman is here to case the bank. She's part of a crew and has designs on twenty thousand seri."

That was unexpected. "They're going to rob the bank? This one, right in the heart of the city?"

Wil shrugged. "It's what Magra says."

"Was there anything else?"

"That's all she told me. Maybe you'd have better luck."

Nera frowned and looked at Magra again. The thought of speaking with that animal sent spiders up her arms, but she had to do it. "Where is the woman now?"

Wil laughed. "One of the bankers tricked her. She's locked in the basement of the bank. He's had her there nearly three quarters of an hour by now."

"We'll get to her in a moment." Nera left Wil and took the steps up to the bank door with dread that she hid behind squared shoulders and the mantle of her rank. Magra swiveled her eyes back to look at Nera as she approached. The mage's overlarge head cocked to a tilt.

"Tell me what you know, halflock."

The voice came out low and breathy, almost a whisper but somehow guttural. "The woman. She play at being nobility, eh. She know magic, yes?"

"She knows magic? Do you mean she's a mage?"

Magra shook her head once, twice, in jerky motions. "No, don't know, yes, no." Her eyes somehow widened even more. "She close to magic maybe, yes? She know magic."

Half of the Imperial mages Nera encountered had ended up like this, functional but fried. They were useful, she admitted, but getting the information out of a halflock was like trying to read a wet scroll with half the words bleeding off it. "Tell me about the robbery," Nera said.

"Twenty thousand seri, that's what she want. She look here and then tell them back."

"Who are her associates? Who is robbing the bank with her?"

"Mm, not a thing Magra know, no, know, no." The mage's tongue darted out to lick at her lips, and she cocked her head at Nera again. "She hate her shoes, ha!"

Nera pressed her lips together and exhaled through her nose. This was getting nowhere. "Tomos, bring the halflock. Wil, with me." She stepped past Magra and shoved the bank door open.

Nera was halfway out of her chair when the woman disappeared through the tiny window. She had knocked the glass out, likely with the chair, long before Nera arrived. How had they missed that?

"Tomos! Wil! Go!" They were already out the door and running up the hallway, but Nera knew they would be too late. She spun on the mage, who now had shrunken into the corner opposite the one where the banker was cowering. "You! Find her!"

Magra shook her head and held her hands out in supplication, her palms up and her wrists pressed together. "No, can't do that. Can't find."

"Can you call more guards outside? Can you do anything useful?"

"Just tell thoughts, yes. Tell them, tell thoughts ought thoughts think."

Nera shoved the mage's shoulder hard, slamming her back against the wall, and left her slumping to the floor as she headed into the hallway. Nera looked both ways in frustration. She knew there would be no catching that woman. She cursed and stepped back into the vault. The mage was sitting on the floor now, pouting, and rubbing at her shoulder. Her eyes rolled toward Nera in accusation, but Nera refused to meet them this time. The banker had pulled himself to his feet but was trembling.

He looked to the window and then to Nera. "Was… was that magic?"

"No," Nera said. "That was a great amount of skill and training. No magic was involved in what just happened."

"How can you be sure?"

"It's my business to know magic, and what she did was her own physical, natural ability."

"But—"

"You will put additional security into place immediately. Do you understand?"

"Yes, but—"

"That woman has a team, and they are desperate for money. They will be back, and you must be ready for them. What contingencies do you have? How many guards?"

The banker shook his head and spread his hands. "You'll need to speak with the manager. I have nothing to do with that. I—I am sorry."

Nera snorted and looked at the window again. Its bottom sill was at least eight feet above the floor. The power in that jump, the fluidity in the spin, and the precision in the slide through the opening all seemed impossible. If Nera didn't know better, she'd have thought it was magic as well. But what she had witnessed was the result of years of experience, not spellwork. It impressed Nera. Mages took the easy way around, the fastest path to their goals. Not so with ordinary people. They had to practice, to hone skills, to prepare themselves for moments such as these. The escape was a frustrating setback, but Nera could admit that she admired the woman's capabilities.

What she did not admire was a useless, wide-eyed abomination who could not provide decent information beyond a basic identification. She glared at Magra and then took two quick steps toward her. The mage flinched away from the first slap, but the second one bounced her head against the wall. "Get up!" Nera barked at her. She grabbed a fistful of material at the front of the mage's dress and yanked her to her feet. "Go!"

Magra led the way out of the vault with tiny steps, her big head lolling forward with each step. Nera followed behind and could see the large square of shaved skin at the back of the mage's head, bordered by crude straight scars. It was not recent. Magra had been converted years ago, but she continued shaving her head, showing the world where the Empire had reached into her brain and reconfigured her life. The madness of mages.

"Get the manager," Nera told the banker before pushing Magra to a faster pace. She waited for the halflock to gain enough of her footing to begin the climb up the stairs. While waiting, Nera felt a warm trickle run past her nose, and then she tasted the faint tang of copper. She wiped at her face, and her hand came away red. Puzzled, she felt higher, and her fingers brushed at something just under her left eye. She pulled, and two thick sewing pins came free into her palm.

Nera closed her hand over the pins, careful not to prick herself again. Besides escaping, the woman had managed to strike back. Another inch, and she would have blinded Nera. Admirable, but it begged a response.

Night had fallen, and they had still not found the woman from the bank. Tomos and Wil had provided descriptions to the other Kites, but it was difficult, given the obvious but effective disguise she'd been wearing. Nera wasn't even sure whether the woman's hair had been a wig, but she erred on the side of it being real, reasoning that no wig would have withstood the acrobatic escape. They were searching the city for any sign of a disheveled young woman with white-blonde hair, around five and a half feet tall, slim, and athletic, with pale skin. That was all they had. It was unlikely that she'd kept the rest of the costume, given that she had already disassembled the skirt and flung it at Wil while making her exit.

Nera covered her weary eyes with her hand and rubbed her

fingertips over the small bumps left where the needles had struck her. "This is a disaster," she murmured and dropped her head onto the desk in front of her.

"What's that?"

Lucian was there, and he sat something on the desk beside her. Without looking, she grasped out and felt a wooden stein. Liquid fortification, always his answer. Nera knew it wouldn't work in this debacle, but she sat back and gave him a weak smile of thanks, anyway.

"I said it's a disaster. We had her in our grasp, and we let her slip away."

He sat next to her and angled his chair toward hers. "Come now, it can't be all bad, can it?"

"If only you had seen it. I thought we had her. I thought we had them all. And then—" She clapped her hands together. "Just like that, she was gone. This was the opportunity we've been waiting for, and I wasted it."

"Tell me what happened. It was the mage that found her, yes? Maggis?"

"Magra." Nera dropped her hands into her lap and stared at the stein before her. "That was a whole other issue. I lost control. I am ashamed of myself, Lucian."

"There, now. Drink up, and tell me about it."

She rolled her eyes at him but relented and took a sip. It was awful, but he smiled encouragement at her, and she took a deeper drink of the swill. Nera was not a frequent drinker, and this concoction was potent enough for her already to feel the zing at the front of her head after one swallow.

"The halflock found the woman, and the banker trapped her. But when she escaped, I was so... so angry. I was furious." Nera hesitated. She felt that she could tell him anything, but how would he judge her for this? Lucian, who always knew the answers and who always kept his composure. Lucian, sometimes too zealous in his duties, but never one to step over the line. When he had to use violence, he could, but it was only as a last resort.

She knew he still regretted the way the situation with Moeply Raseul had turned out. She didn't blame Lucian, not after Raseul had made a lunge for a weapon and tried to escape. Lucian had given him a sword to the neck, and while Nera wished they had gotten more information from the scoundrel, she knew Lucian had done the right thing. The only thing he could have done under the circumstances. He had been so tentative and apologetic when he reported back to her, and now how would he feel about her after this?

"What did you do?" he asked and leaned closer to her.

"I pushed her down. She was on the floor, and I struck her. Twice. It happened in front of the banker, even." Nera pressed her hand over her eyes again. "By the High Lord, Lucian, what was I thinking?"

"She—you hit her? Where is she now?"

"I don't know. Wherever they sent her. I got her out of the bank and gave her over to Tomos to deal with. How could I have shown such a lack of control?"

Lucian's forehead wrinkled. "What else did you do to her? After you struck her?"

"Nothing. Nothing, but I wanted to. I hated her so much. I hate all of them." She rapped her knuckles hard on the desktop, and her stein vibrated. "No mage should be suffered to live. They are the downfall of our society. You see it, Lucian. Tell me you see it."

"You know I do." The sincerity in his eyes and his words softened her mood a bit, and she could feel some tension leaving her shoulders. "We are in a better position to do something about that than anyone else," he added. And then, after a long pause, "We should execute every one of them."

Nera stared into his green eyes. She had already memorized the flecks and patterns in them, but still she stared, studying them. At last, she snorted, and her mouth broke into a grin. "You almost had me that time."

The corners of his mouth flinched, and he joined her with his own laugh. "I... very nearly did."

Nera put a hand on his arm and favored him with a genuine smile. "How do you always know what to say?"

"Your talent is knowing what our soldiers need. Mine is knowing what you need." He placed his hand over hers, and she felt a shiver dance up her arm. Then his hand was gone, and she exhaled.

"They're planning a robbery," she said. "The mage was able to pull that much from the woman's mind. They need twenty thousand seri."

That caught him by surprise. "Twenty thousand? What do they need that for?"

"I have suspicions but no proof. I believe the spy we are hunting already is in Klubridge. They are seeding a resistance cell right here in the city."

"And they're using the money to pay for recruits and supplies," he said. "That's a lot of recruits and a lot of supplies."

"It is, but what else could it be? They wouldn't need that kind of funding if they simply were planning an attack. This is something deeper, something more involved."

"How does the woman at the bank fit into this? You said earlier that she is part of a team?"

Nera nodded. "I believe she works for the contact in the city that the spy is meeting."

"Akithar, the magician."

"That's what I think."

"Why don't we take him down now, then? You know where he is. You've talked to him, even."

"We can't move on him before we know the full shape of this thing."

"Are you certain he's the contact?" Lucian asked.

"I believe he is. I believe he is a mage and is hiding in plain sight behind this stage magic of his. It would be so easy for him to slip through the cracks, all while plotting against the Empire. We know for a fact that he worships Ikarna. He had her icon in his office when I went there."

Lucian opened a hand. "There you go. That's all you need to arrest him. Bring him in on possession of a false icon, and we can wring the rest of it out of him."

"Not yet," she said. "We must find the spy before we take Akithar."

"You know, his religion is a punishable crime, but worshiping Ikarna does not make him a mage. We've taken down plenty of ordinary people stockpiling religious relics. That woman just two months ago in Millshade. What makes you think he has magic?"

Nera's chin wrinkled as she pushed her lips together, and she spoke softly. "It's because of Raseul. He was protecting a mage, and his boy pointed us straight to Akithar. It's as simple as that. I'm sorry to bring him up again. I know how difficult that situation was."

Lucian jerked his head in a quick nod, and she knew he didn't want to talk about it. He was so sensitive, one of the things she admired most about him. She had to ask, though, "Still no sign of the boy?"

"None," he said. "He vanished into the city and could be anywhere by now. I'd say we've seen the last of him."

"A pity," she said. "But we must find the woman from the bank, and we must know how she fits into this. She could lead us to the spy."

"And if not, we already know how the spy will be leaving the city."

"By the harbor, yes, but we need to find them before they get that far."

"If they do, don't worry," Lucian said. "I have eyes on every ship in and out of that port. The spy will have to take a ship since we've closed all other avenues out of Klubridge. We've paid every captain we could find, and we know exactly who boards every ship docked at those piers."

"I still want you to increase patrols, especially at night and around the banks and municipal buildings. The rebels still need their money, and they will try for it again."

"Already done," he said. "We'll catch them if they make another attempt. And, if they don't, they will fall into our trap as soon as they try to sail out of this forsaken city."

CHAPTER 16

Reykas was outside the bank when the Kites arrived. There already was one, a tall and broad soldier with salt and pepper hair, waiting near the entrance. Reykas had not encountered this squad since they arrived in Klubridge, but there was no mistaking the red uniform and weaponry of an agent of the High Lord. Lizandra had to be inside, and this meant they had found her out. Somehow they knew what she was doing, and she was caught.

He watched the Kite with a keen eye, appraising his stance, his posture, even the sword that hung at his belt. Would he be able to take him down on his own? The morning had been a rough one, with the chills threatening to overpower him, but they had lessened at last, and Reykas had made his way across town to the bank. He trusted that Lizandra could take care of herself, but he knew he still would feel better if he could see her safely out and home.

Samira had not tried to stop him. She had left the theater shortly before Reykas and said she had something to take care of at home. Taking that as a tacit blessing, Reykas had begun his trek, and now it found him leaning halfway around the corner of a grocer, diagonally up the street from the bank.

Reykas had just decided to make a run at the Kite when he saw the two additional soldiers turn the corner on horseback, making a quick sprint to the front of the bank. He held himself back and watched their approach. The one in front had to be the commander. Caius and Samira had described her, and even Dorrin had talked about the awful woman in red. In his mind, Reykas had conjured her up as some sort of monster, a creature hunting them down, but he now saw that she was, of course, just a woman.

She dismounted and headed straight for the Kite who was waiting near the entrance. The other soldier, younger than the first, followed in her wake. Reykas was too far away to hear them, but they all soon disappeared into the bank with another woman he hadn't noticed until now.

What now? He kept his eyes on the entrance, but all he saw were ordinary patrons going in and out. Lizandra was trapped somewhere inside, and there were at least three Scarlet Kites in there with her. He might have been able to take one of them, but three trained killers were too many for Reykas, especially when he was not in top fighting form. But he couldn't just leave her in there.

He squatted in place and thought through the situation. He couldn't leave to get help. As soon as he took his eyes off the bank, they could leave with her, and he would have no idea where they took her. Could he get a message to Caius? To Samira? He probably could pay someone to find them, but how could he trust a stranger, particularly in this part of the city? It was down to him alone.

Surely they would not kill her outright. They would want to arrest her, question her, and learn what they could about her intentions in the bank, maybe even about Caius if they had identified her. Reykas could not imagine a proper interrogation happening in the bank. They would bring her out and transport her somewhere else, probably to the Henburn Estate at the middle of the city. He could wait here and watch for them to emerge, but after that he had no plan. He could try to ambush the guards, but the most likely result of that would have both of them dead in the street. He could—

A quick movement down the road caught his eye and derailed his thoughts. A slender form had dropped onto the roadway from no apparent origin. It lay still for a second before kicking up to its feet. Lizandra! She was too far away for him to see her properly, but he knew it had to be her. She looked up and down the street with fast glances before taking off, barefoot, at full speed.

Reykas wanted to call out to her but knew he shouldn't draw attention to himself. Whatever had happened inside the bank, she had escaped, and he had to find her now. As he turned the corner to go down the street after her, the door to the bank banged open, and the two Kite soldiers sprinted out. They rounded the corner, headed for the spot where Lizandra had emerged.

Reykas altered his course and dipped into an alley on the right, heading parallel to the one Lizandra must have taken. She had a lead of only a few seconds on him, but that would be enough for her to lose him entirely if he were not fast. Once out of sight of the guards, Reykas pumped his legs and sped down the alleyway. He leaped at the wall where it dead ended, and he was up and onto it with an easy scramble.

Rather than dropping to the opposite side, he jogged up to the angled roof that connected to the wall and ran in the general direction he imagined Lizandra must have taken. He made a quick leap to a neighboring roof and ran along the edge, his eyes constantly moving down at street level. Behind him, he could hear the shouts of the guards as they tried to coordinate a search. They never would catch up to her. But would he?

There! A pale flash, as Lizandra ducked around a corner, still moving at full speed. Even during crisis, Reykas admired her grace and the fluidity of her movements. She took the next corner without slowing, drawing both of them ever deeper into the mazes of streets and alleys that led out of the city center. He realized she was making a roundabout course back toward the theater. He had to catch her before she got too close. The Kites surely would be watching.

He had her in sight again, now just a quarter of a block away. She came to the edge of two buildings, about to vault out into the street, but she brought herself up short and reversed into the alley, pressing her back against the dark wall. A pair of city watch guards passed the entrance to the alley without seeing her. That was just enough of a delay for Reykas to close the gap. He made a final leap and tucked into a roll before hitting the ground. He went down on his shoulder and sprang up again, just like old times.

Lizandra gasped before seeing that it was Reykas. She grabbed him into her arms and pressed her face against his chest. Her breathing was ragged, and she held him tight against her, the back of his shirt balled into her tight fists. "You stupid, stupid man," she was wheezing into his chest. "You shouldn't be here."

"I could say the same. Are you all right?"

It was a silly question. Clearly she was not. Half her costume was torn away. She still wore the bodice, but the laces were ripped out of one side so it hung loose on her. The lower green part of the dress was gone, leaving only the silky white skirt above her bare and dirty feet. Her hair, so immaculate after Samira had finished with it, now hung in sweaty tendrils, and her makeup smeared across her face, giving her the look of a crazed clown.

"The Kites have mages," she said. She looked down the alley, back the way they had come. "We have to move."

"Mages?" But she already was moving again, and he had to hurry to keep up. "Is that how they caught you?"

"Yes. They don't know everything, but I think they know about Caius. We have to warn him."

"Wait." Reykas caught her arm. She looked down at his hand, surprised, and yanked away. "They will be watching the theater," he said.

She was about to run again but stopped. "You're right. I should have thought about that."

"Samira is at her house. We can go there."

"You don't think they'll have watchers there, too?"

"It is less likely than the theater."

"Okay, follow me." And she was off again, this time angling away from the theater and toward Samira's home to the west.

❧

S amira lived in a small house in a residential row west of the theater. She often spent the night in her office after a late show, but the Chamberlain wasn't her home, as much as she might love the place. Her home was the little stone cottage jammed between two others identical to it in a row of dozens alike. Reykas had been there many times, and he knew the way better than Lizandra. Nevertheless, Lizandra was in the lead.

They had avoided three watch patrols since leaving the bank, but there had been no Scarlet Kites in view. No doubt they were canvassing a radius around the bank, working their way out. That was how the military operated, and that worked in Lizandra's favor this day. Reykas imagined they had already sent a rider to the theater, where there probably already was someone watching the doors. Going to Samira's was the right move, at least until things calmed down.

Lizandra got them to the right street but could not remember which house belonged to Samira. Reykas led her a quarter of the way down the road and up three ancient steps to knock at the wooden door. Lizandra pressed herself against the outer wall, partially obscured by simple stonework on the front stoop. No one had stopped the strange half-dressed girl on the way there, and they couldn't afford to draw attention now that they were so close to safety.

It didn't take long for Samira to answer the knock. She opened the door half an inch, and Reykas saw her eye peering out.

"Let us in. There has been trouble," he said.

She pushed the door shut again, and he heard the slide bar rattle on the other side. When the door reopened a moment later, Samira pulled it wide and motioned for them to come in.

"What happened?" She looked from Reykas to Lizandra, and her eyes widened in concern. "Are you all right?"

The door opened into a sitting area with a thick rug in between a plush settee and two ornamented chairs. There was a fireplace at the back of the room, but it was dark that day. Several books lay scattered across a plain table that was pushed against the nearest wall, and a blue cloak draped off the edge. Samira took Lizandra's hands and pulled her to one of the chairs. "Sit, Lizzie. Are you okay?" she asked again.

"I think so, but it was a near thing," Lizandra said. "They were waiting for me. The Kites have brought Imperial mages to the city. Halflocks. One of them read my mind when I was coming into the bank."

"How much did they get?" Samira dropped onto the edge of the settee, near Lizandra, and Reykas stood next to the other chair. The adrenaline was still there and wouldn't let him sit.

Lizandra shook her head, and more of her hair tumbled free of the elaborate design Samira had built. "Not much, but enough to know I was there for a robbery. They misunderstood and thought I was after money. They know I have a team, but they don't know about the haranium."

Samira glanced over her shoulder and looked like she was about to say something. She hesitated and then asked, "How did they know to watch the bank?"

Reykas had been thinking about that on the flight away from the building. "I do not think they did. I believe multiple mages have been sent here, and they are patrolling the city."

"They could be anywhere," Samira mumbled. "How can we be safe if we don't know how many there are or where they might turn up? Our own thoughts will betray us now."

"This mage had a shaved head. The back part, anyway. All of them must have been conditioned, so we should be able to pick them out like that," Lizandra said.

"That's one piece of good news, at least. What else do they know? Is that all?"

"There's one more thing. The Kite commander was there."

"Mollor."

"Yes. She interrogated me herself." Lizandra dropped her head for a moment and then looked into Samira's eyes. "She asked me if I worked for Akithar."

"No."

"I don't think the mage got that from me. I think they already were after him. She was asking me about some spy in the city and a contact the spy was meeting, all kinds of nonsense I wouldn't have answered even if I'd known what she was talking about."

Reykas rubbed at his chin. "This goes beyond a mage hunt. This is something political."

Lizandra nodded. "I think they are hunting for rebels, not just mages."

"That would explain why they've shut down the city," Samira said. She gave a weak laugh. "They have the wrong man, and they don't even know it. But we can't tell them that, because they'd still want Caius if they knew the truth about him. Do they know who he is?"

"I don't think so. She just called him Akithar. I don't think they have his name or anything beyond that."

"Why haven't they come after him in force, then?" Samira asked.

"Perhaps the task is more complicated than that," Reykas said. "If the Kites are trying to quell a rebellion, it is unlikely that they would be hasty. They would want to ensure that all the pieces were in place before they moved."

Samira nodded in agreement. "That gives us some time, at least. But we can't get the haranium now. They'll be watching all the banks, even if they think we're going after money. It's too dangerous."

"Apak won't be happy about that," Reykas said. "He still needs the haranium for his contraption."

Samira asked, "Where else can we get it? He said there might be small numbers of the message cannisters in the houses of nobility, but we'd have to hit several of them, even to have a chance at finding one that had the cannisters. And we'd need to strike all at once. After we go into one house, all the others will be on heavy guard, just like the banks."

"If they are not already," Reykas said. "If this commander knows her business, she already will have ordered extra patrols anywhere we might be able to steal seri."

"So we'd need somewhere that has haranium but not money," Lizandra said. "That's a tall order."

"I may be able to help." The voice was soft and tentative, but Reykas spun, ready to fight, and Lizandra was on her feet in an instant.

In the back doorway, the one that led to the kitchen, stood a stranger. She was thin but looked athletic, from what Reykas could see of her arms. She wore a patterned green dress of a material similar to the blue cloak on the table. Reykas looked back to the cloak as his mind tried to assemble what was happening. "Who are you?"

"She heard us," Lizandra said. Her eyes were wide with fright, and she shifted toward the front door.

"Wait," Samira said. She put a hand on Lizandra's shoulder and motioned for Reykas to be calm. "This is Aquin. She's a friend." Samira delivered a pointed look to Reykas. "She's my friend."

Understanding came. "Your librarian," he said, and Lizandra raised an eyebrow at him.

"I am sorry," Aquin said. She stepped into the room, and Reykas noticed that she was barefoot. "I didn't mean to startle you. I overheard your conversation, and for that I apologize. But I believe I can help you."

Lizandra looked to Reykas with doubtful eyes, but she lowered herself back onto the settee with Samira's hand still on her shoulder. "How do you know this woman, Samira?"

"Aquin works at the library. I met her a couple of weeks ago."

"When you were retrieving a book for me," Reykas added and glanced back to Aquin. Somehow she was both exactly how he'd expected her and entirely different.

"So you've known her for just a couple of weeks. It all comes back to haranium," Lizandra said.

Aquin's expression was pained. "I don't want to cause trouble. Perhaps I should leave."

It was Reykas that stopped her. "No, please stay. Samira trusts you, and so we must."

Samira's smile was brief, but Aquin visibly relaxed. "Thank you… Reykas?"

"I am Reykas."

"And you are Lizzie?"

"Lizandra," she said without a smile.

"I see. I wish we could have met under more ordinary circumstances, but I suppose this is what we have."

"You said you could help us?" Reykas asked.

"Maybe." Aquin crossed the room to stand behind the settee. "Samira, after you left the library, I did more research on my own. I was intrigued."

"Do you know why we need haranium?" Lizandra asked.

"Only what Reykas said, that it is to be used in a device of some sort."

Samira prompted her. "What did you learn?"

"Well," she began, "as you know, haranium is outlawed from most uses under Imperial edict number seven five seven point nine. They still use it as an alloy in certain construction, even though it is volatile. The most common use is in these message cylinders that you already have been looking for."

"We know all of that," Lizandra said.

"Yes, of course. What I meant to say is that I was curious after learning about these document cylinders. It sounded familiar, so I looked into our own records."

Samira's mouth dropped open. "You mean…"

Aquin smiled back. "We have an archive of documents housed in those cylinders in the library itself. And, the last time I checked, we store no money there. Goddess knows I don't get paid any of it, if there is."

Lizandra had taken some convincing, but once she agreed with Aquin's library plan, the four of them had left Samira's house to come back to the theater. Reykas took the lead and stayed on the roofs, at least half a block ahead of the others the whole way back. They didn't encounter any Kites, but there were a few constables on post that they had to avoid. The chief concern was mages, and Reykas did not know how he would spot one. For all he knew, the Kites could have tucked a mage away in any of the buildings they were passing, and they could be having their minds read at any moment. As he understood it, the halflocks needed to have an unobstructed line of sight in order to hear a person's thoughts. Whatever the Empire did to them diminished their abilities, and those who could read minds no longer could do it with as much range and power as before. That was a safeguard for the Imperials and now a boon for the group of four making its careful way through the city.

Once he had reached the rooftop across from the Chamberlain, Reykas finally spotted a Kite. There was a soldier standing sentinel in an alcove diagonally down the road, partly hidden by a placard at another theater. As hidden as the Kite might think she was, she still was wearing her red uniform, and that thing drew the eye from a mile away. They avoided her by taking the back way in, just like Lizandra had left a few hours earlier.

And now that they all were back and safely reconvened, Caius looked befuddled. "Why should we trust this woman? Why do you trust this woman?"

"She has no love for the Empire," Samira said.

"I don't doubt that. Who does? But is now a good time to be making new friends?"

"I've known her for two weeks. I trust her, and she can help us." Samira crossed her arms. Reykas knew that posture. Once the arms were crossed, there was no moving her.

Caius sighed and rubbed his hands down the sides of his face. He knew that stance, too. "Samira, please listen to me. We are in a more precarious situation than we've been in since we came to Klubridge. Probably a more precarious one than we've ever been in. Don't you think taking this woman's word is a risk?"

"Her name is Aquin, and yes, I think everything we do is a risk. This is one worth taking."

They had gathered in Caius' office—Samira, Caius, Lizandra, Reykas, and Apak. Aquin was somewhere in the theater, too, getting a busy-making tour from Dorrin and Oreth.

Caius looked like he was about to respond to Samira, but Apak was first. "We still need haranium."

"This has gotten too dangerous," Caius said. "Lizzie could have been arrested today. Or worse."

"But she was not." Apak looked across the room to where Lizandra sat on a bare wooden chair. She had changed from the ragged costume into one of her own white gowns and scrubbed the makeup from her face. She looked tired now, but at least like herself again. "What do you think, Lizandra?"

"I think we don't have many options. Mollor is after you, Caius. It's only a matter of time until they're kicking the door in and taking you away."

"And it will not be just you," Reykas said. "When they come, they will take all of us. We all will be conspirators. Not just those of us in this office, but also Oreth. The stage grips. The costumers. Dorrin."

Caius steepled his fingers under his chin, his elbows resting on the arms of his chair. "Can we even continue our performances at this point?"

"They haven't come for you yet," Samira said. "They're waiting for something. We need to use that time, and, as much as I hate to admit it, we need to stick to the plan. Drass needs to be paid, and we need to be on that ship sooner rather than later. Earning the money seems to be the only option now. It's too late to steal it, even if we were open to that possibility, now that they're watching all the banks and probably the exchange house as well."

"Are you all in agreement that this is what we should do?" Caius asked. "Trust Aquin and take the haranium from the library?"

They were unanimous, and he nodded. "All right, then. But we're going to be careful. I still don't like it, but you're right. It's the only way now. We need a plan."

"I've already been working on one," Samira said. She wasted no time savoring the victory and pitched straight into her plot. "The

Kites know you and me. And now they know Lizandra. Our selection of fresh faces is dwindling. Either Apak or Reykas needs to go to the library with Aquin so we'll know what we're dealing with."

"I can do it," Reykas said.

"Reykas, no." Lizandra grabbed his hand and squeezed, staring up at him.

"It will be all right," he said. "This will be easier than what you had to do."

Samira agreed. "He's right. Aquin can walk him right into the library. She can show him where to go, and she'll watch out for him the whole time. He only has to verify that the haranium is there and let us know where it is and how much we can get. Nothing dangerous there."

"Unless another mage is watching the library."

"That is unlikely," Reykas said. "They are going to focus on places with money. You have put them off our trail, at least for a bit."

Lizandra looked like she still wanted to protest, but her exhaustion was winning that battle. She resigned herself to one last reproach. "If you get caught, you know I'll have to kill them all."

Reykas smiled and kissed the top of her hand. "I would expect nothing less."

"You are from Meskia," Aquin said as they slipped out the side exit from the Chamberlain. It wasn't a question, but an observation.

"How did you know?" Reykas scanned the nearby rooftops but saw no sentinels. He knew he wouldn't be able to see mages that might be hiding within the nearby buildings, but he hoped he at least would sense something if his mind were being probed. Lizandra had not known it was happening until it was too late, and he suspected it would be the same for Aquin and for him. Foot traffic still was light but was building as evening approached.

"The way you speak, for one. Your r's are light, and you say your a's like a harsh 'ah.'"

"I do, do I? And that told you I come from Meskia?"

"That, and the way you are with Lizzie." The sun was going down, but Reykas still saw the appraising smile in the shadow of the alley.

"I call her Lizandra."

"That, too. So formal with names," she said.

"What do you mean by the way I am with her?"

"You are protective, but you value her place as you do your own. Strong but soft. It is the custom."

Reykas wasn't sure what to make of that. "Where are you from, then? I would have placed you from the south as well."

"Oh, I am. I was born in Acleau and lived there until I came to school in Klubridge. I was fifteen then."

"And you decided to stay."

"I did. I found that an academic life suited me. How did you find your way out from Meskia? You didn't end up a fisher or a farmer. I assume you aren't a gangster, either."

Reykas was silent as they crossed the street. The crossing was convenient timing, and he held a finger to his lips as he peered down the next block to ensure they would not run afoul of guards or worse. He didn't speak again until they were around the corner and passing the bakery where he bought sweets occasionally for Lizandra.

"You have lost much of the accent," he said. "And you do not seem to have retained the formality you accuse me of keeping."

Aquin laughed. "Formality is not a bad thing, Reykas. It reminds me of home. Of my da. I suppose being away changes a person. Especially being here in Klubridge for so long, and around students from so many places. The pieces fall away, as much as I may try to hold onto them."

"Have you been back since you left?"

"No. I have nothing there now," she said. "You?"

"I have not. Everything I need is here in that theater."

Reykas could feel Aquin looking at him as they walked. "You love her. Truly, I mean. Not just an infatuation."

"Of course I love her."

"How did you meet Lizzie?"

"You call her Lizzie," he said.

"Samira calls her Lizzie. That's how I first knew of her."

"You and Samira…"

"She is a remarkable woman," Aquin said.

"It has been a very long time since she has… cared for someone," Reykas said.

"You disapprove?"

"No," he said. "But as her friend, I must be concerned."

"Concerned about her happiness, you mean."

"And her welfare."

"I am obligated to reassure you about neither of those things. I like you, though, and I can promise you that my intentions are mostly noble."

Reykas couldn't help laughing. "I will have my eye on you."

"Don't let Lizzie know that," Aquin said, and they both laughed.

They had passed through a block of houses similar to the ones on Samira's street, and Reykas kept monitoring the roofs and looking at the windows as they walked. He had still seen no Kites, but there had been a couple of law officers a street or two back. They had been on regular patrols and had paid no attention to him or to Aquin. The guards were less of a concern than the potential mages. As a precaution, he began doing math in his head, as Lizandra had described herself doing.

Aquin interrupted his equations as they took the next street, the one that would lead into the heart of the city. "Tonight you are a historian. I am bringing you into the library to survey some old manuscripts."

"Will there be anyone else working?"

"At this hour, yes. Many students will be there, and most of the staff will be busy with them. They will leave after an hour or two, though. We close the library to the public after the seventh bell, and the librarians all go home by the ninth."

"What about security? Are there guards?"

"Watch guards patrol the campus grounds throughout the night. There usually is someone passing by the library every half to three quarters hour. They never come inside, though."

"And where the document cylinders are kept? Are there safeguards?"

"I've never seen them. I only know that I read we have a vault where they are kept. Vault G3. I can get you into the library and downstairs into the archives. Beyond that, I'm afraid you are on your own."

"I will find them," he said. He had never seen one of the tubes, but Apak had sketched an example for him. It was an ordinary cylinder, likely without external ornamentation. Apak had measured with his hands, showing that they were likely to be only a foot and a half in length. They were thick, though, and dense. The haranium was poured into an alloy with other metals that gave the things a dangerous heft. Apak had warned him not to move or jostle them. Dropping one of the heavy tubes could be enough to activate the haranium. Reykas did not have to ask what that would mean for his own safety.

"How will we get them out?"

Aquin chuckled. "This one is not part of any 'we' in that sentence, Meskian. I will give you access to the library, but my involvement ends there. It is up to you to devise the rest of this scheme."

"That is fair," he said.

They were approaching the library now, and he redoubled his efforts at keeping his brain busy. If mages were posted anywhere along their journey, it would be here, on the school campus. Samira seemed sure that the Kites would have little interest in the library now that they were focused on places with money to be stolen, but he had to be certain.

Aquin led the way through the front doors, and Reykas followed with one last glance across the darkening common area. He saw students, academics, and even one or two youngsters he pegged as cutpurses, but no one suspicious. If a mage were here, they hid themselves well. As long as he could not see them, they could not see him and therefore could not read his mind, at least according to common wisdom. Once inside the library and with most lines of sight to him obscured, Reykas finally allowed himself to relax his guard. It was time to be a historian.

He trailed behind Aquin as she wound through the desks and shelves with a strolling pace that spoke to her familiarity with the building. "To the back," she said over her shoulder, and he nodded.

As much as he read, Reykas had never set foot in the library. Samira often picked up books here and loaned them to him, but he rarely found himself in this part of the city, much less within the halls of academia. His eyes glided over the spines of the books on the endless shelves, and he tried to keep from being too obvious in his interest in the students' work at the tables they passed. One student, a girl with dark hair, was reading something about anatomy. She looked up as Reykas neared, and he gave her a confident nod of greeting. She rolled her eyes and went back into her book.

Two curved staircases at the back of the library ascended to the second floor. Nestled behind and between them was a narrow hallway, mostly hidden from the rest of the library by design. Aquin led him into the short passageway, which soon ended with a thick wooden door. Aquin fished a brass key from a pocket concealed in the folds of her dress and slipped it into the lock. It clicked home, and she pushed the door open. Inside, Reykas could see a flight of stone steps disappearing down into the darkness.

"This is it," she whispered to him. "No one should be down there right now, but make it quick. I will wait here for you."

Reykas didn't take the time to respond and instead slipped past her to go down the stairs. The steps were lit with hooded lanterns mounted on the walls. The flickering gaslight cast eerie shadows around the irregular surfaces of the rocks that built the walls, ceiling, and floor. Unlike the upper levels, which were mostly imported wood, the basement looked more akin to a dungeon carved out of a hillside.

Reykas had to pull his arms in against his body as he went down, and he was thankful he didn't encounter anyone else coming up. One would have to retrace their steps to allow the other to pass. The stairs deposited him in a dark corridor, again lit by evenly spaced flames. It was cooler down here, and he expected the air to smell of dampness. It did not, though, and he suspected something had been done to remove the humidity to preserve the documents stored down there.

Doors opened from all sides of the corridor. Every door was identical, thick and wooden like the one at the top of the stairs, but these had windows built into the upper halves. The window openings were sealed with glass, behind which Reykas could see rows of iron bars. Perhaps this truly was a dungeon and not a library after all. But after looking through the first door he saw that the bars were in place to protect literary artifacts, as suspected.

Each door had a black iron letter and a number attached to it. The one he had just looked through was A4. A5 was to the left, A3 to the right. Reykas followed the wall to the left and watched the numbers ascend. Between A8 and A9, the corridor split into a brief hallway. He took that turn and realized how massive this archive was. It was laid out more or less as a grid, and there was no telling how far it sprawled beneath the school. He was certain that he already was far outside the grounds of the library itself, probably beneath classroom buildings now, if he had his bearings correct.

This chamber was B. He continued through, passing row after row until he found G, the final hallway in the labyrinth. This one was different, with three smooth steps leading down to the last corridor. The corridor itself was octagonal, with five doors, one installed in each of the wall segments to the left and right, one straight ahead, and one on each diagonal segment in between. G3 was the central door, straight ahead of Reykas.

As he approached the door, he saw that the ones on the G block were metal, not wooden. They still had the iron numbers on the front and still had barred windows in the tops, but they looked much sturdier, and he noted three locks in each of them instead of the single lock in each of the wooden doors on the other aisles. Reykas pressed his hands against the surface of the door to vault G3, and it was smooth and cold to the touch. He leaned in to peer through the window.

Between the bars, he could see a chamber similar to the one he had seen back on the A corridor. This one looked to have metal walls, though, from what he could tell by the light that came through the window. The floor was out of his view, but he imagined it would be metal as well. These were the vaults where they stored the most important artifacts, or at least the most dangerous ones.

There was a rack against the far wall, and he squinted into the gloom to try and make out the details. Reykas pressed a hand against the vault door and considered trying somehow to breach it now. But no. That was too dangerous without a proper plan, and spotting the quarry was enough for this night. There they were, stacked, one atop another. He counted ten cylinders logged in the rack, each speckled with red traces of haranium.

CHAPTER 17

A second Scarlet Kite showed up outside the Chamberlain less than an hour after Reykas and Aquin left for the library. Samira was in her office above the entrance and saw her when she arrived. This one was a young woman with dark, asymmetrical hair. She was in the red uniform, now all too familiar in Klubridge, but her arms were bare. Samira squinted through the mirrored window and saw that the Kite had unlaced and removed the sleeves. That didn't seem like it would fit regulations, but Samira wasn't about to go out and tell her that.

The woman was standing in the middle of the street and looking up at the Chamberlain. Samira's stomach felt heavy, and she was sure the Kite knew she was being watched and didn't care. Pedestrians streamed around her, but she stood still in the flow, forcing the others to go around her. Continuing to stare up toward Samira's window, she moved closer to the building. Samira leaned forward to see her trying the front doors. She pulled on each of them before taking two steps back and staring at the windows again. Of course, the doors were locked to the public since they were between seasons and had no off-season show scheduled tonight, but that didn't keep Samira's pulse from quickening as the Kite tugged on each door handle.

With a last look up to the windows, the woman glared and raised her right hand, pointing directly at Samira. Samira gasped and pulled back before remembering that the windows were reflective from the outside. The Kite couldn't possibly see her. Could she? Either way, she'd turned her back now and crossed the street. She reached the other side and propped her back against the front of the Monument Concert Hall, also closed for the seasonal break. Her shoulders slumped as she settled in to wait, and she bent her left knee up to brace her foot against the wall behind her. She was there to stay, and she wanted them to know she wasn't leaving.

Samira checked the side entrance but couldn't see anyone monitoring the alley or the nearby rooftops. Why would they have two Kites on the front door and no one on the back? Surely they weren't that sloppy. Maybe they had a mage somewhere nearby to watch the side door. If that were the case, then they truly were in trouble.

Reykas knew to return by the side door, and Samira knew he would be careful, but she wasn't able to relax until she heard his key in the alley lock. It was, by then, fully dark outside.

"Any trouble?" Samira asked before they even were through the door.

Aquin smiled at her and put a comforting hand on her shoulder. "None other than putting up with this lug for a few hours."

"There is another Kite at the front of the theater," Reykas said.

"I know. She's been there all night, just standing and watching."

"Watching is better than arresting," Reykas said, and Samira had to agree.

She led them through the back hallway and into the room they used for staff meetings. Caius and Apak already sat at the table, deep in discussion no doubt about Apak's monstrous machine. Lizzie was sitting sideways in a plush chair, her legs dangling off the side. She leapt to her feet as soon as she saw Samira coming in with the others.

"Are you all right? Any trouble?" She grabbed Reykas by the arms, then felt his cheeks, laid a hand across his forehead, and kissed his mouth before he had a chance to reply.

Reykas laughed and took her hand in his. "That is a popular question tonight. We are fine, and we were successful."

Caius looked up from his conversation. "You found haranium?"

"Plenty of it. There is a series of tunnels beneath the library. The farthest corridor is the most secure, and I saw several message cylinders inside."

"Is there enough for what we need?" Apak asked.

"Hold up, gentlemen," Aquin said. "This is where I take my leave."

"You're not staying?" Samira sounded disappointed.

Aquin touched her face with her thumb. "I have no desire to know any more about this than I already know. After your scheming is finished, you can let me know what to do, but it is best if I know no more than that."

"The mages," Samira said.

"They can't read what's not there." Aquin squeezed Samira's hand. "I will see you after this. Plot well." With that, she was gone. Samira stared at the door for another moment, part of her wishing she could leave as well. But her place was here, and her role was to help her family survive the coming weeks.

"Can you describe the room where the haranium is held?" Apak asked.

"It is underground," Reykas said. "Not directly beneath the library, though. It was a long walk from the bottom of the library stairs to the room where they keep it. The vault itself is metal. I believe it is metal all around, the door as well. I counted three locks on it."

Apak was scratching notes onto a leaf of paper as Reykas talked. "We will need a means to transport the cylinders out of the vault."

"A wheelbarrow?" Caius suggested.

"That will not work," Reykas said. "The staircase down to the basement is too narrow. And there are too many stairs between the vault and the library door. It is my understanding that we do not wish to jostle these things."

"Right, you are," Apak said. He had an elbow propped on the table and stroked at his beard with that hand.

Samira had an idea. "You said the vault isn't directly below the

215

library. If we knew where it was, could we dig down to it somehow?"

Apak grunted. "There are many unknown factors. The ground-level location of the vault. The depth of it. The material in the ceiling. Many unknowns."

"But if we knew, maybe we could do it?" Samira asked.

"We need plans," Apak said. "Blueprints of the library and the catacombs beneath it."

"There might be blueprints in the library itself," Caius said.

Apak shook his head. "Perhaps for the library, but not for what is below it. Those tunnels were here long before the library was built."

"What do you mean?"

"I have heard stories about tunnels beneath Klubridge that were used for smuggling. Slave trade. Who knows what else? I suspect that these catacombs were part of that system. They predate the founding of the entire university, likely by hundreds of years. I doubt that we would find such plans in the library or anywhere else under the eye of the Empire."

"I know about the tunnels." No one had noticed Dorrin come in, but every eye was on him now.

"You know these tunnels? How much did you hear?" Caius asked.

Dorrin stepped the rest of the way into the room. "I heard some of it. I don't know those exact tunnels, but I know about the network. Scrounger told us all about it. I think he wanted us to use them, eventually. He might still be planning on that." His voice trailed off, and Samira knew he was thinking about the other children he had left behind with Scrounger.

She said, "Tell us what you know, Dorrin. Every bit could help."

Encouraged, he continued. "Scrounger has maps. I don't know if it's the whole thing or just sections or what, but my friend Fairy's seen them. She told me."

Apak looked at Caius, and Samira read their faces. "Wait, no. We're not sending Dorrin back to that monster. It is out of the question."

"It's okay," Dorrin said. "I want to help. I can find Fairy and ask her about it. I've been wanting to see her, anyway."

"You can't tell her what we're doing," Caius said. "It would put her in danger."

"I know. But…" Dorrin hesitated.

"What is it, honey?" Samira stroked his hair.

"I was just wondering. If Fairy can help us… can we bring her with us when we leave? On the ship?"

Samira shot a stern look at Caius and Apak before they could say anything. "One more wouldn't hurt. But it's important that you not tell her why we need the maps. Will she be in danger if she gets them for you?"

"I don't know. Maybe." Dorrin was frowning now, likely rethinking his plan.

"You don't have to do this," Samira said.

He took another moment but then looked up at her. It was decided. "I'll do it. Fairy will help us."

It was another hour and a half of talking, plotting, arguing, and eventually agreeing before Samira left for the night. Before anyone went home, Samira checked out the upstairs window again. As expected, there stood the Kite, still propped against the Monument wall opposite the Chamberlain, now looking somewhere between tired and annoyed. She was watching the people of the city pass with lazy turns of the head, but the entrance to the Chamberlain never was out of her sight. Samira wondered whether the woman would be there all night. Surely she couldn't keep the vigil if she already was getting bored.

When Samira went out the side door, she wasn't surprised to find that it still was unguarded. These Kites were dangerous, but nobody would accuse them of being the most responsible soldiers in Klubridge. There still was the chance that an Imperial mage was lurking somewhere nearby, though, and the thought of having her mind read without even knowing she was being watched made her quicken her pace.

She took a winding route back home, dipping through familiar cross streets and doubling back twice for good measure. She didn't think the Kites had found her house yet, and she had no intention of helping them locate it. Once she was reasonably certain that no one had followed her, Samira turned onto her own street and took the steps up to her door.

She fished in her pocket for the key but stopped. In the slight crack beneath the door, she could see light vibrating with the irregularity of flame. Samira tried the doorknob, and it turned in her hand. She pushed the door inward and smelled the smoky scent of her fireplace.

"If you're going to break into my house, at least let me give you a key."

"It would hardly be breaking in, then, wouldn't it?" Aquin had angled one of the chairs toward the hearth and had her bare feet propped on the edge of the short table that was centered before the settee.

Samira tossed her own key onto the table to her right, next to a stack of novels she'd been meaning to share with Reykas but had forgotten about amid all the recent scheming and peril. She came around the back of the chair and ran a hand through the back of Aquin's thick hair before pressing a kiss into the top of her head. "By all means, make yourself at home," Samira said. She dropped onto the settee and watched the fire dancing in front of her.

"How did things go after I left?" Aquin asked.

"I thought you didn't want to know."

"Not all the details. Just generally, how did it go?"

"We have a plan of sorts," Samira said. "Nothing is settled, and I'm not at all comfortable with how we'll be getting the next piece of information we need. But I suppose it's as good as could be expected at this point."

Aquin slid her hand off the arm of her chair over to rest it on top of Samira's. "You look worried. And tired."

"I am worried. And I guess more weary than tired. I'm just ready for all of this to be done."

"Is this the first time you have dealt with the Empire?"

"No." Samira was silent and watched the fire long enough to

convince herself to keep talking. "There have been other run-ins over the years. You get used to that when you travel with Caius. This is the worst it's been since we came to Klubridge, though."

"How long have you known Caius?"

"Practically my entire life," Samira said, and she smiled for the first time that night. "We grew up together, and we left together. We've been on the run ever since, one way or another."

"On the run?"

"I was barely sixteen when the Kites came the first time. Those were green. Caius was fourteen. We fled and didn't stop moving until we found Klubridge, years later."

"You've always taken care of him, haven't you?"

Had she? "I suppose so. It's funny, in a way. As strong as he is, and I still look after him. I guess that's what family is."

"How has he been in Klubridge for this long without drawing attention? The magic act is a bit brazen, you know."

Samira smirked. "He's drawn plenty of attention. Just not the wrong kind, until now. Who would think that a true mage would be stupid enough to buy a theater and put on a public magic show? Everyone loved to get wrapped up in the fantasy, to believe for a night that they were skating on the edge, watching a mage perform his dark and forbidden spells for them. But none of them really believed in it. It was just play acting for them, and they went home satisfied."

"I'd heard of him, you know. The Great Akithar. His reputation is a strange one."

"Did you come see the show?"

Aquin threw her head back and laughed. "At the prices you charge for tickets? Hardly."

"What kind of reputation does he have, then?"

"People like to think he's a boogeyman. They talk about him with fear, but there's some admiration too. He's crafted quite a persona."

Samira nodded. "That's what he's been trying to do for the past decade. And it's worked until now."

"What put these red Kites onto him?"

"I don't even know." The weariness felt solid, like a block pressing down on her shoulders now. She rolled her head, and her neck gave a deep crack. "You hear what it's doing to me."

"Poor thing," Aquin said and stroked the back of Samira's hand with her fingers. "So you and Caius never…"

Samira swung her head back around to look at Aquin. "Are you serious? Of course not."

"You can't blame me for asking."

"I can and will. That's practically incestuous. Ugh!" Samira stuck her tongue out. "Besides, it's been a very long time since either of us has had anything like… this."

"This?"

"Whatever this is," Samira said. She turned her hand over and slipped her fingers through Aquin's. "I like this."

"As do I." She squeezed Samira's hand. "It hasn't been nearly as long for me," she added with a grin.

"Well, then." Samira leaned her head back again and rested it on the top cushion on the settee. She watched the orange and yellow light play across Aquin's face in the darkness. "Come with us."

"I told you I can't."

"We have a ship."

"I also told you I don't want to know the details."

"You need to know this one. We're leaving, and soon. I don't want to leave you behind."

Aquin looked into Samira's eyes, and Samira wondered what she saw. Aquin gave a sad smile. "I have a life here. It's not perfect, but I can't just leave."

"But we only just found each other. It's not right."

"It is what it is," Aquin said. "Now, we can spend this time happy or we can spend it crying about the future. I know which I prefer."

Samira sighed and returned her own sad smile. "Me too." She surprised herself with a sudden yawn.

"You do look exhausted," Aquin said. She stood and pulled Samira's hand. "Come along. It is time for bed."

"I'm really not sleepy yet," Samira said.

Aquin grinned back. "Neither am I."

CHAPTER 18

Dorrin slipped away under the cover of night. It had been several weeks since he'd been living at the theater, but it already felt like a lifetime. Still, the path back to the East Ward was familiar. It didn't take long for Dorrin to reach the edge of the old neighborhood, marked by a burned-out row of houses. They'd been that way for as long as Dorrin could remember, and they still were empty and untouched. Skink had told Dorrin they were haunted, and he believed it. Everybody else did, too, and that's why nobody had claimed them or tried to do anything about them.

Past the scorched fronts of the housing row, the street angled down into a gradual hill. Dorrin felt the descent more emotionally than physically. It was the first time he'd been here since the night Samira had caught him outside the Chamberlain. What had happened since he'd been gone? Surely Scrounger wasn't happy about his absence. Skink probably was glad to see him gone, but what about Fairy? Dorrin had thought about her every day since he'd left, and he'd been waiting for an excuse to get back to the Ward and check on her.

There wasn't much foot traffic here at this time of night. Everyone who lived in the Ward was out scheming and thieving, and all the people who didn't live there knew better than to be in the Ward at all, much less past dark. Dorrin had never felt like the Ward was a dangerous place when he lived there, but something had shifted in the weeks since he'd left. It felt like the place had changed, but Dorrin knew it was more likely that he had changed. Scrounger would say he'd gotten soft. Maybe he had. Maybe that wasn't so bad. But he did feel a heaviness in the Ward that he'd never felt before.

Dorrin reached the corner with the old, bent lamppost and scampered up it and onto the roof of the ancient tavern. The worn shingles were familiar to his feet, and he leapt across a small gap to another roof, and then another. He never took the street in this part of town. That belonged to Barween Drach, and he knew not to get caught down there, especially after he no longer had his own crew to protect him.

It was only after his destination was in sight that Dorrin considered how he was going to handle this. He couldn't very well just march right into the place. Most everybody would be out, running cons and cutting purses, but Scrounger might still be there. Fairy always stayed behind, except for that one night when she didn't, the night Dorrin left. But who knew how things were handled now that he was gone? Things had a way of turning in the East Ward, and a few weeks in the theater district could be five years down there.

Dorrin crouched on the edge of the roof overlooking the door into Scrounger's den. It was quiet there. He didn't see any movement, no light, nothing. There wasn't anybody else out on this block, either. Dorrin had an eye for the streets, and he knew when he was being watched or followed. He'd never felt more alone here than he did just then. Something wasn't right.

He dropped from the roof to the street and landed in a soundless crouch. His movements were stealthy, but someone still would have spotted him on any other night. Not this one, though. Something was wrong.

Dorrin crept to the broken doorway and listened. Nothing. Swallowing hard, he gave the door a gentle push, and it slid open a few inches, the bottom scrubbing along the floor just like it always had.

Inside was pitch blackness. Dorrin squinted into the dark but could see only as far as the dim moonlight through the door allowed, and that was only a couple of feet of warped floorboards.

Keeping low, he slipped through the doorway and into the front room, where they all slept. His foot caught on something, and for an instant he thought it had to be Skink, catching hold of him and pulling him in to some awful fate. But when he dropped into a squat and slapped at his foot, he realized it was just the old and moth-eaten blanket they hung over the doorway sometimes to keep out the flies. Somebody had pulled it down and left it in a pile on the floor.

Even without being able to see anything, he knew he was alone. There was no sound of bodies shifting, no sound of breathing. He couldn't even smell the stench of perpetually unwashed children, a scent he hadn't even considered until he'd had a week or so of regular baths. There was another smell, though. Something unfamiliar and rank, but faint.

He slid his hand along the wall and felt his way to the mounted lamp he knew would be there. With his other hand, he found the little cannister of matches. He pulled two out and struck one on the rough wall. He used that one to light the lantern mounted in the sconce and slipped the other one into his pocket. The burst of light was so sudden in the black room that it left Dorrin blinded for another few seconds. He blinked away the daze and finally could see.

There was Scrounger's chair, just like always, the only piece of furniture in the room. The same old ratty blankets and rags were in piles in the corners, but he'd been right. No one else was there. Dorrin took a risk and was ready to bolt out the front door if the wrong response came. In a tentative voice, he called, "Fairy?" But there was no answer. Where was she? Where was Scrounger, for that matter?

Dorrin looked around the room for any sign of what might have happened in his absence, and he froze when his gaze fell on the floor at the front of the room. The boards were stained dark there in a way he was certain they hadn't been before he left. He moved closer and squatted next to the stains. It was black in the lamplight, but Dorrin knew it hadn't always been like that. He shuddered and backed away from what must have been a pool of blood. As he moved away from it, he saw more of it on the wall, speckled in the darkness but standing out in a strange pattern. What had happened here?

"Fairy!" Dorrin called louder this time. He no longer worried about Scrounger or Skink or anyone else hearing him. He came around Scrounger's chair and stopped at the door in the back wall, the one covered by the heavy hanging tarp. He'd never been allowed back there, and Scrounger surely would beat him if he found Dorrin in the back area. He had to chance it.

Dorrin pulled the material aside, and it snapped free from its hangings. He cried out and jumped back as the whole makeshift curtain crumpled into a dirty heap at his feet. It had already been hanging loose and was just waiting for the last tug to rip it free. Who had done that?

Fear tingled the back of Dorrin's neck, and uncertainty held him back, but his concern for Fairy pushed harder and propelled him through the opening and into the unfamiliar room. It was dark there, even darker than the front room had been, but he could see another lantern on the wall directly in front of him. He lit it with the second match and wasn't surprised to see that he was still alone.

The back room was smaller than he'd imagined, consisting only of a rickety table, a couple of old chairs, and a sleeping mat shoved against the far wall. That probably was Fairy's. That awful smell was worse back here. He sniffed the air and coughed in regret. Much worse here. He pulled the neck of his shirt up and over his nose and mouth in a feeble attempt to mask the putridity.

There was a door to the right, and Dorrin could tell from the faint moonlight under the edge that it led outside. On the other side of the room, a narrow wooden staircase went down. He unhooked the lantern from the wall and carried it with him to the top of the stairs.

Looking down, he thought those stairs might never end. What could be down there? He wanted to call for Fairy again, but he found that his voice no longer worked. The hand holding the lantern shook, and he had to hold it steady with the other one to keep from dropping out any of the oil. Setting the whole place on fire would not help him or Fairy.

Dorrin forced his feet down one step, and then another. He moved down the stairs with quiet precision, but there was nothing he could do about the boards that groaned under his weight every couple of steps. Before he knew it, though, the stairs ended, and he was in some sort of basement. The stench was worst of all down here, and the shirt did little to keep it out of his nose and mouth.

He held the lantern up and shined it around the unfamiliar room. This must have been Scrounger's office. There was a rotting desk against one wall and a few cabinets flanking it. He still was alone, which came as both a relief and a reminder of how wrong everything felt. Dorrin went toward the desk intending to search for clues, but he stopped midway there. Something didn't look right on the side wall.

Dorrin angled the lantern in that direction, and he saw it was the boards. The walls were nailed up in the same sloppy fashion as in the main room above, but the boards were in a little better condition down here. Still, two of the boards were crooked on that wall, while all the others hung in approximations of straightness.

He changed his course and went to the wall, curiosity overcoming the dread that had been mounting ever since he saw the bloodstains upstairs. It looked like someone had pried the boards off the wall and then stuck them back on without any care. The edges were scarred where they had been pulled, and several nails were missing. Was something hidden back there? Maybe a hint as to what had happened here?

Dorrin traced the edge of one board with his fingertips. There was just enough space to fit his fingers through, so he grasped the board and gave it a pull. It came free easier than he'd expected, and he stumbled back a step. The first board fell out of the wall and pulled the second one beside it down as well. The wood thudded onto the floor, and one of the planks knocked into Dorrin's shin, but he didn't even notice.

In an instant, a lifetime of memories flooded through Dorrin's mind. All the beatings. The mockery. The threats. The fear. All of that was distilled into the horrible shape behind the boards, into the gray and rotting but unmistakable face of Skink.

~

D orrin didn't remember leaving the basement, but he was in a full sprint out the front door by the time his senses came back to him. He staggered onto the broken stones, fell to his knees, and vomited in the middle of the roadway. His entire body heaved as he gagged, and for an instant he believed he could purge what he'd just seen as surely as he was losing everything else. Once there was nothing left to throw up, he replaced it with sobs. The image was still there, and he knew it would be there for the rest of his life.

Skink had been awful. He was mean, violent, and vicious. He also might have been the stupidest person Dorrin ever knew. But he'd been family, of a sort. He'd been there for so long, a specter looming over Dorrin, directing his little band of scoundrels to their own cruel mischief. As awful as he'd made Dorrin's life, he didn't deserve to be dead. Not dead and stuffed into a basement wall, never to be found.

Another sob shook Dorrin, and he forced himself to his feet, up and away from the sickness in the street. He wiped at his face with the back of his hand, trying to get rid of the snot and bile that reminded him of that moment. When the boards fell away and he was staring into the milky eyes of his dead... friend? No, he hadn't been that. Dorrin wasn't sure what he and Skink had been, but now Skink was nothing more than filthy ragged skin disintegrating over a skeleton.

Dorrin shook his head and slapped at his cheeks. He knew he was in shock. He'd seen it happen to people before, but he'd never seen a dead body himself. That was a miracle, given his upbringing, but somehow he'd avoided it until now. But there it was, the first one, Skink. Dead and crawling with shiny things that were in Dorrin's vision just long enough to be seen, but mercifully not long enough to be identified.

He was on the opposite side of the street from Scrounger's den now, and Dorrin knew he'd never go back in there. Had Scrounger done that to him? And where were the others? Was Fairy—

No, she couldn't be. He wouldn't allow it.

Dorrin set off at a run. He didn't know where he was going, and it didn't matter, as long as it was away from that hovel, away from that basement. The street was empty, and he nearly fell as he barreled around a corner. He had to find someone, anyone, but especially Fairy.

"Ey!" The voice stopped Dorrin cold, and he spun around, looking for its source.

It was a teenage girl, thin and dressed in a torn shirt and trousers. The only thing about her that looked clean was the narrow brimmed green hat she'd shoved down over her greasy blonde hair. Dorrin heard movement from behind, and he turned to find two more, one a boy that had just dropped from a rooftop and the other a bigger boy with a narrow and wicked piece of wood resting over one shoulder.

"You in the wrong place," the girl said. She stepped out into the street, and Dorrin saw she was carrying a cane. Her hand wrapped around a knob at the top that looked like a large gemstone, but he knew it couldn't be real. Nothing like that would survive down here for long.

"I don't want trouble," he said and put his hands up in front of him. He hoped that would make him look sincere and not like someone who needed a beating. But he knew better.

"Gim your shoes."

"What?"

She slapped the pavement with the end of her cane, and Dorrin flinched. She pointed the cane at his feet and then at the boy with the club. "Gim your shoes," she repeated.

He looked at the bigger boy, coming up from behind him, and the boy flashed a smile that was more tongue than teeth. He could hand his shoes over, but he knew how that would go. Dorrin had never robbed anyone like this, but he'd heard plenty. If he gave them anything, they'd know they had him. He'd be lucky to make it out alive. He would not give them his shoes. Besides, they were nice leather ones Lizzie had found for him.

Dorrin bent as if to remove his shoes and turned that into a duck beneath the big boy's arms. He was through and tensed to run, but he'd forgotten the third one, the other boy. A swift kick knocked Dorrin off balance, and he spun onto his side in the gutter. As he hit the ground, Dorrin saw the boy who'd kicked him. Short, wiry, malnourished, and hungry for pain if he couldn't get a meal. He was sizing Dorrin up, and Dorrin wasn't sure whether the intention was going to be the former or the latter.

Caving to thugs' demands was a bad thing, but getting caught while denying them was even worse. Dorrin slid backwards, away from the trio and pushed himself up to a sitting position. The big boy was turning now, and he'd taken the club off his shoulder. Behind that one, Dorrin could see the girl, clearly the leader, strolling his way with the nonchalance of a predator confident that she'd run her prey to ground.

"Not smart, boy. You learn, though, see."

Dorrin looked behind him, up, around, but there was no help. The four of them were alone on that street. They'd beat him, and if he were lucky, it would only be half to death. He might die in that street, just around the corner from Skink's rotting corpse. A fierce desperation gripped Dorrin. He would not die. Not here, not like this. The desperation became a buzzing in the back of his brain. He thought he could feel it vibrating through his neck, down his arms, even into his legs, stronger as the girl and two boys drew nearer.

Everything stopped.

Dorrin's eyes were wide, and they took in the dark street as it changed. Everything faded to a pale, luminescent blue. He could hear the night breeze clearer than before, as if all the other sounds had disappeared to focus him on that one rustling breath. It echoed in his ears, and he thought for a moment he might faint.

Dorrin's hands raised, and he watched in terror as threads extended from his fingers. Thin, yellow, shimmering threads, just like the ones he had followed so many times on the street. They had led him to the perfect purses, the best marks to strike. They had guided him, and now they flowed out of his body in a way he'd never seen or imagined. They felt almost tangible, like real threads extending out into the night.

His ears popped, and all the sound came rushing back in at the same time the world lost the blue glow. The street, the night, and the thugs all were back to normal, but somehow nothing was as it had been before.

"What the bleeding—" The girl jumped back, and Dorrin realized they could see the golden threads, too.

The big one reached to touch the glowing strings. His hand passed right through them with a sizzling sound, and he looked at Dorrin, his brow creased in confusion. The boy's fingers dropped off his hand and hit the ground with soft, bloodless thuds.

Just then, the threads pulled taut and shot out past the thugs, up towards the top of the bar where the girl had been hiding. Dorrin felt his whole body jerk forward, and he was up, pulled into the air, soaring over the girl's head, shooting into the night sky. He was flying.

The threads had pulled Dorrin onto the roof of the bar and then past that, beyond more buildings, faster and faster, the wind whipping cold through his hair and making his shirt slap hard against his skin. It was at once both terrifying and exhilarating. He'd experienced nothing like this in his life and had never dreamed that those threads that had guided him on his nightly thieving and kept him safe would be able to physically lift and propel him through the air. His unbelievable journey ended unceremoniously when the threads vanished, and he tumbled end over end onto the roof of what he guessed was someone's home.

He lay on the cold roof tiles and didn't move while he caught his breath. When he could sit up, he looked at his hands. They were normal. There was no sign of the shining lines that had flowed out from them. Dorrin remembered the boy they had maimed, and he swallowed hard. What was happening to him? He seemed to have no control over the things. It was like they sensed he was in danger, and they got him out of there. In the past, the threads had led him through the streets, but they had never become real. No one else had seen them, as far as he knew. Until now, he'd always thought they were imaginary, just something he'd come up with to help him visualize his path through the crowd. Now he knew better.

Dorrin went to the edge of the roof and looked over, down to the street. He had no idea where he was now. He still had to find Fairy, though. He looked at his right hand again. How could there be no sign of those things? Dare he even try what he was thinking?

He took a deep breath and held his hand out over the side of the building. Dorrin closed his eyes, and in his mind he saw Fairy. He remembered her face, her hair, the way she laughed at him. And he felt a tug.

His eyes opened to a faint golden glow, much dimmer than the shine of the threads that had pulled him away from the robbers. This time there was just one thread, exactly like he used to see in the streets. It extended out not from Dorrin's hand but from his chest. He looked down, startled, to see the shimmering string growing out from the center of his shirt. It passed right through the clothes without damaging them, and it flew out into the air. The thread flickered, less steady and constant than the ones from just a few moments ago, and Dorrin suspected he would be the only one who could see this one. The thread dipped from the edge of the roof and disappeared into the street.

Dorrin slid to sit on the side of the house and then dropped himself down to a windowsill, down again to a railing, and finally down to the street. There were a few people out on this street, and he knew he no longer was in the Ward. This wasn't a nice neighborhood by any means, but it at least was a place where people felt safe to walk at night. He weaved between them and picked up his pace to follow the trail set by the golden string.

He still wasn't sure where he was fifteen minutes later, when the thread led him down a backstreet lined with shuttered businesses, a victim of Klubridge's volatile economy. There were signs for restaurants, booksellers, and tool emporiums, all hanging over darkened windows, some of them with boards nailed over the showroom glass. The thread angled to the left across the street, disappearing into a closed grocer's storefront. The glow dissipated, and the string disappeared entirely as Dorrin approached the building. He didn't know how it worked or what he had done, but he was certain that the thread had led him to where he needed to be. To Fairy.

Dorrin tried the front door and found it unlocked. He pushed it open a couple of inches and recalled the door to Scrounger's lair that he had pushed open just a little while ago. Had that really been the same night? This door opened without the scrubbing of wood on wood, and Dorrin was able to slip inside. The front room had been where the produce was sold, but now it was all empty, just rows of wooden bins and a counter, all abandoned to dust and time. From the back, through another door, he could see the warm glow of a candle.

He waited until he was at the door and could see inside before he called out. But there, inside the back room, sat Fairy. She was on the floor and leaning against the far wall, talking in a low voice to a child next to her. Dorrin recognized a young girl from Scrounger's gang. He thought her name might be Miri, but he wasn't sure. There also was a little boy on the other side. He'd heard him called Gad, he was sure. And he saw someone else, also small, curled into a sleeping ball in the corner.

"Fairy," he said.

She stopped talking to the little girl, and they both looked at the door, eyes wide. Startled fear gave way to relief, and Fairy was on her feet and across the gap in a flash. She scooped Dorrin into her arms, and he nearly lost his footing. Fairy said nothing at first but held onto Dorrin like she was afraid he would disappear again. Dorrin hugged her back with an awkward flailing of arms, and she finally stepped back and looked at him.

"How did you find us? Are you all right?"

"I think so. I think I'm okay. But, Fairy, I have no idea how I found you. Something strange is happening to me." He held out his hands again, as if he thought the threads would spring to life, but nothing happened. And, just like that, the story poured out of him. He told her about being attacked, the golden strings, his flight into the sky, even about the boy's fingers. As he was finishing, he realized that he'd left out the instigating factor, the most traumatic part of the whole night. "Fairy, Skink's dead. I saw him." He was seeing the body again, and he shook his head to banish it.

Fairy pulled him down onto the floor, and the little boy and girl looked at him with curious expressions. The third child continued sleeping, oblivious to anything that was happening in the room. "I know," Fairy said. "Scrounger's dead, too."

Seeing Skink's body had shaken Dorrin, but hearing that Scrounger was gone seemed impossible. "No. Scrounger too?"

"There were soldiers who came after you left. They were asking questions about the magician, Akithar."

"Scarlet Kites," he said.

"I guess so? Scrounger wouldn't tell them what they wanted to know, and they killed him. Skink was there and saw it, and they killed him, too."

"You saw it happen?"

She nodded. "I was hiding in the back with the other kids. We made it out the back door before they found us." She took Dorrin's hand in hers and touched his fingers as if she were trying to convince herself that he was real.

"Where did you go? And where's everybody else?" He looked at the three children, only a fraction of the whole gang.

"I tried to take care of everybody, but the group broke apart. Skink's lot took off first. I don't know where they went. I was able to keep the rest together for a few days, but then they started drifting off. The older ones first, and then some of the younger ones wandered away, too. Usually while I was asleep or getting food. We're all that's left now."

The little girl curled up next to Fairy and rested her head against Fairy's arm. She slipped a thumb into her mouth, older than Dorrin thought kids usually were when they stopped doing that. But who knew how damaged this child was?

"I think Scrounger was trying to protect you, Dorrin."

His attention jumped back to Fairy, and his eyebrows went up. "What do you mean? Why would he do that?"

"You were special to him. I think he knew you were a mage all along."

"But I'm not a mage."

Fairy smiled at him. "I've suspected for some time, and I think it's hard for you to argue that you're not after what you just told me."

"That's ridiculous. I can't... I just..." But he stopped, because he felt the truth. There was no other explanation for what he had experienced. For what he had always been experiencing.

"I think Scrounger had other plans for you, and that's why he always treated you different from the others. He saw something in you, and that's a fact. Skink and I saw you going into the magic theater, and Skink was going to sell out that magician to the Kites. That's what brought them to Scrounger, and he died without giving them anything. He was afraid they'd find you."

Everything made sense now. The Kites were after a mage, and Skink had put them onto Caius' trail. That's why he was in trouble now and why the whole theater company was about to give everything up and flee the city. All because of Dorrin.

"Are you okay?" Fairy asked.

He shrugged. "So much has happened since I saw you. I feel like I've messed everything up."

"Don't say that. You're safe now, aren't you?"

"I don't know. The Kites found the theater after all. They're coming after Ca—Akithar now. They think he's some kind of spy or something. I don't even understand half of it. But now everybody has to leave the city, and it's all because of Skink wanting to get me." The words were out before Dorrin remembered his promise not to tell Fairy any of the details about what was happening. Too late to take it back now.

Fairy frowned in sympathy. "They're leaving the city? Are you going with them?"

Here with Fairy now, he wasn't as sure as he'd been earlier that night. "They want me to come. They have a ship that will be leaving soon, but I don't know now."

"Nonsense. You will go with them. You will be on that ship when it sets sail."

Dorrin brightened. "You can come with me. I already asked, and they said you could."

Fairy blinked at him and opened her mouth to speak, but then she shook her head. "I can't, Dorrin. I'm responsible for them now." She nodded to the three children. "They depend on me."

"They can come, too!" He hadn't expected or asked about bringing three young kids along, but he said it anyway.

"We're not going to uproot these children. They've already been through enough. The best I can do for them now is to take care of them and try to find a good home for them. Try to salvage whatever I can of their lives."

Dorrin wanted to protest, but he knew she was right. These children hadn't asked for a life with Scrounger any more than he or Fairy had. They deserved better, and they'd have no chance at that without Fairy. And sailing away with a rogue band of fugitives was not the start to a better life.

Instead of pushing the point again, he resigned himself to the reason he'd gone out that night in the first place. "I need your help, Fairy. They all do, really."

"My help? What can I do?"

"Do you remember the tunnels Scrounger used to talk about?"

She rolled her eyes. "It's practically all he ever talked about when you all were out each night. He was convinced there was treasure hidden down there somewhere."

"Treasure?"

"Coins, jewels, some kind of nonsense. I don't know. But yes, I remember far too much about Scrounger and his blasted tunnels."

"He had maps and drawings of the tunnels. I remember you said you saw them sometimes. Do you know where those are?"

She frowned and hesitated before answering. "They're all in his office. He kept them in cabinets down there."

The basement office, down in the putrid dark, where Dorrin had found Skink. He was about to speak when Fairy cut him off. "Is that what you need? The maps?"

"It is, but you can't go back there, Fairy. The body—"

"It's okay. If that's what you need to get out of here, I'll get them for you." She stood and put a hand on his shoulder. "Watch after them for me, will you? I'll be back as fast as I can."

She leaned down and kissed Dorrin's forehead, and then she was out the door, gone into the night.

CHAPTER 19

Dorrin came back to the theater in the early hours of the morning with a satchel packed full of maps, drawings, and scribblings. The poor boy looked exhausted, so Apak took possession of the papers and sent him to bed in the loft that Samira had turned into Dorrin's room. Dorrin had not offered an explanation of how the documents came to him or where he had been, and Apak did not ask. The task was completed, and the boy had earned his rest.

Apak unbuckled the satchel and poured the papers onto his desk, being careful not to let them overflow onto the floor. He tossed the empty bag into the corner and stepped back to appraise the pile he would have to work through. This Scrounger had been diligent and dogged in collecting every scrap of information he could about the tunnels that ran beneath Klubridge. Apak hoped the man's obsession would prove to be to his own benefit. Surely the blueprints to the library vault Reykas had described were somewhere among those pages.

Apak spent the first hours sorting the documents into piles. He first divided them into maps, drawings, and text. He then set about the work of finding correlations between individual maps, sketches, and accounts related in the written pages. Scrounger's methods emerged as Apak worked. The man would begin by writing any rumors he encountered in exhaustive detail. If he heard about a new entrance to the underground network, he would fill several pages with precise notes about the entrance's location, the grade of the ground's descent, a list of any nearby buildings, what had stood in that place prior to the current structures, on and on and on. Anyone else might find such painstaking elaboration tiring, but it energized Apak. If the man had been so detailed about every bit of information he obtained over the many years he had investigated, it was even more likely that the above ground location of the library vault would be in the collection.

After writing his account, Scrounger then would illustrate the section of tunnels he had described with as much precision as possible. His chosen medium sometimes was charcoal and sometimes ink. Apak was no art scholar, but he had to admit that the scoundrel had a knack for rendering stone walls and brickwork. His flora could have used more practice.

The final step in Scrounger's process had been to plot out a map of the region being studied. As he looked through the blueprints and maps, Apak realized that it was unlikely that Scrounger had been inside any of these tunnels. Notations in the margins of the maps showed scribbled math, indicating that the cartographer had worked out his proportions by comparisons and equations rather than personal observation or actual measurements. Everything on the desk was the product of second- and third-hand information, but the papers seemed to cross verify each other well enough for Apak to accept the conclusions as being mostly accurate. It should be accurate enough for their purposes, at least.

Apak often could match pages from the three piles based on the look and feel of the physical pages. The oldest entries in Scrounger's collection had yellowed over the years, and the more recent papers still retained an off-white sheen. By searching back for the most colored entries, Apak was able to establish a chronology and match written accounts with drawings and blueprints. The selection of paper composition itself had changed over time, as well. Sometimes

Scrounger had used thin, cheap pages, and other times it was thick, almost like playing card stock. A few of the records had been written on linen fabric. There was no discernible pattern for when or why he had used one type of paper rather than another, but all the material concerning a given section of the tunnels was consistent.

Shortly after Apak finished collating the pages into newly sorted stacks, Oreth arrived for his morning tasks.

"Morning, boss," he said as he came in. "What's all this?" He came over to the desk and reached for one of the stacks.

"Do not touch! These are recorded accounts of rumors and research concerning the network of tunnels beneath Klubridge."

"The ones we're busting into?"

"The very same. Our task now is to identify the grid structure of corridors and vaults that Reykas encountered beneath the library. It is somewhere within these stacks."

"Have you been at this all night?" Oreth was not touching the pages now, but he leaned over the table to look at the top pages on the various stacks.

Apak ignored the question. "Do you believe that you could be useful in this task, or should I assign you something less intellectually demanding?"

"I think you just insulted me, but I don't know for sure, so I'll help you. Just tell me what to look for."

Apak told him, and they worked side by side for another three hours, poring through every rumor that had a collection of pages. In the end, it was Oreth that found it.

"Hey, Apak. You said we're looking for a grid, right? Is this like what you wanted?" Oreth held up one of the maps in his left hand and one of the drawings in his right. Scrounger had drawn both on pieces of parchment that had aged to a light brown around the edges, but the center still was crisp and white on both pages.

"That is not a grid, Oreth. That is..." Apak's voice trailed off as he squinted at the pages. It took him a second to see what Oreth already had identified. This map showed a large, open chamber, cut into parallel corridors running from north to south but no connection between them. It looked like the bars in a cell. The second page, the drawing accompanying the map, was an isometric rendering of channels being dug horizontally, west to east, through rows of identical rock walls. Apak leaned forward. "Of course! He drew the map based on the original orientation of the tunnels. They were independent and parallel corridors. It was only later that the connecting hallways were dug."

"So this is good?" Oreth asked.

"This is very good, indeed."

Apak elbowed the door open and made a quick scan of the room before dropping his stack of pages onto the meeting table. "Good, you all are here. The vault we seek is beneath a dormitory on the campus."

Caius laughed. "Never any preamble with you, is there?"

Oreth came in behind Apak and stifled a yawn. "He's had us working on this all day. I think he was at it all night. Oh, hi, Lizzie."

Lizandra was sitting sideways in one of the chairs with her arm propped over the back. "Hello, Oreth." Her smile was genuine, if long suffering, and Apak knew he was going to have to have that talk with Oreth. Again.

Samira had arrived just before Apak and was only now taking her seat next to Caius. "Are you sure about that, Apak? The dorms are a long way from the library. At least three classroom buildings away."

"That would make sense," Reykas said. "It was a long walk from the stairs. Seven corridors over, and each corridor had storage rooms on both sides to pad it out. It's a big area."

Caius steepled his fingers under his chin. "How did you figure that out, Apak?"

"A great amount of the credit belongs to Oreth for identifying the chamber's blueprints. The initial tunnels seem to have been built as evacuation routes. Before the university was funded, the main class building seems to have been a prison."

Lizandra said, "There's a shock."

"Parallel tunnels lead from the various jail blocks underground and into the larger network."

"Where did they exit?" Samira asked.

"That is both unknown and irrelevant," Apak said. "If I might continue, we were able to identify the hill on which the dormitory is built by overlaying its topography on the relative depths of the evacuation tunnels. Taking ground erosion into account, I have found the location directly above the tunnel that Reykas called the 'G' corridor."

"I don't need all the details," Caius said. "I just need to know how sure you are."

Apak wrinkled his chin and looked at the blueprints one more time. "My certainty is within... ninety-eight percent."

"Good enough for me. Show me." Caius stood and came around the table.

Apak shifted the tunnel blueprint to the side. "Aha, here it is." He pulled a large sheet before him and smoothed it on the table. "The dormitory in question."

Caius peered at the paper. "These are students' bedrooms?"

"The uniform rooms are sleeping quarters. This smaller one appears to be a storage room. Fortunately, that is the room we need to access."

"The vault with the haranium is directly beneath that closet?"

"I am certain of it."

"Ninety-eight percent certain," Samira said with a smile.

Apak chose not to respond, even though he was fairly confident that was a joke. "The floor will be poured stone. It should be porous and therefore easy to breach. I believe the ground beneath the dormitory and above the vault is largely composed of packed dirt, perhaps with some small rocks mixed in. According to Reykas, the roof of the vault is metallic, and it likely also is rock or poured stone above that."

"That's a lot to dig through," Lizandra said.

"You are correct. Fortunately," Apak said, shuffling the papers again, "I have developed a solution."

Caius leaned over the drawings on the table. "Isn't that the vibration machine from the earthquake illusion we did last year?"

"It is, and this will be the device that takes us through the floor of the dormitory, displaces the earth beneath the building, and breaches the ceiling of the vault."

"How does it do that?"

"I developed the machine to simulate a localized earthquake. It will be able to disrupt the stone and metal through emitting varied audio oscillations. I merely dampened the oscillations for your illusion."

"Hold on," Caius said. "You gave me a machine that causes actual earthquakes, and we set it off in the theater every night for three months?"

"Precisely." Apak continued, "Of chief concern here is the collateral vibrations that will be generated in the metal walls and possibly the floor of the vault. You likely are thinking that such vibrations could trigger the haranium to explode, and you would be correct."

Caius' eyes were wide, and he gave Samira a look. She shook her head and shrugged back at him.

"This issue is what I plan to address for the remainder of the day and evening."

"So you can make this thing get us into the vault without blowing us all up?" Caius asked.

"I will have the machine's modifications completed tonight."

Lizandra pulled the drawing of the machine closer to her. "What about noise? You said this thing causes audio something or others. Won't that be loud?"

Apak tilted his head. "Well, yes. There will be some sound involved, but I believe I can minimize that as well."

"If you can't, we'll have the police all over us, and that's if we're lucky. Kites, more likely," Lizandra said.

"What is near this building?" Caius asked. "Anything the Kites will be watching?"

Samira said, "The bank is probably the closest place with money, but it's pretty far from the campus. I don't think there's anything on the school grounds that they'd suspect we'd be after."

"There are security patrols on the campus, though," Reykas added. "Aquin mentioned them when we were there."

Caius nodded. "We'll have to be ready for that. We need to keep eyes outside the dormitory, and we should be ready with a distraction, just in case this ends up being louder than we want it to be."

"What kind of distraction?" Samira asked.

"We can do it," Lizandra said. "Reykas and I will watch the building, and we can draw any attention away if needed."

Reykas raised his eyebrows when Lizandra volunteered but smiled at her and agreed. "Distraction is what we have provided every night before your performance, Caius. We can do it again this time."

"Okay. We have the distraction set. Now we need to get the haranium. Who will be in the building with me?"

"No, I do not think that is how we will do this," Apak said.

"What do you mean?"

"You are too valuable to the overall plan. To us. I will be in the dormitory. You will be nowhere near this operation." Apak looked at Samira. "I will trust you to ensure that Caius does not try to involve himself directly in this excursion."

"Now wait—" Caius began.

Samira cut him off. "I'll keep him safe. We will meet you at your workshop after you've finished."

Apak nodded. "That is acceptable."

"It's not acceptable to me," Caius said.

"Do you know how to operate my machine within safe parameters? Do you know how to target the precise vector we will need to breach the vault? Will you be able to dampen the vibrations to limit the chance of igniting the haranium? I think not, and I will not be showing you how to do any of those things. I will be operating the machine, and you will be in the Downsteps with Samira."

Caius was the leader of their troupe, but Apak appreciated the moments when he could step back and allow logic to prevail. This was one of those moments, and Caius sighed with acceptance. "All right, but you can't do it alone."

"Of course not. Oreth, you will accompany me into the dormitory.

We will require one additional strong body to lift the haranium up through the well we will create."

"One of the stagehands?" Samira asked.

"That will be acceptable. A team of three will be sufficient for extracting the haranium to a cart, which will be waiting outside the dormitory. Once we have finished, we will bring the cart to my workshop."

Caius sank into the chair next to Apak and pushed his forehead into his hands. "There are so many ways this will go wrong."

Apak smiled in response. "And exactly one way that it will succeed. Shall we plan for tomorrow evening?"

The earthquake machine was a square metal box that measured about two feet on each side and from top to bottom. When they used it in the nightly performances, it sat under the stage, the open end facing out toward the audience, and rumbled the floorboards and their chairs from its stationary position. It now needed to be mobile, and Apak had laid four selections of handles on the worktable beside the box.

"Can you tell me the benefits and detriments of each of these handles?" he asked Dorrin, who was studying the layout before him.

Dorrin took a flat metal handle and turned it over in his hands. "This one seems like it would hurt to hold it, if the machine's going to be shaking around."

"An astute observation. The flat edges would be likely to cut the holder's palms." Apak pointed across the table. "And you, Oreth? Which handle would you select?"

Oreth was working on removing the fasteners from one of the internal components. When set to a task, he was diligent in accomplishing it, as long as his attention could be kept. He glanced up and then at the handles on the table. "That one on the right?"

Apak shook his head. "The handle you have selected is the same one Dorrin just eliminated. You must pay attention."

"Sorry, Apak, but my attention needs to be on this thing if you expect this to get done in time for tomorrow night."

"What's tomorrow night?" Dorrin asked.

Oreth grinned across the table. "That's when we're robbing the library."

Apak cleared his throat. "You have a task before you, Oreth."

The younger man frowned back. "Whatever, man." He dug back into the machinery, and a fastener popped out and skittered across the floor.

"Carefully, please."

Dorrin had forgotten the handles. "You're robbing the library?"

Apak selected the second handle from the left, a big one with a thick cylinder of wood between the two metal hinges. "This would be the most appropriate handle. The wood is able to absorb the vibrations naturally, and the holder's hands would be protected better than they would by metal handles."

"Is this part of it? You're taking this to the library?"

"And so we shall attach one of these handles on either side of the housing."

"Is it for the haranium stuff? Is that what you're stealing?"

At last, Apak placed the part back onto the table and gave Dorrin his attention. "Yes, we will be obtaining the haranium, but we are not robbing the library, as Oreth chose to describe it."

Dorrin's eyes sparkled. "I can help! If there's one thing I'm good at, it's thieving. Well, I guess I shouldn't call it that. But it's true. I just did purse-cutting on the streets, but I'm really good at sneaking and getting into places."

Oreth grinned at Dorrin. "Well, well, little man."

"Oreth, please." Apak lowered himself into the chair next to Dorrin. "You will not be a part of anything that may or may not be occurring tomorrow night."

"But—"

"That is the end of the discussion. I will not have you involved in this. The plan is set, and it would be too dangerous for you to be there."

"I know how to take care of myself." Dorrin sulked and pushed at one of the handles.

"I am sure that you do, but tomorrow is too important for testing that assertion. You will stay with Caius and Samira, and you may rejoin us in my workshop once the plan has been executed."

Dorrin did not reply but did not look happy. He would learn to accept disappointment, Apak was certain. It was an inevitability in this world, particularly with the lives they were living.

When Dorrin did speak, he took Apak by surprise. "Apak, why is magic outlawed?"

Oreth stopped working again and looked at Dorrin. Apak motioned for him to get back to his task and then asked Dorrin, "Why do you ask?"

"Is magic evil? What does Ikarna say about it?"

"Ikarna does not believe that magic is evil. She, along with her siblings, brought magic to us. Before they made themselves known, we had only the natural elements. Ikarna trusted humans enough to bestow abilities upon a select number. She sees magic as a gift."

"Like what Caius does?"

"I am not sure how this is relevant to our current project, Dorrin."

"It's just, if Ikarna says it's okay, it seems like it must be okay. But then it's illegal, and we're in danger because of it. Why do the Kites want Caius? Why can't people be mages?"

Apak considered his words for a long moment before speaking. "This is a topic that bears a longer discussion at another time. For now, I can assure you that, while magic itself is not evil, it can be used for evil things."

"And that's why it's illegal? To keep people from doing bad things with it?"

"Well, no. That is why people like this Commander Mollor say it is illegal. But the true evil comes from the only one who can wield magic with impunity."

"Impunity?"

"Without getting in trouble," Oreth said and gave Dorrin a wink.

Apak said, "The High Lord Peregrine is a mage. Did you know that?"

Dorrin shook his head.

"He has been doing magic since time immemorial, and he does terrible things with it. His mastery of magical forces is what has kept him in power for so long."

"That's not what Ikarna wanted," Dorrin said in a serious tone.

"No, young man, it is not. The High Lord is jealous with his abilities, and, like any corrupt man in power, the thing he fears the most is losing that power."

"So he doesn't want anybody else using magic."

"Precisely."

Dorrin considered this new knowledge in silence. Apak watched his face, interested to see the conclusion he would reach. The boy was looking at his own hands, splayed on the tabletop in front of him. After a few moments, he folded his hands into his lap and looked up at Apak. "That's messed up."

CHAPTER 20

The dormitory building was at the head of a long, green lawn bordered by three other similar buildings. Lizandra and Reykas arrived together from the southwest just as dusk was settling over Klubridge. It was going to be a clear night, with just a light breeze to rustle the grass and sway the trees. Students were out on the benches or sitting on the ground, some of them rushing from building to building, but it wouldn't be long before night arrived and they disappeared into their rooms to sleep or to study or to sneak out for some mischief.

"This could have been you," Lizandra said.

"Me?" They were standing at the corner of the southernmost building, obscured by the early evening shadows.

"You said you'd thought about going to school once. This is what it would have been like." Lizandra leaned into his chest, and he put an arm around her to hold her back against him. "What would you have become?" she asked.

"I don't know. A poet, perhaps?"

She laughed and craned her neck to look at him in the dark.

"You mock me," he said. He sounded hurt, but she knew better.

"Recite one to me, then. Give me one of your poems."

He smiled back. "Lizandra, your eyes are sparkling pools. Your hair, fine thread from... spools..."

She cackled. "That might be the single worst poem I've ever heard."

"I am not finished."

"Oh, there's more?"

"Your grace is unmatched as you spin and fly..."

She finished it for him. "I guess you really are a lucky guy."

Reykas touched her nose with his and grinned. "I suppose I am."

Lizandra reached a hand up to pull his face to hers, and she kissed him. "I want you to be safe tonight. No unnecessary risks."

"Of course." He didn't give her the same warning, and she suspected it was because he knew better than that. She worried enough for the both of them, between his illness and their stunts and now this utterly mad plan.

Reykas looked at the sky. "It is time for us to be in position."

"I'll take the west building, you take the east?"

He nodded. "You know the signals?"

"Chirp once if I see guards, twice if I'm in trouble, three times if it's all clear again."

"Right." He started to leave her, but he stopped and came back. One more kiss, and he looked into her eyes. "Be careful." And he was away.

Watching Reykas disappear around the corner, headed for his building, Lizandra felt her stomach tense. They had been in love since practically the first moment they saw each other, and they had been performing acrobatics together for just as long. She had taken care of him when he was ill, helped him hide his sickness from prying eyes, and even run away with him when they no longer could stay with her family's carnival. So many moments, so much that seemed to defy death, but this night was the first time she truly feared for him and for herself. They'd never done anything like this before. It had been a long time since Lizandra had given much thought to the gods she was raised to believe in, but she spared them a brief and silent prayer before she took off for her building in a crouching run.

Apak had told Dorrin to go wait at the workshop in the Downsteps, but he had also told Dorrin that people have an obligation to do good where they can. On balance, it seemed more important to do good and then make apologies later. Besides, Apak didn't know about this new thing Dorrin could do, whatever it was. Dorrin had tried to tell him, started to, but in the end he couldn't. Not until he knew more about it himself. He wouldn't learn anything cooped up in the workshop with Caius and Samira, and that's why he crept out of the Chamberlain just after Lizzie and Reykas left.

Dorrin scrambled up to the roofs at the first chance he got, and he trailed behind them all the way to the university. Their pace was slow and casual, and Dorrin had to hold himself back from his usual speed. He thought more than once about trying to propel himself across the rooftops with those strange golden threads, but he knew that was too risky. It would draw attention to him, and he still wasn't sure how to control them. He didn't even know if he could summon them at all. They'd appeared and become solid when he was in trouble and needed help, but every other time he'd seen the threads, they had been dimmer and unreal.

He settled into the slow pace, often crouching on a roof corner or a gable to wait for Lizzie and Reykas to catch up with him. He wasn't positive exactly where they were going, but he knew it was somewhere around the school. He'd gotten a look at the maps but couldn't make sense of them. Dorrin would just rely on his friends to guide him to where he needed to be.

Once they reached the school, Lizzie and Reykas shrank into the shadows behind a building at the bottom end of a wide quad. He hadn't been able to read all the details of the maps and other documents, but he recognized this place from one of the sketches. This was where they were going to use that device of Apak's, and Dorrin was going to make sure they didn't get caught. He didn't need to follow behind anymore, so he dropped to the ground and ran behind one of the long buildings and around the corner to the far one, the one they were planning to break into.

He counted four stories' worth of windows, but a huge tree behind the dormitory stood even taller. Dorrin considered both options and chose the tree. He waited until he was sure that no one was near, and he scurried up the side, his fingers and toes grabbing at the thick bark. Most of Dorrin's climbing had been up and down the sides of brick, stone, and wooden urban landscapes, but that had prepared him well for scaling that tree. It wasn't long until he was sitting on a sturdy branch that overhung the dormitory roof.

Dorrin saw Reykas appear on the roof of a neighboring building, and soon Lizzie was up on the top of the one across the quad from that one. They both came to their respective roof corners and crouched to wait. Up the tree, Dorrin had a better view than either of them. He could see into the lawn, all the way down to the far building, but he also could see the backside of the dormitory they were about to storm.

A breeze made the leaves around Dorrin whisper, and he shivered when a sudden chill ran up his back. He knew what he was doing was dangerous, but that's what you had to do to be a good person, right? Especially if you had magic. You had to learn to use it as well as you could, and make sure you used it to undo some of the bad that others had done with and because of magic. He felt a responsibility, and he rubbed the charm that hung on a leather thread around his neck.

"I'll do it right, Ikarna."

Night had fallen by the time Apak saw the first dormitory ahead. It stood in silhouette, backed by a half moon hanging in the cloudless sky. The water tower anchored to the top of it loomed heavy against the oncoming darkness. Oreth led the dappled gray horse along the stone path that wound through the campus, and behind it rolled a wooden cart carrying the earthquake machine, which they had covered with a dusty dark blanket. Apak walked alongside the cart on the left, and to the right was Zerva, a big woman who had worked with the company as a stagehand for the past year. She stood more than a head taller than Apak, and he had no doubt that she could hoist him over her head if the notion struck her. Thankfully, such a notion had not struck.

Before leaving the theater, Apak had exchanged his usual work clothes for black trousers and a black buttoned shirt. He had recommended the same for Oreth and Zerva. When it was time to depart, Oreth had shown up in the same green pants and brown smock he had worn earlier in the day, and Apak had to send him back to change. Zerva was a better listener and had arrived in a tight-fitting black outfit with no loose fabric to get caught or to impede her movements. Her choice of dress was so well selected for the night's escapades that Apak wondered whether she might have begun her career as a burglar before moving into the arts. Her hair was long and sandy brown, and she had wound it into a tight bun, secured under a black kerchief.

The horse, Genie, was Zerva's. They lived in a small house on the outskirts of the Downsteps with a tiny barn attached to the back. When she was not working at the Chamberlain, Zerva made extra money taking deliveries around Klubridge with the help of Genie, a second horse named Leaner, and the little cart. Apak had noted that the cart's right wheel had a slight wobble, but it was too late to do anything about that. He hoped it would not be significant enough to jostle their delicate cargo on the way back.

Apak tapped Oreth's shoulder and motioned to the left. Oreth nodded and led Genie in that direction as the path split. The small roadway took them behind the first dormitory, which Apak knew from the maps was the one farthest from their goal. They had encountered no students or other pedestrians since arriving on the campus grounds, and he hoped it would stay that way once they were in the midst of the student housing.

He had tinkered with the machine to remove the safeguards that had been in place during Caius' performances. Without those guards, the whole theater would have shaken to pieces on the very first night. Now, with a bit of luck, the directed vibrations would be sufficient to shatter the stone and metal that they were about to encounter. Apak also had worked to dampen the rumble the machine would make when switched on. Relying on the forces of audible sound, it would be impossible to make the device entirely silent, but he had been able to take measures to lessen the resulting noise. He hoped it would lessen the noise, at least. It was difficult to test the thing fully without blowing apart his workshop, and Apak preferred not to do that.

Apak looked up toward the sky as the cart rolled in front of the second building in the grassy quad. He could see a form perched on the edge of the far roof, across the way. That would be Lizandra or Reykas, and he knew the other one should be in a similar position atop the building he was passing just now. They were his sentries, and he trusted that they would spot any trouble before it fell upon him and his two helpers.

Based on his appraisal of distances on the blueprints, Apak had determined that the fastest route into the dormitory building and to the storage room was through the front door. He acknowledged that walking straight through the entrance was a risk, but time was of the essence.

Zerva tethered Genie to a post at the front of the building and rubbed a big hand through her mane. She leaned to whisper something into the horse's ear and then gave Genie a gentle pat on the neck. Apak felt certain that the horse was incapable of understanding whatever Zerva had told her, as horses relied more on physical cues than the intricacies of speech. Nevertheless, he held his tongue and pulled the blanket off the machine.

Zerva reached over the wall of the cart and lifted the contraption out without hesitation. Her strong hands gripped the thick wooden handles, and she held the box in front of her body as she waited for direction from Apak. He motioned for her to follow, and the three moved up the steps to the front of the building. Apak tried the door and found it unlocked. Oreth had crafted a set of lockpicks on a lark a few months ago. Apak had chastised him for wasting time and materials, but this night he had instructed Oreth to bring the tools along, in case they met with any impedance.

"That's a good sign," Oreth whispered as the door swung open.

Apak knew there was no such thing as good or bad signs or luck. He refrained from pointing out Oreth's folly and knew the unlocked door was because of Ikarna's providence. Apak put a finger to his lips and stepped through the doorway. He waved Oreth and Zerva in behind him.

The storage closet was straight ahead on the ground floor, just down this hallway and on the left. Apak marched at the front of the group, Oreth in the middle, and Zerva toting the earthquake machine at the back. Apak had determined the exact location where they would position the machine, give or take a few inches. With a clear shot down through the earth, they should be able to make fast work of the tunneling. Then it would be a matter of hauling the haranium up, carrying it out to the cart, and leaving without alerting anyone. If the machine were quiet enough, they might even be able to accomplish the goal while waking no students.

Apak looked up and down the dark hallway. They were alone, and he heard no movements. Satisfied, he turned the knob to the closet and pushed it inward. The storage room would be too dark for working, so Apak had brought two lanterns with enough oil to last them the night, if needed. He struck the first one alight and held it forward to survey the room. He grunted.

Apak recalled the browning around the edges of the maps and wondered how old the dormitory blueprints had been. At some point after the time when Scrounger drew the map, the floor of the storage room had been dug up, and modern piping had been set into place. The room now was a lavatory, not a closet.

"Well," Oreth said, peering over Apak's shoulder. "That's not what we expected."

Reykas had told Lizandra to be careful. And yet, here they both were, waiting on top of school buildings for their friends to rob a library. He gave a quiet laugh at the situation and looked across the quad, toward the building where he knew Lizandra was positioned. The moon provided dim light that played across the side of the dormitory, but it was not quite enough. He could not see her on the roof, but he thought he could feel her there.

His left hand shook, and he took it in his right hand to hold it steady. That is how the chills began, always with the left hand shaking. It didn't always get bad when his hand shook, but it happened often enough to be a concern. Reykas counted to twenty and released his fingers. He held his hand up again, the palm parallel to the roof. It was steady. Perhaps that would hold, or perhaps he was on the verge of another fit of sweating and convulsing. Either way, it was too late to second guess the plan now. He was committed and would do his part to see his friends safely through the night.

There was movement down in the quad, and Reykas leaned out to get a better look. Someone had come around the side of the far building and now was moving up the path next to Lizandra's dormitory. The figures were in shadow, but Reykas could hear the clopping of the horse's feet on the pathway. Genie. He squinted into the dark and could make out three figures accompanying her. That would be Apak, Oreth, and Zerva.

Reykas winced each time the horse took a step. The noise echoed between the buildings and funneled up to the rooftops. He hoped it was not loud enough to wake any of the students. He looked across the fronts of the four buildings. Windows lined every story, and there likely was a bedroom behind each of those windows. How many students were slumbering just feet away from this wild scheme? Too many, and it would take only one to throw the whole thing into chaos.

It was lighter near the front of the fourth building, for better or for worse, and Reykas had a clear view of Genie being tied to the post, Zerva hauling the machine out of the cart, and the trio heading up and into the housing unit. As the door closed behind Zerva, Reykas felt the night become closer, more oppressive. They were inside now, and there would be no backing away from whatever happened in there.

The night was silent for several minutes, perhaps ten or fifteen.

Plenty of time for Apak to have put his machine in place and begun work. Had the man silenced the box after all? Reykas strained to hear any hint of the thing breaking through the hard floor of the school building, but there was nothing.

And then Reykas heard a low thump. It didn't sound like a machine, but it wasn't exactly organic, either. It came again, and he realized it was in a regular rhythm. Whud... Whud... Whud... Again and again, that low, monotonous thudding sound. It had to be the machine. Reykas cursed and scanned the windows again. It was not a jarring noise, but it was unusual enough to draw attention and to invite investigation. Surely there would be a lantern appearing any moment now.

He looked across the gap to where Lizandra was perched but still could not see her. She had to be hearing this as well. Reykas looked to the left, and his heart jumped into his throat. There, entering the quad, was another figure.

Reykas squinted but could not see any details in the dark. The person had turned toward Reykas' building and was about to pass out of sight as they walked the perimeter. Their pace was steady and slow, despite the strange thudding noise. That they were not in a hurry seemed like a good sign that this was not a guard. Perhaps a student sneaking back into the dormitory after a night of revelry?

A single chirp broke through the cool air. Lizandra. She had a better view of the walker than he did. It was a guard.

Reykas growled another curse and slipped his legs over the edge of the roof. Time for a diversion.

Oreth said something, and Apak leaned away from the hole in the floor. "What?"

"I said it seems pretty loud, don't you think?"

Apak shook his head. "It will be fine."

"What?"

Apak shook his head again and looked back down into the hole.

The original plan had been for Apak to handle the earthquake machine himself. He had designed it, had built it, and was most familiar with its operation. In previous uses, however, the machine had been stationary while running. Now it needed to be held and constantly lowered into the tunnel, and Apak had not anticipated the physical strain involved in wrangling the unwieldy contraption as it vibrated and bucked. In the end, Zerva had volunteered to handle the box. Apak had been reluctant to hand such a machine over to someone else, but he would be the first to acknowledge his own shortcomings.

Getting around the pipes had not been as insurmountable an obstacle as it first had appeared. Oreth had located areas of poured stone that had been laid more recently than the rest of the room, based on the lightness of the floor's coloring in those areas. That told Apak that the renovations had taken out only the back quarter of the room's floor to install plumbing. That area ran near the space in the middle of the room where he had determined they would need to dig, but it was far enough away that no pipes were directly in the path of the excavation. They had to dismantle and move a large metal basin that had been hooked into the plumbing, but once it was out of the way, the digging could begin.

Apak had had concerns that vibrations emitted from the machine might dislodge some nearby pipes once they reached them, but so far there had been no leaks. Zerva had proven adept at maneuvering the device in a circular pattern while making her way deeper into the hole that was forming. She now stood waist deep, and her thick arms bulged under the tight sleeves with the effort of keeping the box on target and away from her feet. As cumbersome as the task seemed, she had not voiced a single complaint and even now had not broken a sweat.

Apak, on the other hand, felt his shirt dampening under the arms, and he wiped a bead of sweat off his forehead before it could run down to smudge his glasses. He thought he had solved the machine's noise problem, and while it was not as loud as it otherwise would have been, it still emitted a rumbling drone at regular intervals. He hated to admit that it was loud, but there was no denying that clamor.

Oreth looked equally troubled by the sound. Zerva was making excellent progress and had completely cleared through the foundation of the dormitory and was well on her way through the earth beneath it. The design of the machine obliterated the refuse she dug out of the ground, leaving only fine piles of dust instead of mounds of dirt. Zerva still had the metal roof of the vault to get through, though, and Apak was uncertain how much resistance that would give, when compared to what she already had encountered.

Every few seconds, a small rock would fly up and out of the hole, dislodged by the sonic blasts. The first one had come close to pinging Apak in the side of the head. After that, he took a few steps back from the hole and motioned for Oreth to do the same. Zerva was undeterred by the debris. The work had spattered her face, neck, and the entire front of her outfit with dirt, and Apak flinched every time he saw a rock or pebble ricochet off her chest or chin. Her determination never flagged, and she never reacted to any of the mess. She continued working, disappearing bit by bit into the new tunnel.

The farther down Zerva went, the more muffled the droning sound became. Perhaps they would make it through without drawing attention, as astoundingly unlikely as that seemed. No sooner had Apak felt a glimmer of hope than the door to the lavatory opened. "People are trying to sleep!"

A young woman, probably no older than eighteen or nineteen years old, stood framed in the doorway. Her blond hair was matted from sleep, and her long nightgown was twisted around the waist. She stood motionless, only now taking in the scene before her. Apak stared back with wide eyes, unsure what to say. Zerva switched the machine off and turned her head to look at the girl. Covered in dirt, Zerva looked like little more than two white eyes peering out of the darkness. Only Oreth spoke. "Er. Hello."

The girl blinked twice before she bolted. Apak heard her shout for help before she even reached the end of the hallway.

~

L izandra spotted the figure as he entered the quad, but she wasn't positive he was a threat until he neared the opposite building and walked between the shadows of two trees. A shaft of moonlight hit him, and there was no mistaking the uniform of the uptown constabulary. Between that awful throbbing noise that had to be coming from Apak's machine and this new arrival, the entire plan was teetering dangerously close to disaster.

She looked across the breach but couldn't make out Reykas' form in the dark. Had he seen the guard yet? She jammed her fingers into the corners of her mouth and blew a sharp chirp that echoed across the quad. Surely he'd heard that. Without waiting to make sure, Lizandra dropped off the side of the building. She caught the edge of the roof with her fingertips, slowing her fall only for an instant, and then dropped the rest of the way onto the grass.

Lizandra rolled into a crouch and launched herself across the quad. The officer was midway past the other building now, and from the corner of her eye she saw movement above that she knew would be Reykas coming down. At her current pace, she'd reach the guard before he did. A shout rang out across the campus, and Lizandra nearly lost her footing.

A woman was running out the front door of the dormitory to the left, the one Apak's crew had entered. Not good. Lizandra swung around a slim tree, and the guard was straight ahead of her. It was a youngish officer in a plain uniform with no badges or medals. A rookie, then. That could be a good thing. As Lizandra approached, still at a dead sprint, she saw him blinking and turning around, trying to identify either the source of the woman's shout or the cause of the loud droning sound. He hadn't seen the woman yet, also a good thing.

"Hey!" Lizandra shouted as she came upon him from behind.

The guard half turned, and she leaped first onto the side of the building and then pounced off, past him. As Lizandra whizzed past his head, she scooped his hat off and slapped it onto her own head. It was a ridiculous thing, tall and rounded, with tassels hanging off both sides, but she knew the penalty a city guard would face for losing any part of his uniform was a stiff one.

"You! Stop!" He made a grab for her, but she danced back out of his grasp.

Lizandra snarled a wicked grin at him and backed away, the hat tilted on her head at a jaunty angle. "Why don't you see if you can make me, eh?"

He rushed at her, and she spun away again. She had his full attention, and he didn't even see the other woman, now heading their way. Time to rush things along. Lizandra broke into a run back down the quad, away from Apak's building. She heard the guard swear behind her, and then there was the sound of his feet pounding on the pathway. She knew he'd never catch her, but she had to stay just slow enough to make him think he had a chance.

She reached the far corner of the building before she checked his progress. When she turned back to look, the guard was right there, on her heels, now knocking into her at full speed. How had he been so fast? She had time to curse her underestimating him before she took the fall hard on her left side. The police hat bounced off into the lawn, and she rolled after it, getting herself out from under the officer.

"Get off her!" Reykas was there, coming up right behind the guard. Lizandra would have told him she was okay, but she couldn't catch her breath. The fall had knocked the wind out of her, and she wheezed on the ground.

She crawled to her knees and looked back just as Reykas delivered a sharp kick to the young officer's side. The guard crumpled to hold his ribs, and Reykas was past him, now scooping Lizandra up. "Are you all right?"

She nodded, still unable to speak, but her eyes widened when she looked past Reykas. He spun to face the guard, looking as if he expected an attack, but Lizandra knew it was something worse than that. The rookie, still folded on the ground in pain, had raised his arm high into the air. Something glowed white and orange in his hand, shooting sparks down onto the walkway, and Reykas seemed puzzled. Lizandra tried to tell him what it was, but all she could do was tug at his sleeve. A shimmering jet of light shot into the sky, passing the tops of the dormitories, and exploded with a loud crack. The shape of a red bird hung above them, illuminating the whole campus.

A flare. The Scarlet Kites were on the way.

"Boss, look!" Kela yelled through the open doorway. The flare was bright enough to see from nearly any point in Klubridge, and she had spied it from just outside the door of one of the city's uptown brothels. The place was seedy enough to be on the low end of clientele but expensive enough to cater only to the upper class. It was a bit above Lucian Gieck's normal price range, but he often found that Kites got what they wanted, regardless of the coin.

Gieck knew Kela wouldn't bother him if it were not important, but he still was not pleased. All intentions of barking at his soldier fled when he spotted the signal glimmering in the night sky. His tabard was in his hand, and he threw it over his head as he ran out to the street. It looked like they were only a block or two away from the source.

"Come on." They had not brought horses, so they had to leg it across the road and through the intersection. Gieck heard Kela running behind him, and he knew Eyral would not be far behind. He thought they must be heading for the university an instant before turning the corner and running through the iron archway bearing the school's seal.

Buildings loomed ahead, and just above them the flare was fading into the air. Gieck heard shouts coming from the other side of the first structure before them. And what was that other sound? It was like the booming heartbeat of a demon, deep enough to rattle his teeth as he ran.

Whatever it was, whoever had interrupted his night, he would make certain they paid, and dearly. He grabbed the strap around his wrist and tugged at the cord hidden and wound within. It gave a satisfying zipping sound, and he held the metal weight at the end of the cord in his palm in preparation. His own pulse quickened with hunger and an eagerness to quench it. Perhaps he could salvage the night after all.

Dorrin heard the chirp before he saw the guard in the quad. It sounded like Lizzie. She had taught him to make the sound one night while they were waiting for the audience to fill the theater. It was a lot like whistling, which he'd picked up from the other kids, but this was more subtle and sharper at the same time. It sounded like a bird, but he couldn't remember what kind she had told him.

He saw Lizzie drop from the building on his right, and he could see Reykas shimmying down the one on the left. They had to stop that man before he reached the dormitory. Dorrin had been sitting on his branch, but now he hopped up to a squat, ready to slide down the tree and jump to the dormitory roof if needed. But he wouldn't need to do that. They'd take care of the guard.

Lizzie spun around the man and grabbed his hat, and Dorrin laughed at her guts. He might have been able to pull off that wall jump, but he never would have thought to take the hat. Then she was running, and the guard was right after her. He was faster than Dorrin expected, and the boy leaned forward, urging Lizzie to go faster. But then she stopped, and they both tumbled to the ground. Reykas was on them a second later, and Dorrin no longer could make out what was happening.

Something bright flew up from the guard's hand, and there was a huge popping noise. Dorrin flinched as the entire sky seemed to explode. It wasn't a weapon, though. It was a flare. He recognized it from the yearly Merchant's Festival, when celebrants would shoot them into the sky above the city, leaving colorful designs floating for a few moments before the wind took them away. This one was red and brighter than the ones Dorrin was used to. He still couldn't remember what bird Lizzie's chirp mimicked, but he definitely knew the bird hanging in front of him now. This one was a kite.

Not good, not good.

Dorrin spun around, searching the ground far below. They would see that flare, and they'd be coming. But from where?

Windows along the quad began lighting up as students awoke to the uproar. Dorrin was surprised the noise from Apak's digging machine hadn't already roused them, but they were sure to hear it now. Whatever else happened, Apak had to get into that vault, and they had to take the haranium.

Someone yelled down in the quad, and Dorrin snapped his attention back to his friends. It was the guard, now on his feet again. Reykas had Lizzie by the hand and was practically dragging her away. Something was wrong with her. Was she hurt?

Now someone else was on the walkway, running toward them. A woman in a nightgown? Where had she come from? Dorrin hissed at Lizzie to run, and his hand closed over Apak's charm. "Help her, Ikarna," he said and closed his eyes. Ikarna didn't answer, but two more figures did, rushing into the quad from the left side. Dorrin could see they wore hats and uniforms like the first man. More city watch!

Reykas and Lizzie were at the front of the dormitory on the far end now, and they were climbing. Dorrin urged them forward, fast and far away from the building where Apak still was working his way down to the vault. "Keep their attention," he whispered, and they did. All four officers were rushing away now, and Reykas was halfway up the building. Lizzie was lagging behind, but still she climbed.

Dorrin was bouncing on the balls of his feet, aching to help, but there was nothing he could do from this far away. They were all the way across the lawn, and going after them would only draw attention back toward the very building they didn't want the guards investigating. He felt helpless and rocked back against the tree trunk.

"Around the side!" The voice came from behind and below Dorrin, and he spun to find the speaker.

It was still dark, but the combination of the moonlight and the red glow of the flare provided enough light for him to see three more people coming up from behind his tree. They were about to go around the trunk, and then they'd head straight for Apak's building.

They couldn't see what was going on in the quad from where they were, and they would follow the sound of the machine instead of Lizzie and Reykas.

Dorrin leaned down, and that's when he saw the uniforms. They were Kites, answering the flare.

He looked back across the quad. Lizzie and Reykas were playing their parts, and they had pulled the city watch away from Apak. But they didn't know about these newcomers, and there was nothing they could do about them if they did. Dorrin knew what he had to do.

He closed his eyes and took a deep breath through his nose, held it, and then let it escape his mouth. When he opened his eyes, the world no longer was lit red. It was shaded blue, and the shouts from below had faded into a pin drop of sound behind the rushing voice of the wind. Dorrin stood on the limb, took a step forward, and allowed himself to fall forward into the night.

Zerva had started the machine again as soon as the girl fled from the room. Apak knew Reykas and Lizandra were on watch for just this sort of situation, and he hoped they were taking care of it. Nevertheless, it was likely that if that young woman did not raise an alarm, someone else soon would. They had to hurry.

The tone of the excavation made an abrupt change from an organic rumbling to a sudden, echoing thickness. Zerva had reached the metal in the ceiling of the vault. The hole was deep enough by then that she had disappeared from view a few moments before. Apak went to the edge of the pit and looked in just as the last of the metal let go. It fell into the vault with a loud clang, and Zerva switched off the machine again. She looked up, still covered in debris, and grinned. "That's it. We're through."

"Here, Oreth, take the machine. Zerva, begin passing the cylinders up."

Oreth stooped and reached into the hole as Zerva handed her equipment up. She relinquished the device without a sound, but he grunted and heaved as he pulled it up from the tunnel. Apak watched Zerva drop through the hole she had made, and she was into the vault. She was gone from his sight as soon as she passed through the opening, and it was pitch black in the room below.

"Do you need light?" Apak called down.

"I'm okay," she called back. "I think I feel them."

"Be careful. If you drop or so much as jostle one—"

"I know, kaboom."

"As you say." Apak wiped at his forehead and glanced at Oreth, who was beside him now and looking down the hole. "Oreth, take the cylinders as she passes them up. We must make haste, but be careful."

Oreth dropped to his knees and reached down into the pit as Zerva's hand appeared from the darkness. Clasped in her firm grip was something cylindrical. It was still too far down and too dark for Apak to see it clearly, but he knew it was a document cannister. Oreth stretched his arms down, and he could reach just far enough to grab the end of the tube.

"Careful," Apak warned again.

Oreth pulled it up with both hands. "Thing's heavy!" he said as he brought it up. "Where do you want them?"

"Stack them there," Apak said. "Be quick. She has the next one ready."

Oreth placed the first one on the floor with care, and Apak saw that it was the prize they sought. The tube was black and plain, with a hinged door on one end that had been sealed with blue wax. Reddish specks and streaks dotted the cylinder in a haphazard pattern. The haranium.

Apak looked back into the hole as Oreth reached for the second cylinder. His hands grabbed the end again, and he started to pull it up. Oreth gave another grunt and tried to jerk the weight up and out of the hole in one motion. Apak was about to scold him when the unthinkable happened.

The cylinder slipped out from between Oreth's hands.

"No!" Oreth yelped and tried to grab for the tube, but it was too late. Apak watched it fall back into the tunnel and knew they were done for.

The cylinder made a soft thud as Zerva caught it in one hand. Her laugh echoed up from the vault. "That was a close one, eh?"

Apak covered his face with his hands and stumbled back from the hole. Oreth was still on the floor and looked up at him, horrified. "I didn't mean—I just—"

"I warned you. You do not listen!" Apak wanted to chastize him again but knew there was no use. They had to hurry, and there would be time for recriminations later.

"What's going on in here?"

For the second time that night, a voice coming from the same doorway froze him in place. Oreth's eyes widened, and Apak turned slowly to see the city watchman standing in the dormitory hall, just outside the lavatory. The officer had a confused frown on his face, and his hand hovered over the regulation baton strapped to his belt.

Without answering the question or taking a step in any direction, Apak grabbed the door and slammed it in the guard's face.

L izandra could climb, but her breathing was ragged, and the center of her chest, just above her stomach, ached with a shooting pain. Reykas was above her, nearly to the roof. Her own progress was slower, but she was making it bit by bit. She cast a quick glance behind her and saw the guards gathered at the base of the building below them. One of the guards, the young one that had bowled her over, was climbing after them.

"Take my hand!" Reykas was at the top now and was reaching down for her.

She shoved herself upward, struggling to pull her own weight, something that ordinarily was a simple feat. Reykas still was half a floor above her, too far to reach, so she kept going.

Another look down, and the guard was gaining fast. She cursed and focused all of her will on her arms and legs. She told herself to ignore the pain in her core, ignore the breathing. She could address that later. For now, just climb. Climb like never before.

Before she realized she was within reach, Lizandra felt Reykas' hand close around her wrist. He hauled her up, and the last few feet of the climb passed in an instant. She tumbled onto the roof beside him and pushed herself to her hands and knees. "He's right behind me," she said. Her voice was a rough wheeze, but Reykas understood her. He looked over the edge, his face lit by the red flare that still burned in the sky, even as the bird shape lost its form in the night breeze.

"Can you run?" Reykas asked. "Can you jump?"

Lizandra pushed herself up to her feet and took an experimental breath. Nothing seemed broken. She'd just lost her wind, and it was coming back now, even if it hurt like hells. "I think so." She was used to tumbling, contorting, and performing. She was not a fighter, and neither was he. They had to be away from there and draw the guards with them as they went.

She looked down the length of the quad, toward the building where Apak and his crew were working. How much longer did they need? She was looking at Genie, tied next to the door, when she saw figures moving toward her. More watch guards. An officer was inspecting Genie and the cart now, and another was going up the stairs to the entrance of the building. "They're going inside! We have to divert them."

Reykas nodded and pulled her to the left. The guard was nearly onto the roof now. Lizandra ran. She shoved the pain down, pushed her breathing to as normal a pace as she could manage, and she ran harder than she ever had. Reykas was three steps ahead of her and had already reached the western edge of the roof. He sprang off it with a grace that still astounded her, even after years of watching him work.

Lizandra heard a shout from behind her and knew the guard was there. She didn't slow her pace and planted a foot on the corner of the ledge, leaping after Reykas. She covered the gap between buildings and rolled into her landing. She doubted the guard could do that, but she knew better than to underestimate him after the strike down on the ground. Instead of looking back, she hopped up to her feet and ran after Reykas again.

The guards were still at the front of the building with Genie, and Lizandra thought only one had gone inside. That was better than it could have been, but they had to draw the others away before they found Apak.

As she ran, Lizandra dipped low and scooped a handful of loose gravel off the roof. She had nearly caught up to Reykas, and they would be coming upon the northern edge of the roof soon. Without slowing, she drew her arm back and sent the tiny rocks hurtling off the rooftop. She prayed a few of them would strike true and get the guards' attention.

Reykas slid to a stop at the edge of the building and looked down. She knew he was judging where they should go next, and she risked a look behind them. The rooftop guard had not attempted the jump. He was off the other roof now, and she saw him leading the first group of police after them on the ground. She turned back to see whether the second group of guards had spotted them just as motion at the far edge of Apak's building caught her eye.

A slight form flew around the corner, and she recognized him in an instant. Lizandra grabbed Reykas' sleeve and pointed. "Dorrin!"

Dorrin's eyes were closed, and he felt the wind rushing past his face as he fell. His hair whipped back from his forehead, and he felt the snap as sound returned. When his eyes opened, he was gliding over the Kites' heads. They were so focused on getting around that building that they hadn't seen him yet. He'd have to do something about that.

The golden threads swung him in a fast arc so he outpaced them, and as he looked to the right, another tendril shot out from his body to anchor in the side of the building. It brought him around the corner, and a chunk of brick broke free. He wobbled in the air and dropped, coming down to the ground in a hard crouch. The shock of the impact evaporated the threads, but it wasn't hard enough to stun him. He was used to making bigger jumps nightly.

The Kites saw him now, for sure. The one in front was big, with a mean snarl on his face. Dorrin wouldn't want to tangle with him in close quarters, but he had to keep his attention. He bent to grab the piece of brick that had fallen with him, and he yelled at the Kites. Before they could respond, he chucked the brick at the front one, and it cracked straight into his face. Dorrin yelped and hopped backwards. He'd just meant to get their attention, not do any actual damage, but he saw now that he'd drawn blood.

The lead Kite staggered and rubbed at his face. The two behind him drew to a fast halt. They looked even less sure about what was happening than Dorrin was.

The injured Kite, the leader, saw the blood on his hand and wiped at his nose with a ferocious swipe. He pointed his bloody finger at Dorrin and gave the order. "Get him."

Dorrin spun away and sprinted around the corner of the building. For a second he lost track of where he was and what he was trying to do, and he angled toward the front entrance, where he saw Genie tethered. Several city watch guards had gathered around her. Past them, up on the next building over, he saw two people running against the darkened sky and coming to a halt on the edge of the roof. Lizzie and Reykas.

He planted a foot and made an abrupt change in direction, now heading away from the building where Apak was. He didn't know whether the watch guards had seen him, but he couldn't worry about them just then. The Kites were his focus now. He looked over his shoulder and saw them coming fast, the big one in the lead and the other two, a man and a woman, following behind. The one he'd hit was yelling something, but Dorrin was too far away and moving too fast to understand him.

The whole lawn was bathed in fading red light, giving everything a wild and fiery look. Dorrin needed to move faster. He tried to conjure the threads again, but they wouldn't come. He was learning that magic was not an exact science. He angled to the left, toward the next dormitory, and the Kites were on his heels. Dorrin had to get away and stay ahead of them, but his magic wasn't working. He had to rely on his old tricks, then.

He jumped against the side of the building and caught between the brickwork with his fingers. His feet scrambled for purchase, and he was going up the wall, hand over hand, just like when he needed a fast exit after cutting a purse. He knew the Kites would be right on his heels, and he didn't know how well they could climb, so he clambered up and onto the roof as fast as he could.

Once on the top, he looked across the lawn and saw Reykas and Lizzie running back along their roof in the direction they'd come from, toward the far building. A small group of guards was after them on the ground, and all the officers that had been in front of Apak's building now were heading for them as well. That was good. They could divert the guards, and he could handle the Kites. He hoped.

Dorrin flinched away from a cracking noise behind him. He turned to see a cable wrapped around a beam supporting the water tower on the roof and pulled tight over the edge. It vibrated with a humming sound, and he realized someone was coming up it, probably that big soldier. Dorrin had no desire to be around when he arrived. He thought it should take a few moments for the Kite to climb the distance, and he risked a glance over the side. Dorrin blinked and tried to process what he was seeing. The Kite was coming up the wall, but he wasn't climbing. He had both hands extended above his head, and that strange cable ran up his sleeve. It was reeling in like Dorrin had seen fishing rods do down by the docks. Instead of pulling in a fish, though, it was dragging the Kite upwards at an alarming speed.

Dorrin spun and ran, heading for the end of the building. If he made it there, maybe he could clear the jump to the next building. As his plan formed, he saw Reykas and Lizzie both make that same jump from their own rooftop across the way. They were on the far building now and heading his way. That gave him a flicker of comfort, but that also meant all the guards were heading that way, too. No time to change things, though. He had to run.

As the end of the roof neared, Dorrin realized the gap was farther than he'd expected. Lizzie and Reykas had taken it without a problem, but they were trained acrobats. He was just a thief who happened to be good at getting away. He hoped that held out for him tonight.

Dorrin stopped at the edge and looked down. The other two Kites were coming around the corner below him. He looked back, and the big one, the Kite leader was on the roof and coming at him fast. He could feel the rooftop vibrate under the pounding boots. Ahead of him, Lizzie had nearly reached the other side.

"Jump, Dorrin!" she shouted. She held her hands out to him, and Reykas had nearly caught up with her.

Dorrin swallowed hard and looked back one more time. He had to do it. He told himself he could do it. He took three steps back and then launched into a short sprint. His lead foot hit the edge of the roof and propelled him forward, up, out. As soon as he was in the air, Dorrin knew he'd never reach the other side. It was just too far, and he had already reached the peak of his jump. His arms and legs pinwheeled in midair, and Lizzie's hands were right there, but still too far.

He was going to fall.

He shut his eyes tight and tried to brace himself, but the fall didn't happen.

Dorrin hung in the air between the buildings, somehow motionless in the night. His eyes opened again, and Lizzie was still right there, her eyes widening and her mouth falling open. Reykas was there with her, and his eyebrows drew down in confusion. Dorrin could see both of them lit by a warm, golden light, and that was when he saw the threads. They arced out of his chest and out of his back, bridging the gap between the two buildings, holding him steady above the scrambling soldiers far below.

Hope swelled, and Dorrin willed himself forward. The threads pulled him, and he swung toward Lizzie. "Take my hands!" she yelled. The magic hadn't failed him after all.

Dorrin grinned at her and reached for her hands. He heard another crack, this time much closer. The cable whizzed past Dorrin's right ear and looped back, encircling his neck, and his fingers stopped an inch short of touching hers. Lizzie's face shifted from amazement to horror, and she screamed, "Dorrin, no!"

His leap carried him another couple of inches toward Lizzie, and then the threads vanished. Dorrin flew backwards, yanked by the cable, and he heard another pop, this one somehow different and even closer, as his head snapped forward with arrested momentum. Lizzie still was reaching for him, now so far away, when his back crashed into the side of the building. As his head slammed back against the roof at an impossible angle, Dorrin saw the last remnants of the red bird in the sky, and then he saw nothing else ever again.

PART IV
THE DOWNSTEPS

CHAPTER 21

As he stared down at the small shape before him, Gieck knew he'd made a mistake and possibly a fatal one. He waited on the roof with the body while Eyral got a wagon, and he turned the situation over in his mind, trying to find the right spin and hoping he'd already taken the right steps to handle this thing before Nera got involved. Kela was on top of the building with him now, looking down at the bent form of the child. He lay on his back, his head twisted too far back and to the left, and a wicked dagger stood embedded in his chest.

"What happened?" she asked.

"It was the magician," he said. "Akithar."

"He was here?"

Kela moved toward the edge of the roof and started to look over the edge, but Gieck snapped at her. "Get back here. Stay out of sight. We don't need more attention."

She looked at him with a frown but didn't argue. That's why he kept her close. She knew better than to challenge him, especially on a night like this one. "Eyral and I saw something glowing," she said. "The boy was hanging over us, and it looked like strings or ropes."

"It was the magic. Akithar was on the opposite roof with a girl. I believe it was the same girl from the bank who escaped from the commander. The wizard grabbed the boy with his magic and conjured that knife from nothing. He killed the boy and threw him back at me."

Kela opened her mouth and closed it again. Gieck could tell she had more questions but was afraid to ask them. Good girl to know when to shut up, but he'd have to keep an eye on her.

The truth was, there really were two other people on the opposite roof, and Gieck was certain one of them had to be the acrobat girl from the bank. She fit the description Mollor had given, minus the noble trappings. Slim, pale, blond hair. He wouldn't mind giving her a try himself. The other one, though, the one that came up from behind her, wasn't Akithar. The man on the roof had dark skin, and Mollor had described the wizard as being pale. That wasn't him, but it made for a better narrative.

One of the two truly had conjured golden threads out of thin air, and they'd caught the boy with it. It was one of the most incredible things Gieck had seen in his life. The boy was going over the edge, sure to fall to his death, and they'd stopped him there between the rooftops. The girl had had her hands thrust out when the threads appeared, so it could have been her, but Mollor had been insistent when she said the acrobat in the bank hadn't used magic. So either she'd saved up her skills for an emergency like this one, or the dark man behind her was the mage. Gieck's money was on the man, but either way, he had seen magic that night. There no longer was any question about whether they were on the right track.

Gieck thought a stabbing sold the story better than a magical strangling would. He'd lifted that knife from a vendor earlier that day, and it was a nice one, too. He'd miss having it in his collection, but it looked like something a mage might call up, all ornamented with a red jewel in the hilt. And, truth be told, it was going to end up in somebody eventually anyway, so it might as well be this street rat.

"Why were they here?" Kela asked.

Gieck looked up from the body and squinted at her. Another question or two, and she might be the second casualty of Akithar that night. "Whatever it was, we stopped them."

"Shouldn't we talk to the guards? They're still in the quad now."

"There's no need. We can handle this, and we will report back to the commander."

"But the flare in the sky—"

Gieck took a fast step toward Kela, and she stumbled backwards in response. Another step, and she'd be off the roof and no longer his problem.

"We can handle this," he said again, his eyes burning into hers. "We will report back to the commander."

She broke the gaze first and bowed her head. "Yes, sir."

Tomos, one of Mollor's lapdogs, threw the door open to the chamber. He stepped aside, and there she was, the grand lady herself. Mollor was wearing her red cloak, and it billowed behind her as she swept into the room. Gieck took that as a good sign. She only wore that cloak when there was serious business to attend to, and this business couldn't get any more serious.

"Tell me what happened." No greeting, straight to the matter at hand. Gieck could handle that.

"I was near the school campus with Kela and Eyral. We were patrolling the perimeter, and there was a commotion near the dormitories, so we went to investigate."

"What sort of commotion?" Mollor was still looking at the boy, but her eyes flicked to Gieck for an answer.

"There was a flare."

Her eyes flicked over to Kela, standing against the wall. Gieck ground his teeth and glared at the girl but kept quiet.

"One of our flares?" Mollor asked.

Kela nodded. "Yes, commander. I believe it was one of the city watch."

"Why did they send up a flare? What was happening?"

"We… did not have the opportunity to question the watch."

"Explain this, Lieutenant."

Gieck didn't like the tone in Mollor's voice. She might outrank him, but she still had some things to learn about respect. "As I was saying, we heard shouting near the dormitories, and a red flare went up. When we arrived on the scene, three people were fleeing. One was this boy. I'd wager the second was your acrobat girl. The third was the mage, Akithar."

Mollor's eyes widened. "You saw him there? With your own eyes?"

"I did. We weren't able to talk to the city watch, because we gave chase. They climbed one of the dormitories—"

"They climbed it? Straight up the wall?"

"The girl is an acrobat, you know."

Mollor tilted her head for him to continue, and so he did. "I went up in pursuit, and Eyral and Kela came around on the ground. Akithar and the girl jumped across to the next roof over. The boy couldn't make the jump, and they left him behind. They had to know I'd stop to help him, and they'd be able to get away. I'm just sorry there was nothing I could do. He was dead by the time I reached him."

"How did he end up like this?" She gestured to the body that had now turned pale. The knife still protruded from his chest, and Gieck had made sure it stayed there as they lowered him down from the roof and made the bumpy ride back to the castle in the wagon.

"Akithar killed him. He caught the boy up in a sort of..." Gieck struggled to describe what he had seen. It was easier to talk about the parts he'd made up. "The knife is some kind of magic. He summoned it up from nothing and threw it at the boy. Then he tossed him back at me like he was nothing. A sack of potatoes."

Mollor was frowning now, but not just because she was outraged at the crime. There was something else. What hadn't he accounted for? She turned to Kela again. "You saw all of this?"

Now she was second guessing him. What was this? To her credit, Kela nodded but looked at Gieck with wary eyes before answering. "Eyral and I were down below, between the two buildings. We saw the boy try to make the jump. The other two were already on the other side by then. I saw the boy stop in the middle of the jump. They caught him in... I don't know what it was. It looked like a bunch of shiny strings. Or ropes, even. Then they disappeared all at once, and the boy went flying back onto the roof with the lieutenant."

Gieck watched Mollor's face as she listened to Kela's account. Her nostrils flared at the mention of the golden strings. It was barely enough to notice, but he'd known her for enough years to know how to read her face, especially when it came to magic. He had her hooked now.

"This makes no sense," she said, almost too low to hear.

"What do you mean?" Gieck asked.

"I know this boy. He was in the theater the day I went and questioned Akithar. I'm positive, this has to be the same boy." She paused, and her eyebrows pulled together. She tugged at the collar of the boy's shirt, dragging it down an inch or two. The boy's throat was discolored where the cord had grabbed him, but that wasn't what had drawn her attention. Below the bruising, laying on the boy's pale chest was a pendant, hanging on a brown string. Mollor closed her hand over it and jerked at it, breaking the cord. She held it up in front of Gieck.

"I don't understand," he said, and for once he wasn't lying.

"This is an icon of Ikarna. It belongs to Akithar. I saw it in his office. This boy was one of his own people."

Gieck had to stifle a laugh. "That seals it, then. We should go arrest him now."

"Why would he kill one of his own? And so brutally? It makes no sense."

"Does anything they do make sense? Mages are wild animals. We have to put him down before he kills anybody else."

Mollor stared past Gieck. He could see her mind at work. Could she be coming around to his simple solution at last? But no. She shook her head. "We will arrest him, and we will silence his magic. He will not be executed. He has information about the rebellion that is vital for the High Lord to possess. He will not be executed," she repeated. "Is that clear?"

"It's clear."

"Go to the Chamberlain. If he's not in the theater, find him. The acrobat, too. Arrest them, and bring them to me."

"Where will you be?"

Mollor motioned for Tomos to follow, and he fell in behind her. "I'm going back to the campus. There are questions that beg answers."

CHAPTER 22

Nera had kept her composure in the castle chamber where the boy's body lay on the cold, stone table, but she felt her rage rising as she stepped through the huge double doors, crossed the bridge, and walked into the street. It was palpable, beginning at her head, radiating heat to her ears, down her neck, into her torso and arms. Her breathing came harder, and she felt the pulse throbbing in her throat.

That boy had been alive when she went to the theater. He'd been an innocent, caught up in something he didn't understand. Something he likely had no choice about. And now he was dead, his corpse bruised and bent and a knife still skewered through his chest.

Nera had heard about magical weaponry, swords and bows and staves conjured from nothingness, but this was the first one she had seen with her own eyes. Previously she'd put no more stock in those stories than she had in tales of magical creatures bestowing gifts or raining fire down from the sky. And yet, here a weapon summoned from magic. Somehow she felt that if magic weapons existed, they should glow. That was what magic usually looked like when she'd witnessed it, at least. Bright, colorful, shining with malevolence like the spell Lucian and Kela had described. They'd seen shining threads materialize around the boy, threads that had left their vicious marks around his neck. The dagger had none of that glow. It was ordinary steel, perhaps more ornamental than the regulation blades her Kites carried, but still more mundane than she would have expected.

Why had Akithar killed his own boy? Was it meant as some sort of message for her, or was he truly that ruthless? In her years of tracking mages, Nera had encountered all manner of disgusting humanity. She'd seen wives betray husbands to save their own necks. She'd watched a woman flay the skin from one of Nera's trusted soldiers with the flick of a wrist. She'd seen mages immolate an entire building full of humans, just to make a political statement.

But this? Never. The casual brutality of stringing an innocent child up and stabbing him to death was foreign to Nera. There was no blood visible around the knife wound, and that gave her hope that the poor child had died quickly, as soon as the first spell had hit him. Perhaps his neck broke, and he was gone long before the villain created a blade for the express purpose of passing it through his body.

She clenched her fists as she walked, and a woman sidestepped to get out of her way. Nera gave her no notice and had ignored every other citizen that had scrambled out of her path on her trail out from the castle. She was too furious to care about anything but that monster now.

The boy had been working in the theater. He had trusted Akithar, had been part of his company. She wondered whether the child even knew anything about the horrors that mages had brought into the world. It was unlikely. Everyone in that theater lived and worked under the sway of Akithar, and they had probably groomed the boy to believe that his patron was misunderstood or oppressed or dozens of other equally blatant lies. Akithar was a mage, and this is how it always went with mages.

Nera opened her hand and looked at the charm in her palm. She'd first seen it in Akithar's office on the same day she'd first seen the boy. The amulet was the last piece she had needed to confirm her suspicion that she was on the right trail, that the Chamberlain was a den of sedition against the Empire. How had this icon ended up around the boy's neck? She again wondered whether it was a message, a threat directed at her. Or was there something even more insidious at play? It would not surprise her if Akithar had brainwashed the boy into worshiping Ikarna alongside him. Ikarna, the sea hag that drew the superstitious devotion of so many rebellious dogs.

She slipped the charm into the pouch strapped to her belt as she made the left turn onto Broom Street. She'd been in no mood for crowds and had taken a side street to this point, but there was no avoiding the traffic as she neared the courts. Still, the people saw her coming and read hatred in her face, and a pathway opened before her as they pushed to either side. The buildings here were pale stone, built early in Klubridge's ignominious life, when there had still been hope for the city to be a beacon of something, anything other than the squalor and excess that it ended up embracing in equal measure.

Nera knew that the barrister's office on the left was one of the oldest buildings in the entire city. On any other day, she'd have taken the time to step inside and admire the ancient stonework and the history within. Today was not that day, and she gave the building barely a glance, her red cloak whipping behind her in a sudden gust.

Tomos was nearly at a jog to keep up with her. He'd been following in her wake the whole way from the castle, but now he moved up beside her. "Where are we going?"

Instead of answering, she shot a fierce look at Tomos, and he flinched. She regretted it. He was a good soldier and was learning well. He didn't deserve her rancor any more than that boy deserved the mage's dagger. "Did Eyral say anything to you about what he saw last night? Anything other than what the lieutenant told me?"

Tomos shook his head. "He didn't say much other than telling me Lieutenant Gieck had him find a cart to bring the boy back. He had to help get the body off the roof."

Lucian had done his best with a bad situation. She wished he'd had the presence of mind to pursue Akithar and the girl, but she knew that tending to the boy was the correct move. As rough as he might seem to others, Lucian had a soft heart. Of that, she was sure, and her own heart ached for the horror he must have felt when Akithar murdered the boy just to slow him down. Nera's sympathy for Lucian fed her anger, and she felt her cheeks flare with its fire.

The only mistake Lucian had made the previous night was not following up with the city guards who had summoned him with the flare. She would address that soon enough.

"Tomos, please wait by the entrance."

"Yes, Commander."

She left him on the street and climbed the white stone steps to the Watch House, the central headquarters for the city guard.

Nera had known Wilhelm Bonner since she first came to the Imperial Academy at eighteen. He'd been stationed there, technically at the garrison just outside the campus, but he led a few classes in the academy and spent most of his time in and around the classroom buildings. Back then he had seemed like an old man, but Nera guessed he had probably been in his mid-fifties. More than a decade later, his hair had fled back to a wispy white wreath around the back of his head, and age spots pocked his sun darkened skin. He seemed smaller now, too, somehow shrunken and more hollowed than Nera remembered, but his blue eyes still twinkled with a cunning brilliance.

Bonner had taught Nera's first lessons in criminal investigation, and he'd recognized her as the brightest pupil in a class that otherwise consisted mostly of bored students waiting for weapons practice. Nera had excelled at weaponry as well, of course, but she had a special knack that her classmates lacked for working her way through puzzles and problems. Bonner had appreciated that in her and recommended her for accelerated courses. That track brought her into the Kites and eventually to her position as commander of her unit. She hadn't forgotten how this clever little man had helped guide her future, but more than that, Nera liked him. Liking a person with no ulterior motive was a rare thing in these times.

Long after Nera graduated from the academy and began serving the Kites, Bonner had retired from both the military life and teaching, and his wife Rasla left her post as an associate dean. They'd moved south to Lakeband, where they had planned to live the rest of their lives in a cabin on the edge of the waters. Wilhelm fished most days, and his wife took to gardening. They'd had a happy life, and Nera made it a point to visit them whenever her duties brought her near.

Nera had been training recruits west of Sandwallow when the news came, only two years after the Bonners left academia. Wilhelm had come home from the lake to find Rasla collapsed in her garden. It had been the void sickness, and it came on fast. She was gone within a day. It took a couple of months for Bonner to sell the cabin, and he'd moved into a small government sponsored apartment here in Klubridge, where he'd taken on the position of watch captain. The town had run the old one into the stocks for stealing money from drug peddlers he should have been arresting. Nera had heard that a bit of corruption was acceptable in Klubridge, but once his own addiction to flurium had become public knowledge, he was finished. All of Wilhelm's old students liked him, and most had gone on to Imperial posts, so it hadn't been hard for him to secure his position. That's where Nera found him when a young guard brought her down a bright hallway to the captain's office.

"Miss Mollor." He greeted her exactly as he had in her school days. Titles meant little to this man, and Nera didn't mind.

"Don't get up," she said, closing the door behind her.

"If I don't get up now and again, I might forget how." He came around his desk with a limp and put a hand on her shoulder. "Look at you now. How long has it been?"

"I last saw you in Ornamen."

"Ah, yes. That unpleasant business with the duke. How has life found you since then?"

"Very much the same as it did before. I follow my orders. I preserve the Empire."

He grunted a friendly agreement and went back to his chair, a tall one with twisted wooden spindles across the back. "You didn't come see me when you got to town."

"I did, but you were away. I spoke with your deputy."

"Tasa, yes. They told me you were about. This spy you're looking for, is that connected with the excitement from last night?"

"It is," she said and lowered herself into the chair across from him. Her cloak draped off the sides, and she clasped her hands in her lap. "That's why I'm here now. What can you tell me about what happened at the university? My Kites were there, but their account of the events is… less complete than I would like."

Bonner leaned into the desk. "The report I received was equally disappointing. I suspect you and I can help each other fill in some details. The first incident involved a cadet. He'd been assigned a patrol route around the school. He wasn't supposed to be at the dormitories, but that's where he ended up. I suspect he has a sweetheart there, but you know how that is."

She didn't, but she nodded anyway.

"He reported a strange noise coming from one of the buildings."

Nera frowned. "What kind of noise?"

"He described it as something like a loud hum, but going in and out. He'd never heard the like."

Magic, Nera would wager. Some sort of spellcraft had been going on at the school. "Is that when he called for us?"

"Not just yet," Bonner said. "He was going to investigate the noise when a woman attacked him. He gave us a thorough description of her."

"Slim, blond, pale, athletic?" Nera asked.

Bonner smiled. "It seems we do have things to discuss."

"I encountered her recently myself. She's part of a gang that tried to rob the central bank."

"I heard about that. That was her?"

"If it's not, then we have a pair of wicked twins roaming the city."

"Let us hope it's not that. One of her was enough for my lad. She taunted him and ran. He was able to catch her, but an accomplice blindsided him and helped her get away."

"What did the accomplice look like?"

"Strong, male, that's just about the entirety of it. He got a better look at the woman. Do you know the man?"

"I may. I believe he's a man who goes by the name Akithar."

Bonner sat back in the chair and raised his eyebrows. "The stage magician? You can't be serious."

"I've been watching him since shortly after we arrived in the city. I have reasons—sound reasons—to believe that he is involved in the plot we were sent here to stop."

"The one you're looking for, you said it was a mage? You think Akithar truly is a magic user?"

Nera nodded. "I feel certain."

"Hmm." Bonner didn't like something. Nera knew that look from her days at the academy, and she suddenly felt eighteen years old and green again.

"What?"

"You latched onto this stage magician soon after you arrived in the city. What evidence do you have that he is the one you seek? Have you seen him do magic?"

"Well, no," she said. "My lieutenant and two other soldiers saw magic last night, though. They all described a web of golden threads that he made on the roof of one of the dormitories. I also know that he follows Ikarna. And the boy who died last night worked at his theater."

"A boy died? What do you mean?"

For the first time, Nera realized no one had notified the watch about the murder. Of course they hadn't, if Lucian had neglected to meet with them. She shook her head. "It was a chaotic night. My lieutenant came to the dormitories in response to the flare. The boy was there with the other two that you described. My lieutenant—"

"Gieck," he said with a frown. Nera knew that Bonner had never approved of Lucian, but she ignored the implied jab this time.

"He pursued the three to the rooftops. Akithar murdered the boy, apparently as a diversion. While my Kites tended to the body, Akithar and the woman escaped."

Bonner's frown deepened, and he leaned forward again. "Miss

Mollor, why is this the first that I am hearing about a murder in my city? And why did your Kites not report to my guards after they saw the flare?"

Chastened, Nera knew he was right. She outranked her old instructor and friend by virtue of her position in the Kites, but she never would use her rank to shirk a shortcoming in her own command. "I am sorry, Wilhelm. I do not know why you weren't notified last night, but I will find out, and I will make amends. We have the boy's body in the castle, if you'd like to have it inspected. In the meantime, is there anything else you know about what happened last night?"

He stared at her for a hard moment before shaking his head. "One of my officers went into South Housing to investigate the noise. He claimed to see two men hiding in a lavatory on the first floor. He says they locked the door when he approached them."

"Says? Claims? You sound skeptical."

"Well, he eventually knocked the door open, and there was no sign of them by then. And I'm not one to cast aspersions on two men meeting in the night."

"Do you think they were students?"

"I don't know." He rubbed a tired hand over his face. "I didn't take these reports with the gravity they seem to deserve. I might have been more attentive if I'd known that a murder had occurred."

"Again, I apologize. I can't undo the mistakes my soldiers made last night, but I can help you set things right."

"How do you propose we do that?"

"I'd like to begin by getting a look at the dormitories, if you wouldn't mind."

The horse whinnied and cast a suspicious look their way as Nera and Bonner approached the dormitory. She was pretty, gray with spots of black, and a dark mane, though a bit skittish. She kicked at the ground but didn't resist when Nera put a hand on her neck.

Nera had grown up with horses, both tending to them and learning to ride them. It had been one part of her childhood that had survived the trauma and carried forward with her into the academy and military. Nera had a respect for horses and liked to think she understood them better than most. She liked most horses more than she liked many people, at least.

"Whose horse is this?" she asked.

The officer accompanying them shrugged. Bonner had introduced him as Guerin. "She's been out here all morning."

Nera looked into the small cart behind the horse. There was a checked blanket of dark green and blue stuffed into the side, but otherwise it was empty. The horse had been out here too long. Nera wished she knew who to blame for that and gave her neck another rub.

"Are we here to make animal friends or to investigate?"

Nera smiled at Bonner and patted the horse once more before following him up the steps to the front doors. "You know me and horses," she said.

"I do remember." He held the door open for her. "This is the building where my officers heard the sound last night."

"I heard it," Guerin said. He came through the door behind them. "Everybody around couldn't help but hear it. Like a scobis dying."

Nera smirked. "You've heard a scobis die, then?"

"Well, no, but it's how I'd imagine."

"This is the lavatory where the two men were seen," Bonner said. He pushed the door open, and Nera saw that the lock had been broken off it. The wood on the inside was splintered where the guard had kicked the bolt through.

She led the way into the room and wrinkled her nose at the telltale stench of human waste. It was not as bad as some privies she'd encountered, but it still lingered enough to encourage a quick investigation. There were shelves built into the wall on the left, and she saw empty brackets where more shelves were installed on the opposite wall as well. This had been a closet before its conversion.

A small walled compartment enclosed the toilet, and Nera peeked around the corner. It was cleaner than she'd expected, despite the odor. Outside the stall was a long and wide trough with a drain in the bottom and a faucet overhanging it. It looked like it might have once fed horses, but now it washed the hands of the privileged students of Klubridge. With the amount of money that poured into schools like this one, Nera was unsurprised that even the dormitories had running water.

She pulled the lever on the side of the faucet, but no water poured out. She tried it twice more, and still nothing.

"Find something?" Bonner had been next to the door but came over to see what she was doing.

"I'm not sure." She stepped back and looked at the faucet. It was at the end of a tall pipe that arced up from the back of the basin before turning downward to aim into the trough. Nera moved to the side of the trough and ran her hand along the back of the pipe. It disappeared behind the back wall of the trough and ended abruptly. She felt around the end of the pipe with her fingers. There had been another section of plumbing here, but it was missing now.

"Guerin, yes?"

"Yes, ma'am."

"Commander will do. Help me with this." She motioned him around to the other side of the trough. Together, they lifted it a couple of inches off the floor, and Nera jerked her head to the side. "Out that way."

Guerin nodded, and they stepped the fixture out and away from the wall. Nera sat her end in the middle of the floor, and Guerin dropped his with a resounding clang. "Sorry," he muttered, but Nera ignored both the clang and the apology. All her attention was on the gaping hole in the floor that the trough had been covering.

"What's below this?" she asked Bonner.

"I have no idea." He looked past her and into the hole. "There used to be tunnels under the city, but most of those have been filled in or converted into new construction."

"Do you have light?"

Bonner felt his pockets, but Guerin was the one who produced a small box of matches. "You never know when you might need them," he said with a sheepish smile.

Nera took the box and looked into the hole again. Bonner put a hand on her arm. "You're not thinking of going down there, surely."

"Wait here," she said and squatted to lower herself through the hole.

The tunnel was crude but big enough for her to pass through with ease. Below the stone floor of the dormitory was a long section of bare earth, and Nera dug her fingers and toes into the dirt on both sides as she climbed downward. She could see into the hole as far as the earth extended, but then there was another floor beneath her, this time metal. A hole gaped in the center of the metal, and it looked like it had somehow been blown inward. Beyond that makeshift entrance was complete blackness.

There could be anything down there, Nera told herself. But she also told herself that her old mentor and friend was watching her descent, and she had to make reparations to him for the mistakes her Kites had made the previous night. Getting to the bottom of what Akithar was doing on the campus likely meant getting to the bottom of this hole, and she wasn't about to back out. Nera tucked her elbows and slid down into the darkness.

She bent her knees with the fall but still nearly fell over when she hit the ground. A few moments too late, she realized she should have tested the depth before jumping in. It could have been a deep well, and she could be lying at the bottom with a broken neck by now. That reminded her of the boy with the shattered body, and she made herself focus on what she was doing. Nera looked up and could see Bonner and Guerin peering down from far above her. Everything else around her was black.

Nera retrieved the box of matches from her belt pouch and fumbled one stick out. She struck it blindly, and it flared to life, sending the chamber where she stood into sudden light and dancing shadows. Where was she?

There were shelves on three sides of her, all bare, and the fourth wall held a thick metal door with a small window in the top. Was this a storage room? One of the tunnels Bonner had mentioned? If so, it was empty, but she didn't see the usual signs of disuse. No perceptible dust, and there weren't any webs or detritus that she would have expected in a long-abandoned nook like this. There was a dusting of dirt on the floor, alongside the remnants of stone and metal particles from above, but the small room was otherwise clean.

She tried the door, expecting it to be locked, but it pushed open with ease. As it swung outward, Nera realized there was another light source outside the small metal room. Dim gaslight flickered on the floor, visible only now that the door was open. She waved the match to put out the flame and dropped it on the floor among the remains of the excavation. Her hand moved to the sword at her side, and she took a cautious step through the doorway.

It was a chamber of some sort, with similar doors along the other walls. The one she had just exited was marked G3. A lamp burned low next to that door, its light unattended and likely to disappear before long. But there was more light ahead, through an open doorway opposite the door she'd just exited, leading into a hallway. Nera went into the hall and took care to step silently. She didn't hear movement other than her own, and she thought she was alone, but she would be prudent.

The hallway led her into a corridor with similar doors, all locked, but these were wooden instead of metal. Through the small windows, she could see dim shapes but could not make out details. Was this a secret warehouse? The storage place of some band of urban brigands? Unlikely. It was too well-constructed and too well-kept to belong to that sort of rabble. What, then?

She pressed forward and moved through one identical hallway after another. Surely this place had an end. Just as Nera was considering turning back and clambering up the hole again, she emerged from the strange catacombs at the foot of a narrow staircase. The door at the top was closed, but she could see more light through a barred window in the top of it. This light was brighter than any she'd encountered in her underground excursion, so she headed up toward it.

Voices were on the other side of the door. The window's glass was hazy and opaque, but Nera could see movement in the next room. She slipped her hand around the doorknob and tried it. Locked. She glanced back down the stairs and considered returning to Bonner after all. It would be wiser to tell him what she'd seen and hope that they could trace what this place was and where this door might deposit her. But no. The time for prudence had come and gone, and Nera was ready to be finished with this dungeon.

She drew her sword, braced the opposite arm on the wall, and delivered a sharp kick to the door, just above the knob. The wood cracked but did not yield. The voices on the other side ceased. They'd be expecting her now. She held herself steady and sent her boot into the door once more, and this time it burst outward, spewing splinters into the air. Nera rushed forward, sword at the ready, and stopped herself before she could take a swing at a teenage girl holding a stack of books.

Every eye in the room was on Nera, staring from the bewildered faces of students gathered around tables and sitting at desks. The room was a chamber lined and filled with bookshelves. The campus library. Nera lowered her sword and slid it back into the sheath, which she now saw was streaked with dirt from her trip through the tunnel. Her tabard was similarly soiled, as were her hands and arms. The girl with the books gaped at Nera, mortified.

Someone in the library laughed, and then someone else. Nera's eyes jumped from face to face, but she couldn't find who it was. She scowled and pushed past the book girl, cutting a rapid path down the center aisle and out the front door. By the time she made it out of the library, the laughter had spread to five, six, maybe a dozen people. By all rights, Nera could have quieted them with the authority of the High Lord, but she didn't. She wanted nothing more than to be out of there, away from anyone who had seen her dirt-smeared, reddening face.

Once outside, navigation back to the dormitories was not a hard task. Students moved out of her way, and she knew she must look every bit the horror she imagined. As she approached the entrance, she saw Bonner outside, holding something dark and oblong.

"Miss Mollor! What happened to you?"

She was in no mood to recount the whole debacle, so she simply said, "The tunnel leads to the library. There are catacombs beneath it. That must be where the two men went last night." She looked at the object in Bonner's hands and saw that it was a dark tube of some sort. The remnants of a wax seal rimmed one end, where Bonner had pulled the container open. "What's that?"

Bonner's blue eyes widened, and he ignored her question. "You were in the basement beneath the library? Where were you? Precisely?"

Nera sensed the urgency in his tone. "The tunnel went down into a small, empty room with metal walls. There was a metal door. G3, it said on it."

Bonner took a step toward her. "You are certain that this room was empty? G3?"

"Yes. There were shelves, but there was nothing else in the room."

Bonner had never addressed Nera by rank, but he did so now. "Commander, you must find those men."

"What was in that room? It's a vault, isn't it?" She remembered the bank vault where she had encountered the acrobat woman. "That was their target. Everything else last night was a distraction. Was it money? Did they get seri?"

Bonner had been unflappable throughout his grief after Rasla died. He had faced every challenge Nera had seen him face with aplomb. But now she saw fear on his face. He held the black cylinder out to her. "Do you see this, Commander?" She extended her hand to take it, but before she could reach it, Bonner lobbed it toward the lawn with a swift underhanded pitch.

The cylinder tumbled end over end through the air and came down hard on the grass. The tube vaporized with a roar, and in its place a fireball grew, instantly scorching the lawn in a circle that had to be at least six feet in diameter. Nera flinched back from the explosion and felt the shockwave and its heat pound against her face.

Students cried out, and the horse ripped free of her tether and galloped out of the quad, the little cart rattling behind her.

Nera spun to challenge Bonner as low flames rippled on the quad and someone called for water. Bonner stared back at her, defiant. "This is far worse than money, Miss Mollor." He pointed to the space where the tube had disappeared. "There were sixty-three of those in the vault below the library. My men found that one in the lavatory. By my reckoning, the people you are hunting now have sixty-two of them."

Nera's skin turned cold, even as the fire continued to burn a few feet away from her. "That's—"

"Enough to bring down this entire city."

CHAPTER 23

Apak shoved the lock home after slamming the door in the guard's face. He turned to Oreth, who was standing near the hole with his mouth hanging open. "We have a situation."

"That was a city guard!"

"I know what that was, Oreth. Ergo, we have a situation." Apak hurried to the edge of the hole, where Zerva was holding the second cylinder up again.

"Anybody up there?" she asked with a laugh.

"Zerva, can you come up? We need help."

Her arm disappeared back into the darkness, and then her hands poked out of the opening without the document cylinder. She hauled herself up into the earthen tunnel and climbed out into the lavatory. "What's up, boss?"

The doorknob to the hallway jiggled, and Oreth pointed. "There's a guard!"

Apak motioned Oreth to silence. "We have been discovered, but all is not yet lost. We cannot exit through the dormitory, so we all must go down the tunnel into the vault."

She looked skeptical. "It's going to be a tight fit."

"We shall become better friends, then." Apak pointed to the earthquake machine. "That needs to go down first. We cannot leave it to be found. Please take it down, and then come back up to help us with our own exits." A drop of sweat fell off the arm of Apak's glasses, betraying his calm and polite facade. "With all speed, if you will."

"Open up in there!" The voice was followed by a pounding and jerked all three heads around to see whether the door would hold.

It did, and Zerva asked, "Why don't I just deal with the guard?"

Apak gaped at the gigantic woman. "Deal with—No. No, no, no. There will be no dealing with the city's constabulary. We already are courting enough trouble."

She looked to Oreth, and he shrugged. She returned the gesture and bent to heave the metal device up into her arms once more. Zerva carried it to the edge of the hole, dropped to sit on the edge, and slipped the rest of the way in. Apak heard her boots scraping against the tunnel walls as she slid down, and then came the distant thud of her feet landing in the vault. The guard was pounding at the door again when she emerged from the hole once more, just a few seconds later.

"What now?"

Apak motioned for Oreth to go ahead of him. "Oreth will go down first, and then I will follow. Once we are down, you will come last. Can you cover the hole with the basin after you climb in?"

"Not a problem," she said. Oreth already was climbing down, and Zerva grabbed the side of the long metal tub and gave it a tug to bring it closer to the edge of the hole. It scraped across the stone floor, but Apak suspected the guard could not hear it over the din of his own knocking.

Oreth disappeared into the hole, and it was Apak's turn. He was reluctant to clamber down into that filthy passage, but he suspected the guard would switch from knocking to ramming before long, and Apak had no intention of being aboveground when that happened. He squatted next to the hole, shifted onto his knees, and slid his short legs off the edge. As he dangled at the side, his belly caught on the rim and nearly yanked his shirt off. Zerva stooped and grabbed him under the arms.

297

"What—"

"Just go limp," she said.

He tried to do that, and whatever he did must have helped. Zerva scooped him away from the tunnel's edge and lowered him down to the top of the library vault with quick care. Once he was down, Zerva gave him a wink. "Time to get cozy."

She dropped into the hole but held half her body above the rim with her left arm. She hooked her right arm over the edge of the trough. It made another loud groan as she dragged it toward the hole. Apak watched it cover half the hole, then three quarters, and finally the entire opening. It reminded him of the darkening of the moon he had watched from his father's shop as a boy. Back then, the sight had filled him with curiosity and wonder. Now it was pure dread. Apak squatted again and allowed Oreth to help lower him from the tunnel the last few feet into the vault.

As Apak's feet touched the floor, he felt Zerva climbing down the rest of the distance. It was pitch black down here, now that the hole above was covered. Apak sensed Oreth on the other side of the small room, and he felt Zerva's bulk as she worked her way through the ceiling and into the vault. She turned as she reached the floor, and her shoulder shoved Apak into the shelves at the side of the room. He caught himself and realized an instant later that his hands were resting on hard, metallic cylinders.

"Be very careful," he told the darkness. "We seem to be surrounded by haranium. One false move—"

"And kablooie," Oreth said.

The guard above punctuated the advice with an expected but still jarring kick to the door. The sound of wood splintering was distant beyond the tunnel and the trough, but it was loud enough for Apak to know that the watch guard was directly above them now, and they were one inquisitive idea away from being discovered.

～

Apak thought at least twenty minutes must have passed since the door to the hallway crashed open. He had heard the guard enter the room, and then there were confused and halting footsteps as the man paced. Apak held his breath when he heard hands clamp onto the sides of the trough above them, and he was certain their tunnel would be exposed. But no, the officer must have simply looked into the tub and moved along. The sounds of searching disappeared fairly quickly, but Apak made the other two remain silent and unmoving until he felt certain the danger had passed.

The vault was too small for three adults to stand inside with comfort, and much less so when one of them was the size of Zerva. Apak had twisted into the side shelves throughout the ordeal, and his head was smashed into either Zerva's elbow or her shoulder blade. Apak thought Oreth was standing on one of his feet, but there was no space to move and no light to see, and he dared not say anything until sufficient time had passed.

How much time would be sufficient, though? Apak thought it prudent that they wait for at least another half hour, but that was when he realized that his legs were going to sleep. The prickling sensation started in his left foot, the one upon which Oreth was not standing, and worked its way up until he could feel the ache creeping into his lower back. He tried to speak, but his words came out muffled against Zerva's filthy shirt.

She shifted, and he discovered that his face had indeed been compressed into her back. "What's that, boss?" she asked, keeping her voice low.

"I said that I believe we can extricate ourselves from this uncomfortable situation without the worry of being overheard."

"Got it." She started turning, and she dragged Apak along in her wake. He now was pressed face first into a corner and felt the cold metal of the walls on both cheeks. His glasses had been pushed off at some time during their incarceration, but at this point he was more worried about being ground into paste against the walls than he was about losing his eyewear. "Think I found the door," Zerva said.

Apak felt Zerva moving behind him, no doubt feeling for an exit. "There we go!" The door gave a clang as she slid the locks open. Of course the mechanisms would unlock manually from within. This was a vault, not a cell, and the designers no doubt wanted to prevent careless archivists from shutting themselves inside with no way out.

The door swung open to the outside with a sigh of polished metal on metal, and Zerva stumbled out of the vault. Left free in the vacuum, Apak and Oreth both staggered away from opposite walls and bumped shoulders before regaining their balance. With the door open, Apak fumbled in his pockets and at last came up with the matches he sought. He flicked one alight and moved it around the small room.

The interior of the vault jumped into his vision, and he failed to suppress a gasp. He had known there were document cylinders on the shelves, but the sheer number of them had eluded him until now. He swept the light around the collection and made a quick estimate that there were at least fifty, likely sixty, all piled into this chamber. What was this stockpile? More importantly, how could they get it out?

"I think there's a lamp out here," Zerva said, and Apak followed her voice out the door and into the larger room Reykas had described. He saw the other similar doors built into the walls, and the light from the match revealed that Zerva was correct. A sconce protruded from the masonry just to the right of the door to the vault they had exited. Apak leaned up and touched his match to the housing, and the lantern flared to life with a sudden whoosh. Gaslight flooded the room, and he shook the flame out from the dwindling match.

Apak went to the next door past the lantern and squinted through the window. It was dark inside, but he could make out shelves on the opposite wall. He could see shapes on the shelves, but they did not look cylindrical. He moved on to the next door and looked through that window. More shelves and more stored valuables, but once again he did not see document tubes. This one held what looked like books, more appropriate for the basement of a library than explosive cylinders, but Apak wondered why these were shut away in a metal vault. He tried the door and was unsurprised to find it locked.

"We need to get out of here," Oreth said.

Apak looked at him and then at Zerva. He walked a circuit around the room and cast a glance down the hallway that he knew eventually would lead up to the library itself. Everything else was dark and silent. He looked back at the open door to the vault and at the trove of haranium waiting inside.

"Zerva, how many of these tubes would you be able to carry safely and without a risk of dropping or bumping them?"

She leaned her left forearm against the wall next to the vault and looked inside. "I don't know. Maybe eight? Nine? I can tie some around my waist, but you and Oreth would need to carry the machine."

"I believe we can manage that," Apak said and gestured for Oreth to bring the contraption out of the vault, where Zerva had left it on the floor.

Zerva waited for Oreth to get clear of the chamber, and she stepped back in. She lifted one of the tubes off a shelf and tested its weight again. "Shouldn't be a problem," she said. She looked out through the door at Apak, standing in the antechamber, lit by the flickering gaslamp. "How many do you want?"

Apak smiled back. "All of them, if you would please."

CHAPTER 24

I t had been so long, it seemed like a lifetime ago, since Samira had
seen Caius cry. The last time was the day they buried Henrik in
the woods beside the Norster River. It was a cool day in autumn, and
she had never forgotten the way the wind covered the fresh grave with
orange and red leaves as Caius knelt in the dirt. They had both been
teenagers, and he was only two years younger than she was, but he'd
seemed so small then. She'd held him as he shook with the tears. And
now the tears Caius shed were for Dorrin, and Samira's chest ached.

"How did it happen?" she asked, her voice strained.

"The Kites did it," Lizzie said. Her own eyes were red but dry.
Samira thought she must have emptied herself of tears on the way
from the campus back here, to the workshop hidden in the
Downsteps.

Reykas was pacing, fury in his eyes. "One Kite," he said. His voice
was rough with anger. "A big one, long hair. He killed Dorrin. It
happened right there. We were so close."

"I almost had him." Lizandra's hands were reaching out in front of
her, and she stared at them with incredulity. "We were across the gap,
and Dorrin was running. He jumped to us, and we almost had him."

Her hands closed into soft fists. She dropped them onto the table and closed her eyes.

"There was no time." Reykas wiped a big hand down his face and shook his head. "It happened too quickly. There was no time for me to do anything. He was gone before I knew it."

"Are you sure?" Caius asked. The tears he cried for Dorrin were silent, but Samira could hear his sorrow when he spoke. "Are you positive he's… gone?"

Lizzie's eyes squeezed tighter, and she whispered, "He broke Dorrin's neck. I heard it snap."

Samira doubled with pain and hugged her arms across her stomach. How could this have happened? "He wasn't even supposed to be there. Why was he there?"

"There were guards from the city watch," Lizzie said. "Reykas and I pulled them away and had them chasing us, but we didn't see the Kites until they already got there. They were chasing Dorrin, and he kept them from finding Apak." She held a hand over her mouth. "He must have followed us there. Reykas and me. We didn't even know he was there."

The three sat in silence while Reykas continued pacing. Lizzie and Reykas had arrived at the workshop only moments before, and there had been no sign of Apak and his crew. Samira didn't think she could handle any more losses that night. She was lapsed in her faith, but she said a silent prayer for Apak, Oreth, and Zerva, that Ikarna would see them safely home. Apak would appreciate that.

"What did the Kite do to Dorrin? Exactly?" Caius asked. Samira looked across the table at him with a pained expression, but she knew he had to know. He would shoulder the burden, as he always did, and he wanted to know exactly what he had allowed to happen under his watch.

Lizzie swallowed and spread her hands on the table, palms down. She couldn't look at Caius or at Samira. She stared down at her hands as she answered. "The Kite had a cable. Some kind of strange thing that looked like it spooled into a bracelet he was wearing. He threw it and caught Dorrin around the neck while he was jumping to us. That was it."

Caius didn't answer immediately but stared straight ahead, unblinking. Samira knew what he would say before he spoke. "This is my fault. I knew this plan was bad, and I never should have allowed it. We've lost Dorrin, and who knows what's happened to Apak by now?"

Samira reached for Caius' hand, but Reykas interrupted the gesture.

"Did you know that Dorrin was a mage?"

Samira froze, and Caius looked up, startled. "What do you mean?"

Reykas had stopped pacing and stood now with his hands on the back of an empty chair. His knuckles bulged as he squeezed the wood. "Dorrin had magic. Did you know about this?"

"No," Caius said. "I had no idea. How do you know?"

Lizzie propped her elbows on the table and ran her hands through her hair. "Reykas is right. When he jumped, Dorrin didn't have enough speed. He wasn't going to make it to us. I tried to grab him, to pull him up, but it was too far. Just barely too far. I thought he was going to fall, but then he just stopped. Right there in the air, he just stopped."

Reykas said, "There was light coming out from him. Gold light, and it held him up and kept him from falling. It was for just a moment, but it was there. And then the Kite took him."

Caius gaped at Reykas and then at Samira. "Did you know about this?"

"I suspected," she said.

"And you didn't say anything? You didn't tell me?"

"The night I met him, Dorrin was picking pockets in front of the theater. There was something about the way he moved that didn't seem right, not natural. It reminded me of… other things I've seen." She looked at Caius. "I suspected that night, and I knew what would happen if he got caught. I thought he would be safer here, with us. With you."

"You should have told me."

"I know that now. But then, I wasn't sure. I couldn't have known for certain. I thought it was likely, though, and I should have told you. This is not your fault. It's mine."

"No," Caius said, but Lizzie interrupted him.

"If it's anyone's fault, it's ours," she said. "Reykas and I should have seen him. We were the lookouts. That was our job. We couldn't even see our own boy, our friend." She lowered her head to the table and buried her face in the crook of her arm.

Reykas picked the chair up and slammed it on the floor. "This is no one's fault but the Kite's. He didn't have to kill Dorrin. He could have caught him, arrested him, arrested us. He could have done any number of things to stop us, and he chose to kill a defenseless child." He pointed at Lizzie, Samira, and Caius, each in turn. "This is not your fault, nor yours, nor yours. The blame for this lies with the Scarlet Kites, and this cannot go unaddressed."

"What would you have us do, Reykas?" Caius asked. "Go after the Kites? Launch an attack on them? We're not an army. They are."

Reykas' anger simmered, and he growled a curse in his native tongue. "It is not right."

"It's not," Caius said. "We have no choice but to save everyone else, though. Everyone who works with us is in danger, and it's only a matter of time before the Kites come for the rest of us. We have to get everyone out of the city, and the only way we can do that is to stick to the plan."

Dread tempered Samira's grief. She asked Lizzie, "Did the Kite see you?"

"I think so. He must have, just across the roofs."

Samira looked to Caius. "If they identified Lizzie and Reykas, they could recognize them from their act."

His eyes widened. "The theater."

Lizzie said, "I'll go check the Chamberlain."

Samira stood. "I'm going with you. The stagehands should be away now that we're not running a show, but we need to make sure. We have to get anyone who's still there out and bring them here." Caius moved to stand, but she stopped him. "You and Reykas should wait here for Apak and his crew. This is where they are supposed to come, and someone needs to be here." She hesitated. Apak often was frustrating and usually was an enigma, but there was no mistaking his fondness for Dorrin. "To tell him," she said.

Caius winced and nodded. "Be careful, Samira. Both of you."

She gave his arm a squeeze and managed a tight smile before she led Lizzie out the workshop door and into the Downsteps.

T he Downsteps was poor but not dangerous. Samira wouldn't have ventured out at night in seedier districts like the East Ward, but she felt comfortable in the Downsteps. That part of the city had once been a promising spot for new bakeries, clothiers, and any assortment of other vendors to set up their shops, and there had been plenty of hope and promise. That was long before Samira and Caius had arrived in Klubridge. She didn't know what had happened, but the Downsteps had fallen on hard times and never recovered. It now was where most of the city's less fortunate ended up if they weren't interested in a life of crime. The community helped each other, and these streets had a genuineness that was absent from most of the rest of the city. It also fell beneath the notice of the Empire and the city watch, and Samira didn't mind those benefits, either.

The thieves knew there was nothing worth stealing in the Downsteps, and the residents had nowhere to go, so the streets were empty at night. Samira felt like she and Lizzie were walking through an abandoned city, the last people remaining after a mass exodus. The moon was bright and lit their way up Beacon Row, all the way to the foot of the stairs that had earned the Downsteps its name.

To the north and west, Klubridge sat high on natural hills that rolled down as the city spread to the south and east. Most of the descent from uptown was gradual, barely noticeable, but the dropoff in the southern central area of the city was sudden. Rather than moving earth and building out a more natural slope, the early builders had put in a long stone staircase that led from the edge of the Downsteps up into the Midtown Cross. Perhaps it had been those very steps that had doomed the commerce. Who wanted to go up and down those things just to buy goods, when there were innumerable other shops that didn't require an endless descent? Horses could handle the stairs if they went slowly, but there was no hope for carts. There was an old wooden elevator that could raise and lower wagons and cargo, but that was far too slow to support buzzing commerce.

Lizzie led the way up the steps, Samira right behind her. They didn't speak until they reached the top and came out in a little plaza in the Cross. Lizzie asked, "What are we going to do?"

"What do you mean?"

"They killed Dorrin for no reason. When they come for Caius, do you think they'll hesitate to go through us?"

Samira didn't have to respond. They both knew the answer.

"So what are we going to do?" Lizzie asked again.

"We're going to leave this city and never look back," Samira said.

"You think we still can earn the money for the ship? I doubt we'll ever perform in this city again. If anywhere, ever."

"The commander, Mollor, seemed hesitant to move. She's sent Kites to watch the theater, but they haven't tried to take Caius yet."

"Yet," Lizzie said with doubt in her voice. "But they saw Dorrin do magic tonight. That's all the confirmation they'll need."

"If they identified you."

Lizzie slowed her pace to walk beside Samira. Now in Midtown, they were passing some late-night walkers, so she lowered her voice. "If they identified me, then we're done. There will be no performing, no money, no ship."

"We'll find another way."

"What way is there? We all agreed this was the only route out of Klubridge. That's the only reason we all went with this awful plan."

Samira didn't disagree. It was a terrible plan, and they all had known it from the start. Apak was a brilliant engineer but a horrid strategist. All of this had been borne of desperation, and with no other available options they'd thought they could solve their troubles with a heist. Now Dorrin was dead, and who knew what might have happened to Apak, Oreth, and Zerva? Everything was falling apart, and Lizzie was right. They needed a backup plan.

"Have you fought before?" she asked Lizzie.

Lizzie laughed bitterly. "Fought my brother for a piece of cake, maybe. No, I'm a runner. I'm no fighter."

"We may have to be fighters. If we have no other choice, we could have to fight our way out of the city."

Lizzie looked at her as if Samira had sprouted a second head. "Who, exactly, will be taking on the Imperial military? You? Me? Reykas in the middle of one of his fits? Caius or Apak? Oreth? We have no training, no weapons, no experience."

"Still, we need to be ready. If we can't leave the city, they'll find us, eventually. This is too big for the Kites to leave empty-handed. They'll put out bounties, they'll run us down. If cornered, we may have to fight."

Lizzie huffed a frustrated sigh. They were nearly to the edge of the theater district, and without needing to consult each other, they stepped off the main streets and into the narrow side alleys that ran between and behind the big playhouses. "They may not even be after us," Lizzie said.

"What do you mean?"

Lizzie started to answer, stopped, and then pushed her thoughts out. "Caius is the one they're after. If they got him—"

Samira grabbed Lizzie's arm and pulled her to a stop. She stepped close to the younger woman, their faces less than a foot apart, and she stared into Lizzie's dark blue eyes. "You will not finish that thought. I'm going to pretend I didn't hear what you just said, and you're not even going to think that sort of thing."

Lizzie's lip trembled, and Samira felt her arm tense. "I... I'm sorry, Samira. You know I didn't mean it. I just—It's been a trying night."

Samira let go of her arm and nodded down the alley. "We're almost there. We should come in from behind the theater."

Lizzie nodded without another word and followed Samira between two small puppet theaters. Samira led the way now and didn't dare look at Lizzie again. She was furious at the suggestion the girl had almost made but also terrified at the possibility that it could make some sort of awful sense.

But no, she had told Lizzie not to think about that sort of thing, and she would make sure that she adhered to her own admonition. Anyway, they would find the theater safe and secure, and they would be back to performing on the season's opening night, in just a few days' time. They would earn the money they needed, they would pay that pirate, Drass, and they would sail away from this city without a look back.

That thought was in Samira's mind when they came within sight of the Chamberlain, and her hopes died like overripe apples dropping from the tree. They were in the street parallel to the main one, and even from here Samira could see a crowd gathering. She pulled Lizzie into the next alley, and they stopped at the far end before it deposited them into the street.

Samira peeked around the corner, and she could hear the people murmuring from a block away. They'd formed a mob in front of the Chamberlain, all craning their necks to see what was happening. The city watch held the passersby back, and Samira counted three, no, four Scarlet Kites standing outside the front door of her theater. The doors were open, likely broken in by booted feet, and a fifth Kite emerged to consult with his comrades outside. Then there was a sixth one, the woman with the asymmetrical hair. She came out the doors and slammed a piece of paper with a nail into the front of the building.

That was it. The Empire had claimed ownership of the theater. The Chamberlain was lost, and with it went Samira's feeble, fleeting hope.

The first light had turned the edge of the sky from black to red, but the sun was not yet visible when Reykas tilted his head toward the door.

Exhaustion had dulled Samira nearly into a doze, but she was immediately alert now. "What is it?"

"Hooves in the street." He got up and moved to the side of the door and pulled it open a hair. He laid his head against the wall to peek out into the still darkened street.

"Caius," Samira said. She shook his arm, and his head jerked up. It amazed her that any of them had slept, but the twin weights of sorrow and uncertainty had pulled all of them but Reykas down. Lizzie shifted in her chair, and now she was looking toward the door as well.

Samira held her breath and listened toward the street, and she thought Caius and Lizzie were doing the same. They watched Reykas for any sign, but he was motionless. After a moment, Samira could hear the clopping of hooves on stone, approaching at a slow pace. Reykas had always had better ears than any of them.

Samira stood as quietly as she could, even though she knew no one in the street, much less on horseback, could hear her inside the workshop. Nevertheless, she remained quiet and padded around the table to join Reykas at the door. He glanced at her and held up a finger for her to wait. She leaned to look past him just as the silhouette of a horse came into view. It was too dark to see any details, but Samira now heard the rolling wheels of a cart as well. Apak!

She moved toward the door and pulled it another couple of inches open before Reykas could stop her. She would have opened it all the way and gone out into the street, had the light from inside the workshop not shown her the horse first. It was brown, not dappled gray. This wasn't Genie.

Samira lurched back from the door in doubt just as a big hand grabbed it and pushed it all the way open. Reykas danced back, ready to defend the workshop. Then he froze and looked as confused as Samira. The great figure filling the door was covered in dried mud, from its head down to its feet. Only the eyes remained bright and unobscured.

"Zerva?" Samira asked.

"Well, it's not the High Lord," the woman said with a laugh and turned to motion the others in. Oreth pushed the second door open and led the horse inside, Apak following behind.

"Where's Genie?" Samira asked.

Zerva frowned and rubbed the brown horse's light mane. She left a dusting of dirt there but didn't seem to notice. "Tied outside the dormitory, last I saw her. Likely still there. I'll have to collect the poor girl in the morning. This is Leaner. I had to get all the way back home and fetch him when we knew we couldn't get back to Genie."

The horse and cart were fully inside the workshop now, and Oreth was barring the door shut. "It was a near thing," he said. "We got spotted, but Apak was quick with his thinking, and Zerva got us out of there."

Caius rose from his seat and looked past Leaner, toward the cart. A burgundy blanket stretched tight across a small mountain that peaked higher than the edges of the wagon. Samira could see the wheels straining under the weight of the load.

"Is this the haranium?" Caius asked as he reached for the edge of the blanket.

Apak swatted at his hand and grinned back. "Carefully, please. We did not bring this all the way here, only to have you explode the full cartload."

"How much did you get? You said you only needed a few cannisters."

"I did say that, did I not?" Apak now reached for that same edge of cloth, and Samira knew he'd been looking forward to unveiling the spoils of his night, his moment of glory. With a flourish, Apak whipped the blanket back.

Samira gaped at the stacks of tubes. "Apak, that's—"

"Sixty-two document tubes," he said. "The entire stock of the library, I would wager."

"How did you get out with those?" Lizzie asked. "We tried to divert the guards, but we saw one get inside."

"He did," Apak said, "but that is another story for another day. For now, I suggest that we rest. It has been a long but successful evening, and I can begin my work in earnest after a bit of sleep."

His words hung in the room, and Samira looked to Caius. He was staring back at her, and she could tell he didn't know what to say to Apak. Oreth noticed the look. "What is it? What happened?" He stepped closer to the table and looked from one of their faces to another. "Lizzie?"

She looked to Samira for guidance. Samira closed her eyes and drew a deep breath. "Things happened while you were gone. We need to talk."

"What is it?" Oreth asked again. He knew something terrible had transpired, but Apak still seemed oblivious. It was hard to read Zerva's face, covered in muck as it was, but even she shifted with unease, waiting for the news.

Samira said, "We can't go home. None of us can. And we won't be building the machine. Or any machines. The Kites have seized the Chamberlain. It's Imperial property now."

Apak's brow creased, and he finally lost his grin. He rested a hand on the side of the cart. "What about our property? My tools. My designs—"

"Everything is gone. It was all in the theater, and we can't go back there. We can never go back."

"What about the crew?" Zerva asked.

Lizzie spoke up. "We don't think anyone was there when they raided the place, but we can't be certain. Samira and I were watching, and we didn't see anyone taken away."

Apak's eyes moved around the room, and he asked Lizzie, "Where is Dorrin?"

She tried to answer, but no words would come. Samira saw her throat working, and tears filled her eyes again. Reykas moved to her side and wrapped her in his arms.

"Where is Dorrin?" Apak asked again, this time to Samira.

She felt like crying, too, but she didn't. She dug into that well that she relied on, that Caius had always relied on, and she told him. "He's gone, Apak. It was the Kites."

"Gone?" He removed his glasses and blinked at her as if he didn't understand.

"Dorrin died, Apak. The Kites killed him tonight."

Apak stared through Samira, his eyes unfocused and his face looking like he was trying to work out some problem, trying to find an answer to an arcane equation. It was Oreth who broke. Apak jolted out of his trance when his apprentice moaned a wrenching cry. Oreth fell to his knees, and Samira knew everyone in the workshop felt his pain.

CHAPTER 25

Gieck looked up at the front of the Chamberlain. Nera had told him about the place when she'd made her visit shortly after they arrived in the city, and she'd instructed him to have eyes on the comings and goings here ever since. He'd delegated that task to Jona, and she had scheduled watches for herself and the other Kites in rotation. What she had failed to do was set someone up on the back entrance in the alley around the right side of the building. Sloppy, but it didn't surprise Gieck.

The wizard and his clan had probably spotted Jona and the others as soon as they took their posts, and they'd been using that side entrance the whole time. It probably was just as well, because if she'd put eyes on that side door, they likely would have that bastard Akithar in custody by now. Gieck had some work to take care of before he could allow that to happen, and if he had his way, there would be nothing left to arrest by the time Nera caught up with the mage. She didn't know that Akithar wasn't the only wizard in the bunch, though. She and Kela and whoever else listened to that version of the story thought Akithar was the one who conjured up those golden threads. Gieck knew better. It was one of the other two, probably the man, and he'd make that work to his own advantage.

The locks on the front doors were broken, pried off in the raid the night before. Gieck went through into the lobby and took in the atmosphere. He'd heard plenty about this place from the locals. It was among the oldest and biggest theaters in the city but still managed to lose itself in the midst of the ninety or so other establishments that surrounded it. It was fancy, too. Marble floors here in the front area and red velvet curtains on the walls, tied back with gold ropes.

He walked to the archway on the left that led into the theater itself. The room yawned open before him like a giant red mouth lined with rows of seats at the bottom and metal walkways at the top. The stage was far away, down the aisle and up a small rise. Nothing useful there, most likely. He didn't even really know what he was looking for. Nera had finally given the order to bring down Akithar, but weeks too late, if Gieck were asked his opinion.

She still wanted him brought in alive so she could interrogate him about the rebels' hideout. Gieck wanted that information, too, but he was less concerned with the wizard's health upon delivery. In fact, it would benefit Gieck to get the location of the hideout and deliver it himself, along with Akithar's unspeaking corpse. No way that Nera could steal that victory from him, when he could present the Empire with the most valuable information they'd collected in years.

He took a step back from the house entrance and went to a door in the side wall marked "Staff Only" with gilded letters on the dark wood. He tried the door, found it unlocked, and pushed through into a small vestibule. There was a staircase leading up, alongside what looked like a supply closet. Gieck was less interested in that closet than in what he might find upstairs in this place. Sometimes the actors and managers lived in their theaters, and he hoped that would be the case here. At the very least, there should be some offices he could rifle through.

At the top of the stairs he came to a branching hallway, and there was a door standing open right in front of him. "Beat me to it, eh?" he asked as he came in.

Jona squatted next to a cabinet and was digging through a pile of paperwork that she had already scattered around the floor. She looked over her shoulder and smirked at him. "Can't have you getting there first with everything, can I?"

Gieck shut the door behind him and looked out the windows in the wall on the right. The light coming through was dim, and he realized they must be mirrored on the other side. The view looked down past the theater sign, into the street where two other Kites stood guard to keep nosy civilians from wandering in.

Jona stepped up beside him to look out the windows. "This was her office, the manager."

"Tandogan," Gieck said. Nera had met her when she came to the theater.

"I'll wager she stood right here and watched me," Jona said. "I was right there." She pointed across the street to the opposite theater where she'd taken her post. Straight across, in plain view of anyone looking out from the Chamberlain.

"You didn't try to be subtle, did you?"

"Where's the fun in that?" She turned her back to the window and leaned against the outer wall. "You had quite a night. Tell me about it."

"What's to tell?"

She put a finger on his chest and hooked it under the top of his tabard. "I heard a boy died. You were there for it."

"I was. The wizard killed him."

"I want to see."

Gieck raised an eyebrow at her. Jona's head tilted forward, the long dark hair hanging down on one side, partly obscuring her right eye, but he could see the wicked curiosity in the left one. "You want to see what? The boy?"

"I want to see his body." She pulled at the tabard, and Gieck had to take a step toward her to keep from going off balance. "Eyral says he has a magic knife in him."

Eyral needed to keep his mouth shut. "He does. Why do you want to see it? It's just a dead boy."

"He said his neck's broken, too. All crunched to the side." She jerked her head to the side and stuck out her tongue in pantomime.

Gieck stared at her and then shook his head. "He's being handed over to the city watch. I don't have anything to do with that."

Jona pouted and released the top of his jerkin. "That's no fun. I heard you saw magic, too. That the mage choked him."

"I did. It was fast, so I didn't see much." That much was true. He'd seen the flash of golden light, but it had been too brief for him to pinpoint the source or see how it had been cast. The spell had fallen apart when he'd hooked the boy back to the roof. Those were details he didn't need to share with Jona or anyone else. He pulled away from her and took two steps over to the woman's desk, left untouched since she had last left her office the previous night or whenever she'd vacated the premises.

"I know what's wrong with you," Jona said, and Gieck felt her behind him now, pressing into his back. He was bent over the desk, and she leaned in close to his ear. "You're under too much stress. You have to dance for her ladyship." That was what Jona often called Nera when they were alone, and he turned his head to protest, but Jona was quicker. She caught his ear in her teeth and gave it a sharp bite.

"What!" His hand flew to the side of his head, and it came away bloody. "You're insane."

"You know I can help you with that stress." She wiped the back of her hand across her mouth, and Gieck saw a smear of his own blood on her light skin. His pulse quickened, and he spun on her. Gieck grabbed her bloody hand and used it to turn her to face the wall. He shoved her forward, and she slammed into the thick window, her cheek turned to press against the glass. Looking back, she parted her lips and bared her teeth at him in a savage grin. He pulled her wrist up behind her back, and her grin became a snarl. She goaded him. "Is that the best you can do?"

He let go of her wrist and ripped her tabard over her head. He heard some threads popping in the seams as it came, and he tossed it on the floor. Her hands were up now, palms flat against the window. "Look at them," she said. "Such stupid little people. If only they could see us now."

"Shut up." Gieck grabbed her throat with his left hand and yanked her head back toward him. She craned her neck, and he pushed his face against hers, kissing her hard enough to bruise. She grasped his wrist with her hand, but not to free herself. She squeezed his hand tighter into her throat.

Gieck growled and reached around her with his other hand, trying to find the clasps and buttons that held that confounded uniform together. As he groped, Jona ran her fingers around the leather bracelet on his wrist. She pulled at the end of the cable and then let it zip back into its holster. "You are a monster," she whispered against the side of his face. He didn't respond but had finally undone the lacing at the front of her trousers. His hand froze when she then whispered, "Did you kill the little gutter rat yourself?"

Gieck felt the hair at the back of his neck tingle, and he pulled his face away from hers. "What did you say?"

She spun around and draped her hands around his neck. Her eyebrows drew down, and the corner of her mouth quirked upward in fierce mirth. "You choked him out with your little toy here and then skewered him, didn't you?" She leaned closer to kiss him, but he shoved her chest. Jona fell back away from him and hit the window hard enough to clack her teeth together.

"That hurt!" She scowled at him. "What's wrong with you?"

"What's wrong with you?" he spat back.

"I was joking, you ass. You know how I am." She rubbed at the back of her head, where it had bounced off the glass. Gieck scowled at her and took a step back. She followed him with her eyes, confused until realization dawned. Her eyes widened. "You did do it, didn't you? You killed him."

Part of him wanted to tell her he had done it. That he had broken the boy's neck and would do it again. If there was anyone he would tell, it would be Jona. She'd be more likely to ask what it felt like and to have him show her than she'd be to turn him in. But no, even that would be a risk, and this was a perilous time.

Gieck pointed a finger at Jona. "You will not speak about that again. It isn't funny."

But she was already there. Her upper lip pulled up, and her smile was feral. "You killed him. You're the one." She reached for him, and he swatted her hands down.

"Stop it, Jona." And something in his tone did stop her. She knew how dangerous he was. She'd seen it firsthand on many occasions. That he'd killed a child was less surprising to her than his insistence that she not talk about it. Gieck studied her face, trying to gauge how much and what she had worked out. Plenty, by the sound of it. He couldn't kill her, too, though. The death of a few assorted drunkards in the city was one thing, and the death of a boy associated with a known mage was another, but the death of a Scarlet Kite was something else entirely. He couldn't handle that as easily as he always handled the others. He had to deal with it another way.

"That woman in Gramery, at the school."

"What about her?"

"I saw what you did to her," he said.

Jona frowned. "Yeah? And what? You didn't have a problem with it at the time."

"I saw what you did. There and before. In Teusas, too, and in Ordport before that. You just remember I know what you've done."

"What is this, Lucian?" The fun was gone now, and she was looking afraid. Good.

"You're not to mention that boy again. Or this." He held up his hand to show her the bracelet with the cable wound inside. She flinched away from it. She'd never done that before. Gieck felt something break between himself and Jona. There was some regret, but it would be for the best. "Do you understand me?"

Jona squinted at him and answered through clenched teeth. "Better than I did before."

By the time Gieck slammed his forearm against the door and pushed his way back into the street, he was second guessing his decision to let Jona live. He had Nera under his thumb, but if she learned that he was the one who killed the kid, it would all be over.

Nera and her damnably strict code. His cabler was not an authorized and regimented part of the Kites' armory. He wasn't even supposed to have it strapped to his arm. She likely would turn him in to the governing board herself. Bekam had gotten him out of some jams in the past, but this kind of thing? Not a chance.

Why had he killed the boy in the first place? Yes, his blood was up, and he needed to kill something last night, but why did it have to be that kid? All he'd been thinking about was stopping the brat, and then he'd been thinking about how to use it to get Nera to finally move on the wizard. Well, that part had worked, at least. She had them scouring the city, but it was too late. Akithar and his whole company had gone to ground. They had to know they were being hunted by now. If only he'd been able to convince Nera to move faster. They could have collected the wizard, gotten his information, and seen the last of this city.

The order was to apprehend Akithar and any of his compatriots. The acrobat girl was the primary target among them, but any would do. Nera had been very specific about not killing any of them, but Gieck still fully intended to slay the wizard once he found him. He'd learn the destination of that accursed spy that they still had not found, and then he'd put an end to the man before he could say anything else. Let him die with the murder of his own boy sitting atop him. Better that than giving him a chance to tell his version of the story, which would go very differently than Gieck's had gone.

Even if Akithar talked to Nera, Gieck wasn't certain that she would believe that version of the story. Her insane and single-minded hatred of all things magic would disincline her to trust Akithar, and she still was smitten with Gieck. He still had that hold over her, and he hoped it was strong enough to blind her to any protestations she might hear.

Ordinarily he'd feel safe with the backing of his Kites, but even that didn't seem like a sure thing anymore. The more he thought about it, the worse he thought he'd handled that confrontation with Jona. She wasn't one to run off tattling to Nera. She was the one person he could impress with his drive to murder the kid, and he'd likely burned that bridge.

"Sir." It was Vam, waiting outside the theater with Eyral and Kela.

"What?" Gieck snapped and looked around the street. The people of Klubridge streamed past, half of them craning their necks to see what had happened at the Chamberlain. The other half quickened their paces, wanting no part of whatever was going on there.

"You're bleeding." Vam gestured to his own ear, and Gieck swiped at the side of his head again. His hand came away bloody from where Jona had bitten him. He was lucky she hadn't done worse.

"It's nothing. Anything to report?"

"No, Lieutenant. I was just with the watch captain, and he's made the entire watch available to us. We'll find them."

Gieck nodded and wiped his hand across his tabard. It was red on red, but he knew the blood would dry darker. Not what he needed to be worrying about just then. He looked at Vam, short, young, tanned, his hair pulled back in a tight ponytail. Vam hadn't been at the campus last night and had yet to be poisoned by doubt. He was still one Gieck could count on. Right? He looked at Kela, waiting just past the shorter Kite.

He snapped at her. "What are you looking at?"

"Nothing, sir." She'd been looking, though. Looking at him like she knew things. What did she know? Nothing. Just like she said. Nothing.

And Eyral? What about him? He looked uneasy now, his eyes shifting between Kela and Gieck. What had he heard? He'd been there last night. Did he know that wasn't Akithar on the other roof? Had he seen the cable snap around the boy's neck?

Gieck stepped close enough to Eyral that he could feel the other man's breath on his face. "You have something to say to me, soldier?"

Eyral's eyes grew wide, and he tried to step back from his superior, but Gieck wouldn't let him. He caught a handful of Eyral's tabard and held him in place. Gieck stared into his eyes for a long moment and finally let him go, shoving him back. Eyral nearly tumbled to the ground, but Kela caught his arm. What did that mean?

Gieck stared at Kela again and tried to sense what she was thinking. He was no mage, but he could see it in her face. Her eyes were wide like Eyral's. Her mouth was parted, and there was a deep line between her eyebrows. She was thinking something. He could see it, and Eyral was doing it, too. Probably Jona as well.

He stepped into the middle of the street and looked up to the windows over the theater sign. They were mirrored, just like he'd thought. She was probably up there behind them, even now. He could feel her looking down at him, suspecting him, accusing him. Eyral was looking at him, too, and Kela now. Even Vam was frowning at him. Did they all know? How had they found out?

Kela. She was the one who stepped out of line last night when Nera was there. She was the one causing this. His skin felt hot, and a bead of sweat rolled down the back of his neck.

Gieck's lips peeled back from his gritted teeth, and he pointed a shaking finger at Kela. "You don't know anything," he said. But then his own bracelet caught his attention. The zephyr spool he'd gotten in Dushouca. That was the only evidence they'd have. They couldn't pin anything on him. Not without evidence, and he was on top of that. Always.

He unbuckled the bracelet and slipped it off his arm and into his waist pouch. It took three tries before he got the pouch fastened again, but when he had it shut, he looked back at Kela. He wiped a wet strand of hair out of his eyes and snarled at her. "You know nothing."

CHAPTER 26

Samira Tandogan's house was nondescript, hidden away in a row of identical homes. Nera never would have found it without Bonner's involvement. After the Kites took the Chamberlain, Nera had her soldiers turn over every document in the theater. Morcan had a head for accounting, and he'd gone through the bookkeeping Jona had found in the office above the entrance. The books were remarkably detailed and thorough, and Morcan had found nothing untoward in the ledgers. The person who handled money for the Chamberlain was at least as astute as he was, and they had left no seri unaccounted for.

What Morcan did find were names, and a lot of them. There was a decade's worth of pay documented to grips, assistants, costumers, prop makers, and ticket takers, all enumerated and listed by name. Every last one of them had received their payment from the same person who kept the books, one Samira Tandogan. Nera remembered meeting Tandogan when she came to the theater. She'd been brusque and less than welcoming. The woman likely knew why Nera was there, and she was not keen on seeing her primary attraction hauled away.

Nera had assumed that Akithar was the proprietor, but all the paperwork showed that Tandogan owned the theater and also managed it. There was no mention of the mage on the management payroll or business documents. Was that to keep his proper name unconnected to the Akithar identity, or was he merely another hire like the rest of the crew? Was his name mixed in among all the rest? She intended to find out, and the best lead she had was Samira Tandogan herself.

Bonner had become invested when he learned of the boy's murder, and he'd had the body transported to the city watch's facilities, where his own investigators had access to more resources in Klubridge than the visiting Kites would have. The theft from the library had been the event that sparked Bonner's urgency, though. He was keen to get those document cylinders back into Imperial hands, and he had offered Nera all his own resources for tracking down the thieves. Given Lucian's account, they both were convinced that the thieves and the murderer were in league with each other and, furthermore, that Akithar was at the center of the whole thing.

Nera was impressed by the speed with which Bonner located the Tandogan woman's address once the gears started turning. Nera didn't expect to find her there, but every step forward was a step closer to identifying, capturing, and finally imprisoning the murderous wizard known as Akithar.

Wil had accompanied her to the house. He was more experienced than any of the other soldiers under her command, but perhaps more importantly, he was bigger than most of the others. If Tandogan or any of her lackeys turned up at that address, Nera and Wil would be ready for them.

Nera tried the front door and was not surprised to find it bolted. She stepped back and nodded to Wil. His bushy gray mustache twitched, and he returned her nod. With casual strength, he kicked just above the doorknob, and the door bashed inward. He let the momentum carry him into the house, and Nera was two steps behind him. Her hand hovered over the hilt of her sword, but she doubted she would need it. The house looked empty, and she suspected Tandogan was smart enough to have gone to ground after the events of the previous night. She wouldn't be hunkered in her bedroom, waiting for them to come get her.

Wil moved through the front room into the kitchen, and Nera followed, her scan of each area quick but thorough. They went in and out of the remaining spaces to cover the ground floor, and Nera took the lead up the stairs just past the front room. Upstairs was a smaller area, just a couple of rooms. They found no one in the bedroom or the accompanying closet.

Wil confirmed her suspicions. "No one here. Nobody was here last night, either. She's been gone for a day or two."

Nera agreed. "Look through everything you can find. If she's not here, she has to have somewhere else she can hide. A friend, a relative, someone who would take her in. She could own other property, too. Look for any papers, any letters, anything that can direct us."

Nera thought Wil was smiling at her, but his mustache hid his mouth. "Not my first time."

"Nor mine, my friend."

Wil started upstairs, and Nera began downstairs in the front room. The house was tidy, kept clean but with the right amount of clutter that every inhabited space accumulated. She could see that Tandogan liked books. Fiction, mostly. There were several novels stacked on the front table, and more were arranged in a bookcase next to the hearth.

Nera riffled the pages of each book but found nothing more substantial than a couple of bookmarks. The books were well-read, but Tandogan was not a note taker. The pages were pristine and unmarked, and she had stuck no keepsakes or important papers into the covers. Nera had seen books hollowed out to hide contraband, but no such luck here. If she didn't know better, Nera would think this woman lived a quiet life, well removed from political intrigue and the harboring of fugitive mages.

She gave the front room one more pass but still found nothing incriminating or even useful. No personal letters, nothing that referenced her work at the theater, not a shred of proof that she even knew Akithar, much less employed him. She was about to move through to the kitchen when she heard Wil's heavy and slow tread on the stairs.

"Anything?"

"Maybe. Come up and have a look?"

She followed him upstairs again and into the bedroom. It looked just as it had when they first arrived, but Nera knew Wil had been thorough in his search. He had a delicate touch but wasn't one to miss details. He'd taken the opposite career path that Bonner had, starting his work as an investigator for a local constabulary. He'd moved into the service of the Kites later in life than most, but the experience and deliberation he brought with him made him an instantly appealing recruit. He had a steady and sure way of approaching every problem, and that was what Nera saw in him as he watched her enter the bedroom.

"What did you find?"

"Before I tell you, I want to see if you agree. What do you see here?"

She looked around the room. It was painted a light blue, with a green rug that covered most of the wooden floor. The bed was large but not ostentatious, with a quilt that looked expensive. There was a polished dresser against the wall opposite the bed, just below a window that let the midday light into the room. A blue garment draped off the edge of the dresser, something silky and patterned. Nera looked across to the other side of the room, where the door to a closet stood open.

Inside, Nera could see that Tandogan's wardrobe was divided into two distinct flavors: working clothes and presenting clothes. There were rough shirts and breeches hanging to the left, and to the right there were several dresses, all similar in design. They were nice but, like the rest of the trappings in the house, not ornate. Nera imagined the woman wore the casual and work clothing when she was about the business of running the theater, and she wore the dresses when she wanted to look just a couple of steps down from the nobility when she handled her public.

"Do you see it?" Wil asked.

Nera frowned. She didn't like being rushed, but she needed to know what he'd seen. She was about to ask him when it clicked. Nera ran her hand along the material of the dresses hanging in the closet. All of them were thick, plain, and cheaper than Tandogan would hope people would notice.

"The blue gown," she said.

Wil nodded as she crossed the room again. "It's too nice," she continued. "And it's different from anything else in here. It's not hers."

"That's what I think, too," Wil said. "But there's more. Pick it up."

Nera lifted the gown from the top of the dresser, and it was every bit as airy and light as she'd imagined. But then she picked up the whole garment and felt the weight. There was a pocket sewn into one side, and something was pulling at the fabric. Nera slipped her hand inside. Her fingers felt something unyielding and metal. They closed around a key. Nera pulled it out and turned it over in her hand.

"Oh, Wil," she said. "You've earned your supper tonight."

Stamped in the metal at the top of the key was the Klubridge campus insignia, with an opened book engraved below it. The university library.

~

After fumbling through secondhand accounts and no physical evidence, Nera finally had something solid to link Akithar to the attack at the campus the previous night. From there, linking him to the intrigue with the rebel spy should be elementary. Standing in Samira Tandogan's bedroom with the library key in her hand, Nera wanted to leave immediately for the campus to establish a firm connection between the woman, the key, and the burglary and murder.

"You need a plan first," Wil said. "It won't do you any good to show up at the library again armed only with this key."

She knew he was right. "We have to find the owner of this gown. Is it a gown?" Nera held it up by the shoulders and let it hang before her. It had sleeves that probably ended at the elbow and a sash attached that came together to tie at the waist, but it was too thin to wear as a dress on its own. Some kind of drape or overwear? Something caught her eye, and she stepped closer to the window with the garment.

"Are we positive it doesn't belong to Tandogan?" Wil gestured to the closet. "It is different from everything else she owns, but perhaps she was trying something new."

"It's not hers," Nera said. "Look."

Wil joined her at the window as she carefully pulled the fabric at the neck tight. There, laying across a patch of pale blue silk, was a long, thick black hair.

"I met Tandogan. Her hair is much shorter than this, and lighter. This is someone else."

Wil squinted at the hair and nodded. "What do you think?"

"I think we need to find a woman with long, black hair and a penchant for patterned silks."

"How will we find her?"

Nera looked at the key for a long moment and sighed. "We need the halflock."

"Magra?" Wil sounded surprised.

"I don't have to like a tool to see its use," Nera said.

Wil shrugged. "I'll round her up."

By the time they found Magra, they had added two more Kites to their party. Nera rode at the front, followed by Tomos and then Morcan, who rode beside Magra on the old mare the city watch had scrounged up for her. Wil brought up the rear, and Nera knew his gaze was jumping from building to building and from face to face in the crowds they passed. The citizens parted the way for them, some of them bowing respectfully but others glaring up at them. It was rare for the commoners to pick fights with the Kites, but on the occasions when they did, Nera could think of no soldier she'd rather have at her back than Wil.

Klubridge had been in lockdown for weeks now, and the populace was feeling the box, large though it was. The eyes looking back at Nera had been fearful when her Scarlet Kites first arrived, but now they were giving way to resignation and even indignation. These people were growing tired of military rule. That was good. The more desperate the siege made them, the more likely they'd be to share information. Anything to get back to their old way of life. Someone out there knew Akithar. They knew where to find him and who he really was, and he knew the location of the hidden stronghold at Stormbreak. It was only a matter of time until they broke and shared the information. Press long enough, and even his friends would turn on him. Nera had done it before, and she knew it would work again here, unless she found him first.

Something flew past Nera's head. She heard it more than felt it, and she turned in time to see what looked like a cabbage smashing into the street behind her. Before she could turn back around, she felt the thud against her chest. When she looked down, she first thought the wetness was her own blood, red and soaking into the insignia of the Kites. But no, there was no wound, no weapon. The culprit tomato tumbled into her lap and fell off to the side, into the road.

"Who—"

Another one sailed past, barely missing her, and she heard swords unsheathe behind her. The crowds backed away, now showing more fear than anger, but she had no idea who had thrown the vegetables.

"Hold!" she called back to her soldiers. Her primary mandate was that her Scarlet Kites would not kill innocent civilians. The last thing she needed was for Wil to start taking heads. A full-blown riot would not be far behind. Nera looked over her shoulder to make sure they were following her order, and she saw Tomos sliding his blade back into its sheath with reluctance. He met her eyes, and she saw concern, but there was fear, too. He also recognized the sheer number of civilians surrounding them. Things could go very badly, very quickly.

"Pick up the pace," she told him, and he nodded back. She gave her horse a light spurring, and its walk turned into a trot. The sounds of hooves at her back became louder, and she knew they were following her directions. No heads would fall today. There would be no riots, either.

The crowds thinned as they neared the university, and there were fewer angry faces among the people on the streets. Mobs bred discontent, and isolation bred compliance. That was something she had learned at the academy, and it had stayed with her through the years. If you want to get someone to obey you, isolate them. That's what she had planned for the owner of the key.

The small band slowed and stopped in front of the library. Morcan was off his horse first and helped Magra off hers. The wretched witch's eyes rolled around their huge sockets, taking in the unexpected greenery of the trees and campus lawn in the middle of the city. Tomos and Wil were securing their horses now, but Nera hesitated before dismounting.

She looked down at the front of her uniform again, and she could see the wet stain of tomato juice that had soaked into the tabard. It made a faint, blobby outline around the embroidered bird. Nera knew it wouldn't be as noticeable as she felt like it was, but still her hand covered it and felt the wetness. That just as easily could have been a dagger or an arrow.

She took her hand away and saw seeds from the tomato stuck to her fingers. Filth, thrown at her for doing her job. For upholding the safety of the Empire. Nera never strayed from her duties, and this was how the people saw her. She remembered the students laughing at her when she burst into the library, covered in dirt. Would any of those same students be inside now? Would they remember and laugh again, seeing that she had traded her dirt for vegetable innards?

Nera wiped her palm against her leg, furiously scrubbing the seeds and juice off her fingers. She regretted it as soon as she saw the new stains on her trousers. More stains, more to laugh at. All she wanted was to protect these people, but nothing ever was good enough. Even Lucian—

"Ready, Commander?"

It was Wil, waiting at her side. He had recognized her distress. He'd seen it enough times in the past to know when and how to interrupt her thoughts before she spiraled into panic. His eyes were hard but kind under his thick white brows. Nera nodded to him. "Just collecting my thoughts."

He grunted agreement and offered his hand. She took it and dropped down from her horse. For an instant her knees felt like they would buckle, but Wil had her elbow and kept her upright. None of the others had noticed, but the witch was looking at her with those vacant, owlish eyes. Nera snapped her own eyes away and asked Wil, "You have the garment and the key?"

"Right here." He handed them to her. Nera took both and breathed in through her nose, out through her mouth. There was one key in her hand. There were two doors in the front of the library. Three steps up to the doors. Four legs to a horse. Five people in her party. Six dark gray stones among the lighter ones in the wall before her. Seven letters to "library". She was ready.

"Morcan, bring the mage. Wil, you're with me. Tomos, watch the horses and the entrance. If anyone tries to escape, be ready."

"Yes, Commander." Tomos rested his hand on the hilt of his sword and stepped aside to let the others pass. They entered the library together, Nera at the front, Morcan and the witch behind, and Wil once again watching the back.

The panic tried to rise again when she stepped through the door, but she quelled it by focusing on the hard sharpness of the key in her fingers. Focus there, not on the curious young faces staring up at them from tables and cubicles. The library always was a quiet place, but now it was a tomb. A single Kite might be worth laughing at, but three Kites and an Imperial mage commanded the attention, respect, and perhaps fear of every eye in the building.

Ahead, midway down the center aisle, Nera saw a man frozen in place. He was too old to be a student, perhaps forty, and dressed in a vest and tie. "You," Nera said, leading her entourage through the vaulted room. "You work here?"

He touched his glasses and then his sandy mustache. "I, yes, I'm a faculty advisor. How may I help?"

Nera held out the key. He took it from her and turned it over in his hands. "I don't understand," he said.

"This key is from this library, yes?"

"I suppose so. It looks like our keys. I'd have to try it in—"

"Who has access to keys like that one?"

"Any of our staff, I suppose. All of us have to get in early or late every now and then."

"Who wears clothing like this?" Nera held up the garment but pulled it back when he reached to take it.

"I'm sorry," he said. "I don't know what—"

Nera interrupted. "We are looking for a woman who works here. She has long, black hair, and this belongs to her. Who is she?"

The man blinked at the clothing, and something passed across his face. Recognition? But then he shook his head. "We don't have anyone here like that. I'm sorry."

Nera turned to look back at Morcan. "What did she get?"

The witch, Magra, grimaced. It might have been a smile, but there were too many teeth, and it was too tight. Nera wanted to look away but forced herself to lock eyes with the abominable creature. Magra hissed between those teeth and said, "Mirada. Aquin Mirada, yes. She is on the upstair, up, up, stair, there, where, third floor, more, door."

Nera's attention shifted back to the librarian. His mouth trembled, and he held his hands out in supplication. "I didn't want any trouble."

Nera plucked the key from his fingers. "Arrest this man. Deliver him to the city watch for obstruction." Without waiting for a confirmation or for the man's inevitable protest, Nera brushed past him and headed for the stairs. She took them two at a time and knew the rest of the library still was watching her. The eyes felt heavy, but she bore them. They seemed heavier than the mantle and the cloak that fluttered behind her as she took the second landing. More books here, no offices, so she continued up to the top floor. It was an open hallway that ringed the building, looking down onto the students and books that filled the ground floor. She saw Wil pulling the library worker toward the front door. Morcan had followed Nera, dragging the mage along behind.

A woman, surely another library worker, had been about to go down the stairs, but she backed away, a book clasped to her chest. Nera studied her but knew this wasn't who she wanted. This woman's hair was too light, too thin. "Aquin Mirada," she said.

The woman extended a shaking hand and pointed to the left.

"Thank you." Nera left her and found the door to Mirada's office.

Without knocking, she turned the knob and pushed it open. It was a small space, just enough room for a desk and a few smaller pieces of furniture. There, sitting at the desk with a stack of papers before her, was the owner of the gown or wrap or whatever it was. The woman was dark and striking, likely tall, but it was hard to judge her height when she was sitting. Her hair was long and thick, a match for the black hair Nera had found. She wore a green blouse, silky like the blue garment, and covered in black patterning. Nera recognized it now. It was an omensand design, common in the south, as were the thin fabrics.

"Does this belong to you?" Nera dropped the gown on the desk atop the papers, and the woman gaped up at her.

"I don't... I..."

"Is this yours?"

"What is this?" the woman asked. "Who are you?"

"Do you know Samira Tandogan?"

The woman's eyes widened briefly, but long enough for Nera to be certain. She looked at the mage. "Does she know Tandogan?"

Magra gave her awful grin and stomped her feet with apparent glee. "Oh yes, she know, she know Tandogan, she know much."

"Commander." It was Morcan. He had stepped through the open door into what Nera assumed was a closet. He tossed something to her, and she caught it.

When Nera opened her fingers, she saw the face of Ikarna staring back up at her from a small, oval icon not unlike the one Akithar owned, the one that had been on the boy's body. The one that, even now, added weight to Nera's belt pouch.

Nera scowled and closed her hand over the relic again. "Arrest this woman. The man will be going to Bonner, but she's coming with us."

"Wait, no, you don't understand," Aquin Mirada said.

Nera shot her a cold look. "I don't yet, but I will."

~

333

W il took Mirada, Tomos left with the other librarian to escort him to the city jail, and Magra remained in Morcan's custody to be taken wherever such creatures were kept when they weren't needed. Nera had let Wil take her horse for Mirada so he could get her back and processed as quickly as possible. With tensions running high in the city, Nera did not want to risk anything preventing that woman from ending up in her dungeon. Wil had protested, of course, not liking leaving Nera on her own in the midst of the city. She had been resolute, though, and he'd eventually been the last to go, leading her horse away with Aquin Mirada.

The truth was that Nera needed some time alone, when she could calm her mind without worrying about how she was presenting herself to her soldiers. If any citizens were unwise enough to accost her, she would handle the situation, but she didn't think it was likely. Nera had told Wil that she needed to check some leads before coming back to the castle, but she really just wanted the time to walk and think. She waited until the last horse was out of sight, and then she began walking after them, down the high street that led out of the university.

How did the librarian fit into the plan? If she were, as Nera suspected, a pawn that Akithar had used for access to the library vault, then she should be easy to break. They simply had to find what was important to her and squeeze. That begged the question of why she had helped Akithar, if she were but a pawn. Was she being forced to help him, or had he lured her into his service? Paid? Tricked? The nuances of those answers would determine how Mirada could be turned from an enemy into a resource.

That was unless, of course, she were one of the faithful. Akithar had surrounded himself with his theater company and indoctrinated them into his service like some sort of twisted family. There was Samira Tandogan, for all purposes his shield from the public. All documents and properties were in her name, and she ostensibly ran the Chamberlain theater. Nera remembered the hostility in the other woman's eyes when she had come to the theater that first day to ask for the performer.

And there was the acrobat, the young woman who had escaped from Nera's grasp in the bank. She also had been at the dormitories and was with Akithar when he killed the boy. Lucian had witnessed the murder and positively identified both of them. That girl likely was a part of Akithar's stage show as well. Nera had heard talk about contortionists who opened the show every night, a man and a woman. She'd bet her blade that woman was this elusive acrobat.

Who else was involved? Everyone connected to the theater? The Chamberlain was suspiciously empty and quiet when the Kites took possession of it. Granted, it was between theater seasons, so no performances were due just then. But wouldn't they ordinarily have been rehearsing? Nera knew nothing about stage magic, but she imagined that it required an extraordinary amount of preparation and practice. It was not the sort of thing one just showed up and did. The lack of any crew indicated that the entire company could be in on Akithar's plans.

What were his plans, exactly? He had been performing in Klubridge for a decade, according to accounts from neighboring theaters. Even Bonner knew about the magic show and attested to how long it had been in residence at the Chamberlain. It must have been Akithar's cover. All that time, he had been the rebels' connection in the city, just as he was supposed to provide this newly arrived spy with critical information. Nera was frustrated by the lack of information they had about the spy, but attacking the problem from the contact's side should render the spy irrelevant. Taking down Akithar and his supports would weaken the rebels' position in the city, and getting the location of that stronghold from him very well could decimate the whole movement.

They simply had to break Aquin Mirada, and all the pieces should fall into place.

Nera was about to take the right turn toward the city center, but a vendor stall at the corner caught her eye. She crossed the street for a closer look. The stall was unremarkable by any standards. It was nothing more than some old pieces of wood nailed together into a semblance of display shelves and a small bin, backed by a rickety shack with a window cut in the front. Similar makeshift storefronts lined many of the streets here. They could be collapsed at night and set back up in the morning with no real construction needed. The proprietor, a man with three days' growth of gray beard and stains from his lunch on the front of his shirt, sat behind the window, following the crowd with sullen disinterest.

He watched Nera approach and was unimpressed with her uniform and rank. "See something you like?"

She ignored his question and studied the merchandise before the man. Trinkets, mostly, nearly all of it junk. A wooden carving of a horse, a metal bird with a wire attached at the top for hanging, assorted screws and unrecognizable components from what might once have been clocks or some more esoteric machinery. But there, amid the jumble, lay three identical knives. Nera traced her finger along the hilt of the one that laid on top.

She had spotted that hilt from across the street, and now she studied the red gem inlaid into the grip. It was identical to the gems in the other two knives lying alongside it in the bin. Identical to the one in the knife's hilt that Akithar had thrust into the chest of that boy atop the campus dormitory.

CHAPTER 27

"Listen closely," Apak said. "You must decant the solution into the vat before you submerge the tubes." Oreth could learn if only he would apply himself.

Oreth looked down into the steel tub and hung his head. "What's the use? What are we even doing?"

"As I told you before, we are extracting the elemental haranium from the document tubes. It is essential that we recover as much of the material as possible." Apak lifted a brown jug from the floor and sat it carefully on the table beside the vat. "This is the lylprine. You will recall using this in another of our recent projects."

Oreth raised his eyes from the vat to look at Apak, and they were empty. Apak saw no spark of understanding or application, only vacant brown orbs. None of this lesson had adhered. Very well. They would begin again.

Apak walked past Oreth's seat and picked up one of the cylinders from the worktable where he had all of them arranged. Apak had laid them out in three rows that covered the entire span of the table, and he had put wooden blocks on both sides to act as makeshift bookends, keeping the tubes from rolling off. Apak shuddered as he imagined the calamity that would result from a cylinder striking the hard floor.

Igniting one of the tubes might yield sufficient force to destroy everything in the workshop. Apak could not conceive of the disaster that would result from dozens of them going off at once.

They had been lucky in the dormitory, but Zerva was not here to catch any errant drops. She had left earlier that day to find Genie. Or was it the previous day? Apak blinked and wiped his fingertips across his eyes, beneath his glasses. Day and night were bleeding together, but he must persevere. There was work to be done.

Apak carried the cylinder back to the table at the middle of the workshop, where he had arranged the vat and various other tools they would need. So many projects were lost in the theater when the Scarlet Kites seized the Chamberlain. Fortunately, they had not gotten Apak's most important tools, which always stayed here in the Downsteps. This is where he built the most complex contraptions and where he had worked out the science for the electrical spotlights that hung even now across the ceiling of the theater. It pained Apak to think of those beautiful creations falling into the unappreciative hands of the Empire, but such was the circumstance. Ever onward and upward, he would march.

He blinked again and squeezed his eyes closed for a longer moment. Moisture was necessary for proper vision when one was… What was one doing? Ah, yes. Apak was holding the message tube. He sat it on the table before Oreth and wiped his sweaty palms on the sides of his vest.

"We shall begin again. Each of these message cylinders was forged with a—"

"Apak," Oreth said.

"—mixture of haranium and other metal alloys. The process for infusing the haranium into—"

"Apak."

"—the greater compound is quite complex, but it can be chemically reversed. Once done, we can recover the trace elements and reconstitute them electrically—"

Oreth stood and kicked the stool across the room. It tumbled into a pile of metallic scrap before crashing to the floor. Apak flinched in surprise but recovered quickly. "You were wise not to kick the stool into the table behind you."

Oreth looked behind him at the table covered with haranium tubes and then back at Apak. His face was pinched tight, and his chin shook in an unfamiliar expression. Was he about to cry again? Is that what this was?

"Why are we doing this?" Oreth asked. His voice shook, but no tears came. "The theater is gone, Dorrin's gone, everything is gone."

"We are doing this," Apak said, "because the extraction of the haranium is essential if we are to be able to use it in our project."

"There is no project. All that's done. Caius isn't doing any more magic shows, and we're not making any more tricks for him. Everything is finished. There's no need to do the… the extracting or whatever this is."

Apak waited for him to finish and gave him a chance to catch his breath before answering. "I am aware of our situation, Oreth. The dire circumstance in which we find ourselves provides no excuse for us to shirk our duties. We will proceed with our plans, as before. We will see to it that Caius has his device. This will be Akithar's greatest trick."

Oreth grabbed the stool by one leg and righted it on the floor next to the pile of metal he had disturbed. He sat on it again, all the fury apparently drained in his outburst. Perhaps he could focus and learn now. But he looked at Apak with an intensity Apak was not even aware that Oreth possessed. "Dorrin is dead."

The words were manifest, tangible things that Apak could feel even as he heard them. They were a hammer to his chest, and it took great effort not to double from the blow. He swallowed the pain and, once he was certain that he could speak without distortion, he said, "I know, Oreth. Dorrin died while making certain that we were not apprehended. He ensured that we would be successful in our mission to obtain these document tubes. And we were successful." He gestured to the table full of tubes, and Oreth followed his gaze. "I ask you, Oreth, would you have Dorrin's sacrifice be for nothing? Should we leave this bounty and flee into the arms of the Scarlet Kites? Do you want for Dorrin to have died, only for us to squander the final gift he gave us?"

Oreth's response was quiet, but Apak heard him say, "No."

"I am certain you will agree, then, that it is time that we resumed our work."

∾

Apak jolted, and suddenly Lizandra was there. She was standing before him, a hand on his shoulder, and concern on her face. "Apak? Are you all right?"

He straightened in his seat and looked around. What time was it? What day was it, even? Oreth was across the large room, working at the steel vat. Only now he was not working. He was looking at Apak and Lizandra, wearing his own look of concern.

"He was telling me how to do this, and then he trailed off. That was maybe twenty minutes ago."

"Have you slept, Apak?" Lizandra asked.

"Of course I have slept," Apak said. "I simply…" Oreth was not looking at him. He was looking at Lizandra again. That silly boy was incorrigible. How many times would Apak have to scold him for mooning over this young woman?

"You simply…?" Lizandra drew Apak's attention back to her.

He removed his glasses and wiped at his eyes with the back of his hand. "There simply is much work to complete, and there never is enough time."

"Tell me the truth," she said. "Have you slept since the school? At all?"

"I believe I was sleeping just now."

Lizandra pressed her lips together and drew her brow down. "Here. Samira sent food. Reykas is having chills again, and she and Caius are with him at our house now. The Kites haven't been there yet, so we think they don't know about Reykas and me, at least not by name. If you're not going to sleep, you at least have to eat." She sat a

340

basket on the table beside him, but Apak had no desire to eat just now. He waved the food away.

"There is too much to do. I will eat when our work is complete."

She squatted next to his stool and met his eyes. Apak noted that she lowered her voice as well. Perhaps she did not wish for Oreth to hear. "You're scaring me. Things are bad enough, Apak. We don't need you losing it now."

"I assure you that I am losing nothing. On the contrary, I have been instructing Oreth in the proper method for extracting haranium from the cylinders we retrieved. It took a few tries, but I am very pleased with his progress. He currently is leaching the element out of the tubes using a chemical bath I designed. We then will use electrical currents to draw the unstable material out of the vat, where we may reconstitute it into a usable form."

She frowned and glanced over her shoulder to where Oreth was working. "Why do you still need the haranium? Isn't that finished now?"

"Oh, no, no. Nothing is finished. We must persevere in our project. I must have the haranium if I am to construct the final illusion for Caius."

"There's not going to be a show, Apak. The Kites took the theater, remember?"

The look Lizandra was giving him was intolerable. It was concern crossed with confusion and laced with pity, of all things. Apak breathed out through his nose and lowered his own voice. "My faculties have not left me, Lizandra. I am aware that we no longer have a stage. I also know that I should be eating and sleeping but am not. I find myself disinclined to do either at the present moment. While my sanity has not fled, my appetite seems to have done just that. And when I attempt sleep, Dorrin awaits me on the other side."

"Oh, Apak." She put her hand over his. He flinched but did not pull away. "We all miss Dorrin. We're all hurting, but you have to pull yourself together. We need you now. All of us do. We need each other."

"I am a builder," he said. "I know how to construct marvelous things. That is where my strength may be found. I have knowledge about craftsmanship, about chemistry, even about electrical wonders. I have found that I do not, however, know how to pay recompense for the loss of that poor boy."

"Pay recompense? You have nothing to feel guilty about. What happened to Dorrin was not your fault."

"Oh, but it was. In so many ways, it was."

"I felt that way, too. I was right there and watched him die, and I couldn't do anything about it. I felt responsible, but so did Caius and Samira and even Reykas, even though he wouldn't say it. We all felt like we were to blame for what happened. But really, nobody was to blame but the Kites. They're the ones who killed him."

Apak put his other hand on top of Lizandra's and gave it a pat. His smile was slow and sad. "Although I may not be the one who murdered Dorrin, I assuredly bear more responsibility than you or any of our friends. Obtaining haranium was my idea, as were many details concerning our excavation at the university." He saw that Lizandra was about to protest, but he forestalled her with a raised hand. "Even before we left, Dorrin came to me and wanted to accompany us on our mission. I was busy with my preparations and would hear nothing of it."

"You did the right thing. Dorrin had no place being with us there. You told him not to come, and he came anyway. That was not your fault."

"Perhaps. Perhaps not. But my greatest sin is that I did not give Dorrin the advice and support he needed when he came to me about his magic."

Lizandra gasped. "You knew he was a mage?"

"No! No, of course not. I should have suspected it, though. In that same visit, when Dorrin wanted to join us, he asked me about magic. He wanted to know whether all mages were evil. He asked me how Ikarna views magic users."

"What did you tell him?" Lizandra whispered.

"Is that food?" Oreth called.

Lizandra smiled at Apak, and he took the expression as a pause in their conversation. She stood and turned. "Samira sent it. She thought you probably hadn't eaten."

"We haven't," Oreth said. He was about to lower the next tube into the bath but instead sat it on the table with enough care that Apak thought some of his instruction finally had gotten through to the young man. "Apak's kept me working through dinner."

Oreth stood and stretched his back with a bit more bend than Apak thought appropriate. "Take care you do not harm yourself," Apak said. Oreth snorted in response and started around his table to come to inspect the food. His hip clipped the corner of the table, and its wooden legs made a brief screech as they slid an inch across the floor.

The haranium tube bumped into motion and rolled away from Oreth. He lunged to grab for it, but it was too late. Apak felt a chill rush through his body, and he was wide awake now, all drowsiness supplanted by horror. As the cylinder tipped off the edge of the table, he threw himself off his stool and into Lizandra.

There was a flash of light, and Apak felt a scalding crush of heat slam into his body an instant before the thunderous crack of the explosion reached his ears.

CHAPTER 28

Gieck shoved the door open, and two of Nera's lapdogs were there. The younger one, Tomos, flinched, but the older one, Wil, stood like marble. "Where is she?"

"Commander Mollor should be returning soon. She sent us ahead with the prisoner," Wil said.

"Not her. Where is the prisoner?"

"Through there," Tomos said, pointing at the next door through the chamber.

Wil gave him a scolding look. "It would be most prudent to wait until the commander returns."

"Open it up," Gieck said.

"But Lieutenant—"

Gieck stared into Wil's eyes, and for the briefest instant he thought the old soldier wasn't going to back down. But of course he did. Wil nodded and produced the key from his pocket. "I will let the commander know you went ahead with the interrogation." He was deathly slow in getting the thing into the lock, and Gieck felt like ripping it out of his hand and doing it himself.

He'd been a few blocks west of here, patrolling with Kela and Shoy, when Eyral rode up, his eyes excited. "The commander caught one of them!"

"Is it the wizard?" Gieck had asked, his pulse quickening.

"No. It's a librarian. The mage—our mage—says she knows about the attack on the campus."

Gieck had turned to Kela. "Finish showing Shoy the rounds. Have her report to me if you find anything." And then, to Eyral, "Has the librarian talked?"

"Not yet. The commander isn't back at the castle yet. Wil is guarding the prisoner until she returns."

This was his chance to get a step ahead of Nera. If he could find Akithar before she did, he could get the location of the Stormbreak Sanctuary and kill the man before Nera asked him anything about the boy. He still had to worry about Jona's suspicions and whatever Eyral and Kela might have seen, but eliminating Akithar would destroy his greatest threat. If he could secure the rebels' information in the process, all the better. The man who delivered the uprising to the High Lord would be untouchable.

He wasn't sure whether he could beat Nera back to the castle, but he rode hard through the city, leaving Eyral far behind and knocking into anyone who lacked the sense to stay out of his way. The bizarre witch with the colossal head lingered outside the keep. Gieck knew Nera hated her, and that made the halflock even more useful. He had not been positive that he'd made it in time until just now, when he burst into the chamber to find these two pathetic Kites awaiting their mistress's return.

His impatience finally got the better of him, and he shoved Wil aside once he heard the lock clack open. He'd been fuming about the old man being slow, but the look Wil gave him as Gieck pushed him out of the way told him the slowness was intentional. He had been delaying Gieck and hoping for Nera to return. Gieck narrowed his eyes at Wil but would have to deal with him later.

Inside the chamber, the woman sat at a wooden table. Her hands were bound in front of her and shackled through a hole in the center of the table. Gieck was familiar enough with procedures to know that the other end of those shackles under the table bound her feet. She wouldn't be able to stand or even move very much. Having her sitting in that position, the chain pulling her arms out and attaching them to her legs would wear on her back. The standard method was to wait long enough for the muscle cramps to begin, and only then should the interrogator begin working. Gieck had no time for that.

"Aquin Mirada," he said.

She stared back at him with large, dark eyes.

"You are Aquin Mirada," he said again.

She set her jaw in defiance, but he saw it quiver. She was terrified. She wanted him to think she was tough, cunning, resourceful, but if there was one thing Gieck could smell on a person, it was fear.

He straddled the chair opposite hers and leaned toward her with his arms crossed on the table. "You are in a lot of trouble."

She tightened her jaw, and her eyes moistened. This was going to be easier than he liked. Expediency was necessary if he wanted to get the information out of her before Nera arrived, but he never liked to hurry with these kinds of things. Interrogations should be slow and excruciating. They should be entertaining.

"How do you know Samira Tandogan?"

"I don't know her," she said. Her voice was tentative, compressed by doubt and despair.

Gieck shoved his chair backward and stood. Mirada blinked at the suddenness of his movement, and a single tear escaped down her cheek. She moved her hand to wipe at it, and the chain caught her in place. The woman's eyebrows drew together as she looked down at her predicament, and another tear rolled down the other side of her face. Gieck was around the table by then and squatted next to her. He pressed a thick thumb into the side of her chin and scrubbed it upward, slowly tracing the tear's track up her cheek. She whimpered, and he stopped just short of shoving his thumb into her eye.

He leaned in close and closed his hand around her face, keeping his thumb in place. Gieck turned her head toward his own, and he could feel her breath on his face now, coming fast and hitching.

"Don't toy with me," he hissed, close enough to kiss her. "We know where you're from. We know you have family there, and you do not want for me to find them. Do you know what I would do to them?" It was a lie, but it was the kind that was the most effective. He had no idea who this woman's people might be or where she came from, short of somewhere in the south of Teshovar.

She said nothing, and probably couldn't say anything with the grip Gieck had on her face, but her moan was answer enough.

"How do you know Samira Tandogan? I'm asking you again, but I won't ask a third time."

He loosened his fingers but kept them wrapped around her chin, cupping her face so she had to look directly into his eyes, only inches away. She inhaled twice, fast, before she whispered, "I met her at the library. Not long ago."

"Did she use you to get the haranium?"

"No! No, I—"

"We know what you did. You can't lie to us. That'll make it worse for you. Tell me about the haranium."

Mirada began, stuttered, stopped, and began again. "We have haranium in the basement. Had it. In the message tubes."

"Do you know where those document tubes are?"

"No!" She was insistent, begging him to believe her, and he did. But not knowing where the loot ended up didn't mean she was not a part of the theft.

"The robbery was Akithar, wasn't it?" He rocked her head with a violent shake. "Tell me it was Akithar."

"It was Akithar," she said. She shut her eyes tight and clamped her mouth shut. She might have said it just to appease Gieck, but he didn't think so. He'd seen enough people in this situation to know when they were telling the truth. He'd put enough people in this situation himself.

"What does he want with the haranium?"

"I don't know. I didn't want to know. I wouldn't let them tell me." The words poured out alongside more tears. They wet Gieck's fingers, and he scowled in disgust at the audacity of this southerner dirtying his hand.

There were voices outside the door. Gieck recognized Nera's and knew his time was up. He squeezed Mirada's face again, this time so hard that her jaw made a popping sound and she squeaked a confused protest of pain and fear. He leaned even closer and pressed his forehead against hers. "Where is Akithar?"

"I don't know! I swear I don't know," she said, her voice stripped to sobs now.

"Is he a mage?"

She sniffed and sputtered, and he shook her once more. "Yes! Yes, he is a mage."

"How do you know?"

"Samira told me. She told me he's a mage. He looks after them. All of them."

The door clanked behind Gieck, and he released Mirada's face and leaned back away from her. "That's all for now. What you said matches what the witch told me."

She blinked at him, startled. "She read all that from my mind? Why did you put me through that if you already knew? Why did you hurt me?"

Gieck winked at her and whispered, "Everybody needs a little fun now and then." He stood and went around the table to meet Nera as she was coming through the door.

"Lieutenant," she said. "Wil told me you began the interrogation without me."

"She confirmed that Akithar is a mage and that she was in on the heist, but she doesn't know where he is." Nera could get that much information herself, so he might as well play the dutiful servant.

"Was there anything else? Anything we didn't know?"

"Nothing," he said. While it was true that Mirada hadn't given up more information, the witch Magra had been happy to spill a few additional details, but there was no need to share those. Nera wouldn't be conversing with that old sorceress.

"I'll want to talk to her myself," Nera said. She looked past Gieck to the shackled woman with a tear-stained face. "What happened?"

"She feels guilty for giving up her friends," he said.

She stepped closer to him, her voice lowered. "Before I interview her, I need to talk with you. I don't think the knife—"

The sound of a distant blast cut her off mid-sentence, and Gieck felt the ground vibrate. "Was that thunder?" he asked.

"No, that was an explosion." She looked at Mirada again, hesitated, and then motioned to Gieck. "Follow me." She made a quick pace through the hallway and out to the front of the castle.

People had stopped in the street, all looking to the eastern sky. Gieck stepped past Nera and backed into the street himself. Above the rooftops of buildings that obscured his view, he could see the night sky illuminated in that direction, brighter than it should be even with the moon. "There's a fire," he said.

"The people are saying it's in the Downsteps," Eyral said. He had been waiting outside and was next to Gieck now. "What should we do?"

"It's the haranium," Nera said. "It's happening now. This is their attack."

CHAPTER 29

Apak knew he was not dead when he inhaled a lungful of smoke and gagged on the acrid stench. He began coughing and rolled himself onto his left side to spit the sooty taste out. It came out dark but not red. There was no blood, and for that he was both surprised and thankful. Less promising was the shooting pain in his torso. He ran a hand down his side, probing for wounds, but found no cuts or punctures. It could be bruising, but he thought it more likely that he had broken ribs.

He pushed up to kneel and could see the flicker of flames across the room. Everything was blurred, and he blinked a couple of times before realizing he had lost his glasses in the explosion. Apak dropped back to the floor and swiped his hands around the area near him, sweeping debris out of the way as he went. If he had been able to reason properly, he would have taken extra precautions not to jab splinters of wood, metal, and glass into his palms. Luck favored him in that regard, and he managed not to injure himself further but could not find the glasses.

He did not realize at first that his hearing had been replaced by a keen whistling riding atop an incessant roar. Lizandra might have spoken to him, but he was not even aware she was there until she grabbed a handful of his shirt and pulled him around in her direction. She pressed something into his hand. Ah, his glasses. Apak settled them on the bridge of his nose, and his vision returned to him, albeit split by a crack in the left lens. That would have to be good enough for now.

Lizandra was on her knees next to him, and her previously white dress now was ripped and stained red. She was holding her left hand tight against her right bicep, where Apak could see a long cut. Blood also covered the side of her face, coming from another cut somewhere higher, perhaps in her scalp. Her eyes were wide, and she was saying something to him as she pointed away from them, but the roar persisted.

"I can not hear you," he tried to say. He could hear his voice within his own head, but nothing else. That gave him some assurance that he would not be entirely or permanently deaf. He tapped his ear. What had happened here? Why could he not hear, and why was Lizandra bleeding?

Lizandra pushed herself to her feet with her right hand, keeping the left clamped on her wound. Standing, she wobbled, unsteady for a moment, but gained her balance and reached down for Apak. He took her hand and, with her assistance, made his own shaky way up to his feet. He let go of Lizandra's hand and held himself up on the edge of the table where he had been sitting. It had blown over to shield them and likely was the reason they had not sustained worse injuries.

The explosion. The past seconds rushed back to him in a fearful torrent of fire and debris. Where was Oreth?

Standing now, he got his first look at the other side of the workshop and realized that was what Lizandra had been attempting to show him. The table where Oreth had been at work now was little more than blasted splinters. Apak saw the steel tub was still in one piece but lay crumpled on the floor, the front and bottom dented up into the body. It was hard to even discern what else had been on that side of the room. Everything else was wreckage, burning with increasing intensity.

Apak headed toward the fire and noted that he had to favor his right leg, as the left was stiff and largely unresponsive. That was a concern for later. For now, he had to find Oreth. Lizandra passed Apak and shoved a demolished shelf out of the way. Apak heard a distant thud when it hit the floor, and he knew his hearing was returning, but slowly. He joined Lizandra and helped her haul a piece of smashed equipment up and over to crash down on the floor. He realized that had been part of an experiment he had begun involving electricity and magnetism. It was lost now, all gone, but that was not his focus.

"Apak!" He heard Lizandra yell his name next to him, but she sounded twenty feet away. She was pointing again, and he followed her finger to the back wall, where rubble had piled high but not breached the side of the building. A pale and dirty hand lay limp, barely visible out of the mound of broken stone, glass, and metal.

The pile had not yet caught fire, and Apak pulled himself over the debris. His left leg was dragging, but it at least could support him. When he reached the spot where Lizandra had seen the hand, he had a dizzying fear that the hand would be all that was left. But no, he now could see the arm and the shape of the rest of the body, all covered with the ruins of the workshop.

"Help me." He did not know how loud his voice might be, but it echoed in his aching head.

Lizandra was over the wreckage in an instant and pulled up on the wooden beam Apak already was trying to lift. The task felt impossible, but the two of them moved it up enough to shove it off to the side. The beam leveraged a chunk of heavy stone and a sheet of metal that also fell free from the pile.

Lizandra fell to her knees beside Oreth, heedless of the sharp and jagged edges of the debris. Her own wound was forgotten as she covered her mouth with her bloody hand. Tears streamed from her eyes, likely as much a reaction to the growing cloud of smoke as it was to finding this poor boy, this poor young man who had been so smitten with her. Oreth was crushed, his chest now unnervingly concave and his left arm and left leg bent in unnatural directions. His clothes had shredded, hanging off him in rags, and Apak could see the burned skin beneath. Shrapnel punctuated his left side, the side that had been facing the explosion.

The blast somehow had left his face untouched. Oreth's head had tilted back, the top resting against the hard wall, and he looked as though he might be sleeping. Apak clamped his teeth together as he felt the smoke drawing tears into his own eyes. He dropped to his knees beside Lizandra and ignored the pain that shot through his left leg. Apak put his hand to the side of Oreth's cheek, more gently than he believed he ever had addressed the young man. A faint puff of air grazed Apak's palm.

Somehow, impossibly, Oreth was alive.

～

It took Samira less than five minutes to burst into the workshop. She took in the scene in a glance and asked Apak, "What happened?"

Enough of his hearing had returned that he could respond with reasonable confidence that he had understood her correctly. "Oreth had an accident." Apak and Lizandra had dragged his unmoving body out of the rubble, clearing the area only seconds before a section of the roof gave way and dropped a flaming beam across the mound where Oreth had lain. It was hard work, between Lizandra's injured arm and Apak's wounded leg, but they were able to pull Oreth across the floor and up a makeshift ramp onto a small cart Zerva had left behind. The blast had demolished the far end of the workshop, but this end, the one nearest where Apak and Lizandra had been talking, had escaped with less severe damage.

Samira spotted Oreth on the cart and rushed to his side. "Is he alive?"

"He is," Apak said, "but I do not believe he has long."

Lizandra lifted Oreth's broken arm onto the cart with a gentleness that made Apak's chest ache. She looked up from Oreth's still face to Samira. "Where is Caius? Is he still at my house with Reykas?"

Samira nodded. "He wanted to come, but I made him stay behind."

And then, to Apak, "We have to get Oreth out of here. He needs healing, and there's no time."

"He will not survive transport," Apak said. "We must take the time."

"This place is burning down, and the city watch is probably on the way. Maybe even the Kites. If we stay here, we're all done for."

Apak scowled and looked at the ruined building. He had purchased it many years ago, after he first arrived in Klubridge. It was where he built his business, long before he met and joined with Caius and Samira. So much time spent here, all gone now. Even as he watched, another piece of the roof fell in, this time closer, and he felt the heat from the growing fire becoming more intense by the second.

He turned back to Oreth and put a hand on the young man's forehead. He knew that Samira was correct. This place would not stand for much longer, and it was an unsuitable infirmary, even in a time of crisis like this. "Go ahead," he said. "The cart should still be intact for transporting him."

"You're not coming?" Samira asked.

"There is too much remaining here that the Empire must not see or possess. It will take only a moment, but I must remain behind. I will rejoin you soon." He clasped Oreth's uninjured hand and squeezed it. "Take him to Caius."

"Hurry," Samira said, giving Apak a meaningful stare.

"Can magic even heal this?" Lizandra asked. "Oreth is… It's not good." Her eyes were brave, but her mouth trembled.

"It has to. Can you help me with the cart?"

"I think so." Lizandra took one side, and Samira grabbed the other. It was obvious that Samira had to do most of the work, but together they were able to roll the cart through the front door. As they went out into the street, Samira shot another look back at Apak. "Hurry," she said again. He intended to do just that.

Apak waded into the heat and pulled up the front of his shirt to cover his mouth and nose. His eyes stung from the smoke, and unbidden tears streamed down his face. The side of the workshop where Oreth had been was well and truly destroyed. The explosion had reduced the remaining equipment to unrecognizable lumps of metal, shattered glass, and burning wood. Apak looked over his shoulder, back to where he and Lizandra had been at the time of the explosion. His eyes widened. Just past them, on the far table that somehow was still undisturbed, sat the remainder of the haranium cylinders.

He remembered it now. He and Oreth had transported the cylinders from Oreth's worktable over to the other one, specifically because Apak had been concerned that having Oreth work with the full complement of tubes at hand would pose too great a risk. He had Oreth extracting the haranium from them one at a time, venturing across the room to retrieve the next tube when he was finished with the last one. The only cylinders that had exploded were the one Oreth had dropped and a second one that had been on his table. If the others had gone up... Apak did not even wish to imagine the calamity.

Apak stepped over the remains of the steel vat and made his way back across to the far table. The room was full of smoke now, and the fire was spreading to the nearer sections of the roof and the adjoining walls. It would burn out the frame and all the wooden supports, but the bricks and metal construction would remain, protecting what was left of Apak's tools and equipment. It was an inferno, but there might be enough left afterward for the Empire to benefit from Apak's work.

He shook his head. That would not happen as long as he had anything to say about it. He worked quickly now, finding an old pack discarded in the back corner and gathering what odds and ends he could salvage and that would be useful. Earlier in the evening, Oreth already had succeeded in extracting the haranium from several of the tubes. The base element was stored in an insulated jar, and Apak tucked that into the pack with extra gentleness.

What else might he need? What else could be saved? The books already were going up in flames, and there simply were too many tools and devices to bring even a fraction of them. At last he spotted the earthquake machine sitting alone by the door, where they had deposited it after the night at the university. He did not know what use he might have for it at this point, but Apak felt compelled to save the contraption, even if it broke his back to drag the heavy thing out of there. At least one of his inventions would survive that night.

Satisfied with his selection, Apak moved toward the exit and the clear air that waited outside. His hand on the door, he hesitated and looked once more at the table loaded with the remaining tubes. The roof eventually would fall in and crush that table, setting off a secondary blast that would wipe out the entire building and everything in it. Not for the first time, Apak was thankful that he had no immediate neighbors. But how long would it take for the remaining haranium to ignite? Long enough for the city watch or worse to arrive?

Apak looked out and into the night and sighed. He pushed the door closed and faced the blazing interior again. With new determination, he placed his pack on the floor beside the earthquake machine and stepped into the chaos. There still was one more project to complete before his workshop could be retired.

CHAPTER 30

Oreth would survive. Samira wasn't sure that he would walk unaided or that he would have full strength in his broken arm, but he at least would live, and that was better than she might have hoped for just a couple of hours ago. He lay in the middle of Lizzie and Reykas' bed, swaddled in makeshift bandages that finally were not leaking red onto the white sheets. Samira had had to change the dressings twice already, but the bleeding seemed under control now. She had no formal medical training but had done the best she could do, and that seemed to suffice.

She felt Oreth's head once more, and there still was no fever. She wasn't sure what it would mean, exactly, if he had had a fever, but she knew that wouldn't have been good. Caius knew so much more about that sort of thing, and she had planned to tend to Oreth alongside him. And yet, Caius was nowhere to be found.

When she left the house to investigate the explosion, she had instructed Caius to keep watch over Reykas while she was away. He had agreed, but when she and Lizzie got back with Oreth in tow, Reykas was asleep on the lounge in the front room, and Caius had disappeared. There was no note, no indication of where he had gone or what had happened. Samira didn't know whether to be worried or angry, so she hovered somewhere in between the two. Reykas' chills had subsided in her absence, and he was sleeping in peace now. Fortunately, he hadn't needed someone after being left on his own.

Samira looked at her hands, covered in her friend's blood. How had this become her life? It was supposed to be simpler now. There had been years of running, years of violence and fear, but all of that should have ended with Klubridge. Now the fear was back, and the violence, and they would run if they could, but every part of that plan had fallen apart. What was left but to wait for the Kites to close in on them?

She washed her hands in the basin in the next room and propped herself on the edge of it to look at her reflection in the mirror. She was wearing a borrowed shirt from Lizandra, her own shirt now turning brittle from Oreth's blood that had soaked into it as they wrestled him off the cart, up the stairs, and into the bedroom. It was fortunate that Lizzie wore loose-fitting clothes, because Samira was positive she wouldn't have fit into anything that actually fit the slim girl. There were a couple of streaks of blood, now brown, on Samira's pants, but she tried to ignore the stains. She had a lot more to be concerned about right now, such as when the Kites would kick the door in to carry them all away and where in the ageless realm Caius has gotten off to.

And Aquin.

Samira gasped at her own face in the mirror and saw the blood drain from it. During everything else that was happening, she hadn't checked on Aquin. It had been three days since they had seen each other. The Kites had identified Samira, and they soon would find Apak's workshop, but surely they hadn't connected Samira to Aquin. She had to be all right. The smart thing would be to wait for Caius to return and discuss it with him. It wouldn't be wise to go poking about in the city, especially when the guards would be on high alert and looking for her and Caius in particular. Sometimes what was wise didn't agree with what was right, and Samira knew she was going, anyway.

She checked on Oreth once more before pulling the door open and stepping out into the short upstairs hallway. She left the door ajar so that Lizzie could look in on Oreth. She knew she couldn't depend on Apak for that. He'd arrived at the house not long after Lizzie and Samira, laden with a bulging pack on his back and dragging that bizarre square machine behind him on a small, wheeled cart. Samira had tried to talk to him about what had happened, but he shook his head, said something about work to be done, and closed himself away in the spare room next to Oreth's. Apak was a strange man at the best of times, but something had changed in him, broken maybe, after Dorrin's death. Samira worried about how that would continue to devolve after Oreth's injury and losing the workshop, but there wasn't much she could do for Apak just now. She had to find Aquin.

Lizzie looked up from Reykas when she heard Samira coming down the stairs. "How is he?"

"He'll make it. He's resting now. I did what I could, but I wish Caius had been here."

"I doubt he could have helped much more than you did."

Samira sighed. "Sometimes magic can do what traditional medicine can't. Usually, in fact." She put a hand on Lizzie's shoulder and looked past her to Reykas. "How is he?"

"No chills for now. With luck, he'll be better after this sleep."

Samira nodded. "I have to go out."

"What? Now?"

"It's Aquin. I don't know whether she's safe."

Lizzie looked like she wanted to protest, and Samira wouldn't have blamed her if she did. But they both knew what it meant to care for someone who was in danger, and Lizzie simply nodded. "Be careful. Don't take any unnecessary risks."

"If Caius comes back while I'm gone, keep him here."

"I'll try. You know Caius."

There were more people in the street tonight than usual. There had been more every night for a while. The people of Klubridge didn't enjoy being trapped, and the city gates had been under Kite control for weeks now. It was a siege that the populace had humored at first, but their humor was wearing thin.

Samira stepped into the flow of foot traffic and hoped no one would notice the blood on her trousers. If they did, she might pass it off as dirt or grease or something equally innocuous and not at all nefarious. She kept a hand low, partly covering the streaks, just in case. But mostly she kept an eye out for the city watch and the Kites. They knew what she looked like, and they would have her name and an order to arrest her by now. The guard presence was low here, and that allowed her to make quicker time through the main streets instead of having to take back alleys.

She suspected most of the official law presence was in the Down-steps, trying to make sense of the burned-out warehouse. There had been a second explosion shortly after Apak returned, this one much larger than the first one. Samira had poked her head outside and had seen the glow of the flames illuminating clouds in the sky above the city. She didn't know what Apak had done, but she thought that second blast was his doing. Surely he had taken precautions to make sure no innocents were killed, and certainly he would have made sure the fire didn't spread through the whole city.

But she no longer was certain about what Apak would or wouldn't do. He was a haunted man now. He didn't process his emotions well in the best of times, and now he was struggling with loss and grief keener than he ever had encountered. Samira had lost loved ones before and knew the impossible weight that came after. Apak felt that weight now, and she thought he didn't know what to do with it. She'd have to talk to him again, once there was a spare moment. If there ever were any more spare moments, which seemed less likely by the hour.

～

Samira crossed paths with six city guards and one Kite, but she had to duck into alleys to avoid only two of them. The rest were busy trying to quell the unruly crowds that were becoming more and more common in the streets. The sounds of the explosions seemed to have rocked the entire city, and the roadways were full of the curious, the angry, and the afraid. Samira heard more than a few people she passed speculating about what had caused the blasts. The popular opinion was that the High Lord had ordered an attack on the city after his Scarlet Kites had failed to accomplish whatever mission they were sent to complete.

Aquin lived in an apartment house near the university. All the windows were dark at the front as Samira approached. She lingered outside, looking up to the second-floor window she knew to be Aquin's. Surely she would be inside, safely asleep. Either that, or she would have been awakened by the explosions, but Samira knew Aquin wouldn't venture out into the street like so many others did. No, she would crouch in the darkness before her secret altar with a single candle, clutching her icon and praying that Ikarna deliver this violence from her city.

If she were home, Samira was tempted to ask Aquin to accompany her back to Lizzie's house. She knew that would be foolish, though. If Aquin had avoided detection from the Kites for this long, there was no reason to drag her into the very place they wanted to find. And if she were not at home? If she'd already been taken? That would be a bridge to cross only if necessary.

Samira cast a last glance around the street before taking the stairs up to the front door. There was no sign of authorities, but she still kept her face averted from passersby. She had heard nothing about a bounty, but it would only be a matter of time before there was a price on her head, Caius' head, probably all of their heads. That's when things truly would become interesting. The people of Klubridge hated living under the thumb of the Empire, but they loved money more. She knew that most of the city would sell out their mothers for a few shiny coins.

The front door was mostly glass, and she could see into the empty entryway before she pulled it open. A lamp glowed on the far wall, illuminating the closed postal boxes along the right side. Samira let the door close behind her and glanced at the boxes as she passed. Aquin's name, "A. Mirada," was right there on the middle one. There were three apartments in this building, one per floor. Samira passed the door to the first one and took the stairs on the left. The light from the entryway was not enough to dispel the shadows from the entire passage, so she took the stairs up in darkness. At the top of the staircase was a window, but the light from the moon was feeble tonight, obscured by the clouds.

Samira turned left, onto the second-floor landing. She had been here only once, in the daytime. She remembered the burgundy rug that ran the length of the second-floor hallway, but she couldn't see it clearly in the darkness. There was a lamp on the back wall here, like the one below, but this one was not burning.

Her eyes had adjusted to the gloom, and even in the darkness Samira could make out the basic shapes of the hallway. She trailed her fingertips along the right-hand wall until she reached Aquin's door. There she paused, now unsure about how to proceed. Should she knock? Call out? She felt foolish for even coming all this way, when Aquin probably was just on the other side of that door, sound asleep. She would laugh at Samira's concern.

Samira placed her hand on the door, still trying to decide whether to knock, and it pushed inward. She sucked in a quick breath and held it as a chill ran up her arms. Aquin had been careless with leaving her office door unlocked at the library. She'd speculated about how bad a situation she would have been in, if it had been someone other than Samira who'd found her in prayer. Since then, Aquin had become compulsive about locking doors. She would not have left this one open.

Samira's heart sank, and she found herself hoping Aquin was not inside after all. She pushed the door again, gently, and it swung inward, slowly opening all the way. Samira swallowed hard before stepping inside. There was more light in there, coming through the window that faced the street. It was just enough for her to see that the entire room had been ransacked. The Kites had already been here.

Fear drove Samira forward two more steps, and it was fear that halted her mid-stride as well. Silhouetted against the window, a figure stepped out from Aquin's bedroom. A lantern flared to life in the hands of a stranger, a short and lean man with his hair pulled back into a ponytail. He didn't move toward Samira, but he held the lantern to the side and squinted at her. When his hand moved, Samira saw the red uniform with the dark bird on the chest.

"You're her," he said. He sounded stunned, as if he couldn't believe what he was seeing. "Samira Tandogan."

Still too afraid to move, she asked, "What did you do to her?"

The Kite blinked at her and then understood. "The Mirada woman. We have her, and you'll see her soon." He took a step toward her, and that was enough to jar Samira into motion. Her feet shuffled backwards, nearly tumbling over each other, and she was into the hallway, spinning first right and then left, remembering the way back to the stairs. She had to go down, out from here. It was stupid for her to have come.

"Wait!" the Kite called after her, and she heard him behind her, now moving into the hallway. She was already at the stairs, spinning around the corner. "Kela!" he yelled, "Stop this woman!"

Samira was halfway down the stairs when the other Kite, Kela, appeared at the bottom. Samira was in darkness and knew the other woman couldn't see her descent. She could see the Kite, though. She was about Samira's age, but broader, stronger. She had light brown hair pulled back in a ponytail similar to the first Kite's.

Kela started up the stairs, and Samira leaped down the final few steps, ramming her body into the woman's shoulder. She'd aimed for her head, but her momentum carried her through to the side. Kela grunted with the impact and spun back against the wall on the left. That gave Samira the space she needed to slip through to the right. Samira stumbled out into the entryway, seeing stars for an instant. She shook her head and barreled toward the door. Her flight was so frantic that she nearly crashed through the big window in it. She checked herself just in time and slowed enough to push it open.

"Hey!" The woman was after her now, only a few steps behind.

Samira ran out into the street and made a hasty choice to the right. She didn't know or care where she was going, as long as it was away from those soldiers. They probably were faster than she was, but they also were laden with their uniforms and equipment. Samira hoped that would be enough to let her keep her lead.

She sprinted down the full block, and her feet skidded on the road as she made an abrupt turn to the left. She heard hard soles pounding behind her. They sounded closer than she'd hoped, but she didn't risk the time to look back. She tucked her head and ran.

Up ahead was an intersection, busier than this street. Perhaps she could lose them in a crowd. As she drew nearer, she could see that it wasn't just the usual traffic. People had gathered there, under the streetlamps. They were conversing and looking toward the east, toward the Downsteps where the fire still lit the dark horizon. There were enough people to clog the street, plenty to hide Samira. She was almost there and had a fleeting hope that she'd reach them before the Kite caught her.

That hope died when she was scarcely three feet from the edge of the crowd. A hand shoved the middle of her back, and Samira lost her footing. She staggered, her feet catching on each other, and then she was in the air, going down hard on the street. She fell between two men and rolled with the fall to lessen the impact.

As Samira turned onto her back, she saw the woman named Kela, her red uniform burning brightly in the dark of the night.

"Are you all right?" one of the men asked and reached to help Samira up.

"Do not touch this woman!" Kela shouted. And then, to Samira, "You are under arrest by the authority entrusted to the Scarlet Kites by the High Lord Peregrine."

Samira was still on her back but pushed up to her elbows and tried to crawl backwards, away from Kela. She realized that she'd cut her arms and scrubbed the skin on both palms in the fall. With this soldier looming over her and doom imminent, all Samira could feel was regret that she'd bloodied another shirt that night, this time Lizzie's.

Kela took a step toward her, and Samira saw the other Kite, the man from the second floor, running up behind her.

"You're not taking her."

At first Samira thought it was the other Kite talking, but her confusion deepened when she saw it was one of the men next to her. He stepped in front of her, putting himself between Samira and the two Kites. The other man, the one who had offered to help her, now reached down and pulled her to her feet. "You'll be all right, miss," he said.

"Step aside," Kela told the other one, but he didn't move.

"You've taken enough from us," the man said. "It stops here. You're not taking this woman. Whatever you want her for, you're not getting her. Not this night."

The last few words came out slurred, and Samira saw the bottle hanging loosely from his fingers. She looked around the crowd and saw more bottles, more angry glares. These people were drunk. They'd been in some tavern or other when they heard the explosions, and now they were out here, looking for somewhere to direct their anger.

Samira started, "I don't—"

"Behind us," the man who'd helped her up said, and he pushed her back, through the middle of the crowd. There must have been a dozen and a half bodies in the cluster. As Samira watched, more were joining. The smell of excitement was in the street. Something, anything to quell the impotent resentment they'd been feeling for the weeks the city had been under lockdown. She looked through the crowd, back to the Kites. Kela was looking past the man who was trying to block her.

"This woman is a traitor to the Empire, and we're taking her." She put a gloved hand on the front man's shoulder and shoved him aside. As he staggered to the left, a murmur of protest arose from the crowd. Kela had waded into the middle of it now, headed straight for Samira. The other Kite, the man, was more hesitant.

"Kela," he called after her. "Wait, maybe we shouldn't—"

But it was too late. The man Kela had shoved had regained his balance, and he swung his bottle around in a quick spin. Samira heard the thud as it hit the back of Kela's head, but it didn't break. The Kite winced and lurched forward. In a fury, she turned on the man, and her hand went for the dagger sheathed at her side.

"She's got a knife!" someone in the crowd yelled, and a pair of hands grabbed Kela's arm before she could draw the blade.

"Vam!" she called to the other Kite. The hands pulled her backwards, farther into the mob, and Samira took an involuntary step backwards. This was spiraling out of control.

Unable to pull her blade, Kela jerked her arm away from the crowd and tried to throw an elbow at the person next to her. The people were too close, though, and there was no space for her to land a solid hit. The other Kite, Vam, saw what was happening, and there was nothing he could do but watch. If he tried to intervene, he'd be pulled into the mass of people as well, and Samira didn't blame him for the uncertain dance he was doing, forward and backward.

Samira didn't see it happen, but somehow the dagger was out and in Kela's hand. She was turning left and right, clearly disoriented now, probably still looking for Samira, who by now was clear and out the other side of the mob. Samira should have run, but she couldn't, not while these people were dealing with a problem she had brought to them.

Someone punched Kela, and Samira heard the smack of knuckles against flesh. Kela's head rocked back, and she roared in anger as she came around, reaching out for whichever person had struck her. She lunged forward, and there was a grunt from the woman in front of her, and everything went still. Samira watched Kela's rage melt into uncertainty and then horror as the Kite pulled her bloody hand back, freeing her blade from the woman who had been unlucky enough to be standing beside her.

"She's killed Thallon!"

Kela cried out in protest. "No! I was defending myself! Wait!"

The crowd folded in on itself like nothing Samira had ever seen. As the remaining citizens descended upon Kela and drove her to the ground, Samira moved back quickly, away from the chaos. She saw Vam, still far on the other side. He was watching the mob with haunted eyes. He knew what the outcome of this would be as well as Samira did. At the same time, they turned and ran, Samira in one direction and Vam in the other, both leaving Kela to the street's vengeance.

~

S amira hadn't seen the Kite die, but she knew the crowd would not stop until she was finished. She'd just left the woman there to be torn apart. Even as she hurried through the city back toward Lizzie's house, her arm and hands bleeding from being scraped on the road, Samira felt sick to her stomach. She'd watched a drunken mob destroy that woman, Kela.

If it hadn't happened, Samira could only imagine where Kela and her partner might have taken her and what might have happened to her there. What was happening to Aquin even now. Still, she felt like she should have done something or at least said something. She doubted it would have helped, but she still should have tried. The city was hungry now, starved by the siege, and it had devoured one of its oppressors right there in the middle of the street. Klubridge was changing, mutating into something bestial. It terrified Samira.

She quickened her pace once she was back in the right neighborhood, and the traffic had thinned on the streets around the house where Lizzie was tending to Reykas and Oreth while Apak toiled away at whatever mad project was occupying him. With fewer people out, Samira would be an easy target if she ran afoul of the police or the Kites again. She tried to keep to the shadows and kept her head down, but there was no hiding her injured hands now that they'd bled all over the white shirt she'd borrowed. She had to hope no one would spot her in the darkness, and she was looking back to make sure she wasn't followed when she rounded the corner at Lizzie's house. She collided headfirst into the man waiting next to the door.

Samira lurched back and nearly yelped before she saw who it was. "Where have you been?" She wanted to grab him and shake him, but her hands were still bleeding.

Caius put a finger to his lips and pulled her back around the corner and into the side street she had just left. "What happened to you?" he asked. He took her right hand in his and studied the abrasions in the dim light.

"The Kites were after me. They have Aquin, Caius. They've been through everything in her apartment, turned the whole thing out, and they took her. They came after me, too, but I got away."

Caius grimaced at that. "They won't kill her. They'll want whatever information she has. How much does she know?"

Samira inhaled and dropped her head in shame. "I told her things. She asked if you could do real magic."

"What did you tell her?"

She raised her head and met his eyes. "I told her you could."

"Why did you do that, Samira?"

She shouted back at him, not caring for the moment whether they were spotted or heard. "I don't know! She asked me, and that's what I told her. You disappear and are gone half the time, and I care about her, Caius. I truly do. She asked me a question, and I answered it."

He swore and let go of her hand. "What's done is done. You shouldn't have been out there. What if they'd gotten you?" He looked past her. "You weren't followed, were you?"

"Who are you to tell me where I should or shouldn't be?" She was angry now, but she wasn't even sure whether her anger truly was directed at Caius or whether he was just the most convenient recipient of it. "You were supposed to be with Reykas. There was an explosion at Apak's workshop."

"I know," he said. "I went there and saw it. The whole thing's gone now. Mollor was there, but I don't think they could have found anything. It was all rubble by the time I got there, and they didn't look happy."

"Why did you leave? Oreth was injured, and I had to help him myself. He needed you. We all needed you."

He didn't answer her question, not directly. Instead he said, "After that explosion, the Kites are going to be swarming this area. It's not going to be hard for them to identify Lizzie and Reykas. I'm surprised they haven't already, after the bank and then after what happened at the school. It's no stretch to figure out they're the acrobats from the

Chamberlain, and from there they shouldn't have any trouble finding somebody who could name them. Then the city records can point them to this property that they own. That's how they found your house. Probably how they found Aquin, too."

The hairs on Samira's neck prickled, and she had to check behind herself again, to make sure she truly wasn't followed. "We have to leave here. We have to find somewhere else to hide. But Oreth is in no state to move, and I don't know how long it'll be before Reykas can walk again. Where can we go?"

Caius shook his head. "This is it. There's nowhere else to go. They're going to find all the crew and anyone else we've associated with. They know we can't get out of the city, and they have to know we're getting desperate now."

"There will be bounties," Samira said.

He nodded. "There's no more running. We had a plan, but that's done now. We're in their trap, Samira. They have us."

She scowled at him. "We're not just rolling over and letting them take us, Caius. Don't be ridiculous. Not after all this."

"No, that's not what's going to happen. You're going to be safe. You, Apak, everyone."

"I don't like that tone. What do you mean I'll be safe? What about you?"

"The Kites don't care about you beyond your association with me. I'm the one they want," he said.

Samira remembered Lizzie's moment of doubt, her almost suggesting that they abandon Caius to the Kites. The memory filled her with as much dread and guilt as the implications of what Caius was saying now did. "No," she said. "No, Caius."

He held her shoulders and smiled a sad smile. "It's okay. I've taken steps to make sure it will be okay."

"Where did you go?" she demanded. "What did you do?"

He told her.

CHAPTER 31

Gieck smelled the smoke in the air before they could see the burning building. Nera was ahead on her horse, and he followed behind, and they had roused every Kite they could find to accompany them. Nera seemed sure that this was the moment when she would catch the magician. Gieck doubted it would be that easy, but a little part of him worried that she might be right.

He hadn't been there for the explosive demonstration Bonner gave Nera, but she'd described it in vivid detail. If Akithar's gang truly had sixty-something of those bombs, this might be the beginning of their greater plan. As much as Gieck wanted to catch the mage and choke the life out of him before Nera had a chance to interrogate him, he also was curious to see what that man might accomplish if left to his own devices. It had been a long time since they'd had a good bomber, and never a serial one that he could recall.

The horses had to slow their pace, going down the ancient stairs into the lower part of the city, but once they were in the Downsteps, it was not hard to find the fire. Up to that point, citizens had been scattering to get out of their way, but they were preoccupied here, and a bald man nearly stepped into the side of Gieck's horse. Gieck snarled at him and shoved him away with a boot in his chest.

He wasn't the only one, though. The people here were frightened of something other than the Scarlet Kites, for once. They were coming out from their houses to peer down the street in the direction of the blaze, which Gieck now could see reflected in the night sky. The smoke was stronger here and grew thicker as they neared its source.

The street curved, and there it was. The building was an old warehouse with barn doors at the front. It was stone and brick, and the walls seemed to have withstood the explosion. The roof was a loss, though. Sections of it had already caved in, and the remaining portions blazed bright in the darkness, turning that section of street into a strange and flickering dawn.

Nera already was off her horse by the time Gieck brought his to a halt. She pulled her gloves off as she crossed the street and accosted one of the citizens, an old man in a threadbare shirt, with suspenders holding up his baggy pants. He gawked at the burning building with his jaw hanging open, the flames dancing in his glassy eyes.

"What is this building?" Nera asked him.

"Factory of some kind, I suspect," he said. "You never saw nothing they made, but there was a little man always about. You think he's in there?"

"What does he look like?"

He shrugged. "I don't know. Short man, dark skin. He wears glasses."

"Not the mage," Gieck said. He looked across the street. "One of his agents?"

"Maybe." Nera looked at the old man again. "Were you here when the fire started?"

"Across the way," he said and pointed diagonally down the street. "There was a big bang, like pow! I told Jesmer that sounded like a shot, but he said weren't no firearms in the city. Less, maybe you all brought them in."

"Did you see anything else? Anyone coming out or going in?"

He shook his head. "Just the burning. That's enough for me to see, I tell you."

371

Nera turned her back on the old man. "We need to get that fire stopped. There could be evidence inside. Something that could tell us what they're doing and why they wanted this place destroyed."

It almost felt like a travesty to quell that fire before it reached its full potential, but Gieck nodded. "Eyral," he called, and the soldier ran to meet his summons. "Get your team. Pull in the constabulary if you need to. See if they have a fire brigade in this city. We need that fire put out."

"Right away," Eyral said. He rushed across the street to examine the building before going for help. He laid his palm flat against the left barn door before opening it. Gieck had little experience with fires like this one, so he wasn't sure what Eyral might be feeling for.

Whatever he felt, the Kite seemed satisfied. He slid his hand down the door and pulled the handle. The door didn't move, so he gave it a push. It was unbarred and swung open with ease. The scene inside was stunning. Fire fell from the ceiling, and everything Gieck could see through the doorway glowed in the conflagration. Eyral stood silhouetted against the burning backdrop just long enough for Gieck to spot the wire attached at the top of the door. It ran off to the right, inside the building, and it pulled taut as the door finished opening.

There was no time to move or even to shout a warning. A second after the wire reached its limit and snapped, all the air left the street. It was as if the building itself inhaled a giant lungful of wind, and it sucked Eyral inside with it. He lifted off his feet and flew straight into the burning room. Before he had time to land, the building expelled that breath in an awesome and fiery roar.

The second explosion was like nothing Gieck had ever heard or seen. The brick walls of the building bulged and erupted, spewing stone and mortar into the street. The remainder of the roof ejected itself into the sky, a blazing comet that went up as one piece, blew apart in the air, and rained burning wood and shingles in every direction.

Nera cried out, and the concussion knocked the old man off his feet. The horses tried to stampede, but the other soldiers kept tight grips on their reins. Only one got away and galloped past Gieck. It sprinted through the smoke like a demon, sparks dancing off its mane and its eyes burning with terror.

After the second explosion, there were at least three more, each smaller than the last. Every one of them blasted fire out into the sky and into the street. The nearest walls of the buildings on both sides of the warehouse crumpled inward and fell, taking their roofs with them.

Gieck stood, unmoving before the chaos, even as the hot wind blew over him and the smoke stung his eyes. He refused to look away, even when something wet hit the cobblestones next to his feet and he realized it was a piece of Eyral.

It had taken a spectacular bombing and the death of one of her Kites, but Nera finally found her motivation to act. After Eyral walked into the trap in the warehouse, she became furious, barking orders to the surviving Kites, and even to Gieck. He murmured his solemn agreement to everything she demanded, but he knew her rage was weeks too late. If she'd had this kind of drive when they first arrived in Klubridge, they could have taken Akithar straight away, before any of this nonsense had unfurled. Nera even met with him, knew he was the one they were after, and did nothing. Now he was in the wind, and he'd murdered a Kite. Gieck would be sure to note those facts in his report to Bekam.

Granted, Eyral had been a problem Gieck was going to have to do something about sooner or later, so the loss was less acute than Nera expected it to be. Eyral had been there when Gieck slaughtered that pig, Scrounger, and he might have witnessed more than he'd admitted the night of the boy's death. Loose ends needed snipping, but the opportunity hadn't presented itself until now. Eyral's death left only Jona and Kela among those who might spoil Gieck's career. And even they had no evidence, just suspicions.

Nera stood now in the glow of the fire, her hair blown out of its tight bun so that a red tendril hung in front of her left eye. Soot marked her face and her uniform, and the snarl she showed the first members of the fire brigade was ferocious. Gieck's pulse quickened, and in another time, another place, he might be tempted. But not here and not now. She was incompetent, and he needed to focus on displacing her, not bedding her. She snapped her head around to face him, and he blinked, wondering whether his thoughts had been palpable.

"Lucian, beat down every door in the Downsteps. Somebody knows something. He's not operating alone."

He nodded. "Who can I take?"

"Take anyone you need. Just get him."

Gieck moved, but she caught his arm. He looked down, into her eyes, and she lowered her voice. "He still has information we need. I want him alive."

"You'll have him." Gieck snapped his fingers and motioned for Vam. "They could be hiding in one of their homes. Take Kela, and go search the Tandogan woman's house again. Find out where Aquin Mirada lives, and go there, too. Search out anybody connected to the theater."

"They might not let us in," Vam said.

Gieck glared at him. "You are an agent of the High Lord. You will enter whether they let you or not."

Vam stammered an agreement and disappeared to find Kela. That left Gieck with seven Kites and a city to search. First, to narrow it down and to get one more problem out from under him. Jona was at the periphery, apart from the others, watching the brigade pass buckets to throw water into the inferno. Gieck forced his usual temerity down before approaching her. She needed to be out of his way, not provoked to cause even more problems.

"Jona."

She didn't take her eyes off the fire. "What do you want?"

He bristled at that. If his position with her were not already precarious, he would teach her a few things about rank and respect. But that was for later, once this ordeal was behind them and Akithar was dead. "I need for you to liaise with the city watch. Have them blockade the Downsteps as quickly as possible."

She rolled her eyes at him. "You think they're still down here? They probably made it up those stairs and into the city five minutes after that trap was set. They could be anywhere."

"And yet, we have orders to search the Downsteps, and that is what we will do." Gieck met her gaze and held it for a long moment.

She finally shrugged and pushed away from the wall where she'd been leaning.

"You'll do it?" he asked.

Without answering, she swept an exaggerated curtsy at him and sauntered into the night. She would do her duty, even if she now hated him. That left him with six Kites, most of whom were more manageable, and all but Wil should be malleable to Gieck's methods. Wil was too old and too entrenched in his loyalty to Nera.

Gieck divided his soldiers into three teams of two and repeated Nera's orders to them. They were to bash in every door in the Downsteps until they found Akithar or someone who knew where Akithar was. There had to be accomplices, and they'd find them that night.

Gieck matched himself with a pair of Klubridge patrolmen who looked sturdy and mean enough for him not to have to worry about. All the groups departed as one, with orders to send up a flare as soon as a breakthrough was made. In truth, Gieck knew Jona was right. Akithar would have been a fool to stay in the Downsteps, and he had proven himself not to be a fool.

While the other Kites were busy on Nera's goose chase, Gieck led his men up the stairs and out toward the city center. There already was a roadblock at the head of the stairs, and Gieck was impressed by Jona's speed. She liked to seem disaffected and lazy, but she could get things done. He regretted losing her loyalty, but only for an instant. Anyone who knew what had happened at the university was an enemy and had to be handled.

Gieck spent the greater part of the night kicking doors and frightening citizens. The officers with him had no complaints and joined in roughing up some less talkative subjects. Ignorance was the claim of the evening, and no one admitted to knowing anything about Akithar or any of his accomplices. It was frustrating work, and more than once Gieck wished someone had thought to bring the bug eyed mindreader along. She could have cut through some of these protestations easier than a beating would, but he admitted that also would have been less enjoyable.

Exhaustion set in after a few hours, and there had been no sign of a flare. Even the watch guards were flagging, and Gieck called it a night. He led them back toward the walls of the Henburn Estate and into the Obedient Helm, a pub Eyral had discovered on their third night in the city. Gieck usually preferred the less trafficked watering holes, the ones where he could show up and leave without notice, but he was tired enough tonight to settle for this place.

A fire was going in the hearth, even though it wasn't a cool night. Still, the fire gave the room a pleasant ambiance that was welcome after they'd stomped all over the blasted city with nothing to show for their efforts. Although it was late, the Helm still did good business. It was well known as the preferred bar for the constabulary, and there were several officers at a round table in the corner. Morcan, one of Nera's lackeys, already was back, propped against the bar with a pint and talking to Asil, his partner for the night's search. Asil was dark, not quite as dark as the Mirada woman, but not quite as alluring, either.

"Nothing?" Gieck asked, settling onto a stool at the bar between Morcan and a sandy-haired stranger in a long coat.

Morcan shook his head. "We covered the whole northern third of the Downsteps, and nobody knew anything."

"You checked all the houses?"

"Every one. There are going to be some doors that need replacing tomorrow."

Gieck chuckled at that and rapped his knuckles to get the barkeep's attention.

"Shame about Eyral," Morcan said. "I know he looked up to you."

Gieck hesitated and glanced at Morcan. Was there something more behind that observation? "We all regret his loss," he said, perhaps a little too stiffly. Had Eyral said something to Morcan? Something about Scrounger or maybe about the gutter rat Eyral had killed himself? Or, worse, about the boy who died on the rooftop?

Gieck grabbed his pint from where the barkeep had left it and leaned so that his shoulder was toward Morcan. Enough of that conversation. Now he was facing the sandy-haired stranger on the other side of him. The man glanced at Gieck and grinned.

Gieck frowned. "Do I know you, friend?"

"Not yet," he said. "Are you a betting man?"

"What is this?"

"Just a question. Do you like a wager now and then?"

"I suppose it depends on what it's for."

"I'll bet you ten seri I can empty your beer before you can take your first sip."

Gieck laughed. He'd dealt with this kind before, but it usually happened when there were girls to impress. He shook his head and raised his pint. His empty pint.

"What in the—" He slammed the glass onto the bar and glared at the man next to him. "What did you do?"

"It looks like he just earned ten seri," Morcan said with a laugh.

"I'm in no mood tonight," Gieck said. "You'll be buying me another pint."

"I'll be happy to, with your ten seri," the stranger said, opening his empty hand. He closed his fist and flicked his wrist, and a ten-note shot out from between his fingers onto the stained wood.

Gieck's hand went to his pouch, still sealed, but he knew that if he opened it he'd find ten seri missing. Behind him, past Morcan, Asil laughed with delight and slapped the bar. "Buy him a drink, Lieutenant!"

Gieck turned his head to glare at Asil, and the smile disappeared from her face. She closed her stupid mouth and let her eyes fall back to her own drink. That was more like it. Before he could turn around again, the stranger was whispering in his ear.

"For my next trick, I'll make you vanish, you child killing bastard."

Gieck's skin turned cold, and he heard his own pulse loud inside his head. With the fear came sudden realization. He spun to look at the stranger, the man with hair that was sandy, not black, his face clean shaven, without a mustache, but mustaches were easy to fake. But the intention behind that sneer was unmistakable.

He grabbed the collar of Akithar's coat and dragged the man off his stool, slamming him to the floor. The bar fell into shocked silence, broken only when Gieck slammed his fist into the magician's face. It came back bloody, and Morcan yelled, "Lieutenant, no!"

"This is Akithar!" he bellowed back. "It's the mage!"

Akithar rolled to the left, and the next punch crashed into the floor next to his head. Gieck winced and drew his fist back, just as the smaller man kicked up, striking his thigh. Gieck staggered back a step but then was on the wizard again. He yanked the man off the ground and ran him against the nearest wall, smashing the glass in front of a painting with Akithar's shoulder. He drove his left forearm into Akithar's back, pushing the man's face into the wall.

This was it. He had to act fast. Gieck grabbed the end of the garrote with his right hand and unspooled it around Akithar's neck with a quick jerk, hidden from the rest of the bar. He saw the man's eyes go wide as he realized what was happening. It was a pity there wasn't time to interrogate him in private. He had to die, and quickly, before Nera got wind of this.

Gieck pulled hard, and Akithar slapped at the wall, trying to push away, trying to get a breath. His mouth worked open and closed, but no sound came. His face was turning pink, and veins raised in his temples. He managed to shove backwards a few inches, but Gieck slammed him back against the wall and pulled tighter. The struggles were weaker now. Only a few more seconds.

Akithar fell limp, and Gieck's grip slacked for an instant. It was long enough for the mage to kick his foot into the wall and piston himself back into the Kite. Gieck grunted when Akithar's elbow smashed into his stomach, and he lost his grip on the cord. It released from Akithar's neck and sped back into its home, wound into the leather housing with a quick zip.

The mage hit the floor on his side and gasped for air, his hands clawing at the ground. Gieck moved to attack him again, but Morcan was between them. He kicked Akithar onto his back and planted a foot on the man's chest. "Excellent work, Lieutenant." And then, to the man on the ground, "Akithar, I am placing you under arrest under the authority of the High Lord and all his realms. You stand accused of wizardry, murder, treason, and terrorism."

Gieck was breathing hard as he watched the scene unfold. He'd missed his chance. Akithar was in custody, and he was still alive. Gieck's fists clenched at his sides, and he imagined smashing one of the pint glasses into the back of Morcan's head and using the shards to cut Asil's throat and then stab Akithar. He probably could take out everyone in the Helm, if needed.

But no, it was done. It was done, and Gieck had lost.

PART V
SILENCE

CHAPTER 32

Apak maneuvered his screwdriver between two blocks of metal inside the box and tightened the tiny screw that attached an internal mounting bracket to the side of the device. It was delicate work, and he still had yet to get proper sleep, but his focus kept his hand steady, and his resolve kept him motivated.

"There," he whispered. He pulled his hand back out of the casing, being careful not to touch the metal end of the tool against either of the electrical components that flanked the bracket. Once clear of the device and all its delicate innards, he laid the screwdriver to the side and sat back in his chair.

The earthquake machine was his only fully formed invention that had survived the workshop fires and still was not in Imperial hands. Apak did not want to think about what devious uses the Scarlet Kites might find for any of his contraptions that they might discover in the theater. With luck, none of their people would be smart enough to use the inventions properly. He knew better, though. The High Lord had endless resources and countless experts ready to fall in line.

The controls Peregrine had imposed on scientific development and the communication of those developments between cities of course did not extend to the Imperial seat itself. As a consequence, most learned scientists and inventors saw better opportunities working for the Empire than outside of it. Most of the top minds in the world served under the High Lord, as it had been for tens of centuries. There were smart and imaginative brains that were not on the governmental payroll, of course, but those who did not bend the knee could not avail themselves of the benefits of the station. Apak had never worked for the Empire, and he always had been a step behind. The advances he and Caius had made in electricity were revolutionary, but he suspected the Empire had gotten there before a stage magician and his trick engineer had.

Still, Apak made good use of what he had, as he was doing with this earthquake machine. In truth, he should not call it by that name any longer, as its days of earthquake generation were far behind it. He had converted it into an excavator when that was needed, and now he was putting it through yet another transformation. He already had gutted most of its inner workings, and the resulting device, while still heavy, now should be easier for him to lift unaided.

Apak pulled off his glasses to rub at his tired eyes. He had replaced the cracked lens with an intact piece of glass, but it did not match the curvature and thickness of his old, precise lens, and so his vision was slightly blurred now. It took some getting used to, and Apak suspected that, coupled with his lack of rest, was a primary contributor to the headache that even now encroached upon him.

He pushed his chair back and stood. He really would have to get some sleep. The room he had claimed on the upper floor of Reykas' and Lizandra's home was a study and had no bed, but Apak suspected he would be quite satisfied with the floor. He had other business first, though.

Apak left the study and stepped into the upstairs hallway. He listened at the top of the stairs but heard no voices below. He was surprised that the others were not deep into conversation, hatching some alternative plan after all the others had fallen apart. Apak had no interest in those plans now. Though his eyewear might be flawed,

Ikarna had focused his vision, and he knew where his path would lead. For now, it led him to the next room down the hall to the right.

The door was open, and he stepped through without knocking. Oreth still was sleeping, and no one could have responded to welcome Apak even if he had announced himself. Instead, he closed the door with care and stepped to the side of the bed, making as little noise as possible.

Oreth lay on his back, a white sheet pulled up to just below his shoulders. His injuries were not visible, but Apak remembered the crumpled and burned body he and Lizandra had found only a few hours before. Oreth would live, but Apak had doubts about how his life after the accident would resemble the one before.

"You did not deserve this," Apak said. He reached a hand toward Oreth but pulled it back. He did not want to wake him. This could be the last restful sleep Oreth got before things changed even more for all of them.

Rather than sit on the mattress and risk disturbing him, Apak sank to the floor beside the bed. His knee still hurt, but he could move it with precision to minimize the pain. Once sitting, he watched Oreth for a moment. The shape beneath the sheet rose and fell with slow regularity. It was miraculous that Oreth even was breathing, given the dire state of his crushed chest when he lay in the pile of burning debris.

"You did not deserve this," Apak repeated. "And neither did Dorrin." His voice hitched on Dorrin's name, and he had to squeeze his eyes shut to impede the flow of tears that wanted to escape. "I grieve for Dorrin, and I grieve for you, as well. But this is not the time for grief. If there is time later, I will serve it, but not now."

Apak rubbed at his nose and sighed. "I know what the others think of me. I know what you thought—think of me, as well. That I am irrational. Distant, eccentric. That I am unable to understand the gravity of what has befallen us." He shook his head with a low chuckle. "That could not be farther from the truth, my friend. I see and I feel what is happening. Perhaps I am not the best among us at expressing my reactions to those feelings, but I do feel, and I hurt for you. I hurt for our friends, our family. I hurt for Dorrin. That poor boy. He did not deserve to die. He did not deserve to be killed as he was. He wanted only to learn and to have friends."

He curled his fingers into the plush rug that lay at the center of the room. "The priority has been to escape the city. I suspect the others have ideas about how to make a run at that plan again, but that no longer is my priority, Oreth. What has happened to you is unconscionable. And what happened to Dorrin is inexcusable. I bear my share of the guilt for his death and for your injury, but the Scarlet Kites are to blame. They are the force that has disrupted and destroyed our lives."

Apak halted when a tear escaped and ran down his cheek. He touched his fingertips to it and looked at the wetness before wiping it away with a fierce swipe of the back of his hand. "I am building something new, Oreth. It would impress you, but I doubt you would approve. The others likely will not. It must be built, though, and Ikarna is guiding my hands like never before. There must be a reckoning for the evil that has been visited upon all of us."

He did not know whether Oreth could hear him, but he thought it wise to err on the side of believing that he could. Apak therefore chose his next words with care.

"I may not depart Klubridge with you, but I will see to it that you survive. I will ensure that all of you do and that these monsters, these barbarians, will take no more of you from me. I may die while procuring that end, but it would be a death worth having lived for. Whether or not I survive the coming days, Oreth, I promise you and I swear by Ikarna that no Kite shall leave this city alive."

The sound of the downstairs door opening awakened Apak. He jolted and then winced as pain shot through his knee and ribs once more. Halfway to sitting, he blinked at his surroundings. It took a moment for him to realize he still was on the floor next to Oreth's bed. He must have dozed off while visiting him. How long had he been there?

He pushed himself onto his good knee and leveraged himself up from there to stand. Oreth still was sleeping silently, undisturbed by Apak's visit and was, to all appearances, napping and unwounded. Apak reached again to pat his friend's hand but stopped himself once more. The rest was more important than sentimentality just now, so he headed for the hallway instead.

Coming down the stairs, Apak could hear voices. Samira was back, but Caius seemed to remain among the missing. Apak ducked his head to see the front room as he took each step with ginger care, favoring his unhurt side.

Reykas was awake now, reclined on the sofa, but he was pushing himself up to sit on the edge. He looked much better than he had earlier. The shaking had subsided, and his fever likely had broken.

Lizandra looked to have been asleep as well but now had roused as Samira was pushing the front door shut. "Did you find Aquin?"

Samira shook her head. "The Kites have her. They had ransacked her apartment, and they nearly got me as well."

"You're bleeding!" Lizandra crossed the room and put a hand on Samira's arm. Only then did Apak notice the blood staining her hands.

"I'm okay, but I think your shirt is done for," Samira said with a sad smile.

"Never mind that. Come, sit."

"Where did they take Aquin?" Reykas asked. His voice sounded stronger now, too. That was good. They needed strength on their side for what was to come.

"I assume to Henburn, somewhere in the keep," Samira said. "I think she's safe. Alive, at least. They tried to catch me, but I ran." She paused, looking as if she were unsure whether to continue. At last, she did. "I only got away because of a crowd that had just come out of a tavern. They... They killed one of the Kites chasing me. The other one ran away."

Apak raised his eyebrows as he finally reached the bottom of the stairs. "The city is tired of being under the heel of these soldiers, it would seem."

The other three had not seen him until then, and Lizandra asked, "Are you okay, Apak? When you came back earlier—"

"I am fine," he said, and it was true. He felt a certainty of purpose that had eluded him for a very long time.

"How will we get Aquin back?" Reykas asked, his attention turned back to Samira. "Does Caius know about this yet?"

Samira was silent again, and her face contorted in a way Apak did not recognize.

"What is it?" Lizandra asked.

Samira pressed a hand over her mouth and shut her eyes. Belatedly, she pulled her hand away and looked at her scraped palm but ignored the fresh smear of blood she left on her cheek. After drawing a deep breath, she stepped farther into the room and sank into a chair that faced Reykas' couch. "I saw Caius," she said. Her voice was low and unsteady. Apak limped around the sofa and rested his hands on the back, but he did not sit.

Samira looked at him. "Apak, when you were working with the haranium, did you look at what was inside any of the cylinders?"

He shook his head. "Letters, household inventories, other assorted writings. There was nothing that seemed important to me. I asked Oreth to dispose of them."

"Somehow Caius got hold of them. You're right. There were plenty of letters, some property deeds, historical documents, all sorts of things. He said he didn't make much of them at first glance, either. But after reading through some of them, he realized what they were. Apak, you stole a stockpile of blackmail from the Empire."

"Blackmail? Of what sort?"

Samira began listing it. "Sazen Nosse, city councilman for the past twenty-odd years. Did you know that he secretly deals in religious paraphernalia?"

Apak did know that and, in fact, had suspected that his own icon of Ikarna had originated from Nosse. He remained quiet on that matter, though, to allow Samira to continue.

"Eldon Dewlon is an assistant tax administrator. His wife is a mage who was active in radical groups before they married." She was counting the Imperial sins on her fingers. "Vila Tegera owns the Fortune Theater."

"That big opera house a few blocks from the Chamberlain," Lizandra said.

"That one. The Fortune is a front for an illegal gambling operation she runs in the back of the house. There are files on nearly everyone of note in Klubridge."

"You and Caius?" Reykas asked, sitting forward.

"No. As far as Caius could tell, these are all about Imperial loyalists. The best he could figure, this is how the Empire keeps a rein on its nobility in Klubridge. If someone steps out of line, they have everything they need to bring them down within the High Lord's law."

Apak frowned. This made no sense. "Why was this in the library? Why not in a bank or in a vault in the castle?"

"There are files on too many people in banking and that have access to the castle. Based on what Aquin said, I think very few people know about that vault under the library. Only a trusted few who weren't included in the blackmail material. The captain of the city guard isn't included in the documents. I'd bet he was safeguarding this stuff."

"And Peregrine probably has separate files on him elsewhere."

"I wouldn't doubt it," Samira said.

"What do we do with this now?" Lizandra asked.

"Caius already has used it. He took it to the port and met with Ergo Drass."

"The pirate."

"The importer," Samira said, but the disdain in her voice was clear. "We have a new deal. Drass is going to accept the documents as our payment to board his ship. He has agreed to take us out of Klubridge."

Lizandra's mouth dropped open. "Just like that? It's done?"

"Not quite," Samira said. She paused again, and Apak sensed that she was nearing the crux of the matter. The great complication that would undo the good news she had delivered.

"Drass told Caius the port is being watched in secret. The Kites have been hunting for a rebel spy. They believe the spy was meeting with a contact in the city, who was going to take them to the rebels' headquarters, to the Stormbreak Sanctuary. This was their chance to end the whole rebellion, and they shut down the city gates in the hope that the ones they're looking for would try to leave by ship."

"It's a trap," Reykas said. "They were funneling us to the port and would have picked us off then and there."

"Well, they were trying to funnel the spy, and they thought Caius was that spy. Or the spy's contact, maybe? They at least believe that he was connected in some way."

Lizandra's next question was halting. "He… isn't, is he?"

Samira snapped an exasperated sigh. "Of course not. But we all know the kinds of secrets Caius does have that the Empire would be interested in getting."

"The magic," Apak said.

"How do you know all this?" Lizandra asked Samira.

"The Kites think they are after Caius, but it turns out that they're just a few steps away from their real target."

"It's Drass, isn't it?"

"It's Drass. He's not a mage, but he's in Klubridge to meet with the spy and provide passage to Stormbreak."

"Who is this spy, then?"

"I don't know, but we are likely to be sharing a ship with them."

"So that's where we're going, too?" Lizandra asked. "To the rebels?"

"Not as long as the Kites are watching the docks," Reykas said, and Lizandra's enthusiasm deflated.

Samira began to speak again but faltered. She finally said, "We leave for the docks in three hours. The Kites should have withdrawn by then, and the docks will be clear."

No one spoke, waiting for Samira to offer more, but she sat in silence, looking down at her damaged hands.

Lizandra broke the silence. "Why would the Kites withdraw, Samira?" Her eyes widened. "Where is Caius?"

Apak answered before Samira could. "He turned himself over to them, did he not? The fool has sacrificed himself so that we could go free."

Lizandra gaped at Apak and turned back to Samira. "Is that true?"

Samira nodded. "I couldn't stop him. He'd already given the blackmail documents to Drass, and he was on his way to the Kites. He made me swear to put all of you on that ship."

Reykas was incredulous. "Did you try to stop him? What did he say?"

"There was no stopping him. Of course I tried. He said the Kites were looking for him, not us, and that it was his duty to protect us."

"And you agree with this?"

"It kills me, Reykas, but what else can we do? It's only a matter of time until the Kites find all of us. Caius—"

"He's not the only one. You said they have Aquin, too."

"Yes," she whispered, her eyes on her hands once more.

"You would have us leave Klubridge, leave our home, and abandon both of them to whatever fate the Empire has designed for them?" Reykas rose from the sofa. His legs were unsteady, but he held himself upright. "This is not how we do things, Samira."

"I promised Caius that we would be on that ship. He already has turned himself in. We can't let that be for nothing."

Apak grunted and looked to Lizandra. "What do you think of this?"

She looked from him to Reykas and finally to Samira. "I... I don't know. I hate to think of leaving them, but Samira is right. If we stay, they're going to find us, and all of this would have been for nothing."

Apak exhaled hard and glared at Samira, then Lizandra. "I am ashamed of both of you. Reykas is correct. This is not how things are done." He pointed a shaking finger at Samira. "You may inform Captain Drass that I will not be on his ship."

Samira stared back. "What are you going to do, Apak? You can't stay in the city. The Kites will still find you, even though they have Caius."

"I agree with Apak," Reykas said. "There has to be another way."

"Caius made me swear—"

"Curse you and Caius and anything you might have sworn!" Apak bellowed. "I am not leaving this city as long as a single Scarlet Kite draws breath. We are owed in blood, and I intend to collect that debt."

CHAPTER 33

Kela was dead. That was two of her Kites in one night, unprecedented for Nera. She had lost soldiers before, but never two at once and never when so much was at stake.

Bonner had come to the scene of the bombing while the fire brigade worked to quell the flames. He was irate, demanding progress on her investigation. Nothing she could tell him was good enough to satisfy him, and in the end she had had to assert her rank, something she had never expected to do to one of her oldest friends and mentors. Bonner had left then, but his fury hadn't lessened. He ordered her to bring him the remaining message cylinders before the morning. She could have been harsher with him, but he was an old man who had grown used to the luxuries of his post. He'd forgotten what it was like to be on the hunt, chasing after an impressive foe. Apparently he had also forgotten that she was a Commander in the Imperial Kites, while he was relegated to a bureaucratic job out of pity. That was not something she would say to him, but he pressed her closer and closer to that line.

No sooner had Bonner left than Vam ran back to the scene of the attack. He was out of breath, and Nera thought he was coming to report good news. But no. "Kela is dead." He gasped it between panting and wringing his hands. She had to wait for him to catch his wind again before he could give her the details. It had been the wizard, Akithar. "He tore her to pieces right in front of me," he said. "There was nothing I could do. I barely escaped with my own life."

"Where is he?"

"He… He vanished! As soon as he was done with her. I don't know where he went."

"Where is she?"

"Who?" He was frantic. There was no time for this.

"Kela. Where is she?"

"Oh, Kela. She…" He pointed back the way he had come but hesitated. The fool didn't even know where his fallen comrade's body was.

"Go back and find her remains. She will get a proper committal."

Vam nodded furiously and jogged backwards, watching Nera before turning and running away again. He was one of the newer recruits, but not as new as Tomos, and Tomos was twice the soldier Vam was proving to be. Nera had left Vam under Lucian's watch, but perhaps she'd better bring him into her own ranks. They were two Kites short now and would need even more recruits to fill out the company. Nera did not look forward to reporting that back to General Bekam.

She folded her arms and watched the firefighters for another few minutes. It had taken great effort and more water than she'd expected, but the fire finally was under control and should be extinguished within the hour. Nera already could see that there would be nothing left of use. The fire had reduced the whole warehouse and most of the two buildings on either side of it to cinders. There were twisted and scorched pieces of metal protruding from the ashes, but there was nothing recognizable. Whatever that building had been, all trace of it was gone now. Gone, just like Akithar. He had disappeared once again, slipping through Nera's grasp after murdering Eyral and now Kela.

Nera sighed in frustration and went to recover her horse from where she had tied it, diagonally down the street. With nothing left for her to do here, she would resume what she'd been doing when the explosion had pulled her away. That reminded her of the knife she had found in the market stall earlier that day. She had been about to tell Lucian about it but had missed the chance. She hoped he could help her understand the strangeness of the duplicate blades, since he had witnessed the murder himself. Either Akithar had summoned one of those blades into his hand the night of the murder, or he had simply killed the boy without the use of his magic. Both possibilities rendered the knife that ended up in the boy as being entirely mundane, without a hint of magical origins.

Aquin Mirada had information about the mage and his gang. She might even be one of them. Lucian had managed to get a confirmation from her that Akithar had real magic, but that was hardly a revelation. Mirada worked for him, and he knew where Stormbreak was located. It was very possible that she could know that as well. And if she didn't know it, she could point them to someone who did. For the moment, preventing more bombings was an even more pressing issue than learning the spy's intelligence, but Mirada might be the key to both.

When Nera made it back to the castle, she found Mirada still shackled to the table. The woman was asleep, her arms stretched on the table in front of her, and her head cradled between her upper arms. She flinched when Nera closed the door, and she raised her head slowly to watch Nera with wary eyes.

Nera didn't speak until she'd sat in the chair directly across from the prisoner. "Your friends have killed two of my officers."

Aquin was still coming awake and wiped at her face with her shoulder. "The one who was questioning me before?"

"No, that's Lieutenant Gieck. He is trying to find the one called Akithar, in order to prevent more violence." Nera clasped her hands on the table and remembered a similar arrangement when the acrobat had escaped her questioning at the bank.

"I don't know anything," Aquin said. "I wouldn't let them tell me anything. I didn't want to know."

"But you helped them get into the library," Nera said. "That's very serious. Do you know why they wanted access to the library?"

The other woman closed her mouth and didn't respond. Nera suspected she knew part of it but not the full story.

"They stole Imperial property. Document cylinders that had been stored in the library vault for safekeeping. Do you know what those cylinders are made from?"

"Haranium," Aquin whispered and looked miserable after the word had left her lips. A small betrayal, but a betrayal nonetheless.

"Very good," Nera said. "The haranium you helped your friends steal now has killed a good man. And Akithar himself murdered a good woman tonight. Those deaths could have been prevented and should have been prevented. Tell me something I can use to stop them."

"I don't believe you. That's not the sort of people they are."

"You seem to know them so well. Or is it just Samira Tandogan that you know?"

Aquin's eyes narrowed, and she leaned away from Nera. It was a barely noticeable tell, and Nera pursued it. "If you help me, I can protect Samira. If you don't, there will be little I can do. My Kites are angry now. They've lost two of their own. They won't show mercy when we find her. And we will find her."

Nera watched Aquin's face for any sign of compliance, any sign that she had more information. Aquin's chin quivered, and she said, "I don't know what you need. All I know is what I told that man, the lieutenant."

The young woman was terrified. But was she still hiding something? Nera felt that she was on the brink, very near getting at something she could use. "What is Akithar's name?" she asked.

"What do you mean?"

"Akithar is his stage name. He has a real name. What is it?"

"I don't know." But her eyes flicked to the left when she said it. There it was.

"Have you ever dealt with mages, Aquin?"

She didn't answer but looked back at Nera.

"My job is to find them and to make sure they don't hurt innocent people. Akithar is hurting people. It's the way mages are. They have more power than any human should possess, and they don't know what to do with it, so they turn it against people like us. People like you and even like Samira. I know she's close to the mage, and she wouldn't betray him. I know you would not betray her. But you have to see that you can protect her. Every minute she spends in his presence is a minute she's in danger."

"That's not how they are," Aquin said. "Having magic doesn't make someone evil."

"If only that were true, the world wouldn't need people like me," Nera said.

Aquin leaned forward and studied Nera's face. "What happened to you? What put you on this path?"

Nera chewed at her bottom lip as she stared back at Aquin. She debated not answering the question, but in the end she said, "My parents. They both died when I was young. I was ten."

"You loved them very much."

"I did. My father was the sheriff in the town where I grew up. My mother was a clerk for the court in the nearest city. They taught me from the time I was very small to respect order."

"No siblings?"

"Only me."

"A mage killed them. Is that what happened?"

Nera hesitated. Was this the best way to get the woman to talk? No living person outside of her superiors and Bonner knew what had happened. She had told Lucian part of the story, but she had left out the worst of it. And now she was telling it to this prisoner who very literally had been sleeping with the enemy?

She took a breath before continuing. "It was just after my tenth birthday. We had come to Klubridge, actually. We saw a play here, and my mother had business in the city. We left here and went to Redwater. My father was sent there to escort prisoners to the jail in Craydon, a few days' ride to the west. That was the first time I saw Kites. They were green, not red like mine, but they were wonderful. So powerful and regal in their colors and with their seriousness. They had a mission and were bound to it. Nothing could sway them. I liked that determination. Even that young, I knew I wanted something like that for myself, something that would give me direction."

"They were escorting a mage?" Aquin asked.

Nera ignored her. She was telling her story now, and it all would come out as it was meant to come out. "One of the prisoners was a man named Khesem. I don't know what he had done to be arrested. I still don't, but he was kind to me. It was unusual to have a child along on that kind of mission, but with the timing, it couldn't be avoided. Or I suppose it could have, but that would have had my mother traveling alone with me back home. My father wouldn't hear of it, so we accompanied him. Khesem liked to tell stories when we camped. He was in a big cage on a wagon, and I would stand next to it and talk to him. My father warned me not to talk to the prisoners, but you can imagine how much good that did."

Aquin nodded and even gave a faint smile. Nera continued. "I was too young to know better. I trusted Khesem, even when he had me sit near his cage, right up until he grabbed me through it and tried to pull me inside."

"By Ik—" Aquin caught herself. She was about to say the goddess's name. Something to make a note of and remember, but it would not stop the story, not now.

"I still don't know what his intention was. He might have been hoping to hold me hostage and win his freedom. He might have had more nefarious designs. I never found out." Nera licked her lower lip and cleared her throat. "He had me by the shoulders, trying to pull me in. I still remember how he started screaming. I didn't know what was happening, so I looked at him, and his whole head was on fire. I saw his hair catch fire, and then it was down his arms and hands and all over. He couldn't let go of me, and I caught fire. And then my father was there, pulling me away and rolling on the ground with me. He saved me from the worst of it, but Khesem was done for. I'll never forget laying on the grass with my father and looking up to see my mother staring at that cage. She had such hate in her eyes. I'd never seen her like that. She was changed."

"Your mother," Aquin whispered.

"The Kites figured out what she was right away. They came after her, but she burned three of them before they took her down. Her hands glowed when it happened, but it wasn't like she threw the flames. Her hands glowed, and the flames just appeared all over the people. They all died screaming, with their skin melting off. The fourth one got her from behind. His sword went all the way through her, from back to front, and the last thing she did before dying was set him on fire, too."

"That's terrible. I'm so—"

"My father left me there on the grass and ran to her. He pulled the Kite off her so that she wouldn't catch fire, too, but I remember thinking that she couldn't burn. The man's body was on her back, and he was burning, but she just lay there, dead, and unburned. My father gathered her in his arms and held her. She was already gone by then, but he screamed at her, begged her to come back. The rest of the Kites were out of their tents by then, and one of them picked me up and turned me away from the scene. I didn't see it, but I heard it when my father killed three other men and two women with shadows. I heard the details later, about how the night's own darkness dissected the Kites, removing their arms, legs, and heads as clean as a blade would have done. Cleaner, probably. And the last one finished my father. I don't know whether he intended it or if it was an accident, but his own magic drew a shadow through his chest and pierced his heart. He collapsed and died with my mother's body in his lap."

Aquin's look of pity had transformed to one of horror. She had no words, and Nera found that she had no more, either. The two women stared at each other across the table, the story lingering in the air between them.

Just as she had claimed, Aquin knew nothing. It was a disappointing interview, but Nera relented after another hour of conversation. Aquin admitted to knowing Akithar and his cohorts and even to being intimate with Samira Tandogan, but she had no knowledge of Akithar's proper name or his current where-abouts. Exhausted and defeated, she had also confessed to being the one who told the mage about the haranium in the library, but she did not know what its intended use would be.

She had isolated herself from that information specifically because she didn't want to be in a position where she could be compelled to betray them. Nera had to admit that Aquin's foresight matched her low estimation of her ability to withstand interrogation. Regardless, there was nothing else to be learned, and the prisoner released a heavy sigh when Nera told her they were finished.

"Can I go now?"

Nera was about to leave but paused midway up from the chair. She raised an eyebrow at Aquin and waited until she'd finished standing before responding. "No, I think not. You have admitted to aiding in treason against the High Lord. You knowingly consorted with a mage, and your actions led to the death of at least one of my soldiers. You'll not be going anywhere for a very long time."

Aquin protested and begged and rattled her chains and cried, but Nera felt no remorse. This was the fate of any who opposed the High Lord and conspired toward his downfall. She remembered the surprised shout from Eyral as the draft pulled him into the doomed warehouse an instant before the whole thing exploded, and she placed a healthy share of the blame for his death squarely on the shoulders of this whimpering young woman.

She might not have known what she was getting herself into, but Nera had no doubt that Eyral still would be alive if not for her showing Akithar the way to the explosives. Kela might still be alive as well, and surely that little boy wouldn't have been in a position to be murdered on the dormitory roof, had Aquin not delivered the university to Akithar and his gang as a beneficial target.

Aquin Mirada was unlikely ever to leave the custody of the Empire, and, if Nera had her way, she'd see justice at the edge of the executioner's blade before the month was out.

It was late, and Nera felt every bit as exhausted as her prisoner had looked. She didn't want to rest until she made some kind of progress, but she knew she'd be no use to anyone if she collapsed from lack of sleep. She was on the way down the corridor to her bedroom when the thick oak door to the soldiers' quarters banged open. She froze in place, and she knew.

She spun on her heel as Asil rounded the corner, nearly at a run.

"Where is he?" Nera demanded, coming back down the hallway, all thoughts of sleep abandoned.

"We caught him! We caught the mage!"

"Where is he?" she asked again as she closed the distance.

"Morcan arrested him. Lieutenant Gieck was with us and subdued him. They took him to the tower cell."

That was good. The tower, the tallest structure in Klubridge, was removed from most of the foot traffic in the castle. If Akithar freed himself with a spell, any damage would be confined to that tower. "Summon the rest of the Kites," Nera told Asil as she passed her. The younger woman hurried to keep pace with the commander. "Also, send a messenger to Captain Bonner. Tell him to deliver every available watch officer to me, upon my command."

Nera stopped beside the door leading out of the soldiers' quarters. She was loath to give the next order, but it had to be done. "Send word to General Bekam that we have caught the mage, and we need Herons. Halflocks won't do."

Asil was nodding along with each command. "Morcan already brought that spooky one up, and I think he's rounded up a couple more to keep watch over Akithar. They'll be making sure he can't use his magic."

"Good. You've done well, Asil. Now go. The other Kites should be somewhere between here and the Downsteps. Bring them back here, and use a flare if you have to."

Asil gave a short and sharp bow before disappearing into the night. Nera realized her hands were sweating, and she wiped her palms down the sides of her uniform. The winding stairs leading up into the tower were at the end of the opposite hallway, and at their top waited the man she had been seeking since being dispatched to Klubridge. Tonight she would get her answers.

~

The tower cell was less a prison and more an elaborately outfitted state suite. With plenty of traditional cells in the city jail, it was rare for Klubridge to need the tower. As she climbed the circular staircase that wound its way up the inside of the tall silo, Nera recalled the list of prisoners she'd heard had lodged up there. All of them were people of note. Dignitaries, nobility, famously connected merchants, all who somehow ran afoul of the law. Nera knew that most of them ended up pardoned by their cronies in the city government or otherwise excused for their seditious behavior, but that would not be happening this time. Not for Akithar, not after the lives lost at his hands.

Because the temporary residents of the tower tended to be known and well-respected members of society, their cell was far cozier than anything Nera felt they should deserve. She'd heard about the plush carpets, the canopied bed, the gilded furniture, and the gas lighting, but this would be her first time looking upon such decadence, wasted upon enemies of the High Lord himself.

Lucian waited at the top of the stairs, in conversation with Morcan. They stopped talking and watched her approach.

"You did well," Nera said and laid a hand on Lucian's shoulder. "You both did," she added with a nod to Morcan.

"He attacked the lieutenant," Morcan said.

Nera looked to Lucian, and he lifted his shoulders in a brief shrug. "He used his magic, and I was able to subdue him before he could hurt anyone."

"Did he have any weapons? Any of the haranium?"

Lucian shook his head. "He showed up at the Obedient Helm. Who knows what he was planning and how many more of us he'd have taken out if we hadn't been there? He probably didn't even need weapons to do the job."

Nera recalled the cheap dagger Akithar had materialized from the street-side shop and into his grasp, and she didn't doubt that he could have done the same with the haranium if the notion struck him. "Is he able to do magic in there?" The idea of him pulling explosives out of thin air and laying waste to the castle was chilling.

"Three Imperial mages are in there with him. They're keeping him in check. For now," Morcan added with a doubtful look.

"I've sent for Herons. Until they arrive, this tower is to be under constant guard. Lieutenant, you will coordinate between the Scarlet Kites and the city watch. I want no fewer than thirty guards watching the tower at all times."

"Thirty!" he exclaimed. "Do you think that's necessary?"

Nera's voice was steel and brooked no further argument. "I would have three thousand if they were available to me. Akithar will not be escaping under my watch. Take care of this."

Lucian gave a halting nod, and Nera felt a quick pang of regret for her sharpness. She knew he would forgive her, but she still felt a moment of shame. Lucian was a good soldier and an even better man, and he did not deserve to be berated, especially in front of one of their troops. He was away and down the stairs now, though, and there was nothing she could do for it.

"What should I do?" Morcan asked.

"Stay here. More guards will be coming, but until then you will keep watch on the stairs. Akithar has a network, and we don't yet know how far it extends beyond the few people Aquin Mirada has described. We need to be ready for them to attempt a rescue."

"You can count on me, Commander."

They had barred the tower door from the outside. Nera pushed the metal rod to the right and pulled the door open. It was heavy wood, similar to the one below in the sleeping quarters, but she knew it wouldn't withstand the fully concentrated powers of a mage. If his abilities were not being dampened, Akithar likely could blow away the door and half the tower wall with it.

For once, Nera was pleased to be in the presence of three halflocks. One was the familiar creature, Magra, her enormous eyes rolling toward Nera as she entered the chamber. The other two, another woman and a bald man, were strangers. The Empire had sent all of them to help find Akithar, but none of them had a fraction of the power he must wield. The Imperial protocols made mages compliant and harmless, but they also robbed them of the full force of their magic. Nera hoped these three, working in concert, would be enough to keep Akithar's substantial power at bay.

"Has he attempted magic?" she asked Magra without looking at the witch.

"Not yet, you bet, set, wet."

Nera's attention shifted to the prisoner. "You look different without the mustache," she said and moved past the guards and into the cell.

"I thought I'd try something new," Akithar said. He was standing at the tower window, looking out across the city. That barred window was the only thing in the room that belied the impression that he was a guest in palatial lodgings.

"You won't get out that way," Nera said. "It's a long way to the ground, and I'd wager that flying isn't among your talents."

His smile was wry, and he left the window to walk towards her, as though greeting a guest. He even gestured to a pair of golden lacquered chairs that sat at an angle to each other. "Please, Commander, have a seat."

"I prefer to stand," she said and immediately regretted it. Akithar took one of the seats and now looked up at her, standing before him like a supplicant. This was not how this meeting would go. Nera felt her neck tighten, and she inhaled through her nose.

One tower window, two chairs, three halflocks, four mages in all.

She let out the breath and pulled the second chair away from the wizard. She positioned it facing him and sat. Akithar watched her, waiting, and she studied his face. When she saw him in the theater, his hair was darker, and he'd worn a mustache and some amount of stage makeup. Now his hair was sandy brown, and his face was clean shaven. He looked at least ten years younger than she'd estimated. It was no wonder that finding him had been a challenge, despite his celebrity across the city.

"Where is the rest of the haranium?" she asked.

"There is no more. An accident earlier tonight saw to that, but I suspect you already know about that."

Nera folded her hands in her lap to keep them from forming fists hard enough for her nails to bloody her own palms. The mage's gall infuriated her, but she kept her temper in check. "I do know about the warehouse, and your trap took the life of a good man. His name was Eyral, and he sent money home to his mother every month."

Akithar's brow furrowed for a brief instant, and then his face was impassive again. He almost looked as if he didn't know what she was talking about, but then he said, "I am truly sorry for your friend's death. I did not intend that."

"Just as you did not intend to tear another of my soldiers apart just a few hours ago?"

Now the confusion was evident on his face. He shook his head. "I don't know anything about that. What are you saying that I did?"

Nera considered pushing the point, but she was not here to get a confession for Kela's murder. She corrected her course and went straight to the point. "Where is the rebel headquarters? Where is Stormbreak?"

At that, he actually laughed. "I have no idea. I haven't left Klubridge in over ten years. You think I would know where the rebellion hides?"

Nera turned her head to Magra. "What do you hear?"

Magra raised her arms in a theatrical shrug. "Nothing there, no rebel place in his face, no trace, race."

"How certain are you?" Nera didn't know how the mindreading worked, but she surmised that Akithar could block it somehow. There was no way to know what a mage could do.

Magra didn't answer that but rolled her enormous head in a full circle, rocking it back, then onto her right shoulder, letting it fall to the front, then to the left shoulder, and back again. Nera bristled at the cracking sound the woman's neck gave when she jerked it back upright. Magra grinned at her and had nothing more to say.

"How can you condone that?"

Nera looked back to Akithar, and he was watching Magra with dismay.

"How do you mean?" she asked.

"These people. The Empire maimed them. They have no identities now, no memories of what came before. How can you support that being done to another human being?"

"That is where you're wrong," she said. "These are not people. They're mages, and human beings are their prey. Just as any beast must be tempered before it can harm an innocent, we have dealt with these mages."

"Is that what you have planned for me? Are you going to cut the back of my head open and stir up my brain?" He didn't look worried, and that concerned Nera more than anything else he'd said so far.

"No, this will not be your fate."

"You're just going to execute me outright, then?"

Nera watched for any sign of fright or dread, but there was nothing. His face was impassive, truly the result of years of performing for audiences. She considered telling him exactly what was to be done with him but instead said, "Tell me about the boy."

That surprised him, at least. "Boy? What boy?"

"The one you murdered. The one who worked in your theater and the one you killed at the university." She threw the heretical icon at him, and he caught it on reflex. "The one around whose neck you hung this cursed thing."

He studied the image of Ikarna in his palm for a long moment before closing his fingers over it. A quick sequence of emotions fought across the magician's face, but the predominant two were confusion and sadness. "I didn't kill Dorrin. I never would have harmed that boy. His death is on your hands, Commander."

"Don't be ridiculous," she said. She had him on the defensive for once. How far could she press the advantage? More importantly, what did this turn in the conversation mean? "I saw his body," she continued. "I saw the wounds your magic left on him, and I saw the dagger you placed in his heart."

Akithar had no response. His mouth was open, and his eyes moved back and forth, as though he were trying to work out a problem. Nera waited for him. He sat forward, his elbows on his knees, and she resisted the urge to lean away from him.

"You're being played, Commander. I didn't kill Dorrin, and I no longer think you had a part in it, either."

He waited for her to respond, but she waited longer. Where was this going?

"Your lieutenant killed that boy. He broke Dorrin's neck with some sort of cable. A wire hidden in his sleeve. In a bracer, maybe."

"Nonsense. No Kite is authorized to carry non-regulation weaponry, and I can assure you that this wire of yours is not among our armaments."

"Check him, Commander. The lieutenant put that cord around my friend's throat and murdered him. It was some sort of grapple. He tried to strangle me with it as well. Here, look." He pulled down his collar and showed her an angry red line that ran across the skin of his throat. "I've done many things that you can imprison and execute me for doing, but I did not murder Dorrin."

His eyes were eager and distressingly earnest. Nera had to remind herself that deception was his stock in trade. He'd made his living tempting an audience to look at his left hand while his right hand conjured tricks. Even his career was a trick, relying on his audience's gullibility to hide true magic behind the facade of staged illusions. That line on his throat was some sort of illusion as well, something designed to trick her into questioning her own man. He was good, but he was not good enough to break her confidence in Lucian with this ridiculous claim about some sort of hidden weapon.

And yet... Something about his insistence made her wonder. Was it at all possible that Lucian had been mistaken in what he saw that night? Could the killer have been one of Akithar's lackeys instead of Akithar himself?

"Where are your people?" Nera asked.

He blinked and sat back. "Which people do you mean?"

"We're beyond the point of playing coy. Where is Samira Tando-gan? Where is the acrobat girl? Where are your cohorts?"

"They have nothing to do with this."

"On the contrary, they are as complicit in this predicament as you are. And if you won't tell me where Stormbreak is located, I'm certain we can find someone else who will. We can be quite persuasive when the need arises. We have Aquin Mirada downstairs. I believe you know her. I am positive your friend Samira does. Aquin currently is shackled to a table in a much less comfortable cell than the one where we're keeping you. I know she'd be happy to share what she knows in exchange for leniency. And, failing that, we can resort to less pleasant but more creative tactics."

Akithar slumped back in his chair. Nera would have sworn that he now was broken if she didn't know better than to trust his appearance. He opened his palms to her, and she steeled herself against whatever spell he might unleash, but instead of giving her magic, he gave her a plea. "Can't you just accept your victory and be done with it? You've caught me, and I'm cooperating with you. Let Aquin go. Let all of them go. I'm the one you want."

Nera smiled at him and shook her head. She rose from her chair and headed for the door. "As much as you might think of yourself, you're not the goal. You are a means to an end. I will have the location of the Stormbreak Sanctuary, and I will have the identity of the spy you were working with. Having you means nothing without that information. You're just another piece of glittery trash."

She rapped twice on the door for Morcan to unbar it, and she left Akithar alone, imprisoned, and powerless.

CHAPTER 34

R eykas rarely needed the cane, but lately he'd taken to bringing it along for walks more often than not. His shakes were becoming more frequent, but they lasted only a couple of hours before subsiding. It was enough to be disruptive but not enough to take him out of the fight. Not yet, anyway. He was not sure whether the chills coming more often were a byproduct of the stress the whole company had been enduring for the last few weeks or a symptom of his condition worsening. There was no denying that his illness was progressing. They'd always known it would, as surely as they knew there was no cure. He only hoped he could keep going for as long as he needed to.

Lizandra wore dark and loose clothes that hid her slender frame. She had pulled her platinum hair back and hidden it in a dark blue head wrap that would not be out of place near the docks. Lizandra was well known to the city guard, the Scarlet Kites, and even to their commander, Mollor, by now. Even if they did not know her name, they knew her by sight, and it was possible—likely, even—that they would be on watch for her. Reykas had blindsided the guard who attacked Lizandra at the campus, and he knew the Kite on the roof had not gotten a good look at him. It would be less likely that anyone would identify him on the street, as long as they didn't have any of their mindreaders active. He was betting they didn't, and the risk was worth the certainty of the information they were after.

"Which ship is it?" Lizandra asked as they descended the old wooden stairs leading down from the street.

Reykas peered through the dark at the vessels bobbing gently at the docks, the lanterns hung on their decks providing pinpoints of light in the cloudy gloom. "Samira said it was near the end of the main pier. She called it unconventional, more like a pleasure yacht than a cargo ship."

The port was less busy than Reykas remembered it being. In ordinary times, the Port of Klubridge bustled night and day, with goods and passengers loading off and on the ships at all hours. Even when the weather was too rough to bring in new ships, there still was a business about the port that defied all but the stormiest weather. Food had to be bought and sold, and money had to change hands. That wasn't happening now, though. The city lockdown had been draining Klubridge's commerce bit by bit, and the hard times had now reached the port. There still were ships at anchor, but their crews stood sullenly on empty decks and leaned over their railings to try to spot opportunities from any passersby.

"I think that's the one." Lizandra pointed to a large and angular ship docked past most of the big haulers. It was too dark to see the flag flying at its mast, but Reykas saw the name *Sephare* burned into the wood of the hull. This was the one.

There was no gangplank or any other visible way to board the ship. Lizandra pulled Reykas onto the small dock jutting off the pier beside the ship, and she called up to someone on deck, barely visible in the darkness. The figure disappeared from view, and a moment later someone else appeared, this one carrying a lantern. He held it above his head and angled the mirrored back to direct the beam of light down onto the dock. "Help you?"

"We are looking for Captain Drass," Reykas called back.

"Do I know you, friend?"

"You know our friends. I'm told you're waiting for us."

Drass examined them with a skeptical eye. Reykas cast a wary glance over his shoulder. The port was completely dark from here. Anyone could be watching or, more importantly, listening. This was when he had to take a risk. "Caius Harrim sent us."

Drass grunted and watched them for another moment before turning and walking toward the back of his ship, leaving them on the dock.

"Well, that didn't work," Lizandra said. But no sooner had the words left her mouth than Reykas heard wood scraping on wood, and in the dim light he saw a railed ramp extending down from the ship's railing to the dock where they stood. Reykas handed his cane to Lizandra and caught the end of the gangway as it neared. He guided it down and slotted it into the metal brackets attached to the dock.

Even though there were rails to guide them, there was something surreal about stepping off the dock and into the darkness, almost as if they were ascending on nothing but air into the night sky above the black water. Reykas reached the ship first and turned to help Lizandra over the rail, but she tilted her head at him and easily made the hop down to the deck on her own.

Drass was waiting for them halfway up the deck, and he turned to enter the forecastle when he saw they were aboard. Reykas led the way, nodding to a pair of sailors propped against the opposite rail. Lizandra followed him through the door into a lit cabin that looked more like it belonged in a country manor than on the rolling seas.

The captain was settling into his seat behind his desk and motioned to the two chairs opposite his. "I understood there would be more of you."

"There will be," Reykas said. "Samira told us that Caius made a deal with you. Would you please recount that deal to us?"

Drass scowled at Reykas and then at Lizandra. "I don't make a practice of kissing and telling."

"I think you can make an exception this time," Lizandra said, "given that we are the ones being kissed."

He bobbed his head in reluctant agreement. "You do make a good point. All right, then. Caius gave me a parcel in exchange for your safe passage out of Klubridge. I'm also expecting Samira Tandogan and that odd little engineer with his assistant. I assume that plan is satisfactory?"

"What about the guards watching the port?" Reykas asked.

Drass shrugged. "They've been gone nearly an hour. One of my crew alerted me when they left. It's the first time they haven't had the port under watch since this whole ordeal began. It was Caius, wasn't it? He turned himself in. Sacrificed his freedom for yours."

"He did, but we are going to get him back."

"Reykas," Lizandra snapped.

Drass' smile now was bemused. "You're going to get yourself killed."

Reykas didn't rise to the warning. "We will be coming back with five more people. You will wait for us and will not leave without us."

"Caius Harrim is an old friend of mine, and I appreciate his bargaining. I will honor the deal I made with him, but the deal was to transport five people, all told, and that we would leave before sunrise."

"You'll wait until we come back, seven people, all told."

Drass pushed his chair back and went to a black metal safe that was bolted to the floor, just below a counter that ran along the back side of the room. He patted the front of the safe but did not open it. "Do you understand the value of what Caius brought me? The importance of what I have in here? Do you even know who else will be sailing on this ship? No, I don't think you understand any of that." He came back to stand behind his chair and placed his hands on the sides of it. "I appreciate Caius, and I consider him a friend, but some things surpass friendship. I will not sacrifice my mission to wait for you."

"You will wait," Reykas said one more time. "We are getting Caius back, and we are getting another friend back. When we return with them, only then may this ship depart." He pushed his own chair back and leaned on his cane to stand. Lizandra was still looking at him with worry in her eyes, but she stood alongside him.

Drass barked a rough laugh at that. "Telling me what I can do with my own ship now?" He scrubbed a hand through his hair and sighed. "I'll do what I can. If you somehow survive and make it back with

Caius and whatever other unfortunates you manage to round up, I'll take you all to sea. But I will not wait forever. You'd best hurry about it."

Reykas smiled back. "Just wait for us." He led the way back out to the deck.

❧

"Reykas, that was not why we came here! We were here to find out whether the guards really had left."

"And so we did," Reykas said and gave Lizandra a brief smile.

"This isn't funny." She grabbed his sleeve and pulled him to the side of the road. They had come back up the steps from the docks, and it was lighter here on the streets, where the gaslamps still were burning. Enough darkness remained, though, to keep them from drawing the attention of any of the unusually large numbers of citizens that were roaming about in the middle of the night.

Reykas sighed and folded his hands on the rail off the side of the street. He leaned into it and looked out at the scant moonlight that played in dim ripples on the water of the bay. "Tell me your mind, my love."

Lizandra kept a hand on his arm but propped next to him on the railing. "Caius turned himself over to the Kites for us. He wanted us to escape."

"What Caius wants and what is the right thing to do are two very different things."

"How do you think we're going to rescue him? Do you even know how ridiculous that sounds?"

Reykas placed his hand over Lizandra's. "I don't believe we will be doing anything of the sort. You will go ahead to the ship and wait for us. I will liberate both Caius and Aquin, and we will meet you there."

Lizandra yanked her hand from under his. "Don't be stupid, Reykas. How do you think you're even going to get close to them? Now that the Kites have Caius, they're going to have every guard in the city watching him. Getting to him would be impossible for a small army, much less you alone."

"I do not believe I will be alone. Apak seems very confident in his new device."

"Apak is grieving and angry. He's not thinking straight, but he's not my priority. You are." She touched his chin and gently turned his face toward her. "You will die if you try to do this. You both will. I think Apak might even want to at this point. I have no idea what's going on in his head."

"He is angry, yes, but he also is unwilling to let these injustices stand, and that is the most sane thing any of us has said during this ordeal. Listen to me, Lizandra. If we run, we lose not only Caius and Aquin but also our chance to do something right. These Kites. These Imperials. They kill with impunity, and they terrorize innocent people. You saw what they did to Dorrin, and now they have Caius. Would you let that stand?"

"Of course I want to stop them. You know I do. But there's nothing we can do but get ourselves killed. You're talking about going up against a team of trained soldiers and every constable in the city. We're acrobats. What do you know about fighting?"

"I know very little about fighting. I know about being fast and agile, and I know about getting into and out of tight situations. I recall that you have some experience in that yourself, my would-be bank robber."

"That's my point! They almost got me, and I barely got away. I was lucky then, and we were lucky to get away at the school. Dorrin wasn't lucky. Next time, that will be you or me or Apak or Samira if we do what you're proposing. We don't know how to use our skills for this."

Reykas glanced at her and then back out at the water. Glass broke somewhere down the street. It sounded like a bottle, maybe a window. "Could you live with yourself if we simply abandoned Caius, Lizandra? I do not believe that I could."

"I don't want to leave Caius here, but I don't see any way to get him out. If I knew we had a chance, of course I'd want to try. But I can't lose you. That's my deepest fear. You're the one I couldn't live without, Reykas."

"And I, you, but there is more in this world than the two of us."

"What will it accomplish for you to go and die? They'll still have Caius and Aquin. You'll just be dead then. I can't have that."

Reykas took her hand again and found her eyes in the darkness. "We both know that will be coming, regardless of what we do now."

Lizandra's face fell, and she shook her head. "Don't you say that. Don't you ever say that. You're sick, but we're going to find a way to make you better."

"Lizandra—"

"And besides, that's even more reason for you to forget this whole thing. What if you have one of your episodes in the middle of it? What will that get you?"

"A good death," he said and waited. When Lizandra didn't respond, he said, "I am dying. I have been for years, since before you knew me. What good is this life if I spend what I have remaining of it in hiding? If I leave my friends behind and selfishly try in vain to find a cure that we know does not exist?" He shook his head. "That is not a life I want. I don't think it is one you want, either."

Clouds still covered the moon, and the gaslight on the street was dim, but it was just enough for Reykas to see the tear roll down Lizandra's cheek. He held his cane in his left hand and used his right to pull her against him.

"I'm still here for now. No tears, my love."

"I just... I can't bear the thought of losing you."

"You never will lose me. I may not be here," he said, gripping the railing, "but I always will be here." He touched his fingers to her chest, and she pressed her hands against his, holding him there.

They stood together in silence, ignoring the crowds passing behind them, sharing this moment in the night on the edge of the water. Someone shouted farther up the street, but they ignored that as well.

Lizandra angled her face up toward Reykas. She wiped at her eyes with the back of her hand and whispered, "If we're doing this, how are we doing it?"

~

When Reykas and Lizandra got home, Apak had moved his makeshift workshop from the upstairs study down to the first floor. His big metal earthquake box was on the front table, tipped on its side, and Apak had his hands deep in its innards, a pair of goggles over his eyes and his usual glasses sitting to the side. He looked up when they entered and smiled apologetically. "I will tidy this up soon."

Samira was watching him from the couch nearby. She had taken over the space Reykas had abandoned and had tucked her feet under her legs. She looked weary but managed a half smile. "He was worried that his work would disturb Oreth."

"How is he now?" Lizandra asked.

Samira tilted her head and shrugged. "He's still sleeping. I don't think he's in any pain. I've been checking on him every few minutes."

Lizandra nodded. She'd been holding Reykas' hand but released it to go sit next to Samira. "The guards have left the port. We talked to Drass."

"That's good. He's willing to take us all? He's not trying to back out on the deal Caius made, is he?"

"No," Reykas said. He wandered over to the table where Apak was working and watched the other man's hands busy at work with tiny tools. "He is waiting for us and will take us. If the city doesn't tear itself apart first, that is."

Samira frowned. "Is it getting worse?"

"It certainly is not getting better."

"They have Caius now, so they should be opening the gates."

"The gates are not open yet. And when they do, it will take time for anything close to normalcy to return to this city. The people have lived under the Scarlet Kites for too long now. What Klubridge has endured will not be forgotten so quickly."

Samira drew a deep breath and looked at Reykas. "Are you still going along with Apak's terrible plan?"

"To rescue our friends? Of course."

"I'm going, too."

Reykas raised his eyebrows, and Apak paused his work to pull up his goggles. "What changed your mind?" Reykas asked.

"We can't leave Caius to them. I can't leave Aquin. We aren't soldiers, and we don't know how to fight them, but we're not helpless. We have to do something." She looked to Lizandra. "I know you didn't like the idea—"

Lizandra stopped her by holding up both hands. "You don't need to sell me. Reykas already did it. We're all in now."

It was Samira's turn for surprise. "I expected more resistance from you."

"So did I," she said. "Reykas can be convincing. If some of us are going to get ourselves killed, we all might as well be included."

"We will need a plan," Reykas said.

Lizandra smirked at him. "That's the first sensible thing you've said all night."

Apak cleared his throat, and the other three turned to him. "Perhaps," he said, "it would be an opportune time for me to tell you what I am building."

CHAPTER 35

Gieck fumed all the way down the stairs from the tower cell. He had caught the bastard, and Nera had the nerve to snap him around like her errand boy. He knew she'd graciously take all the credit for the collar as well, no mention of his being the one to bring Akithar in. And now she wanted thirty guards at all times for him, and she'd called for even more mages from Bekam. If Gieck had had just one more moment with Akithar in the pub, none of that would be necessary, and he'd be acknowledged as the man who took down Akithar.

True, getting the location of the rebel headquarters would have been a career defining bonus, but at this point he'd be happy just to have the man dead and the whole deal done. Who knew what he might be telling Nera even now? Gieck hoped she'd focus on the parts of the interrogation that really mattered—that base location and the scheme with the spy—but he knew she was likely to confront him about the boy's murder. Her bleeding heart wouldn't be able to resist.

What would Akithar say to that? He'd protest his innocence, surely, and he'd likely point the finger at Gieck. Curses. He knew who ended that little brat. He'd made that clear enough in the Helm. His lackeys must have identified Gieck and reported on him. That was the only answer, and now that message would get passed on to Nera. This was exactly what Gieck had dreaded, and it would be the moment when he found out just how far his wooing and her infatuation would get him. He might have to bed her yet, if that's what it would take to get him out of her list of suspects.

At the bottom of the stairs, he paused and ran back through the night of the boy's death. What evidence was there of his involvement? Eyral and Kela had been there and might have seen what happened, but they both had died tonight. Providence had unusual ways of making itself known. Jona suspected but had no proof. He regretted lashing out at her as he had. Perhaps there would be an opportunity for reconciliation after all this had passed. What did that leave? What might Akithar know that could damn Gieck?

He felt his wrist. Nera knew nothing about his zephyr spool. She hadn't been there when he'd gotten it, and she didn't know he wore a non-regulation weapon under his uniform. Akithar knew about it, though. He'd had it wrapped around his own throat, and he likely knew it was the very thing that had ended that boy's life. That was the lingering piece of evidence.

Gieck unbuckled the thick leather bracelet and slid it off his hand. It was heavier than it looked, the spooled wire inside adding heft. He studied the intricate designs burned into the hide one last time before shoving the outer doors open and taking three quick steps to the low battlement overlooking the moat that surrounded the castle. He flung the cabler over the wall, and he listened to the splash below half a second later.

It took a three-block walk in the middle of the night for Gieck to rouse enough city guards to meet Nera's quota of thirty. In the end, he had to go to the captain of the guard's house and bang on the front door for ten minutes before the old man answered it. Gieck knew Bonner had mentored Nera when she was in the Academy, but indications tonight had been that that relationship might be souring. That could be something useful to lean into.

"What do you want?" Bonner asked, stuffing the bottom of his shirt into his trousers. "I'd just gotten to bed. This had better be good."

"We have the magician," Gieck said.

The old man blinked at him a couple of times and rubbed at his scraggly white hair that had thinned to almost nothing. "Do you have the rest of the message cylinders?"

Gieck had no time and no desire to be interrogated in that breezy doorway. "Finish getting dressed. Commander Mollor has him in the tower cell and has ordered a watch of thirty guards at all times."

"Thirty? What does she think he's going to do?"

"Escape or kill someone, I imagine. Do you have enough officers on call?"

Bonner chewed at the inside of his mouth as his eyes worked back and forth. He mumbled a few names under his breath and finally nodded. "I'll have to call in the shift that just went off, but I can get them together."

"Then do it. Make it fast."

Bonner scowled at the tone but said nothing. Gieck knew Bonner had never liked him. He had either heard about Gieck or he was a good enough judge of character on his own that he didn't dare protest. "Right away, lieutenant."

Gieck took backstreets on his return to the castle. Vam had reported to Nera that Akithar had killed Kela, but he'd confided the truth to Gieck. It was the city itself. Shutting the gates had been a practical necessity for the search at first, but Nera had let it go on for too long.

The luxury goods dried up first, and the citizens now were feeling the sting of not having the food they wanted. Without new visitors, many of the city's establishments that thrived on tourism and business travel were hurting, and that was spilling over into the streets.

A city with an upper class that was used to getting what it wanted when it wanted it had been denied. The dissatisfaction trickled down to the lower classes who were put on leave from their jobs, and the already bustling occupation of thieving had gained new life. Nera had strangled the entire city without even realizing what she was doing. Another thing for Gieck to remember in his report to Bekam after the fact, but for now he had no desire to get caught alone by a drunken mob.

Nera had finished her interrogation of the prisoner by the time he got back. She was sitting at a table in the entry hall when Gieck came through the door. "Did you get them?"

He nodded. "Bonner is rounding them up himself. He'll have them here."

"Good." She looked at him with tired eyes and motioned to the chair next to hers. "Have a seat."

"I really—"

"Just for a moment."

He cast a longing glance at the door that would lead to his chamber and his bed, but he stifled that desire before Nera could notice it. He had to humor her, at least for a few more days. "Of course." He pulled out the chair and settled onto it, all his weariness threatening not to let him stand again. "Did the wizard talk?"

"He claims not to know anything about the rebels or their hideout."

"Lies," Gieck said. He clasped his hands, and his head bowed toward them, but from beneath his heavy brow his eyes sought some sort of sign from the woman next to him. What else had Akithar told her?

"I'm sorry I was curt with you, Lucian." She slid her right hand across the table and took his left hand. "It has been a trying night."

"Think nothing of it," he said and squeezed her hand back with what he hoped came through as reassurance.

"I wasn't thinking before, when I sent you away so abruptly. You've lost two of your own tonight. We both have, but I know you were especially close to both Kela and Eyral."

He summoned a pained expression. It took effort, but he pinched his eyes tight and lowered his eyebrows in what should be a suitable response. "It is difficult. I keep telling myself I should have been the one to open that warehouse door."

"No!" She put her left hand on top of his and now had him held there with both of her hands. "Never think that way. Eyral was a good soldier, and he died doing his duty. He would have stepped ahead of you willingly if he'd known that door was a trap."

Gieck wasn't so sure about that, but he didn't argue the point. Nera leaned forward over the table, and then she had his right hand between both of hers. She pulled it toward her, and he had to turn to face her. What did she think she was doing?

"Lucian, how certain are you about what you saw on the dormitory roof?"

He felt his skin go cold, and he wondered whether she could feel it as well. Could she feel his pulse quicken? Her fingers were on his wrist even now, but she looked at him with that dull eyed and innocent earnestness that would be her undoing.

"I know what I saw," he said. He had to be careful here, but she had provided him with an opening. "Did Akithar claim otherwise?"

"He denies killing the boy, of course." She released his hands at last and sat back in her chair. "Can you tell me again what you saw?"

"It's as I told you before. The magician was on the opposite roof, and I was running after the boy. When the boy went to make the jump off the roof I was on, Akithar grabbed him in the air with some sort of magical tendrils. It looked like threads, almost. He threw him back at me."

"When did the knife appear?"

Gieck's mind spun to reassemble the story exactly as he'd told it to her before. "As the boy was being pushed back through the air, Akithar summoned that knife and threw it straight into his chest. That's when the boy hit the roof before me, and I lost my pursuit so I could try to help the poor child. It was too late."

"You didn't see any sort of... wire? Or a retractable cable or some sort?"

Gieck swallowed and forced his face to remain impassive. Of course she knew about the cabler now. It was fortunate he'd chucked it into the moat when he had. "A wire system to catch the boy? You mean you don't think he used his magic?"

"No, no," she said, "I'm certain it happened as you said. I'm simply trying to make sense of some of his wilder claims."

"You should have him put to death and be done with it. I'd even do it for you. For what he did to Eyral and Kela."

"Magic use alone is not punishable by death, Lucian. As much as we might wish the contrary to be true."

"Maybe not just magic, but murder is."

Her finger tapped twice on the table, slowly. She bit at her lower lip, and Gieck imagined her brain churning through what she knew and what she suspected. This was the time to be careful.

Nera shook her head. "We have insufficient evidence to prove him a murderer. And I suspect he's holding back what he knows about the rebels. He will not die."

"You'll have him made compliant, then?"

"No, I do not enjoy half measures. The Herons General Bekam is sending will silence Akithar entirely. Losing his ability to touch magic at all, forever, should be something like a death, don't you think?"

Not nearly enough like a death to suit Gieck, but he gave Nera a grunt of acquiescence. What more could he do? Nera opened her mouth to say something else but shut it again. She was on the verge of telling him something. He could smell it in the space between them, but she held back. She never did that. Not with him.

"What else did he tell you?" Gieck asked.

She looked into his eyes then. Really looked, and not just in the usual mooning way. She was searching, and he thought he could feel her probing in his head, down into his chest, his gut. But then she smiled, and the uncomfortable spell broke. She brushed at the air with her fingers. "It was nothing of substance, and I've kept you awake far too long. You need your rest."

"As do you," he said. Had he betrayed anything to her himself? How much did she suspect about him, and did she truly believe whatever Akithar had told her?

Nera rose from her chair and put a hand on his shoulder. "Good night, Lucian. I will stay up to see that the guards are assigned properly. Go get your sleep, and we will reconvene in the morning." She gave his shoulder one last squeeze before she left toward the tower stairs again.

It was only after she was out of sight through the doorway that Gieck touched his left wrist and rubbed at the empty space where his zephyr spool had been less than an hour before. The very space where Nera had been grasping and probing, searching for his weapon. She knew, and worse yet, she believed Akithar.

$\sim$

It was too hot to sleep. Gieck shoved the rough sheet aside and closed his eyes, uncovered. He had sweat through the linens, and now the air in his tiny bedroom chilled the beads of moisture that still clung to his skin. He cursed and rolled onto one side, then the other. His body felt exhausted, but his mind wouldn't allow rest. Not until something had been decided. Not until this was dealt with, one way or another.

With another curse, he swung his legs off the edge of the bed and sat in the darkness, his back hunched and his elbows on his knees.

Gieck's rise was contingent on his ability to control Nera. Bekam had paired him with her specifically because she was so malleable, so easy to twist around his fingers. He'd been grooming her, building her anticipation and expectation and unanswered desire for years now. She had made a complete mess of this Klubridge affair, and he'd be able to report the whole thing to her superiors in just a few days. Just a few more days, and they'd be back in Aramore, away from this decadent and restless city and under the predictable net of the High Lord once more.

He planned to deliver every delicious detail, from her unwillingness to arrest Akithar when she had him before her in his own office to her losing the acrobat girl in the failed bank heist to her allowing a gang of rebels to run roughshod over the city with a load of bombs. He would talk about the loss of two experienced and trusted Kites, his own right and left hands, both dead because of Nera Mollor's inability to act decisively and her incompetent leadership. He would sweeten the delivery with a heart wrenching account of the young boy's murder at the hands of the wizard, accompanied by the commander's lack of foresight and irresponsibility in allowing Akithar to remain free for so long.

The perfect capstone would be Gieck's surprising revelation of the location of the Stormbreak Sanctuary, information Nera had failed to extract from two prisoners. Gieck was certain Akithar knew where the rebels were hiding, and that was information that would build Gieck's career while demolishing Nera Mollor's. But he, too, had failed to learn the location, and now he was out of time.

All of his plans and all of Nera's missteps hinged on her trusting him and confiding in him just long enough for them to leave this blasted city behind, but it all was falling apart. Whatever Akithar had told her was convincing enough to shake her unwavering belief in Gieck. It had been enough for her to lie to him and even to search him for the weapon she now knew was used to kill that boy. She thought she was so damned clever, running her fingers under his sleeves, poking and prodding at his wrists. Gieck's nostrils flared, and he felt his skin growing hot now in fury.

He no longer could rely on her playing the role he needed her to play, but this was salvageable. He still could make this work, but he had to repair bridges. He rolled off the bed and grabbed his shirt from the back of the chair in the dark.

The lamps still burned in the hallway outside his door, but no one was up and about. Farther down, toward the central area of the keep, he could hear distant voices. No doubt Nera's thirty-odd guards, roused out of sleep by Bonner. Gieck closed his door and headed three rooms down and across the hall. He'd left his boots behind so as not to awaken anyone else. Without knocking, he tried the doorknob and, finding it unlocked, pushed the door open.

Jona had her back to him when he entered, but she saw him in the mirror and cocked her head to the side. "We're back on those terms, then?"

He opened his hands to her. "I come in peace. I took the chance that you might still be awake."

"I am, and you're here, so what do you want?" She turned back to the mirror and laid a towel on the vanity in front of it. She had a lantern on the surface next to it, backlighting her, and Gieck could see her form silhouetted through her thin nightshirt. Her legs and feet were bare, and he forced his focus back to her face in the mirror.

"You understand the stress I'm under," he said.

"Apparently enough stress to threaten me."

"I'd never report on you. You have to know that."

"Do I?" She turned to face him and leaned back against the vanity. Her skin and hair shone in the dim light, and the shirt was damp at the shoulders. She must have just had her bath.

Gieck's eyes wandered down to her tight thighs, visible but in shadow beneath the bottom of the shirt. He sniffed the air. Something earthy and unfamiliar. "Is that perfume?"

She snorted. "It's called soap, you filthy idiot. You might give it a try sometime. Why are you here?"

"It's rare for me to acknowledge that I was wrong."

"Is that what this is, then? An apology?"

"If it were, would you accept it?"

With the lamp behind her, Gieck couldn't see her face in the dark room, but he knew she was staring at him, studying him. It reminded him of how Nera's eyes had bored through him earlier. He was under the scrutiny of too many women lately.

"Do I at least still have your loyalty?" he asked.

"Still? You know where my loyalty always has been and always will be."

"With yourself."

"The same as yours."

"Our own best interests might be intersecting again."

Jona angled her head, and Gieck saw the hint of a smile in the fire-light. "At last we come to the truth."

"After we're finished here, after we leave Klubridge, I will be in ascent. General Bekam will be promoting me to lead the Scarlet Kites."

"You sound so certain of that."

"It will be a promotion of necessity, but I also will have earned it. My plan is coming to fruition, and I can raise you with me. The Kites will need a new lieutenant."

"And what do you expect from me?"

Gieck knew his next words required a leap of faith. He would have to trust that Jona saw her own benefit in this plan and would not betray him. She'd lied and killed for him before. Once more, then. "I expect for you to side with me when I kill Mollor."

Jona stared at him in the dark again. Her hand moved to her wet towel, and she shoved it aside, hopping up to sit on the edge of the vanity. She pulled her shirt over her head and tossed it on the floor in one motion.

"You'd better get over here, then."

CHAPTER 36

Fairy was alone.

It had been five days since she'd seen Miri and longer since Gad left. Gad had talked about finding Barween Drach and joining her crew. He was lonely and miserable and wanted it to be like it had been when they had Scrounger looking after them. Fairy had tried to tell him that Barween Drach was no Scrounger, and Scrounger was no hero, but had he listened? Of course not. So off he went, just dancing out into the city one night after Fairy and Miri were asleep. He hadn't told them he was leaving, but he hadn't needed to. She knew exactly where he'd gone, and she could only hope he found the good sense to keep himself alive.

Miri had been another story entirely. She followed Fairy everywhere and had no complaints about the tiny portions of food they had to split every day. She didn't even complain about having to sleep in abandoned businesses and hidden away in alleys. Things had gotten better in those regards as the city itself went crazy. People were breaking into shops, taking whatever they wanted, and the law didn't seem to care. That left a slew of newly vacated buildings where Fairy could pick up the leavings and find a cozy spot for herself and for Miri inside and away from the madness.

Fairy had found a day-old baguette and some unidentifiable vegetable paste behind the counter in a bakery shortly after the place was looted. She had split it with Miri for dinner that night, and they went to sleep upstairs in the side office room of that same shop, tucked away under a desk. Fairy fell asleep sitting up and leaning against the underside of the desk, and Miri dozed off with her head on Fairy's chest, just like always. But when Fairy woke with the first rays of sun the next morning, Miri was gone.

The next three days were a roaming nightmare of Fairy screaming the girl's name as she wandered from street to street. She asked everyone she saw, and she described Miri a million times, but nobody had seen her. Nobody ever noticed kids like Miri and Fairy, though, and that was a fact. Even if Miri had walked right past them, these people wouldn't have seen her under normal circumstances, much less when the city was in such an uproar.

After those three days, Fairy went back to the bakery, hoping against hope that she'd missed some sign of Miri, but by then one of the local gangs had taken over the storefront. She couldn't get inside past the dirty boy at the front with the mean eyes and the weighted baton, so she'd left, still with no idea about what had happened to the child or where she might have gone.

Miri was her responsibility, and she'd lost her, just like she'd lost Gad and all the rest of them. The only one she knew had gotten away was Dorrin. He'd be on that ship out at sea somewhere by now, having his own adventures. Part of her hoped he'd remember her when he set foot on new lands they'd only ever been able to imagine. The other part of her hoped he'd forget all about Scrounger, Klubridge, even her, and live the life he deserved to live.

It was on the fifth day after Miri disappeared that Fairy found herself near the southwestern gate. The crowds had been huge at all the gates ever since the Kites shut the city down. Everybody was packed in, hoping to be the first to get out whenever the soldiers left, but so far there'd been no sign of them going away. There'd been some kind of big action near the Downsteps, and the Kites themselves had kept mostly in and around the castle since then, but the gates were still closed, and the city watch still wasn't letting anyone through.

The crowds around the gates made for prime picking grounds if you were willing to risk swiping purses that close to the authorities. Fairy hadn't been that desperate until Miri left and her scavenging tactics had failed her. Now, though, she was ready to risk it, and, truth be told, she almost didn't care if she got caught. She doubted she'd be put to death. She might even be thrown in a cell somewhere that she'd be fed at least one meal a day.

As she approached the gatehouses, she was trying to remember all the tactics Scrounger had taught her about making a quick grab and getting out. Starting a block away from the core of the throng, there was a new buzz in the air that grabbed her focus. "What's going on?" she asked an old lady who was watching from the doorway of a bookshop that had stayed open without being vandalized.

"Empire's coming," the lady told her. "My boy spotted them up from the roofs. A whole big processional, it is."

Fairy had never been as good at climbing as Dorrin was, but she scaled the side of the bookshop and scrambled across to the next roof, high enough to see over the city walls. Only one person yelled for her to get down, and she ignored them as she sought a higher perch. And then, once she was way up above the crowds, she saw the caravan. There were three pairs of horses riding in front, leading a series of four strange coaches. The carriages all were bright white, shining in the midday sun, and she thought they might even be gilded, the way they gleamed as they rolled along the road toward the city. In back of the carriages were three more pairs of horses, and she could see that all the riders were armored and armed.

It looked like a guarded escort for the white carriages. Who could be in there? Somebody important, but Fairy didn't think it was a big enough procession for the High Lord himself. She watched the horses and the wheels make their gradual way to the city walls, and they didn't stop once they reached the gate. The guards stood aside and pushed the crowds back, widening the way for them to enter the city.

Fairy hopped across to a neighboring roof and slid down the gable facing the main street. She caught herself before reaching the edge and hung onto the side of a window to watch the caravan approaching. The crowd was parting of its own accord now, the people of Klubridge more curious than angry as they moved out of the way and craned their necks to try and get a look into the carriages. The windows were blocked from the inside, though, and nobody was getting a glimpse of anything.

"It's mages," a voice said behind Fairy. She twisted and looked up to see a boy, nearly her own age, hanging onto a vent pipe above and behind her.

"How do you know?" she asked.

He shrugged. "My mate Gaffy was working the guardhouse earlier. Got a pretty penny, too. Nearly got nicked by some soldier type, but he got away. Anyhow, he heard the guards talking, and they said mages were coming in from Deakem. Imperial ones with guards and all. That's what's happening. Mages in the buggies, guards on the ponies."

She watched one of the carriages going by below them and imagined an Imperial mage shut away inside. The thought sent a chill up the back of her neck. "Why are they coming here, of all places?"

"I expect for Akithar."

Fairy started, and she pulled herself around to face the boy. "Akithar, the magician with the stage show? What about him?"

He laughed at her with a gap-toothed grin. "Where've you been? Everybody knows about him."

"Obviously I don't, so tell me."

"He's the one the Kites were after. They got him a few days ago, locked him up in the tower at Henburn."

Fairy knew of the tower, where Klubridge liked to stow its ne'er-do-well prisoners instead of tossing them in the proper jail. "That's impossible. Akithar left the city a week or more ago. He's long gone."

"Not so. Way I hear, he ain't going anywhere for a long time. They got him on magic and also murder."

"Murder? Come off it."

"It's true, swear it. Everybody in the city knows it but you."

"I've been busy."

"Been having your head in the ground, sounds like."

"So who is he supposed to have killed?"

"Not supposed to, he did it all right. Gaffy snuck us in, and we saw the body. Some scrawny little boy, supposed to have worked for Akithar."

Fairy's heart thudded as dread pressed into her chest. She squeezed the window frame tighter, for fear that she was about to collapse and tumble off the roof into the street below. "You're lying," she said.

The boy wrinkled his nose at her. "You're ugly. Call me a liar now." With one more laugh, he clambered back up the roof and disappeared over the peak.

Fairy leaned back against the rough shingles and felt shock mix with disbelief, but something else was trying to push its way through her confusion. It wasn't grief. She'd known that many times before, and she knew she should feel that if Dorrin truly was gone, but this wasn't it. This was something darker, something more primal. Something begging for it not to be true and swearing vengeance if it were.

By the time night fell, Fairy had gotten the same story from five other people. Akithar had gotten into some kind of trouble at the university, and he had his boy with him. The Scarlet Kites gave chase, and he sacrificed the boy so he could make his own escape. Sacrificed Dorrin.

Some of them had offered the details of exactly how he'd done it, but she didn't want that. She had no room for that, not yet, maybe not ever. For now, it was enough to know that Dorrin, sweet Dorrin, was dead, and the man he trusted to get him away from here had made him that way. The Kites had caught Akithar and jailed him in the tower cell, just as the boy on the roof had told her. Nobody knew why he was jailed there, only that he was under heavy guard.

Fairy thought he surely would be executed for the murder. The thought brought her no peace, though. The man would die in the cold and efficient way of the Empire without truly facing the reality of what he'd done. He'd go to his grave without knowing how the life he'd taken would impact others and what he'd robbed from the world. But then she talked to the man who ran the news broker just outside the East Ward. Akithar wasn't being executed after all. Rumor had it he was too valuable to the Empire to kill, so he would live.

Fairy didn't know whether that made it better or worse. If he died at the hands of the Empire, it would mean nothing. If he lived under Imperial imprisonment, it would be in luxury rather than in a jail-house or dungeon. The tower cell's reputation was not lost on her, and she imagined the magician reclining on a soft chaise and eating grapes while the rest of the city languished. She pushed down the grief, the panic, and the tears. She could fall into those later. For now, she had room only for her anger.

She scavenged a shard of glass from a broken window near the news broker. It took walking up and down three streets of ransacked storefronts before she found what she was looking for. It was thick glass and sharp, long enough to be useful but small enough to conceal. She tore strips of fabric off the ends of her sleeves and wrapped the material around and around the glass, shaping it into a clumsy but usable handle that should keep her from cutting her own hands. Once done, she tested the makeshift knife on her finger and drew a dot of blood with the slightest pressure. It would do.

She waited until well into the night before heading toward the city center. One point of agreement between everybody she'd encountered was that Akithar was under heavy guard, including mages who were keeping him from using his magic to escape. Getting to him would not be easy, but she was determined to get answers or blood. Maybe a little of both.

Fairy arrived at the Henburn Estate from the southwest. She'd been through the city center plenty of times, and the castle was visible from nearly everywhere in Klubridge, but all those other times she'd been trying her best to avoid being brought inside its ancient and rocky white walls. Tonight was different. She was going to get in but hoped she could do it of her own free will.

The city had turned the estate into its own little island at some point. There was a moat dug around it, but it didn't look all that effective. Fairy had been swimming only a handful of times, but she felt confident she could cross that dark water nearly as fast as she could walk across the one bridge that led into the walls. She considered jumping straight into the moat and being done with it, but she reconsidered when she looked up at the wall she was going to have to scale. That tower was tall, and getting up the side would be hard enough without worrying about wet fingers and toes slipping. She couldn't risk the swim. The bridge it was, then.

Fairy crouched next to a shrub that bordered the moat and watched the front of the castle. She saw one guard standing midway across the short bridge. She couldn't see them properly from this distance, but she thought it probably was a city watch. There'd be more guards inside, but she didn't need to get inside. She just had to get past that one guard, and she'd be on the right side of this stupid water.

She looked at the shard of glass for a long moment before pulling its fabric wrapping down to cover the sharp end as well. She didn't need to cut herself getting in. That knife was meant for one person, and it wasn't her. Once satisfied that it was safe, Fairy pulled the pocket of her trousers wide and slid the bundle inside. She then tugged at the laces at her waist and felt the system of cords cinch down her legs. Thank you for that, Dorrin.

Keeping low to the ground, she crept closer to the bridge and didn't halt until she'd reached the nearest side of it. The bridge rail arced up to her right, making a brief hill before connecting to the opposite shore. She peeked around the edge of the rail to see where the guard was, and she froze. The figure was still midway down, currently looking off to the left, Fairy's right, but that was no city watch. Fairy could see the telltale red of a Scarlet Kite uniform. It was a woman with dark hair, short on one side, long on the other. Awesome hair, if Fairy was honest.

Fairy closed her eyes and breathed in. Kite or watch, a guard was a guard, and both types were just people. She let out the breath and slid around the corner. The bridge itself had no lanterns or lamps, but there was enough light coming from the castle to make hiding in shadows impossible. She was committed now, and she willed the Kite not to look her way. Fairy stayed light on the balls of her feet and imagined herself gliding barely above the ground, skimming right past her unnoticed.

She was a quarter of the way across, now halfway, now—

"Hey, kid."

Fairy froze again and squeezed her eyes closed tight. Her shoulders were tense, and she could feel the Kite behind her, looking at her. What to do? If she ran, the woman probably could catch her. If she gave up, it was all done. Unless she could lie her way out of it.

"I'm talking to you," the woman said.

Fairy turned slowly to face the Kite. The woman looked young, probably only seven or eight years older than Fairy, but those years were big ones and counted a lot more than they might if they had both been ten years older.

"Hey," Fairy said.

"Hey yourself. Get back on the other side of this bridge before I have to turn you inside out."

Fairy swallowed and knew her eyes were too big. She forced herself to talk. "I'm supposed to be here. I have a message."

"Give it here, then."

"Nope, it's not for you. It's for… your boss."

"My boss?" The Kite crossed her arms and leaned against the side of the bridge. She smirked at Fairy. "And who might that be?"

Always case the place before you go in. Scrounger had told her that, and if she'd remembered it before now, she might be in a better position. She had no idea who was in charge there. "The… captain?"

The Kite clicked her tongue. "Wrong. You're coming with me." She reached for Fairy, but Fairy danced back a step.

"Wait, here. You can have the message. I'll just leave it with you and go."

"You'll come with me," she said and reached again.

Fairy had the glass out of her pocket just fast enough to slash at the Kite. The shard caught the woman across the back of the hand, and she flinched back. "You little—"

Fairy didn't wait for her to finish. She turned and darted down the slope of the bridge toward the castle. As she ran, the huge doors began to open, and she saw a man, another Kite, coming out. It was the one who killed Scrounger! Before he could see her, she was off the bridge and dove to the left, back into the darkness.

Fairy's foot caught on the grass and she tumbled into a mess of bushes next to the castle wall. The glass knife slipped out of her hand, and she dropped low, feeling around the ground for it. Just around the corner, the man called to the Kite she'd cut. He wasn't loud, but Fairy could hear him. "Jona, what are you doing?"

"Some urchin got across the bridge. She cut me!"

A pause, and Fairy thought he must have been examining her wound. "You're fine. We have work to do."

"The girl is across the bridge and has a shard of glass, Gieck. I'm going after her."

"No, you're coming with me. Leave the child. We've had enough trouble of that sort."

"But—"

"What do you think she's going to do? Assassinate Mollor? We could only hope. Now wrap your hand up before you bleed all over yourself, and follow me."

The woman swore, more impressively than Fairy had heard since Skink was around, and then they were gone. Her heart thudded in her chest, but she had done it. She was across the moat, and her groping hand closed over the wrapped end of the glass in the dirt. Now for the climb.

The tower had seemed tall when she was on the ground, looking up, but it felt immense once she was halfway through scaling it. Midway up the climb, Fairy realized that she'd stand out against the white curved wall for anyone who happened to look up. Even in the darkness of the night and amid the many crevices and ornamentations, those walls shone, and she had to count on any onlookers being tucked away in their beds at that hour. She reached the upper level of the tower without being shot down by arrows or worse, so she counted that as a win. It was only once she was up there, clinging to the side of the structure with her fingertips, that she realized she was on the wrong side.

She'd seen a lit window high up toward the top when she was approaching Henburn, but somehow she'd gotten turned around, either when she was climbing up or when she was scampering through the brush after the Kites nearly caught her. Whenever it happened, she saw no window now and knew she had to work her way around the whole column. The wind whipped at her hair, and she made the mistake of turning her head to look over her shoulder in the direction of the breeze.

Dark space yawned behind and below her. A wave of vertigo made her reel, and she dug her fingers into the gaps between the bricks even tighter. She was not about to get this far and then fall to her death from a dizzy spell. Fairy faced front again and pressed her forehead against the cold wall. She closed her eyes to wait for the feeling to pass. It took several minutes before she felt ready to open her eyes again. Once she did, she kept them locked on the bricks in front of her face and didn't look away.

Her toes probed to the right to find new places to step, and she pulled herself to meet their pace with her fingertips. Circling the tower was terrifying work. She felt like it took hours, but she knew it probably was a matter of just a few minutes.

Fairy felt the edge of the window before she saw it. The bricks jutted out there, making a sort of shelf that protruded from the side of the tower, different from the ornamental arches and columns that ringed the rest of the structure. She nearly slipped when her fingers failed to find more bricks and instead dipped into emptiness. With a gasp, she lunged, and her hand closed around a metal bar. This had to be the cell.

She pulled herself to the right and realized she was going to have to let go of the wall with her feet if she wanted to get up onto the window ledge. This was just like getting into the theater. Just like it, only about a million feet farther from the ground. She closed her eyes for another few seconds, and when she reopened them, she was ready. Fairy pulled herself up with her right hand and swung to the right so she could grab another bar with her left hand. Her feet dropped free from the spaces between the bricks where she had wedged her toes, and she now hung off the edge of the tower by her arm strength and grip alone.

It was then that she considered that the bars in the window might have loosened over the centuries. Surely they could hold her. There was no point in worrying that they couldn't, anyway. If the bars let loose, she wouldn't have long to deal with the results of her actions before the ground far below splatted her.

But the bars held. She grunted and heaved and swung her right leg up onto the window ledge first. That was the one with the knife strapped to it. The left leg swung up next, and she was sitting on the side of the tower now, her back to the window and her feet swinging over the abyss below.

Fairy stayed like that for long enough to catch her breath and to give her aching arms some time to rest. She was going to have to climb all the way back down after she was finished, and she hoped the descent would be easier. For now, though, she looked out across the city and knew she was facing east. The port was ahead of her, and a ship was disembarking as she watched.

The wind whipped a strand of hair across Fairy's face, and she felt it tug at her shirt. Time to get moving. She slid around to face the window and came up onto her knees. Her heart dropped as she looked at the opening. What a fool she'd been. Of course the window's bars would be too small for a person to crawl between. That was the whole point of a prison cell!

Still, she pulled on one of the bars and then tried to press her shoulder between two of them. She could get an arm through, but her head was too big. There was no getting in, after that long climb and the many times she'd almost careened into a gruesome death. Fairy gave the bars a furious shake, but there was no budging them and no getting through them. With a quiet moan, she rested her head against the middle pair of bars.

A man was staring back at her from the other side.

Fairy gasped and jumped back, but the man's hand was quicker. It shot between the bars and grabbed the front of her shirt, catching her just before she would have fallen. He pulled her back in and only let go once she was back on the relative safety of the window ledge. She held the bars again, her eyes wide with the realization of what she'd almost done.

"Are… are you him?" The question came out with a tremble Fairy hated. She was here to exact vengeance, not to wilt in fear.

The man smiled back, and she was no longer as sure that this was the man she was after. This one had a kind face, and his hair was lighter than that of the man she'd seen that night in the theater when she was in the rafters. He also had no mustache, but she guessed that could be shaved off. His hair color could be changed, too, for that matter. "I am a him," he said. "I'm not sure whether I'm the him you're looking for, though. Is there a particular reason you're dangling outside my window?"

"You're Akithar," she said. It had to be him. Who else would be in that room? She looked past him and saw someone else across the room. A woman, she thought, but it was dark on that side of the tower. But it looked like a woman, just standing in the dark and staring at them silently.

"You obviously know me, but I'm sorry that I don't know you. Have we met?"

He was pleasant where she had expected coldness, smiling when she'd prepared for a diabolical scowl. This wasn't going how she'd expected in so many ways, and she had to remind herself. She was there for Dorrin. Dorrin, who was dead because of this man. Her hand slid into her pocket and found the wrapped end of the glass.

"You killed my friend," she hissed and lunged, her hand slipping between the bars, the knife plunging straight at the magician's chest.

He sidestepped the attack with ease and caught her wrist in his hand. She tried to pull it back, but he wasn't letting go. "Is that glass? You came up here to stab me with a piece of glass?"

She tugged at her arm again and fumed at him through the bars, but there was no getting out of his grip. "Let me go!"

"I'll let you go if you'll drop that thing before you get hurt. And if you'll tell me who you are instead of just trying to kill me."

Fairy pulled again, but it was no use. She opened her fingers, and he took the knife away from her. "You killed my friend," she said. "The Kites aren't even going to execute you for that."

Akithar had been looking at the makeshift knife in his hand, but his eyes found hers as she spoke. Fairy was an excellent judge of people, and the pain on his face was unmistakable. "You're Fairy, aren't you?"

She stopped struggling and stared back at him. "How do you know me?"

"Dorrin talked about you. Fairy, I am so sorry—"

"No," she said. "No, you don't get to apologize. Not after what you did. No apology is enough."

"I didn't kill Dorrin," Akithar said. "It was the Kites. I wasn't there that night, but I wish I had been. I don't know whether I could have done any good, but..." His voice trailed off, and he let go of Fairy's wrist.

Fairy pulled her arm back through the bars, and she thought about leaving, just sliding off the edge and climbing all the way back down. She also thought about leaning into the bars and screaming her fury into his face. How dare he take Dorrin away and then lie to her like this? Except... He wasn't lying. He had to be, but he wasn't.

"Where is he?" she asked, her voice small now.

Akithar frowned. "I'm sorry?"

"Dorrin. Where's his body?"

"I don't know. The Kites took him away, and we never saw him after that night. They may still have him."

"He deserves to be treated properly. He shouldn't be just kept around somewhere."

"I agree. Dorrin didn't deserve any of this."

Her anger flared again. "Why didn't you protect him, then? That's why he came to you! You told him he'd be safe."

"I thought we were protecting him. He was supposed to have stayed behind, but he slipped out that night. If I had that whole night to do over again—"

"But you don't, do you? Dorrin is dead, and there's nothing any of us can do." Fairy felt the heat in her eyes, and she cursed it silently. She forbade tears to come now, of all times. Not now, when she was confronting the man she most wanted to blame. But they did come, slow at first and then heavier and harder. She squeezed the bars and pushed her head into them again. She shook with her sobs, but she made no sound.

Dorrin was gone. Really gone and never coming back. It had seemed so distant, like something you heard somebody talking about and you pretended to agree, but you knew it couldn't be true. But now, sitting on that ridiculous window ledge and looking into Akithar's eyes, she knew it had happened. Dorrin was dead, and the Kites had killed him. Not this strange magician, but the Kites. It made a vicious kind of sense that she didn't want to accept, but she knew it was the truth.

Fairy didn't flinch when she felt Akithar's hand on her head. "I'm so sorry," he said, and that only made her cry more. It all poured out of her and onto those metal bars. The rage flowed out in her tears, leaving her emptier than she'd ever felt. She reached through the window and took hold of Akithar's shirt. She squeezed it as the pain rolled over her, and he stood there and let her.

When the sobs had turned dry, and her eyes stung, and there were no more tears, she wiped at her face with her own shirt sleeve. It came away with the wet shape of her eyes, nose, and mouth pressed into it, and she had to stifle a laugh at the bizarre image that accompanied her wildly swinging emotions. She let go of Akithar's shirt and took a deep breath in between sniffles.

"How are you getting out of there?" she asked.

"Out of the tower? I don't think I can."

"Out of there, but also out of this mess. How are you getting out?"

He shook his head. "I don't think there's any getting out of this one. I'm going to have to see this through."

"Can't you just... I don't know... Can't you fly out the window or dissolve the castle or something?"

He smiled sadly. "It doesn't work like that. And it wouldn't do any good if it did. Besides, you said they're not going to execute me."

"They're going to silence you instead," she said. Did he already know that? She should have been more delicate, but it was out there now. She looked at him from the corner of her eyes, not wanting to see his face if he didn't already know. Silencing wasn't a small thing.

But when she looked at him, he didn't look horrified like she expected. He looked more contemplative than anything else. "Silencing," he said, like he was trying the word out on his tongue. "How do you know?"

"I saw the mages today. They came in white coaches with guards. They're supposed to be doing it tomorrow, I hear."

He breathed deeply and nodded. "I should have expected that."

"Aren't you upset? They're going to take your power away!"

"They've already been working on that," he said. He nodded his head back toward the figure standing behind him in the darkness. "I have three friends in here that have been seeing to it that I don't do anything too preposterous."

"Those are halflocks," she said, her eyes wide again as she tried to get a better look. She'd heard about those but never seen one in person. Rumor was that the Empire cut them open and changed their brains around. They left them loyal to the Empire and weaker than before, but still not something she'd want to run afoul of.

Akithar interrupted her thoughts. "Do you see those lights over there?"

He pointed past Fairy, out toward the edge of the city. She followed his finger, and her head managed not to spin when she peered out across the open gulf of air. He was pointing toward the port, toward a trio of lights that stood higher than others. "Those three?" she asked.

"Those three. That's a ship that belongs to a captain I know. He's taking my friends far away from here. They're supposed to already be gone, but they haven't left yet. I'm in here so they can be out there."

"Dorrin told me about the ship. He promised I could come along."

"Why didn't you?"

"There were others I had to take care of. But I told him to go. I told him to have adventures and a good life away from here. And now..."

She sat quietly, and Akithar let her have her thoughts. When some time had passed, he said, "You can still go with them. If you want to get away from this place."

Fairy looked through the bars at his face and tried to find the trick there. He was a magician. There always was a trick. He'd make her look at his right hand while his left shoved her off the perch. But that wasn't really true, was it? She was good with eyes, and his were kind, concerned. "Why are you being nice to me? I came here to kill you."

"It's lucky for me you're a bad assassin."

She laughed into her hands and tucked her knees up under her chin. Her back was against one side of the window's alcove now, and somehow she felt safer than she'd felt in years. Up here, inches away from a speedy and screaming death, up here, facing the most wanted mage in Klubridge, she felt safe.

"Go to the ship," Akithar said. "It's called the *Sephare*. The captain is a man named Ergo Drass. Tell him Caius sent you. He'll take you on board."

"Who's Caius?"

"I'm Caius," he said. "Now you know more than the Kites know."

She felt stupid again, but only for a moment. Of course his real name wouldn't be Akithar. She should have known that, but somehow it had caught her by surprise. Akithar was the person she'd blamed for

Dorrin's death and the misery it had brought her. But she didn't know Caius. He was something new entirely.

"Will you go?" he asked. "Dorrin would want you to leave Klubridge, if that's what you want."

"It's what I want," she said, her voice low.

"Then go. I don't know why they haven't left yet, but they will be leaving anytime now. Hurry, and tell them I'm going to be okay."

Fairy wiped at her face again and nodded. She reached through the bars once more, being careful to do it with the hand that wasn't covered in tears and snot. Akithar, no, Caius looked at it and smiled at her. He took her hand in his and gave it a squeeze and a shake. "Good luck, Fairy."

"Thank you, Caius."

CHAPTER 37

Nera nodded to Morcan as she approached the door at the end of the hallway. Poor Morcan always was the one to handle the mages. He never complained, but it couldn't be a pleasant position, dealing with those wretches every time one was needed. Nera would remember to recommend a commendation of some sort for him after they had finished this business in Klubridge.

"Are they inside?"

Morcan nodded and found the big iron key that fit the lock. "All four of them. They just arrived by coach less than an hour ago. They haven't even eaten yet."

"And their escort?"

"They've been assigned quarters and are probably in the tavern now having a meal."

"Good. I will see them now."

Morcan turned the key, and the lock clanged open. The door scraped on the stone floor as he pushed it open. The room was bigger than Nera had expected. It was a parlor, not a cell, after all. She shouldn't have been surprised, but it felt unusual stepping into the underground room with walls draped in pink and red linens and lanterns in the corners, giving the space a cozy and warm glow. The scent of incense burned Nera's nose, and its vapors clouded the air.

The four mages were waiting within, immersed in the hazy vapors. A woman with straight black hair and suspicious eyes sat on an upholstered chair near the center of the room with her head tilted toward that of a man of middle age with a scruffy salt and pepper beard. They halted their quiet conversation and looked to the door as Nera entered. The third mage, a younger man with curly blond hair down to his shoulders was to the right, leaning against the wall and paging through a small book. He, too, paused as she entered and eyed her with a smirk.

The fourth mage was the only one previously known to Nera. Tall and lean, with dark brown skin and a closely shaved head, Farij Basos had been a Heron for as long as Nera had been alive. He had to be at least seventy years old by now but looked no older than forty. Farij bowed his head to her. "Commander. It has been far too long."

"I trust your journey was unremarkable." Her tone was too curt, too clipped. He was an agent of the Empire and deserved the same respectful tone she would give to any of her colleagues, but he still was a mage. And an untampered one, at that. These creatures had given themselves over to the service of the High Lord without being hunted down. The operations had not been performed on them, and they retained their full powers with none of the cognitive limitations most halflocks ended up having. No matter how many times she'd been around him, Nera always stayed on edge when in the presence of Farij Basos. Having three other Herons in the same room didn't make it any easier.

"We traveled in comfort. And thank you for the concern. Might I inquire as to when we will be eating?"

"I'll see that someone brings you food soon. Were you told why you're here?"

"Only that a silencing was required. We all are quite intrigued by the identity of your prisoner. What can you tell us?"

The others were watching the conversation with keen interest, but Nera tried to ignore them. She spoke only to Farij and had no desire to meet the other three. The sooner they left, the better. "We've caught a magician. He's been running a stage show in Klubridge for many years, and he is connected to the rebels."

Farij touched a fingertip to his lips. "Hiding in plain sight. How extraordinary."

"Is it Akithar?" the woman asked.

Nera's eye twitched, but she forced herself to acknowledge the other mage. "It is."

"I saw his performance six years ago. He was impressive."

"You saw no indication then that he was a true mage?"

The woman gave Nera a smile that either was endearing or mocking, but Nera was uncertain which. "If I had, he would not have been much of a performer, would he?"

Nera turned back to Farij. "We have scheduled the silencing for tomorrow at midday. It's being done publicly, and we have flyers going up in the city now. You should expect an audience. Do you need anything before then?"

"Food will be enough for now. But then there will be the matter of certain accommodations when we return home."

Nera frowned. Herons always were angling to get something extra whenever their skills were needed. "I will have you fed, but you'd be wise not to press me."

Farij gave her a wan smile. "You are aware that a silencing is a significant undertaking, no? It requires a massive amount of our combined willpower to be channeled in just the right way."

"I am aware."

"Just so. Any lack of concentration or distraction that we might suffer could result in unpredictable and disastrous consequences."

Nera's lip curled into a sneer. Herons were agents of the Empire, but they still lived as prisoners, albeit among luxury. Occasionally they needed reminding of their stations. "I hope that wasn't a threat, Farij."

He touched his chest, his fingers splayed, and gasped as though stung. "Of course not, Commander."

"I'm glad. It would be a pity to have to call a second set of Herons to Klubridge in order to have the four of you silenced alongside Akithar. Or maybe I'd just have you made into halflocks. Which would you prefer?"

Farij tilted his head and closed his eyes in acceptance. "I believe food will suffice. Thank you, Commander."

"Tomorrow, then."

Nera pointedly avoided interacting with the Herons after that first and only required meeting. She intended to see them perform the rites and leave straight away. She still needed the location of the Stormbreak Sanctuary, so there was more to do in Klubridge after the silencing. However, getting Akithar dealt with would put her one more step toward being finished with this city. She had no contact with Farij and the others the remainder of that day and night, and she presumed they were prepared for the silencing when she arose the following morning.

She'd be glad not to see Klubridge again for a time, and she'd be especially glad not to have to climb that cursed tower ever again. Wil and Jona accompanied her on that final ascent to collect the prisoner. The thirty guards she'd ordered from the city watch were on post in the tower even now, but it always was better to have cohorts you knew and trusted when dealing with mages.

Morcan had arrived ahead of them and was wrangling his three halflocks when Nera and the other two Kites reached the top of the tower and passed through the doorway. The room was unchanged from the other night, when Nera had interviewed Akithar, and Akithar himself sat on that same chair where she'd left him. Had he even moved in all that time? She knew he must have, but her imagination couldn't stop spinning macabre possibilities about the magician.

"We're ready when you are, Commander," Morcan said, and the strange halflock woman with the egg head peered around his shoulder.

Nera nodded and walked to stand in front of Akithar. He leaned back in his chair and crossed his leg. His air of nonchalance infuriated her, but she kept her outward calm. "Good morning, Akithar."

"Today's the day?" He gave her a smile, but it was a tight one. Good. He had nerves after all.

"Today is the day." Nera stared down at him and forced herself to meet his eyes. Looking into a fully powered mage's eyes was a risk, but with the halflocks in the room, there wasn't much he could do. "This is your last chance to unburden yourself. Tell me what you know about the rebels' plans, and things will go easier for you."

"You won't silence me then?"

Nera snorted. He'd figured out his punishment, then. "Don't misunderstand your situation. You still will be losing your powers, but there are many paths you could take after that. I can guarantee that some are more fraught than others."

He clasped his hands in his lap and pressed his thumbs together. "That is a generous offer, but I'm afraid I'll have to decline."

"It's no matter," she said. "We'll pry your secrets out of your friends instead."

His eyes widened for a fraction of a second, but his face remained otherwise impassive. He still worried for his friends. It was good to know weaknesses, and she'd be sure to exploit that one.

Jona was past them, near the window, when she held something up. "Commander, look at this."

It was a knife of some sort. As Nera came closer, she realized it was a shard of glass with a fabric wrapped hilt. She spun, and her eyes searched the room for a broken mirror or any other source of the glass, but there was nothing. The single barred window looking out from the tower had no glass. "Where did you find that?"

Jona gestured to a low table to the right of the window. "It was just lying there."

"Explain this," Nera commanded.

Akithar turned in his chair and raised his arms in an open-handed shrug. "It's not mine."

She looked from him back to the rudimentary knife. "Is that blood?"

Jona held it up to the window and let sunlight shine through it. "Looks like." She paused and peered at the knife again, then turned her head quickly toward Akithar.

"What is it?" Nera asked.

Jona blinked but shook her head. She held the knife in her left hand and clasped her right hand into a loose fist, moving to hold it behind her back. "Nothing. I was just thinking. Want me to hold onto this?"

"Keep it until after the silencing. Once we're done, we'll decide what to do with it." She cut her eyes to Akithar. "And with him."

The procession at noon marched out the front of the castle and across the bridge. Nera walked at the front, Lucian beside her. Tomos and Wil walked abreast behind them, followed by Farij and the younger mage who had been reading in the salon the previous night. Following close behind them came Akithar, bound with chains securing his hands and feet, guided between Morcan and Jona. The other two Herons came next, forming a sort of magical cage around the condemned man. As Nera understood it, they always enclosed a convicted mage to prevent them from using their magics. She wasn't sure whether the Herons were actively using their own magic to suppress Akithar's or simply were ready to act if he began casting spells. Either way, having that much magical ability at her back failed to reassure her at all.

Trailing behind the Herons came Vam, Shoy, and Asil, with the Heron guards following them. The Heron guards had no magic of their own, of course, but, like the Kites, they were trained in slaying mages. Their regulations were secret, but Nera had heard that the black armor they wore held some sort of enchantments against magical attacks. Having mages enchant armor to make it easier to kill mages had a sort of circular entropy that both satisfied and disturbed Nera. The Herons were there to monitor Akithar, while their guards were prepared to slaughter all four of the Herons at the first sign of their rebellion. In the history of their order, there had been only one instance of Herons turning on their masters. While rebellion from Farij and his cohorts was unlikely, having the mages outnumbered by mage killers did make this spectacle more tolerable.

They made a grand presentation of strength, stomping out the front of the castle and into the roadway, which the city watch had blocked for that purpose. As was customary, they had distributed leaflets throughout the city to bring a crowd to witness the fate of Akithar. Everyone knew that the High Lord suffered no mages to live freely, but occasionally it was necessary to remind them with shows of conviction like this one. The people had gathered at the barricades, but the crowd was less eager than Nera had expected. She'd hosted silencings in smaller cities and with far less notable mages being silenced that had rendered more enthusiasm than she saw here. These faces did not look cowed or excited. They were hateful and defiant, not toward the shackled magician but toward the Kites.

"This is less fanfare than I anticipated," she said to Lucian.

He walked a few paces beside her before responding. "He's a celebrity to them. Maybe the people of Klubridge have forgotten their taste for justice."

"We'll have to remind them."

The walk was a short one to the square that had been designated for the ceremony. It was a broad lane, more rectangular than square in truth, paved with flat stones and with a raised dais in the center. Three stone steps led up all four sides of the square platform, and iron rings had been implanted into the top of it. It usually served as a stage for city meetings and announcements, but it was no stranger to public punishments.

The crowd in the square was more enthusiastic than the one in the surrounding streets. Akithar's admirers wanted a look at the man and his captors but had no interest in seeing him publicly destroyed. When the procession entered the square, jeers went up from the crowd that encircled the dais.

"That's more like it," Lucian murmured to Nera, but she was unsure whether the jeers were directed at the prisoner or at his jailers.

Bonner had stationed constables at the perimeter of the square, watching over the five streets that intersected into it. If the citizens that had shown up proved unruly, the guards should have no trouble getting them in hand and dispersing the mob. The more Nera watched the onlookers, the more she worried about something exactly like that happening.

She leaned toward Lucian again as they crossed the plaza. "We need to get this finished quickly."

He stepped aside with her when they reached the base of the platform. Farij had Akithar by the arm and pulled him up the steps to the center of the stage. The other three mages followed, each taking a position next to one of the rings in the ground. The Heron guards moved alongside them and began securing into the mounted rings the chains that already bound Akithar.

Nera watched the magician accept his fate. He stood at the middle of the guards and mages, not quite defiant, but neither was he afraid. He looked as if everything was unfolding exactly as he had expected. That was not how this was supposed to work.

"Something isn't right," she whispered to Lucian.

"What is it?"

"Akithar. He's up to something."

He looked past her toward the mage and huffed a low laugh. "You worry too much. This is what you've been working toward. Look at this audience."

It was true. She'd been hunting him and waiting for the right time to bring him down, and now was her moment. She would rob him of the obscenity that was his talent, and he'd be left hollow like every other silenced mage. She had hoped that the experience would leave him humbled and willing to tell all his secrets, but now she worried. Did the magician have one more trick?

"Check the perimeter," she said. "Keep an eye out for anything suspicious."

"The watch is already on that."

"I don't know them. I do know you." She put a hand on his arm. "Go, just to set my mind at ease."

"Of course." He motioned for Jona to follow him, and they disappeared beyond the crowd toward the eastern entrance to the square.

"We are prepared, Commander. Did you wish to say some words before we begin?"

Farij was looking down at her from the dais, and she hesitated. Part of her wanted to tell him to get on with it, but she knew haste would make the silencing lose its impact on the observers. She nodded to him and took the first step up to the platform. Her knees wobbled, and her face flushed. Not now, damn it.

One prisoner. Two Kites patrolling the perimeter. Three steps up to the stage. Four Herons surrounding Akithar. Five—

She forced herself up to the platform and walked to the center. Akithar nodded to her as she passed, but she ignored him and turned her back on him to face the audience. The rumbling murmur died when she raised her arms.

"Citizens of Klubridge," she began, and her voice echoed back to her from the far end of the plaza. "Before you stands a traitor. This man has acted against your Empire and against your High Lord. He has used your city and his position in it to harbor and aid rebels, and he is complicit in plans to damage your very way of life." She let the listeners receive her words. They stared back at her, some with blank expressions, others with vicious and eager malice for the doomed wizard.

"This man, who has masqueraded as a stage magician in your city for more than a decade, has hidden his true abilities from you. He used you and your patronage at his theater to hide his true nature." She jabbed a finger at Akithar. "This man is a mage, and under the instilled codes of the High Lord Peregrine's Imperial rule, today he will be silenced."

The crowd roared its approval. These were her people. Imperial loyalists, she hoped, but she knew many of them just wanted to see what a powerless mage looked like. She'd show them. Her confidence returning, Nera spared a glance back toward her prisoner.

Akithar did not look afraid. He met her gaze, and the corner of his mouth quirked up into a brief smirk. The public ceremony had been a mistake. Under ordinary circumstances, Nera would have allowed the accused an opportunity to speak before the ritual began. Now, however, she only wanted for it to be over. She wanted to be out of this whole city. They could interrogate Akithar on the road.

She looked to her right, to Farij. "Do it."

Nera backed down the steps to the left and watched the four Herons clap their hands together in unison. They stood in front of, behind, and to either side of Akithar, and they bowed their heads toward him as one. He stood in the middle of them, chained to the stage, and only now did he look unsure. Nera watched his face, waiting for the moment of terror when he felt his connection to magic snap. His eyes were wider than they had been, and his lower lip trembled.

Farij raised his hands toward Akithar and shouted, "Khagan reosi!" The other three followed him in the chant. Again and again they repeated the phrase. Nera didn't speak Aevash and had no idea what they were saying. She'd seen the ritual performed a handful of times in the past, though, and this is how it always went. Soon they would be past the point of no return, and Akithar's capacity for using magic would be erased. The realization would hit him, and he would despair. It's how it always happened. The magic left, and with it went all hope.

But that's not how this one happened.

The chanting increased in volume and tempo, and the Herons' hands spread wide above their heads and toward Akithar. The look of realization never came, but in its place came a shriek of agony. Nera wasn't even sure that it had come from Akithar until she saw his hands trying to reach upwards. Shackled to the ground, he couldn't raise them past his waist. Veins stood out in his temples, and his eyes squeezed tight, his mouth drawn into a grimace of pain. What was this?

He stumbled and fell to one knee.

"You're killing him!" someone in the crowd shouted, and Nera wasn't sure that they were wrong.

The chanting continued, but Farij looked to his side at Nera, the concern clear on his face. This was not how a silencing happened.

Nera scanned the crowd and looked beyond them. Where was Lucian? She felt the panic rising in her chest, but there was no time to quell it with counting. Akithar screamed again, and this time he fully collapsed onto the ground. He lay on his stomach, his arms and legs splayed out to the sides where they were secured to the iron rings.

Farij lowered his hands and yelled, "Halt!" The chanting stopped with a suddenness that jarred the entire plaza. Nera heard the crowd mumbling, and all eyes were on the prone form before them. As she watched, she realized that dark smoke was drifting up from his body, buoying glittering sparks that snapped purple and blue as they ascended.

She hurried up the steps to Farij. "Is he dead?"

The old wizard shook his head but did not take his eyes off Akithar's crumpled form. "No, he still lives, but barely."

"Is it finished? Did you complete the silencing?"

"That's just it. There was nothing to silence." He looked from Akithar to Nera. "This man is no mage."

Before Nera could respond, the western entrance to the plaza exploded.

CHAPTER 38

Gieck cut a brisk path through the crowd. They were grumbling among themselves, and several of them even sneered at him as he passed. On a better day he'd make them regret that, but there was no time now. He glanced behind to see Jona lagging, so he stepped back and grabbed her elbow. "Faster. Come on."

"What is this?" She stumbled at first but regained her footing and kept up with him to the edge of the crowd and then out to the border of the plaza.

The unrest had touched the whole city by now, and not even the city center was immune. A curio shop that had previously sold knick-knacks to those with more money than discretion now was a yawning and empty storefront. The windows hadn't been broken out, likely because of its nearness to the Henburn Estate, but it was only a matter of time before the looters got the guts to raid this district. Gieck was counting on that and hoping to give them a nudge. He tried the door to the shop and found it open, so he pushed through and pulled Jona in behind him.

"Gieck, what are you doing?"

Before answering, he strode through the store and checked the back room. Empty. Stairs led up to a second floor, but he knew that would be empty as well. Whoever ran this place was long gone, a victim of Klubridge's rapidly tanking economy.

Outside, Nera began speaking to the crowd. He couldn't make out what she was saying, but it would be something full of platitudes and empty threats. That's how her speeches to the common folk always went. She thought they gave a damn about the Empire and suppressing magic and all that business, when they really only cared about where their next meal would come from and whether their family would make it home safely that night.

Jona was in the back of the store now and stared at Gieck, waiting for an answer. He shoved a hand into his uniform pouch and slid a thick metal cylinder out. "Do you know what this is?"

She reached for it, but he pulled his hand back. "Careful. It's explosive."

"Is that haranium? How did you get that?"

"The librarian knew about a few message tubes that might have arrived at the library but hadn't yet been processed into the vault, after Akithar robbed it. The halflock pulled it out of her head."

"You took that from the library? Does Mollor know?"

"Of course she doesn't." He closed his hand over the tube and slid it back into his waist pouch. He pointed to the front of the store. "The crowd out there is ready. They're looking for an excuse to riot."

"And you're going to give it to them?"

"You have to be ready. When the chaos starts, we head straight for Mollor. Pretend we're getting her out of harm's way."

"That's when we kill her?"

"That's when we kill her."

Jona frowned. "Are you just going to lob that thing into the crowd?"

"Do you have a better idea?"

"You'll kill a lot of innocent people that way."

Gieck sniffed. "Is there a better way to make people panic than to make them fear for their lives?"

She started to answer, but he held up his hand. "No time for that.

She's giving her speech now, and they'll silence Akithar immediately after that. We have to do this before that's done. Are you ready?"

Jona chewed at her lower lip and glanced back toward the front of the store but finally nodded. Gieck started past her, but she caught his arm. "Wait," she said. "Wouldn't it be better to throw that out from the second floor?"

She was right. There'd be less chance of his being spotted if he threw it from above. He grunted and took the stairs up two at a time. Jona was right behind him.

The stairs ended at a small landing, and there was a window overlooking the square. One quick pitch, and the crowd would go wild. They'd have to be fast getting down the stairs, but they could make it work. He sat the cylinder on the windowsill and reached to unlatch the window as Jona leaned on the wall behind him.

"I saw you that night."

"What night?" The latch was jammed, and he had to jiggle it. It finally slid.

"The other night, when you came to my room. I saw you earlier that night."

He scowled over his shoulder. "What are you talking about? Help me with this window."

"That smell you asked me about? It was moat water, you stupid ass."

Gieck heard the zip an instant before the cable caught around his neck. He tried to turn, but Jona had it too tight. She spun around with her back to him and leaned forward, dragging his weight up onto her back.

Jona grunted with the effort and yanked hard, pulling him up and off his feet by the throat. Gieck's hands grabbed at the cable and strained back, trying to catch her hands, anything he could grab, but she was out of reach.

"You sadistic bastard," she grunted and heaved with her shoulder. The cable cut into his skin, and his scrambling fingers could get no purchase on it, no way to give himself enough slack to breathe.

Gieck felt his pulse pounding in his neck, then up into his head, and his vision retreated at the edges. His head felt bloated and heavy, like it was swelling in a vise. Jona grunted again and gave him another hard pull, and he heard more than felt the skin tear. Not here, not by her hands. Not by this traitor. He tried to spin around to face her, but the strength was leaving his limbs, and she moved with him, turning as he did, always leaning forward and pulling.

She had him cross-ways in the hallway now, and when she gave another hard pull, his feet came off the floor again. He rocked back with the momentum and planted his boots on the wall in front of him. With the last strength he could muster, Gieck shoved his legs out, pushing off the wall.

Jona cried out in surprise and tumbled forward. Gieck's teeth clacked together from the impact of Jona's face hitting the wall behind him. She went down, and he fell on top of her, his back against hers. At last, the cable went slack, and he gasped a jagged, wheezing breath.

Gieck slipped his fingers between the cable and his throat and pulled hard, slipping the whole thing off his neck. He rolled to the side, landing on his hands and knees on the floor beside her. Jona shook her head, dazed, and he saw blood on her upper lip. More where that came from.

He lurched toward her, but she was faster. Jona rolled to the side and skittered back, away from him, trying to get to her feet.

Gieck hissed at her, and his voice was little more than a hoarse whisper. "I trusted you."

"You're insane," she spat back at him. "Mollor can't see it, but I do. We all do."

He growled and lunged, springing at her and knocking her to the side, into the wall again. He reached for his sword, but there was no room to draw it. Jona kicked at him and missed, and he pushed forward, driving her back onto the floor. She rolled with his momentum, and they crashed through the banister at the top of the landing. Gieck hit the stairs first, on his back, but Jona was right there on top of him, punching and kicking as they tumbled down in a rolling mass of limbs.

Jona came out on bottom, with Gieck straddling her. He reared back and reached for his dagger. It was halfway out of the sheath when her foot made contact with his hand. He felt bones break, and the knife flew free from his grasp, spinning across the floor into the darkness of the abandoned shop.

Jona grabbed at her wrist, and Gieck saw his own cabler there, strapped in place and bulky on her slender arm. Before he could react, she unreeled the wire and had it looped around his neck again. She pulled the ends hard, and the cable sank back into the raw, bleeding tracks it had already created in his flesh. She yanked him down on top of her and raised her head to meet his. Her forehead slammed against his nose, and his vision darkened again with the crack. His blood sprayed Jona's face, but she didn't relent. She pulled him down harder, her hands out to the sides, strangling the life out of him.

He fell forward and caught his weight on his hands, beside her. His face was inches from hers, almost like she was pulling him in for a kiss. The more he tried to resist, the more the cable tightened. His right hand, useless and broken, pawed at his belt, and his dagger was gone anyway. He tried to curse her, but nothing would come out, and no air would go in. Gieck dropped his weight onto his injured right hand and tried to reach for his sword again with the left.

Their bodies tangled together, and he couldn't find his weapon. He'd lost it somewhere, probably on the stairs. His hand tore through fabric, and he realized it was Jona's waist pouch, not his own. No time. Something, anything.

His fingers closed around a hard, flat shape, and he ripped it free from the pouch. Without knowing what he was holding, he slammed his hand at Jona's head. She flinched away at the last second, and Gieck saw her eyes widen as the shard of glass disappeared into her neck.

The end of the cable slipped from Jona's fingers as she grabbed at her throat, and Gieck dragged himself off of her, free once more. He fell onto his back next to her and watched the blood pouring between her frantic fingers. Her mouth opened and closed in dumb appeals, and she tried to sit up. He shoved her back down and grabbed her left hand away from the wound. The glass bobbed weakly with her pulse, and her right hand was feeble now, trying to reach the cut but failing.

Gieck unstrapped the leather bracelet from her arm. "That's mine," he hissed, and shoved her hand back down at her.

Outside, the plaza rocked with an explosion.

A pak strained to hold up the weight of the device. They had loaded it onto a wheelbarrow and pushed that down back alleys and side streets most of the way to the center of Klubridge, but as they neared the castle, he decided it was time to prepare. That was when Reykas had helped load the box onto Apak's chest, held in place by thick leather straps that went around the backs of his shoulders. It was fortunate that Reykas seemed to have regained his strength that day. Otherwise, this equipping might have been an insurmountable task. The straps helped a bit, but it still was an onerous thing to lug around. Given another week, he could have figured out a better system for distributing the weight. But another week was not on offer, and he would make the best of what he had.

Samira stopped them one block away from the city square. "Does everyone know the plan? Any last questions?"

"Let's not throw around words like 'last,'" Lizandra said and glanced at Reykas.

Samira had a tense smile for her but said, "We're going to be okay. We're going to get Caius and Aquin, and we're all coming back to the ship. Then we're leaving this place for good."

"Are you certain that you can do this on your own?" Apak asked. "We three will be together in the square, but you will be alone."

"It'll be easier that way. I'm going to be sneaking, and your part isn't really in that department. The louder you are, the better for me."

"I anticipate unprecedented volumes," Apak said. He had not been able to test this contraption and had finished constructing it only yesterday. He hoped that it would not blow up in his hands, but if it did, he felt certain his departure would be momentous.

Samira put her hand on his shoulder and squeezed, and then she did the same for Lizandra and finally Reykas. "Be careful," she said. "Don't take unnecessary risks. Just get Caius and get out of there."

Reykas put his hand over hers on his arm. "And the same to you for Aquin. Be fast, and be careful."

Samira nodded and hesitated. She looked as if she wanted to say more, but she smiled at her friends and disappeared around the corner in a fast walk.

"Our turn," Lizandra said.

Apak pushed a lever on the side of the big box on his chest, and the whole frame lurched and sizzled.

Lizandra took a step back. "Is it supposed to do that?"

"Absolutely. I have opened the internal bay and released the extracted haranium to mix with a pre-catalyst compound."

"Is that safe?"

Apak laughed hard enough to shake the whole rig. "Not at all!"

Reykas peeked around the corner. "They're in the square now. I see Kites. I think I may see Caius as well."

Apak readjusted the straps on his shoulders. "Then it is time to begin."

"Remember what Samira said, Apak. Be careful. Do not take unnecessary risks."

"I heard her. We all know what must be done."

"I am serious, my friend. Our intention is to rescue our friends and escape, not to extend a fight we cannot win. Use your machine as a diversion. Try to confuse the guards. Do not engage them in battle. You're not mobile enough to escape when you're wearing that box."

"I am quite serious, as well. I know what to do, and it is time that we moved."

Lizandra touched his cheek. "See you soon."

"And you."

Lizandra led the way toward the square, and Reykas followed with one stern glance back at Apak.

Apak's role was to create confusion and to draw attention to everything other than Lizandra and Reykas as they smuggled Caius out of the square. He had agreed not to wade into any unnecessary battles, but his promise to Oreth and to himself hung heavily in his mind. He would provide his diversions, and he would attack no one unnecessarily, but the Scarlet Kites had necessitated recompense.

Apak counted thirty seconds to allow his friends enough time to move into position, and he was ready. He flipped the switch on the left side of the box to prime the ignition mechanism, and the rig vibrated softly against his chest. The moment had arrived. He stepped around the corner and grasped the handles he had installed on both sides of the device. One deep breath, he pointed the outward facing end of the box in the direction of the square, and he closed his eyes. He pulled back on the handles.

Nothing.

This could not be. He had accounted for every possibility and had ensured that the math was correct. What was he forgetting?

Apak inventoried the controls on the outside of the box as he walked up the street, heading for the southwest entrance to the square. The haranium was mixed, the solution was primed for ignition, and the safety mechanism was disengaged. What else was there?

"Hold up there!"

Apak halted in the street and looked up from the machine to see four city watch guards ahead of him.

"What do you have there?" The nearest one was approaching at a slow walk, his hand on the hilt of his saber.

Apak frowned down at the box and pulled at the handles again, but the machine remained silent. One more tug, and realization dawned on him. Of course! How could he have been so careless?

"Put that down," the guard said. He was less than ten feet away now and had his blade half drawn.

The solution was primed, and the primary safety mechanism was disengaged, but the dampener he had installed to regulate the frequency of the audio when the device was being used as an excavator still was very much in place and activated. With a self-admonishing cluck of his tongue, Apak found the dampener's dial with his right hand and twisted it as far clockwise as he could turn it. That should be everything, yes?

He looked back up to see that the guards were but a few paces away. These were city watch, not Kites. He had a quarrel with them, yes, but he had no desire to kill them. Apak stepped to the right and angled the machine away from the guards and toward the entrance to the square. He was sure that everything was correct now, but he still felt relief when he pulled the handles one more time and felt the box jolt to life.

The blast was heavier than he had expected, but the internal regulators succeeded in reducing the kickback. Apak had to take a half step back to stabilize himself, but the box held steady.

The pyramid of light the device emitted hummed with a shrill keening, and it shot out from the box in a wider swathe than Apak had estimated. The front guard disappeared in a flash of white that peeled the paving stones out of the street and melted the windows in the shops on both sides. Two of the other guards were turning to run when the blast caught them, vaporizing them where they stood before it obliterated the gate they were guarding. Apak thought the final guard escaped into the plaza, but he could not be certain. The archway that had spanned that street for centuries exploded into a rain of stone, and thunder cracked throughout Klubridge.

Apak loosened his grip, and the whine dropped to a dormant crackle as the silvery light vanished. He wiped at his forehead, smearing a dot of soot down to his cheek. He stared at the space where the three constables had stood only an instant before, and his heart thudded with a mixture of dread and something else. Could it be excitement? Was that what this was?

It was fortunate that the initial shot had caught no citizens in its arc. Now that he knew the spread of the blast area, he should be able to avoid harming any of the ones already in the square, but they would be best served to flee. Apak strode through the rubble and into the plaza, and he stopped once more, frozen in place by something even more disturbing than the four guards he had obliterated.

High above the central dais, floating in the sky above the crowd, dark tendrils of smoke were pulling upwards and swirling together, forming into a dense mass, the edges sparkling purple and blue. Apak had heard stories about such things but had never witnessed them or even suspected they could be true. "By Ikarna," he whispered. What had they done? His eyes followed the trail of smoke down to the gathered crowd of city officials beneath the magical vortex. There, scattered among them, stood the Scarlet Kites.

The spectacle in the sky all but forgotten, Apak hefted his machine once more and took another step into the plaza. Some of the crimson villains had spotted him, and he had promises to keep.

T he blast from the plaza had bought Samira all the distraction she needed to slip into the castle unobserved. She found the entry emptied of the three guards she'd seen running out in response to the explosion, and she made a quick decision to head through the left door. As soon as she passed through the entrance, she froze in place. A pair of constables was bickering in the hallway, not ten feet in front of her.

The nearest was a slender woman with her head wrapped with a dark gray scarf that matched her uniform. "Don't be ridiculous, Lang. That was an explosion. It has to be the rebels."

An older man, his belly pushing his uniform jacket out over his belt, shook his head. "We have orders to stay inside during the ceremony. I've got no desire to run afoul of the Kites just before they're finally done with this town."

Samira slipped to her right and tucked herself into a narrow alcove beside a potted fern. It brushed her face as she slid past it, and she realized it was artificial, some sort of rubbery fabric instead of true fronds. She barely had time to settle into her hiding place when the castle shook with the force of a second explosion, this one closer than the last. The officers' argument ended with that, and Samira held her breath as the woman took the corner past her at a sprint, headed for the entryway. The older guard, Lang, trundled after her, swearing under his breath.

Once both guards were out of her sight, Samira poked her head out of the alcove and took a quick survey of the hallway. Empty. She slid back out, being careful not to dislodge the fake plant from its stand. The wall on the left had small, slotted windows that looked out across the moat, toward the city square. Samira risked a quick look through it and saw smoke rising from behind the buildings just opposite the castle. She spared a second to hope Apak's devotion to Ikarna would come back to him tenfold that day, but she knew she had to hurry.

Across from the windows were three closed doors, none with any sign of what might be behind it. In her haste to rescue Aquin, Samira knew she had no idea how the building would be laid out, but until now she hadn't considered what it would be like to roam the hallways, never knowing when she'd turn a corner and run into the end of a guard's blade.

She pressed her ear to the first door and heard nothing. She held her breath again and pulled the door open. An empty meeting chamber. That's probably what the other two rooms were, as well. They wouldn't have prisoners this close to the entrance, anyway. She needed to delve deeper, perhaps even literally, if this place had a dungeon.

The hallway ended with a fork, and Samira took the turn to the right, angling her closer to the center of the building. This hallway was identical to the previous one, but it had doors on both sides instead of windows. Too many choices, too many guards, and not enough time. She looked from one door to the next, wishing that she had some sort of map like they'd gotten for the library job, but it was too late for that.

The door immediately to her right swung inward, and Samira flinched to the left. In the open doorway stood a short woman with an unusually round head and bulbous eyes that rolled toward Samira with grotesque slowness. The woman's eyebrows raised, and she opened her mouth to shout. Samira rushed her, pushing the woman back into the side room. It was a small study, the walls lined with mahogany shelves full of dusty books. Samira's momentum carried them all the way to the opposite wall, and she shoved the smaller woman against the bookshelf and clapped her hand over the woman's mouth. She held her in place with her forearm across the woman's chest.

"No screaming," Samira whispered and glared at the woman. The woman nodded back, her huge eyes flicking between Samira and the open door behind her. "Are you going to be good?" She nodded again, so Samira removed her hand from the woman's face. "What's your name?"

The woman licked her lips, and her mouth trembled, but then her eyes lit with newfound energy. "Name, same, game, blame. Magra they call me, see, tea?"

Samira realized she was a halflock, one of those poor wretches the Empire had kidnapped and mutilated. She'd seen them before and knew that half the time they ended up like Magra, sometimes even worse. "I'm not going to hurt you," Samira said. "Are you being kept here against your will?"

Magra pursed her lips and blew a stream of air out from her puffed cheeks. "Nope, fine here, no no."

Samira took her arm away from Magra's chest. This poor woman would not hurt her or anyone else. "I'm here to rescue my friend. If you can help me find her, you can come with me when I leave."

The smaller woman halted her air blowing and shut her mouth. Her head cocked to the side, and she stared at Samira with suspicion. "Who are you?"

"My name is Samira. I'm not your enemy. I can help you be free. Can you help me?"

Magra's round eyes narrowed, and she peered past Samira again, toward the door. She looked back and forth between the exit and Samira twice more before grabbing Samira by the hand. Gone were the vacant stare and ridiculously singsong voice, replaced by cunning determination. "We have to be fast. The guards will not be gone long."

Samira blinked at her. "That was an act?"

Magra turned her head and showed the shaved patch at the back, bordered by an angry horseshoe shaped scar. "We all find ways to survive, don't we? I have my deceptions, and you have yours." Samira balked and didn't have a chance to respond before the little woman pulled her toward the door. She looked back. "Your friend. A pretty woman? Dark-skinned, came from Acleau?"

"That's her!"

"I know where she is. Follow me, and be quiet."

They were back in the hall just as another blast sounded in what Samira assumed was the direction of the plaza. Following on its heels came a gurgling roar unlike anything she'd ever heard. Samira stumbled to look back down the hall and toward the windows, but Magra pulled her by the wrist. "Worry about that later. Come." Samira responded with a nervous nod and stayed close behind the shorter woman. They went through the keep at a fast clip, halting only at intersections where Magra would check for guards before leading them onward. At last they reached a door that looked heavier than the others. It was darker wood and had metal bars reinforcing it from this side.

"She's in there. Chained, the last I saw her."

"Thank you, Magra."

"Don't thank me until we're out of here. Go now, hurry. I'll keep watch."

Samira feared that the door would be locked, but it yielded to a firm push, and she was through to a small vestibule with a matching door in the left wall. That one was unlocked as well, and she gasped as she pushed into that last room.

This was unquestionably a cell used for interrogation. The walls were bare stone, matching the floor and ceiling. A hanging fixture burned with gaslight above the solitary table, and a second gas lantern lit the room from the wall on the right. In the center of the room, at that lone table, sat Aquin, slumped and unconscious. Her hair splayed across the surface so that it obscured her face, but Samira saw the shackles right away. Her legs were bound, and a chain ran from between her ankles up through the table, no doubt binding her hands.

"Aquin!" Samira rushed to her and brushed her hair back from her face.

Her eyes fluttered and opened, but she didn't raise her head from the table. "You came," she whispered. Her voice was distant and hoarse.

"What have they done to you?" Angry tears burned Samira's eyes, but she didn't let them fall. "How long have you been here?"

"I don't know. Too long." She sat up and winced as her spine straightened. Her face looked gaunt, her eyes sunken.

Samira knelt beside her and cupped her face, kissing her forehead, her cheek, her mouth. "I should have found you sooner."

Aquin managed a weak smile. "On that, we agree." The smile vanished then, and she looked at Samira with pained eyes. "One of the Kites hurt me. His name is Gieck. He made me talk, Samira. I'm so sorry. I was so afraid."

"It's okay. You're okay now."

"No, it's not okay. I betrayed you. All of you. I told him Caius is a mage."

Samira exhaled, almost a laugh, and touched Aquin's face again. "It's okay," she said again. "You did nothing wrong. I should be apologizing to you."

Aquin was puzzled. "You?"

"I lied to you. I had to. I hadn't known you nearly as long as I've known Caius, and I had to keep his secret."

"What do you mean?"

"Caius is not a mage. He never was." Samira moved her hand down to the chain that bound Aquin's hands, and it dissolved into dust on the table. "I am."

"Where is he?" Lizandra asked. Reykas was wondering the same thing and had been watching the southwest gate but glanced at Lizandra. She was tense, ready for something to happen, but there was no sign of Apak. They perched side by side on top of the building next to the southeast entrance to the plaza. Three stories below them, mages had gathered around Caius and were chanting.

"What will happen if they finish the ritual?" she asked.

"If he were a mage, he would lose his abilities forever," Reykas said.

"But he's not. What will this do to him?"

Reykas didn't know, and he didn't want to know. The plan was for Apak to blow something up and create a panic so they could rescue Caius before the Herons completed their ritual. Apak had yet to appear, and the mages were increasing their chanting and the intensity of their gestures. Reykas felt the hairs raise on his forearms, pulled by a tingling crackle that originated at the dais. Those mages were channeling a massive amount of willpower into their casting. He had never seen that much magic concentrated in one place.

"I don't—" but Reykas' words were cut off by the scream. Caius flailed against his chains in agony and dropped to his knees.

Lizandra grabbed Reykas' arm. "We have to do something. They're killing him!"

Reykas counted the Imperials in the square below them. The Kite commander, Mollor, was down there, and he counted six other Scarlet Kites. There had been two others, one of them the brute who had killed Dorrin. They had wandered off from the others before the silencing began. Add to them the four Heron mages who presently were preoccupied with their spell, and then there were a handful of Heron guards, recognizable in their gleaming black armor. That wasn't even including the city watch guards that were posted at all the plaza entrances. The plaza was locked down tight, and there would be no getting to Caius alive unless Apak came through with his distraction. Even then, it was questionable.

Lizandra squeezed his arm tighter and pointed. Something black was peeling up and away from Caius' fallen form. It looked like smoke but was denser, thicker, than any smoke Reykas had seen. It drifted up from the dais, and Reykas realized he was watching a massive amount of magic coalesce into something of its own design after the intended spell had failed. Caius had fallen face first below the gathering cloud and still was bound to the four metal rings around him.

One of the Herons spoke to Mollor, and that's when Apak came through. He was too late for Caius, but his entrance was impressive, nonetheless.

Directly across the southern edge of the square from the building where Reykas and Lizandra waited, the opposite gate erupted inward, stone and bricks blasting into the courtyard. Shouts and screams came from the crowd as the debris pelted them, but none of it was big enough to cause actual harm. The same could not be said for the guards on that gate.

"Reykas, look!" Lizandra was pointing, but he'd already seen it. A constable staggered through the gaping hole where the gate had been. Half of his upper body was gone, and yet he walked. Two more steps, and he fell forward onto the pavement.

A shriek went up then, and the mass of onlookers roiled. Bodies pushed and pulled, rushing in all directions. And, out of the cloud of smoke and ash, stepped a squat form with a bizarre contraption strapped to his chest.

"There he is. It's time," Reykas said. He leaned forward to make his descent, but Lizandra held him back. Their eyes met.

"I love you," she said and grabbed the back of his head, pulling his face to hers for a kiss. The kiss was brief, and before Reykas could respond, Lizandra said, "I've got the two on the right. You get the two on the left." And then she was down, dropping over the edge of the building and into the crowd.

He leaned forward again and tried to find her in the mob, but she'd blended into the running legs and flailing arms. He'd have to find her on the ground, then. Reykas outstretched his hand and watched it for a brief moment. It was steady just now. It had better hold. He slid off the edge of the roof and landed in the plaza in a rolling crouch.

Down here, he couldn't see what was happening farther than a few feet on any side of him, but the darkening mass of energy still roiled overhead, sparks of light shooting out of it now and then. People ran, pushed, screamed, and fell. They jostled into him, but he pushed back, moving forward toward the dais where they had chained Caius. He shoved down the possibility that Caius already was dead, and he stalked ever onward, hopping over a fallen man and spinning to avoid being tripped by a woman running past with a cane.

Just then, another blast split the air, this time far to the right and behind Reykas. The ground shook, and the crowd cried out in unison. Most of them had been heading in that direction, but now they reversed and were pushing the other way. Apak had moved northeast, drawing attention to the opposite side of the plaza. That was good, but how long could he hold off without the Imperials bringing him down?

The stampede parted before Reykas, and the dais was seven feet ahead of him. Caius still lay motionless on the ground, and the four Herons had grouped around him, their backs to each other, their wide and frantic eyes trying to make sense of the chaos. Reykas tucked into a run and had just taken the first step up to the platform when Lizandra leaped out of the crowd on the opposite side. She spun in the air and extended a leg, catching one of the Herons in his bearded jaw with the side of her foot. He spun toward Reykas, his eyes dazed, and he went down.

Reykas didn't wait to see whether he would come back up but sprang toward the nearest mage, a woman with long black hair. She saw him coming at the last instant and tried to pull away, but he already was upon her, his shoulder ramming into her stomach. She grunted and flew backwards, cracking the back of her head into another Heron's face. That one looked to be the leader. He had led the silencing and even now was beginning a new chant.

Lizandra was behind the lead Heron now, and she swept her leg under his. The man's hands were glowing with a yellow energy that dissipated as he toppled to the hard ground. She was up again and gave him a hard kick to the head. He wouldn't be getting up anytime soon.

That left one more, a younger mage with honeyed hair that hung to his shoulders. He rounded the platform to keep both Lizandra and Reykas in his sight, and his hands moved in arcane motions, leaving faint sparks in their wake.

Reykas couldn't let him get a spell off. He swung hard with his right fist, and the Heron ducked the punch. His concentration broke long enough for him to lose the spell, and Reykas was upon him. The mage raised his arm to block another punch, and Reykas put his full weight behind the swing. He felt the pop an instant before hearing it, and the Heron crumpled, holding his broken wrist. He turned his pained and spiteful gaze toward Reykas, and his eyes glowed amber. The Heron opened his mouth, but Lizandra put him down with a kick to the back of the head before he could speak.

All four Herons were down, and Caius had yet to move. Lizandra took an unsure step toward him and looked to Reykas. But then her eyes were wide, focused past him, and she was reaching for him. "Look out!"

Reykas had heard the zipping sound before, that night on the roof of the dormitory. He'd seen the cable slip around Dorrin's throat and snap the life out of him. And now it whipped around Reykas' own neck and jerked him backwards. He flew off the platform backwards, grabbing for the cable, trying to unhook it, but it was too tight, too fast.

He hit the ground on his back, and his head bounced against the stones. Reykas tasted blood, and when his eyes opened, he saw the familiar face looming over him. Gieck, the Kite who had killed Dorrin, his own face now bloody and hideous, contorted with rage. Lizandra screamed, but she sounded far away, too far away to help.

Someone jostled Gieck from behind, and he staggered, looking behind him with malice. Another Kite was there, standing over Reykas. A younger man with olive skin and long dark hair pulled back from his face. Gieck jerked his hand back, and the cable slipped from around Reykas' neck. He snapped an order to the other Kite. "Vam, finish this one," and then he disappeared into the crowd.

Reykas could breathe again, but it came ragged. He tried to push himself up, away from the soldier, but his arms were weak. His hands shook and failed him. He slumped onto his back again. The Kite had a sword in his hand now, and he stood over Reykas. He held the blade uncertainly, hesitating before delivering the finishing blow. Reykas grunted in frustration and saw Lizandra coming down his side of the platform, running for him, but she would be too late.

His eyes rolled back up to the Kite, Vam, and focused past him. The black mass in the sky sparked blue again, and it no longer was a tangible object, but now had become a rip in the very air above them. A shape pushed out of the darkness, something big and sleek, black against the blue of the sky. The black shape turned, and Reykas recoiled back against the hard stones of the ground as an amber eye blinked open, split down the middle by a black slit of a pupil. Just as the beast lunged forward, launching the rest of its body into the plaza, the Kite finally gathered his nerve and stabbed downward with the point of his sword.

Reykas raised his weak left arm over his face in reflex, and his right hand came up, palm out to the Kite above him. The split second extended as Reykas concentrated all his will into that hand. He pushed, just like he'd done so many times before. Just like he did every night when Caius needed his props to disappear, but never where anyone else could see. Never in public.

As a third blast ripped apart another corner of the plaza, a purple shimmer rippled across the space between Reykas and the Kite, and the plunging sword disappeared, swallowed by thin air. Vam had only an instant of confusion before his sword reentered the world behind him and shot between his shoulder blades. Carried by Vam's own strength, the blade traveled through his back and out his chest, spearing and bisecting the bird emblazoned on the front of his uniform. The Kite staggered to the side and tumbled to the ground, felled by his own weapon. Reykas slumped back to the ground and, above the sound of his own breathing, he heard the distant beast scream in fury.

～

Lizzie knew Reykas was going to be okay as soon as he raised his hand. She didn't have to watch the rest of it to know how that would play out. He'd been transporting props with his magic every night for years. Never a weapon before now, but how mechanically different could that be?

She spun on her heel and leaped back up the steps toward Caius. Another explosion blew the front off a building ahead and to the right, and something black flew into the air with that one. A helmet. Apak was taking out the soldiers, not just creating a distraction. Surely he wouldn't let his anger turn against the citizens trapped in the plaza with them, but she'd have to worry about that later. For now, she was three steps away from her fallen friend, and one of the Herons was back on his feet. It was the last one, the younger man with the long hair. The one she'd kicked in the back of the head. His right hand hung limp on its broken wrist, but he raised the other and readied it for spellcasting. Lizzie braced for a fight, but he wasn't coming for her. The Heron stared past her, his mouth open, and she risked a glance over her shoulder. What she saw staggered her as well.

"It's a chamir," the Heron said, but she had already recognized it from the stories her parents had told her. The childish legends about bold heroes and the monsters they hunted. And now, here it was before her, this fictional creature made manifest.

"Did you make this? What is this?" She snapped her attention back to the Heron, but he was still watching the thing in the plaza. It was at least ten feet long, from head to tail, the entire thing covered in slick black fur except the head, which glimmered with dark scales.

"I... suppose we did," he said, and she watched his amazement turn to pride. "Have you ever seen such a creature?"

It was impossible to keep him and the chamir in her sight at the same time, so she turned her back on the creature and faced the Heron as the nearer threat. He looked from the monster back to her, and Lizzie stayed low and watched for the telltale signs of impending magic. His left hand was empty and open, and he could begin channeling something at any instant.

"I'm Edian." He smirked at her and winked. "Another time, another place?"

"Any time, any place, I'd still kick you in the head."

"I like you." He grinned, and his uninjured hand shot forward, pouring a stream of amber energy out of his palm.

Lizzie braced her feet in a quick crouch and shoved her hands forward. A flash of green split the gold, and Edian rocked back on his heels. He had to take a step backwards to stabilize himself but laughed as he did it. "How about that? Look at you with your secret magic. It feels good, doesn't it? Letting it go in the open like this? You don't get to do that, do you?"

Don't rise to his taunts. Watch his hand. Focus on his fingers. The chamir screamed somewhere behind her, and Lizzie flinched, but it was far enough away that she could keep her focus on this mage.

Edian cast at her again, searing the pavement beside her and then sweeping his hand in an arc. She leaped over the spell, cartwheeling into the air and spinning to throw green spears of light at Edian. He swatted them down with a casual wave of his other hand. Even with one broken hand, he still was too powerful. She couldn't take him straight ahead like this, not on her own. Where was Reykas?

She risked a quick look over her shoulder, and Reykas was gone. The Kite lay dead, blood pooling around his body, but Reykas wasn't there. The plaza was in widespread turmoil, with Apak's explosions routing the crowd at the gates and the monster still visible through the gaps in the mob. As Lizzie watched, she saw it raise its reptilian head and unhinge its massive jaw before plunging back into the people.

Lizzie looked back just in time to see another spear of light shooting at her. She spun to the side and somersaulted off the dais, away from Edian, but also away from Caius. She had to end this quickly.

She came up to her feet, off to Edian's left and far enough from the base of the platform's stairs that he couldn't reach her as easily. She feinted right, but before she could move back to the left, she heard that whirring sound again, the one from the dormitory and the one that had nearly killed Reykas only a moment before.

The end of the cable sped past Lizandra's face, and she saw it arcing back, moving as if time had slowed, ready to lasso her neck. In a flash of speed, she pivoted and swung her hand in front of her face. Her spell flicked to life for only an instant, long enough to slice through the cable and send its weighted end flying harmlessly into the crowd. She faced Gieck, and he stared at her, his face blank with shock. His left hand was extended, the leather bracelet showing, and the cable pulled back into it of its own accord. Without the weighted end to stop it, the whole cable reeled in and disappeared into its holster, never to spring forth again.

"You're finished," Lizzie said as she launched herself at him. Her hands glowed green, and the magic formed into the vague and flickering shapes of blades as she came down on him.

A foot away from Gieck, her trajectory halted, and she hung in midair, her legs dangling two feet above the ground. She blinked at him in confusion but couldn't move. Her arms and legs had frozen in position as she hung there before him. And then she understood.

Edian circled around her from behind, his left hand extended toward her, dim amber light radiating to envelop her. She tried to curse him, but her mouth wouldn't move. Only her eyes had freedom.

Gieck sneered at her and reached to his side. He felt for a weapon, but his sheath was empty. He patted it with a sigh and took a step forward, bringing his face an inch away from hers. "I want to gut you," he whispered at her. "I want to push my sword into your stomach and pull it all the way up and let you bleed out right here." He took a half step back. "But I appear to have lost my blade." His eyes shifted past her. "Asil, if you would?"

Lizzie didn't see Asil and didn't know the name, but she felt the blade. She couldn't move and hung in place, but she still felt the point pierce her back, and she felt every inch of the cold steel as it slid through her body and out the front, just to the right of her navel. And then the sword withdrew, pulling back through her body, and the amber light blinked away. Lizandra fell.

She landed on her side, and her shaking hands grabbed at her bleeding stomach. It was too much to stop, and she knew she was bleeding out her back as well. Another Kite, it must have been Asil, came around Lizandra, holding her sword down, the blade red with blood. Edian advanced on her as well. Lizzie's vision was going dark, and her hearing retreated to a dim echo, but she heard Edian ask, "Do you want to finish her, or should I?"

Asil didn't have time to answer. Something thick and heavy thudded into her chest, and it took a moment for Lizandra to realize it was the barbed end of a long, black tail. The barbs speared Asil, lifting her off the ground, and then she was away, flung spinning into the crowd. Before Edian could respond, his upper half disappeared into the gaping maw of the thing. It scooped him up, his legs dangling and still kicking, and it leaped away from the platform, back into the surging mob.

Lizzie coughed and felt blood on her lips. She tried to wipe at her face, but her arms were too heavy, and the world shrank away from her.

~

Moments earlier, Nera had learned that Akithar was no mage, and in that same instant, the plaza was under attack. The southwest gate had just exploded, and Nera stood motionless on the platform next to the man's body. She looked to Farij once more. "Are you positive?"

"There is no question. This man has no magic."

How had he deceived her? More to the point, why had he deceived her? Why would anyone willingly submit to the Scarlet Kites when they were not a mage? Those were questions for later. For now, something was ascending from Akithar's prone body, pulling sparkling darkness into the sky above him. "What is this?" she demanded and grabbed Farij by the collar. "What did you do?"

Farij shook his head. "This was unintentional, Commander. We performed the silencing as you instructed, but this man's body rejected the magic. When a casting fails, the willpower must be redirected somewhere, and that is what we are seeing here."

"What is it doing? What is it making?"

"I honestly have no idea."

Farij bowed his head in supplication. Nera looked from the assembling mass of magical energy toward the crowd, where she knew the rebels were likely to strike again. She chose the terror she knew how to address over the nebulous one that hung overhead. She jumped down from the dais to run into the crowd. The onlookers were panicking, and she had to shove the ones who were too afraid or confused to move out of the way. She screamed for them to let her through, but there was no reasoning with these people. They were going to get themselves killed, and it was her responsibility to ensure that didn't happen. The attack had come from the southwest corner, and that was where she headed.

One of the Heron guards was ahead and to the left. She caught his attention and motioned for him to follow. Three more gathered behind, and the crowd was more accommodating of the four armored soldiers than they had been of Nera alone. They'd nearly reached the edge of the crowd on that side when shouts arose behind them and to the right. Nera turned as another explosion took out the gate to the southeast.

"They're coming from both sides," the lead Heron guard yelled at Nera over the roar of the mob.

She looked to the southwest, where they were headed, and then back to the southeast, where smoke was just starting to rise. "Split your unit. Take two east, and give me one to go west."

He nodded and relayed the order to the other guards. Three disappeared east into the mob, and the fourth fell into step beside Nera. The guard reached to unsheathe her sword, but Nera stayed her hand. "Not yet. Not among all these people. Wait until we see the threat."

Nera led the way through the last of the teeming crowd, and the ruined gate was in view. The entire archway was gone, ripped and burned away by some immense force. The haranium. She remembered the devastation at the warehouse and spun, searching the chaos for the rebels. People were pushing, running, and falling in every direction. It was impossible to tell who might be an innocent and who might be an attacker.

She grabbed the guard's pauldron and was leaning in to give a new order when a high-pitched shriek cut through the roar of panicked voices. It was not quite organic, not quite metallic, and not like anything Nera ever had heard. She turned in the direction she thought it was coming from, and a bright cone of light arced out of the edge of the crowd. The front of a building bordering the plaza crumpled. The whole structure leaned in on itself and fell.

There! At the origin of the blast stood a small man, balding, wearing glasses. Nera squinted through the dust and smoke at what resembled an accordion on his chest. What was that thing?

A different sort of roar blasted through the square behind her. More attacks from that direction? She had to focus on what was before her.

The trio of Heron guards she had sent east had circled around by then and pinpointed the little man from the opposite side. They were running up on him from behind, but he saw them before they were even near him. He turned on the guards and grabbed at handles on the sides of the strange device, pointing the face of it in their direction.

It was some sort of weapon. Had they weaponized the haranium into portable cannons? What was this? But when he fired, Nera understood.

The man glared at the approaching guards, and a red glow filled his eyes, radiating out like twin beacons. His hands shimmered with the same energy, and it fed into his weapon like vapors flowing into a vent. He jerked back on the handles, and the light cone blasted out again, catching all three Heron guards in its beam.

"He's a mage," she shouted at the guard next to her. "His weapon is powered by magic. You're trained for this. Take him down."

"Alive?" the woman asked through the slot in her helmet.

"Just take him down."

Heron guards were trained to deal with mages at all costs, and Nera had to trust this one to do her duty. With the attacks coming from multiple directions, the rebels either hoped to trap everyone in the plaza or they were creating a distraction. They wouldn't win anything by killing a square full of citizens alongside Akithar himself, so it had to be a distraction. She shoved a screaming woman away and pushed her way back into the crowd, this time heading back toward the central dais.

There were mages among the rebels, but Akithar, ostensibly their leader, was not one. Nera couldn't help but pick at the mystery as she wove between squabbling men and sidestepped a child that had gotten loose in the crowd. The dais came into view between the jostling bodies, and she saw Farij before she saw the rest of it. He lay on his back, his head tilted back onto the steps leading up to the platform. Akithar still lay collapsed next to him, and Nera saw another of the Herons fallen on the other side of the stage.

She made it clear of the mob and ran toward the scene of the massacre, only to see that whatever had happened there still was ongoing. The younger Heron with long hair threw a swathe of magic at a young woman facing him on the stairs. When the woman leaped and spun out of the way, Nera recognized her immediately. It was the acrobat from the bank, the one who had been with Akithar when he killed the boy. She was gesturing now, and green light flew from her hands. Nera cursed that useless hag, Magra. This woman had been a mage all along. The halflock probably knew it, too.

The acrobat was out of range of the Heron now, and Nera reached for her sword as she tried to close the gap. But then, like a blessing, Lucian parted the crowd behind the young woman. Blood covered half his face, and his uniform hung in tatters, but he was upright and alive. He'd take the acrobat before she could cause any more trouble. Nera changed her approach so she could come from behind Lucian and support him in his attack.

He flicked his left arm out, and Nera stumbled to a halt. What she saw could not be. A cord whipped out from a leather bracelet on his arm, and he yanked back on it with surgical precision to make it loop around the acrobat's throat. It was the experienced maneuver of one well acquainted with a weapon. Of one who had killed with it before.

The girl was faster and cut his cable with her magic. She leaped for him, and Nera took a step forward, but the Heron had her now, and Asil was there as well, running past Nera and coming up behind the trapped acrobat. Lucian said something to the young woman and then spotted Nera beyond her. As Lucian walked toward Nera, Asil ran the mage through with her sword, and she fell to the ground.

"Commander," he called. "I was afraid for what might have happened to you in the chaos."

"What have you done?" Nera's eyes pleaded for some rational explanation, some answer other than the one she feared was true.

"I've killed a mage," he said. "Something we should have been doing since we arrived in this city."

Nera grabbed his wrist and pulled it up, letting his sleeve fall back to expose the cabler. "You lied to me. This is the weapon Akithar described. You killed that boy, Lucian."

He looked down at the bracelet, and his expression was unreadable. Would he lie again or try to deflect the truth somehow? Before he could answer, a shadow passed over the two of them, and Nera spun to see Asil flying away from the dais, her blood spattering the stones. Her sword flung free of her hand and clattered onto the ground, sliding to a stop not two feet away. There was some sort of massive, feline creature with a head like a lizard. It had turned on one of the Herons and consumed him in nearly a single bite, and now it was leaping away again, charging into the crowd.

The moment of shock was all Lucian needed. His huge fist slammed into the back of Nera's head, and she was down on her knees, her skull ringing and her vision threatening to flee. Nera sensed the second blow coming and rolled out of the way before it connected. Something was wrong with Lucian's right hand, and he was swinging from the left. Nera tried to push herself up to her feet, but the dizziness from the blow overcame her, and she fell back to sit on the ground.

Lucian loomed over her, his nose broken, his face ruined with blood. His eyebrows drew down, and he offered no denial. His eyes narrowed, and his face changed. It was something Nera had never seen before. Her stomach lurched as she remembered his touch, his calm reason. As she remembered wanting him.

"Of course I killed him. Look around you. All these people are mages, and they're trying to kill us. I'd do it again in an instant. The child probably was a mage himself. And look at this... this thing they've conjured."

Nera slid backwards and got a foot under her. She came up slowly as she stared at him. "That's not how we operate, Lucian. You know this is not how it's done."

He took a step toward her, and for the first time she felt fear. "Maybe it should be." He shoved her backwards, and she nearly fell again. "These rebels are animals. They'll do whatever they have to do to take us down, but you never have had the heart for this work. You never have been hard enough to get the job done."

"I am an agent of the High Lord, and I do not execute—"

"You had every opportunity to take Akithar before all of this." He gestured to the smoke, the debris, the screaming mob. "You could have arrested him and been done with it. Instead, you allowed him to steal explosives. You let him make bombs and attack this city. This city you've destroyed with your endless embargo. And now you've let these Herons create whatever the hells that thing is. Can't you see what your incompetence has done? Your unwillingness to do what has to be done?"

Nera could hear the blood rushing in her ears, drowning out the sounds of conflict around them. Her legs shook, and the familiar heat crawled up her neck. Lucian still was talking, pointing at her, berating her, but she couldn't hear it. This man she had trusted, this man she had relied on, had deceived her. All the times she had sought his council, he had given her words of encouragement or guided her, but she now knew what was behind his advice. The mask had fallen away, and she saw him for what he was. She saw the pathetic, manipulative murderer who had wormed his way into her confidence. Into her affections.

"I should have dealt with you before." His hand went to his waist, feeling for his sword, but it wasn't there, probably lost somewhere in the fray. His eyes flicked to Asil's blade, resting on the ground by his feet. He turned his back on Nera and stooped to grab the sword, and she knew that would be the last mistake he'd ever make.

Her breath coming hard and fast, her brain spinning with panic,

Nera pulled her own sword from its sheath. She kicked at his legs, and her boot crashed into the back of his right knee. He tripped forward, coming down onto that knee and catching himself with his left hand on the ground. He winced when his broken right hand impacted the paving stones.

Nera came from behind and grabbed his hair and jerked his head up to look at her. With one quick cut, she ran the edge of her blade across his throat. The slice was jagged but effective. Lucian opened his mouth, but his head lolled back toward her in silence, and hot blood poured over her hand that still held the blade. Nera's shoulders shook with panic and fury, and she let the sword fall from her grasp. Lucian's eyes rolled toward her, accusing, begging, and she couldn't look at them for another instant. She released his hair and pushed him away. He teetered on his knees for a long second before falling forward onto his face. His blood filled the lines in the stones, tracing the end of his life in a spreading and angular spiral of red.

A quin's legs were weak, but she could walk between Magra and Samira, with an arm around each of their shoulders. Samira had done her best to heal her, as she'd done for Oreth only days before, but her magic could mend flesh, not spirit. Aquin's wounds were less tangible than the boy's burns and breaks had been.

As they came into the plaza, Samira stopped them short. Smoke hung heavy in the air, and ash and debris floated down from the ruined edifices that surrounded the square. People were fighting to escape the chaos, streaming past them in a terrified flow. But even more people were coming toward the turmoil. Samira saw angry faces lining the streets, peering out of windows, and opening doors to see what was happening. Klubridge was upended, and it was going to get worse before it could get better.

"I have to help my friends."

"In there?" Magra was incredulous. "You'll be killed!"

"Can you take Aquin on your own? I'll meet you at the docks."

Aquin grabbed Samira's arm. "Wait, don't leave me. Please."

Samira held her hand and put her other hand on Aquin's cheek. "You'll be okay, and I will too. Go to the ship with Magra. I'll be there soon. I promise."

Another explosion shattered the front of another building, and Samira stepped back. "Go as fast as you can. Stop for nothing."

Aquin would keep her there and convince her not to leave them if she waited, so she turned and ran into the fray without another look back. She nearly tripped over a piece of black armor, and then over the man who had lost it. He lay on his back on the paved ground, his eyes staring up blankly at the smoke darkened sky.

It wasn't supposed to be like this. They were supposed to get in, create a distraction, get Caius, and get out. This chaos, this death was not in the plan. Not in her plan, at least. Apak had been single-minded in his vengeance. She'd known he would take casualties if the opportunity had presented itself, but she'd hoped it wouldn't. Now she saw her naivete scattered across the central plaza, soldiers dead and dying as Apak continued to fire on them from somewhere beyond the crowd.

"Samira!"

Her head pivoted, and she scanned the faces, searching for Reykas. That had been his voice. And then she saw him, not standing, but sitting at the edge of the raised platform. She recognized the sickness weighing on his slumped shoulders, but there was something else dragging him down as well. Bodies and blood surrounded him, but the one he held in his lap was the one that took Samira's breath.

"Oh no. No, no." She ran to him and dropped to the ground, heedless of the red soaking into the knees of her trousers.

Lizzie was pale, a trickle of blood spilled from the left side of her mouth. It had run along her cheek and into her hair, which hung loose and in white disarray, now nearly a match for her skin. Tears stained Reykas' face, and he held her tight, one hand on her stomach, the other supporting her back.

"Can you save her?"

Samira touched Lizzie's neck and pressed at the side, searching for any sign of life. "Reykas, I don't know. This is bad."

"Please, Samira. Please help her."

A fresh round of shouting broke out beyond Reykas, and Samira looked away to see a new band of citizens storming into the square. Some came armed, but others rushed in with empty hands, ready to fight. The city watch was no match for their numbers, and she watched three guards fall under the onslaught. There was nothing she could do to stop the violence around them, but if she could do anything to help this poor girl, maybe that would be enough.

"If she's already gone—"

"I know," Reykas said. "But she's not. I can feel her heart beating."

Samira felt again, and she found it now. It was slow and faint, but Lizzie was still alive. Her pulse came as a dull throb, there but just barely. It would have to be enough. Samira could pull her back from the threshold as long as she was still on this side of it. Samira began.

She placed her palms flat on Lizzie's body, the left just below the wound on her stomach and the right just above it. She closed her eyes and forced away the shouting, the clanging of metal, and the crush of people colliding with each other. Her focus became a pinpoint, and she directed it down her arms, through her hands, and into Lizzie.

Samira's hands warmed, and a familiar tingle tickled her palms. If she opened her eyes, she would see the faint green glow that always came with the magic. She didn't know how it worked, only that it did. She couldn't feel the healing in her hands beyond that tingle, but she sensed the repairs being done. Tissues bound together, organs made slow adjustments, and debris that remained from the sword made its way to the surface. The healing radiated from the center outward, gradually rebuilding the parts that were hurt, pushing away from the core, reaching, striving for the surface. At last, Samira knew it was complete.

"You can let go," she said and opened her eyes.

Reykas looked doubtful but shifted his hand half an inch. His trembling fingers slid over Lizzie's stomach, still covered in blood, but there was no wound. The skin had sealed as if it had never happened.

"She's going to need more healing, but she'll be okay for now. Can you get her to the ship?"

"I think so, but you'll need help with Caius."

"Where is he?" But then she saw him, just past Reykas. He lay on his chest, his arms and legs out to the sides and still bound to the platform. Samira gasped and crawled up the steps to where he lay. His face was turned to the side, his cheek pressed hard against the stone dais. "What happened to him?"

"Apak didn't fire soon enough. The Herons completed the ritual," Reykas said. "They silenced him, and he collapsed." He hesitated and looked across the plaza. "When it failed, they created some sort of... monster."

That explained the roar she'd heard, at least. Samira looked at Reykas and followed his gaze into the crowd, but she knew she had to keep her focus here, monster or no. She felt Caius' head, and his skin was warm to the touch. Warmer than it should have been.

"Can you help him?" Reykas asked, still cradling Lizzie in his arms.

"I think so. He's still alive." She looked at Lizzie and back again at Caius. "You need to get her out of here. Take Lizzie to safety, and then come back here. I can heal him, but I'll need help carrying him."

Reykas gave her a fast nod and stood, scooping Lizzie into his arms. His legs wobbled but supported him. He was covered in her blood by then but ignored it. "Stay safe, my friend."

"Hurry back."

And he was gone, running with a quick shuffle toward the northeast gate and toting Lizzie's limp form in his arms as if she weighed nothing.

There were shouts behind Samira, and the ground shook with another blast from Apak's contraption, closer this time than before. She flinched at the sound but was grateful for it, because it meant he was still alive.

Before healing Caius, she had to free him. She touched the shackle at his right ankle first and pushed her will into it, watching it dissolve to metal dust like the ones in Aquin's cell. She then freed his left leg and each arm in turn. Now that he wasn't bound to the platform,

Samira could roll him over. She was gentle with his head, taking care not to let it bang on the ground as he turned.

Once Caius was on his back, she placed her hand on his forehead again and put her other hand on his chest. He was breathing, and the breaths came regularly. He would live, even without her intervention, but she had to know the extent of his injuries. Samira had witnessed a silencing before, but she'd never seen it done to someone who already had no magical affinity. She had no idea what that would do to a person.

Samira didn't hear the approach from behind her, but she felt the warm breeze on the back of her neck. Slowly, she turned her head and opened her eyes, and the monster was there. Right there, less than three feet away, staring at her with its golden eyes. Its tail flicked back and forth, the heavy barbed end thudding and scraping across the ground. Samira stayed as motionless as she could, and the creature glared back at her. A long and narrow tongue shot out of its mouth, flapped quickly in front of its face, tasting the air less than a foot away from Samira's, and disappeared again.

Movement in Samira's peripheral vision caught her attention at the same time the beast saw it. She glanced to the left, and a woman with long black hair was clambering down from where she'd fallen at the dais. One of the Herons, by the look of her. The creature's head snapped toward her as well, and in an instant it was away from Samira, pouncing across the platform and headed for the woman.

Samira wasted no time and made the most of the distraction. She grabbed Caius under the arms and heaved him across the platform, dragging him down the short steps and toward the edge of the surging crowd. Anything to get him away from that thing, whatever it was.

Samira couldn't have seen the sword swinging behind her, but somehow she sensed it in the instant before the blade would have cleaved her body from the right shoulder down to the left hip. She ducked and rolled forward over Caius, and the sword danced off the invisible barrier left where she had knelt. Samira came down on her back, but she shuffled her feet backwards and raised to her elbows before the other woman could swing again.

"Commander," she said, pushing herself to her feet.

Nera Mollor had been the picture of calm, bureaucratic malice when they had last faced each other in the theater. It seemed a lifetime ago but had been only weeks. The woman standing before Samira now was the same but changed. Her right hand was covered in blood, but no wounds were visible. Her uniform was dirtied from the falling soot but otherwise seemed intact. Nevertheless, this woman was damaged. Her eyes were hollow and dead, her face contorted in hatred. She raised her sword again, the tip pointing at Samira.

"Look at this. Look what you've done."

"What I've done?" Samira was incredulous. "We lived here in peace for a decade. You brought this here. All of this is your doing."

"I should have known it was you. All along, you hid behind him. You played the innocent, but you were the one."

"What are you talking about?"

Mollor shook her head violently, and her red hair came loose from its tight bun. "You don't get to do that. I know the truth now. You're the mage. All of you are. All but him."

Caius lay between the two women, and Samira took a slow step to the left, hoping to draw Mollor away from him. "We have power, but we're not the ones you're looking for. We never have had anything to do with the rebels. We only wanted to live our lives, and we wouldn't have bothered anyone."

"Lies!" Mollor screamed and made a wild swing with her sword. Samira saw it coming and deflected it with another barrier. The sword bashed into the hard air, and the impact jarred Mollor's entire body. She took a staggering step to the side, away from Caius, following Samira with her weapon and her viciously empty eyes.

"It's true," Samira said. "You did all of this for nothing. You're looking for some sort of spy, and we know nothing about them. We're performers. That's all we've ever been."

"Why the deception? Why did he pretend to have magic?"

"To protect us from you," Samira spat. Her own anger was rising now. This woman dared question her about Caius and the sacrifice he had made of his entire life?

"We weren't even here. This is nonsense."

"There are always people like you." Samira shoved her hands out, and green light flashed between herself and Mollor. The spell buffeted the Kite backwards, and she had to catch her balance to keep from falling.

Samira didn't give her a chance to recover and came at her again, swinging one hand after the other, pounding invisible blows into her. Samira was not a fighter. She couldn't cause serious harm to the commander, but she hoped to keep her busy until Reykas returned. Together, they might take her, at least for long enough to get Caius and Apak out of the square.

But as Samira swung with another strike, the ground behind her jolted. She felt the paving shake with the impact and knew the creature had landed at her back again, having finished whatever it had done to the Heron woman. Samira launched forward, losing her balance, and she landed hard on her hands and knees in front of Mollor. Samira rocked back, knowing the strike was coming. The sword barely missed her and sparked against the ground. Mollor's swings were wild, not at all the practiced swordplay of a trained Kite. Something had shattered inside the woman.

Samira strained to the side, and she saw it then. The beast crouched mere feet away, its muscles tensed and ready to spring. Its eyes met hers, and she knew she couldn't defend against this thing and Mollor at the same time.

Mollor charged in for a closer jab, and Samira kicked out, connecting with her pelvis. Mollor staggered back but did not relent.

"Samira!"

She rolled right to dodge another swing and saw Apak. Covered in sweat, his glasses askew, his legs bowed from the weight of the device he carried in front of him, he stood before the dais with Caius lying behind him. Apak's eyes met hers, and she knew what he was about to do. Fear chilled her, but there was no stopping him.

Samira rolled to her back again, and Mollor had her sword up, coming in for another strike, this time slashing one handed from the side. She heard the roar and knew the creature was coming for her.

Samira shouted in desperation and thrust both hands up. Her magic flashed green again, and she felt the hairs on her arms raise with static as the invisible bubble completely enveloped her.

She had been too slow to stop the strike. Samira winced with her eyes tight as the sword hit her shoulder.

It bounced away without leaving a mark. Samira opened her eyes in confusion and stared up at Mollor, hunched outside the shielding bubble, looking equally perplexed. Samira saw the bleeding stump where the magic had severed the commander's right arm at the same instant Mollor saw her own hand, now lying beside Samira inside the bubble. Blood hit the shield and ran off it like thick water on glass.

Mollor screamed at Samira in the instant before the creature crashed into the invisible shield, stumbling over it and slamming its shoulder into the commander. It was then that Apak's cone of white, searing light engulfed all of them.

CHAPTER 39

Caius felt the earth rocking beneath him, and he opened his eyes to a dim light that still managed to pound pain into his already aching head. The room was dark and unfamiliar, with wooden walls and a thin mattress under him. Was he back in a cell? The room shifted again and pushed him to the right, then left, and the walls creaked with a lazy heaviness. He pushed himself up slowly, getting to his elbows before realizing that every muscle in his body ached at least as much as his head.

"Took you long enough."

He blinked into the darkness and searched the room for the voice until he could focus on the face sitting across from him, watching him.

"Fairy?" He wiped a hand across his face and forced himself up, sliding his legs off the side of the bed. "Where... What happened?"

"You lied to me. That's what happened." She flicked a match and slid it into a gas lantern hanging near her. The lamp blazed to life, and Caius squinted at the sudden brightness.

"Are we on a ship? Is this Drass' ship?"

"Yes, and yes. I came here after you told me to. I think they were glad to see somebody else come aboard. They needed help with Oreth."

"You know Oreth?"

Fairy rolled her eyes. "I do now. I've been tending to him for days."

"Who else is here? Is everyone all right?"

"Lizzie got hurt, but she's going to be okay. Samira's been healing her. Everybody else is on board."

"How long have we been at sea?"

She frowned and counted. "Three days? Maybe four. I don't know. It's hard to tell when I'm cooped up down here watching you."

Caius felt his chest. "Where are my clothes?"

"Here." Fairy tossed him a pile of fabric he didn't recognize.

"These aren't mine."

"They're from Reykas. He's a lot taller than you, but it'll have to do."

"Where are my clothes?" he asked again.

"Samira said they smelled like burned sausages after they found you. I wouldn't be surprised if she threw them overboard." She leaned forward with her elbows on her knees. "I ought to throw you overboard. Liar."

"Because you thought I was a real magician?"

"Liar."

"It's the only way they could survive. You have to understand that, Fairy. If you'd known Dorrin was a mage, what would you have done to protect him?"

She was scowling at him, but she had to admit the truth. "Anything."

"That's how it's always been with Samira and me. Since we were your age. And then we met Apak. Lizzie. Reykas. Even Oreth. They all had power, and they would have been caught if we hadn't worked together. They'd have been killed or worse."

"They'd have been made into halflocks," she said.

He nodded.

"There's a halflock on the ship."

Caius frowned. "I don't know anybody like that."

"Her name's Magra. She's a little weird, but she helped Samira and Aquin, so I guess she's okay."

"Where is everybody?"

"Waiting for you to wake up, you lazy liar."

～

Fairy grumbled but helped Caius onto his feet after he'd put on Reykas' shirt. It was huge, and he had to roll the sleeves up several times just to get his hands free. Leaning on Fairy, he got out of the small cabin where he'd been resting and climbed the short wooden staircase to the deck.

It was night, and only a few lamps lit the deck. That was probably to make the ship less visible from afar, but he knew less about nautical strategy than he did about real spellcasting. He left the actual magic to his friends and would leave the sailing to Drass.

The sky was clear, and he didn't know when he'd seen so many stars in his entire life. He'd spent the last ten years mostly within the walls of a huge city. There'd been little time for stargazing, much less the unobstructed view for it, with buildings climbing to the surrounding sky everywhere he went. The open sea was different. He felt a shiver of excitement and almost dread as he looked out across the black water, unable to see any land or even where the ocean met the sky.

"He arises," Samira said. She was leaning with her back against the railing and smiled as Caius emerged from the hatch.

"I hear you got your librarian after all," he said, taking the space next to Samira and leaning back to look up at the mast far above.

"That's yet to be seen."

"Oh?"

"She didn't exactly have a choice in the matter," Samira said. "She never should have been a part of this, and I don't know whether that's ever going to be forgivable. Or whether I should be forgiven." She sighed and wiped a hand over her eyes. "How are you?"

"Sore. My head hurts, and so does everything else. What happened to me?"

"You have the distinction of being the only person I'm aware of who has been silenced without being a mage."

"I remember being taken into the square, but that's all. I can't remember anything after that."

"That's probably for the best."

"Why did you come back? You were supposed to be on the ship and long gone already."

"We came back for you, you idiot. You and Aquin."

"You shouldn't have risked that. How did you get us out of there?"

Samira stared into the dark for a moment before answering. "It was awful, Caius. I'll have to tell you later, and I don't even think you'll believe half of it. I don't know what we're going to do with Apak."

"Is he okay? Is everyone okay?"

"We are now. Somehow, against all odds, everything came together. But Apak killed a lot of people, Caius. A whole lot of people."

"The Kites?" Caius asked.

"And a lot of the city constabulary. He took down most of the Heron guards as well. There were so many people in that square."

"What about the people? I remember the crowd…"

Samira shook her head. "I don't think he hurt any of the citizens, but a lot of them were trampled or eaten or—"

"Beaten?"

"No, eaten. It's a whole thing." She hesitated. "Nera Mollor is dead, and most of the Scarlet Kites went down with her. Maybe all of them. I'm not sure. Apak killed so many people. At least one Heron is dead, too, probably more."

Caius traced the texture of the old wood on the railing with his fingertips and listened to the waves lapping at the sides of the ship below them. For the first time, he noticed the scent of salt in the air.

He looked toward Samira, and she was staring up at the stars. "They're amazing, aren't they?" she asked, and he followed her eyes. The Small Crown was above them, the center jewel winking faintly.

"You used your magic in public," Caius said.

"We had to."

"All of you?"

"All of us. There was no choice. There was no life for us in Klubridge anymore, even if we'd stayed hidden. You saw what the city had become after Mollor came."

"It's dangerous, Samira. We've always taken care of each other."

She looked at him with a sad smile. "We still will take care of each other. But the time for hiding has passed. Klubridge is in full revolt, Caius."

He frowned. "Revolt? What do you mean?"

"Exactly what she said." Caius hadn't heard Drass approaching, but he was there now and handed mugs to both of them. Caius sniffed his, and it smelled awful. "Drink it," Drass said. "It helps with the rocking."

"It's true," Samira said. "I was in a bad state the first night on the ship."

Drass laughed. "The Empire could have tracked us just by following the trail of puke she threw overboard."

Caius took an experimental sip and wrinkled his nose. It tasted as bad as it smelled. "Tell me about this revolt. What do you mean?"

"The city was ready to turn even before we rescued you," Samira said. "When we attacked the Kites, that was the last push they needed."

Drass nodded. "I got a message by bird yesterday. The city government is under siege, and the constabulary has shut down. I've been working with the rebels for a long time, and I've never seen something like this happen."

"It won't last," Caius said.

Samira shrugged. "Maybe not, but it's a good start."

"We're not rebels, though. We never wanted a part in this. When we were young and you first realized you had power, we promised to keep each other out of trouble and away from either side of this thing."

Drass laughed again. "You may not have wanted to be a rebel, but that's what you are. All the people are talking about Akithar, the wizard who destroyed the Scarlet Kites and freed Klubridge."

"That's not even what happened," Caius said.

"When has anything been that straightforward with you?" Samira asked. "You're a magician. Your stock in trade is trickery."

"And now you're a folk hero," Drass added. "They're saying you're such a threat that the Empire framed you for a boy's murder. They tried to silence your magic, and you overcame that—a historical first, I do believe. And then they tried to kill you with a chamir, and you killed it with your sorcery."

"A what?"

"Part of that whole thing I mentioned," Samira said.

Caius sighed and rubbed at his temples. This wasn't helping his headache. "Did the actual rebel even reach you? The spy you were waiting on? That's who Mollor was actually after."

"She did," Drass said. "She arrived shortly before the rest of you lot, and she wants a word with you."

"Why me?"

Samira lowered her eyebrows at him. "What part of being a hero of the rebellion do you not understand?"

"That's not me! I don't even have magic. I can't do whatever it is people think I did or want me to do."

"Of course you can't," Samira said. "That's why you have me. You have Reykas, Lizzie, Apak, Oreth. Even Drass here. I think Fairy might even come around on liking you."

Caius tilted his head at her. "We're all, what? Going to become rebels? Off to fight the High Lord?"

"Everything starts somewhere," Drass said. "And I suspect you can still pull off a trick or two."

He walked away across the deck with the sure gait of a man born to the sea. He waved for them to follow, and Samira gestured. "After you, folk hero."

Caius swore and dumped his mug over the railing.

AFTERWORD

When it comes to writing, I'm very much an outliner. I plan my plots and character arcs as far in advance as possible, and I put a lot of effort into making sure I know where the train is going before it leaves the station. The consequence of writing that way is that this book has been a long time in coming. The world of Teshovar began with an initial idea of a character and a magic system nearly ten years ago, and I've been developing it ever since then.

Akithar's Greatest Trick is the first book in a planned trilogy of trilogies about this world, its people, its magic, and its secrets. I'm fully committed to writing a core series of nine books, all of which already are at various stages of development, and there absolutely will be spinoffs, interquels, and all sorts of additional stories coming alongside the central books. You won't have to read everything to keep up with what's going on, but you'll get a more complete understanding of Teshovar if you do.

I'm a fantasy fan myself, and I know about the uncertainty that can come with jumping into a new series. That's why it's important to me to unequivocally promise you at the start of this thing that I already know all the big plot developments for all nine books, and I have a conclusion toward which every book will be building. It's a huge story with a lot of things to track, and I keep abundant reference notes about the characters, the timeline, upcoming revelations, and more. Once the series is done, I want for you to be able to look back at this Afterword and see that I've kept my promise.

You can stay in touch and be the first to hear about new releases, get exclusive free stories, and learn more about my writing by signing up for my email list at JasonDorough.com. I appreciate your giving Teshovar a chance, and I look forward to having you join me on this wild and weird journey!

ABOUT THE AUTHOR

Jason Dorough is the author of *Akithar's Greatest Trick,* the first book in the Teshovar series. Originally from Georgia, Jason now lives in Florida, where he works as a voiceover artist when he's not writing. You can visit him online at JasonDorough.com.

Printed in Great Britain
by Amazon

60721bd5-20fa-4cee-807a-3e0ad6eeee3fR01